Where Privacy Dies

A Twin Cities Mystery

Priscilla Paton

coffeetownpress

Kenmore, WA

coffeetownpress

For more information go to: www.coffeetownpress.com
www.priscillapaton.com

This is a work of fiction. Names, characters, places, brands, media, and incidents are either the product of the author's imagination or are used fictitiously.

Cover design by Sabrina Sun
Author photo by Brett Dorrian

Where Privacy Dies
Copyright © 2018 by Priscilla Paton

ISBN: 978-1-60381-665-6 (Trade Paper)
ISBN: 978-1-60381-666-3 (eBook)

Library of Congress Control Number: 2018944689

Printed in the United States of America

For my growing family

ACKNOWLEDGMENTS

❧

Many made the writing of this book possible. First are my mystery-reading husband, David, and my inventive family—James, Ishanaa, Liz, and Seth. Macey, like any trusty Labrador retriever, provided companionship by my desk until her life of unconditional love ended.

For replying to numerous questions, I wish to thank Craig Rice and Carl Lehmann.

I also thank others who provided important expertise: Katie Arnold, Dr. Andrew Baker, Paul Beaumaster, Dr. Jon Hallberg, Eric Knutson, Bob Thielen, and J.B. Tut. For reading raw versions of the manuscript, Nancy Anderson, Rae Chalmers, Jenny Dunning, Gretchen Morgenson, Tom Nelson, and Ellen Rosen. For their insights as writers and teachers, Erin Hart, David Housewright, and Lily King.

I also wish to thank Jennifer McCord and Catherine Treadgold at Coffeetown Press for providing crucial editing and a vision not only for this novel but also for the Twin Cities Mystery series.

There is no privacy that cannot be penetrated. No secret can be kept in the civilized world. Society is a masked ball, where every one hides his real character, and reveals it by hiding.
—Ralph Waldo Emerson

I never said, "I want to be alone." I only said, "I want to be *let* alone! There is all the difference.
—Attributed to Greta Garbo

Chapter I

❧

Death is private. A person can die in front of a video camera, collapse in a massacre, pass surrounded by family, yet only one being crosses that final line of consciousness. Solitude follows, a remembered saying—the grave's a fine and private place.

It was Detective Erik Jansson's duty to violate that privacy and it weighed on him as he knelt by the crude dirt mound covered with branches. The mound, in the flood zone of the Minnesota River, had been obscured by the scrub of the wildlife refuge. The perfect place for final rest. Perfect and perfectly wrong.

The ascending roar of a silver and red plane leaving the nearby Minneapolis/St. Paul airport disrupted Erik's contemplation. He lost the train of dark thoughts he'd summoned to shut out the temptation of the sunny morning to run and kayak and breathe. A gorgeous morning, the second Sunday in April. The landscape was greening, and robins threw outsized energy into their chirrupy defense of territory. Erik pushed a hand through his dark hair to discharge his own energy, but restlessness will out. What had happened? Who dumped a body so unlovingly? Why? Was there more bad to come? There usually was.

He studied the mound again, and the tweed-sleeved elbow uncovered to confirm the find of the cadaver dogs. Then he straightened to stretch his long legs and rub his arms, the morning being brisk for his department fleece. Waiting on the bank above him were the discoverers of the scene, an odd-sock trio—a boy about twelve in a stained jacket with a dirt-bike quite authentically dirty, and a retired couple outfitted as khaki twins with binoculars clutched to their chests. Behind them stood a uniformed officer. Erik looked past the group toward the refuge entry to trace possible routes to this spot. You could hike down the steep trail behind the airport hotels, as the couple had probably done. An unpaved road for bikes and service vehicles took a less dramatic downhill path to merge with the broad trail where the marsh grasses began. Then the trail ran along backwater banks lined with cottonwoods, alders, maples, and oaks. A four-wheel drive vehicle could navigate that route easily. From trailside, it's a six-foot drop down to the narrow flood zone where Erik stood by the mound. Easier to prepare that grave if more than one person had been hurrying the body along on its journey.

Zywieck and his two cadaver dogs returned from the marshes that reached out into the Minnesota River toward the looming smokestack of an old power plant. The team had already searched the stretch that headed northeast toward the main channel of the Mississippi. The handler shook his head—nothing else—and reached into his jacket pocket for the dogs' ball. Zywieck overthrew. Erik caught the ball and flinched with apprehension at a sensation on the back of his neck.

"Isn't it early for ticks?" Erik asked and rubbed the spot with the tennis ball. He liked Zywieck, though the older man put himself in the role of avuncular advisor; and as for advice, it came from too many quarters.

Zywiek misunderstood. "You're right, Erik, I should check the dogs, Scarlett, Rhett, sit. By the way, this isn't human." The handler nudged raccoon-sized remains near the grave where, according to the uniformed officer, the boy had fallen. The old female Labrador retriever watched her handler obediently while the young male whined. The cadaver dogs had been trained, in the case of the younger still being trained, to ignore all but the odor of human, quick or dead.

"Rhett's not sure he likes this game," Zywieck continued and scratched behind the ears of the whining Rhett. The first time Erik worked with Zywieck, the man explained his philosophy—"put two trainers together, and they'll agree that the third trainer is wrong"—and how the dogs direct their energies to the scent that would earn the reward. A ball for a corpse. Zywieck put a hand on the older dog who had been rolling her big brown eyes for equal attention, as his smile down-shifted to a droop. "After Scarlett here found that eleven-year old last fall, the Eakins murder, the old girl wasn't right for a while. I should plant a live find, make them happy."

Erik knew the Eakins corpse hadn't upset Scarlett: it had been her handler's mood at seeing a child's remains. "The next week," he said, "you and the pups found those toddlers, the ones who survived the night on a tub of gummi-bears." He tossed the dogs' ball up and down in his hand. "May I?"

Zywieck grunted consent and the dogs locked on Erik's face.

"Find!" he ordered, and the dogs signaled at the exposed elbow of the corpse. He threw the ball far over the bank, past the onlookers, and the dogs scrambled up, Rhett so excited he lost traction, allowing Scarlett with her sizeable butt to power ahead.

The boy, the woman, and the man stared down, locking on Erik's face as the dogs had done. His chest tightened under the pressure of their gaze. Tall and fit, he appeared younger than his thirty-something years, and occasionally people doubted his authority. Or given his blue-eyed Nordic bearing, they would bluntly ask why he wasn't blond. He was *not* going to explain the Swedish-Norwegian blend with a Sámi strain—Sámis, the people formerly known as Laplanders. He had also become wary of smiling. Smile, and people's expectations rocketed into the ether.

Erik took a measured inhale and hissed it out through his teeth. What is fascinating about the dead is what they bring out in the living.

Following the dogs' path, he grabbed a root to pull up to the higher level. The first officer on the scene, Jakes, stepped forward with a digital recorder clipped to his sleeve and a notepad in hand. The boy's name was Owen; the couple, Erik heard, were Mr. Nelson and Mrs. More-Nelson. On the ground lay a stained wingtip shoe.

"Owen, what brought you here?" Erik began.

"I'm finishing a photo project for school, 'Emerging Spring Wetland Plants.'"

"Finishing?"

"Um, starting. It's due … soon."

"Soon?"

"Tomorrow." The boy's voice snaked up to a squeal and frogged down to bass on that one word. Oh how Erik remembered being that age. He turned to the couple, and the man spoke up without being asked.

"Spring migration is underway, Detective. The number of bird species explodes"—

"Yes, wonderful, I'm sorry to interrupt, Mr. Nelson, but the shoe, who found it? Mrs. More-Nelson?"

"*Murre*-Nelson, Ms. M-u-r-r-e-Nelson, May Murre-Nelson."

"Ah, we'll correct that in the notes." Erik glanced sideways at Jakes, whose eyes stayed on his pad. Jakes had said in the initial call that there would be Nelsons and More Nelsons. "Please tell me about the shoe, Ms. Murre-Nelson, Mr. Nelson?"

Mr. Nelson displayed his excitement. "We heard wood duck near the water and started down the bank, but it was too steep. May and I were pulling ourselves back onto the path when this young man and his bike came *racing* along and the handle bar caught me"—

"You jumped out like deer," the boy interjected, "dumb deer!"

"Feckless," Mr. Nelson said but Ms. Murre-More Nelson spoke over him, "I was pulling my husband up when *I* slipped, and the three of us *mud*-wrestled, I see your expression, Detective. I grabbed for anything that would hold us, only we kept sliding to that pile where Owen, it's Owen?"—she looked directly at the boy and softened—"where Owen fell and screamed."

"I didn't scream, I called for help."

"May grabbed a shoe, not a root," Mr. Nelson cheerfully concluded and then shook a finger at the boy. "We called 911; we did not *text*." Oh, Owen, Erik thought, nothing's going your way.

"A blood-soaked shoe," Ms. Murre-Nelson said, "though the officer doubted me." Jakes exemplified forbearance. "He asked if I imagined that because I read books. I *think* that because I'm a pharmaceutical chemist."

"Thank you. The lab will check it." Erik smiled at her as the crime scene van came bumping down the trail.

Owen turned his smelly cheek to the group. "Is this evidence? Should I skip a shower?"

"I believe you should take a shower at the first opportunity. Those remains are a coincidental find. The dogs went right past it. First rule, trust the dogs." As Erik said this, Rhett whizzed after a ball, nearly knocking over the Owen-Nelson grouping. Zywieck liked to stay until satisfied that the crime scene team no longer needed, or tolerated, his presence. "Owen, Ms. Murre-Nelson, Mr. Nelson, please verify your contact information with Officer Jakes."

"We're reliable," the Nelson-More-Nelsons self-testified.

"Can I see what's dead, sir?" Owen had yet to learn that near silent compliance created more possibilities for subterfuge.

"Out of respect for what—whoever may be there, there are no spectators. Listen, we'll need a detailed account of the surroundings. Mr. Nelson, do you know plants as well as birds?"

"I not only blog about the piscivorous kingfisher, I detail the life cycle of *Sanguinaria canadensias*"—

"Excellent. Owen, is your phone camera intact? When you rode down the hill, did any birds flush? Retrace your steps, the three of you, take photos, share them to cover everything. Send a digital file to me, then you're free to use the photos as you wish." Erik felt that should finish it.

Except Mr. Nelson grabbed his shoulder. "You remind me of our son!"

"Except our son is blond, short, and round," Ms. Murre-Nelson demurred. "It's the smile, Detective."

"Just like him!" Mr. Nelson insisted as his wife grasped his hand to pull him and mud-coated Owen away. This freed Erik to join the crime scene team working on the flats.

A large branch challenged them. The high winds that had driven the rain days ago had likely wrenched it from a towering cottonwood. That pushed aside, the team speculated that the rest of the debris obscuring the grave could have been pulled in place by a single man or a fit woman, like the newest team member who was demonstrating her capabilities. The team then unburied the dead at an archaeological pace. As the silt was moved aside, an odor seeped into the air. Erik involuntarily stepped back. Injured animals crawl to a hidden spot to die alone, only they didn't stay alone, attracting insects, crows, vultures. Re-use mattered, not dignity. Dignity no longer had meaning for the shape being uncovered. As the odor increased, the team slowed. The lead M.E. handed Erik a mask and gloves. Another creeping thing tried attaching itself to his scalp, making him shudder as the team brushed the last layer from the body. Erik repositioned his mask and knelt again by the grave.

This couldn't be the site of death. The man, the rotting semblance of one, was brought here, dragged and hidden. He wasn't outfitted for bike adventures or birding excursions. The bloodied necktie retained its knotted symmetry, and the muck-saturated suit suggested formality and fussiness. The skull was damaged, the face already food for worms. When the team lifted the body, the footed shoe became unfooted. Erik picked up the shoe and two items fell out. One a custom orthotic. The hairs on his neck stiffened. The other was a laminated photo of a girl, an adolescent curled in the fetal position. She did not look like the live find that would please Zywieck's dogs.

CHAPTER 2

❧

The second Sunday in April was not a typical time to hold a lavish work-related gala in Chicago. Jonathan Lewis knew that the host, the Allston Teague Carlson Group, never wanted to be typical. Allston Teague Carlson, aka ATC, specialized in Public Relations and Reputation Management; and in the four months Jonathan had worked in the group's Minneapolis office, acquired when Allston Groups took over Teague Carlson, he had been hoping to advance his own reputation. He hurried across Michigan Avenue from his budget lodging to the elegant four-star hotel where the evening event had already started. Arriving early suggested you were an underling, while barely late seemed fashionable by Midwest standards. Jonathan had been deemed important enough to have a free flight, more accurately a cheap one, on the company's dime. He had selected the Saturday fare and spent the previous afternoon looking at dead things in the Field Museum. He assured himself as he entered the hotel and took the elevator to the 34th floor that his days of modest solitary activities were over. He was in his twenties, in a tux he'd bought, not rented, and he'd tamed his Huck-Finn thatch of towheaded hair into a smooth style. He was neither tall enough to stand out awkwardly nor short enough to be lost in the crowd. And with his ATC supervisor Niland Harrington not around to nip at his heels, Jonathan could float into the gala on a balloon of confidence.

Then inside he froze. An elite mob swarmed the ballroom, people who used their passports for more than a fishing trip to Canada with a knucklehead cousin, for more than a church-sponsored mission to impoverished Central America. Jonathan whispered a mantra picked up from a TED talk: *fake it until you make it.*

He caught the eye of an attractive woman in her forties, wearing a low-cut royal blue slip. Obligingly, she grabbed two wine glasses from a passing waiter, offered him one, and asked with a smile, "I'm Denise. And you are?"

"Jonathan Lewis."

Denise took the hand he'd offered. "From?"

"North Dakota," Jonathan said before realizing what she meant. "Oh, uh, the new Minneapolis office."

"Well, Jonathan from North Dakota, that's stunning country. I'm an associate partner with Allston Groups here in Chicago. Oh, excuse me, I haven't adjusted to the new name that came out of the Minneapolis merger, 'Allston ...'"

"Teague Carlson, or ATC," Jonathan finished for her. "I think of it as 'All Things Cutting Edge.'"

Denise drank her wine efficiently before responding with a small laugh. "All Things Cutting Edge—good for you! Tell me, have Niland Harrington and Stephen Drexler killed each other yet? Oh, don't look so shocked. I don't see either man tonight, how strange. Especially since they were both based here in Chicago until the Minneapolis acquisition."

"Mr. Drexler, our director, went to New York and Paris, said it was 'business and pleasure' in an office email." Stephen Drexler's full title was a mouthful which translated into a high income—Regional Principal and Director, Crisis Management Expert. Harrington's title was Director of Project Management and Internal Communication. The two men controlled his destiny. Jonathan's title of Public Relations Specialist apparently meant a half-step above office gopher.

Drexler, at thirty-nine-years old, was extremely successful and handsome. He was also the first responder for clients desperate for damage control; he spread words like oil on troubled waters. It was Drexler who had vetoed Allston's proposed motto, *we make you look the way you deserve to look*, for reasons Jonathan didn't quite comprehend. Jonathan quickly downed some wine before mentioning Niland Harrington, older than Drexler but lesser in physical and professional stature. "Harrington, who's my immediate supervisor, took a vacation."

Denise nodded. "Oh, I can imagine handsome, suave Drexler mixing business and pleasure and beautiful women in a capital city. Harrington—our paths crossed a few times and he struck me as obsessive about work, likes to know everything. Our fearless leader Ted Allston values him for that reason." Denise exchanged her empty wine glass for a full one as a server passed—she did not take one for Jonathan and began to turn away.

He spoke quickly. "Mr. Harrington seems *committed* to ATC and *incredibly* attentive to Mr. Drexler and his vision."

"Oh, is he now." Denise swiveled back. "They say that Harrington was all set to be *the* director in Minneapolis, a significant promotion *and* significant raise for him. Then at the last minute, our mighty leader Ted Allston tapped Drexler. Harrington, usually so eager to please, was beside himself." She leaned into Jonathan, the alcohol on her breath drifting up to his nostrils. "Allston's new trophy-bride, Charm, was quite taken with our Mr. Drexler, most women are. They were seen together. Stephen Drexler's too good for Allston to toss out the door, and Harrington's real job may be to keep an eye on Drexler."

Jonathan had nothing to say.

"Anyway, I should let you mingle." Denise waved at a stout man across the room. "My husband, networking. Enjoy as much as you can before the speeches start."

Had he failed a test already? Jonathan had been sure gossip was in his wheelhouse.

It did feel good to be liberated from Harrington's nagging oversight, though the original plan had been for Harrington to attend the gala and introduce Jonathan to the culture of Allston enterprises. Then two weeks ago the email made its way around the Minneapolis ATC office that Niland Harrington was staying home to nurse a cough. Unrelenting Harrington didn't seem like he'd give in to sickness, though it was plausible since several employees, including Jonathan, had been stricken by a respiratory curse. The less plausible email circulated a few days later: Harrington was en route to the Caribbean to ensure recovery. It was strange that both Harrington and Drexler would miss the event celebrating the acquisition responsible for their current positions.

A blunt-figured woman rushed past Jonathan, and for a second he panicked that it was his college girlfriend. He had adored that plain practical girlfriend, even though she seemed, well, old. During their nearly sexless relationship (dry as a cornstalk was her complaint), she repeatedly asked with maternal concern if really he might not be gay. Once her no-filters roommate barged in on their birds or bees talk and bleated that Jonathan was bi-curious. What he had felt was bi-threatened.

He kept himself from touching his hair and destroying its order. Members of the press in hopes of expletive-rich sound-bites rushed to Chicago's new mayor as he appeared at an entrance. Jonathan surveyed the room of polished men and stylish women drinking and chatting at high-top tables covered in white linen. No sign of Ted Allston yet. Allston was short, with the physique of an angry ancient garden gnome, but would be guarded by a tell-tale entourage.

A hulked-up man in an off-brand suit butted Jonathan's shoulder hard, adjusted his ear-piece, and moved on. Security. Three men sinking with age into their velvet vests paused by Jonathan as if he were invisible. If only Sandy

Sweetser had come, with his gift for puncturing pretense. Sandy generally looked like the rumpled reporter he once was, though he too had an inflated ATC title—Project Researcher and Media Strategist. He worked part-time on a contract basis, ferreting out the skeletons in clients' closets that could undo all PR efforts. All smoke and mirrors, Sandy had described ATC's reputation unit. He hadn't been invited, and this wasn't the place for his wit. Instead of saying "good-bye," he'd quip "I'm off like a prom dress."

The dresses here had more digits in their price than any prom dress, Jonathan guessed. Approachable, that's my asset, he reminded himself. And he was approached by a genial group. He didn't need to remember all the names at once: the important people would sort themselves out.

A jazz ensemble played softly enough that people could talk and fast enough that they remained animated, and after a pleasant chat, the group moved on. Jonathan felt the best he had in months—the hors d'oeuvres of tapenade crostinis and berries marinated in passion-fruit liqueur, the quality drink, the acceptance. A woman approached, in an elegant suit rather than a gown. One of the old men in velvet detained her, and as she talked to the fossil she faced Jonathan. He noticed the point of her chin and understood what was meant by a heart-shaped face. She had a slight widow's peak, round cheeks, a small bow mouth, and a child's chin. Surrounding this heart was a frizzy mass of strawberry-blond hair, like the filigree edging of a valentine had been shocked into gravity-defying strands.

She gently touched the old man's arm before leaving him to his trembling martini, and then placed her hand on Jonathan's arm. "You're Jonathan Lewis. Denise pointed you out," she said. "Melanie Genereux. I'd love to talk, when I'm not being summoned." She glanced toward the podium. "Perhaps you'll have time later?"

Melanie Genereux, Director of Allston Philanthropies, asking if *he* had time. She was responsible for moving Allston out of his rust-belt sensibility into the internet era of data and philanthropic commitment. She oversaw Allston like a brilliant nanny, and his arrival was the cause of her summoning.

Theodore "Ted" Allston entered like the man who owned the room, which he was. A current crackled as he took the podium and gestured to the retired founders of Tigue Carlson who, like Jonathan, had flown in from the Cities. Allston rejected a microphone until Melanie smilingly held it forward again.

"Old Warriors of Chicago! You stand strong in your ability to determine what is best for our clients and ourselves." Allston gargled in his throat for a few seconds then boomed out: "We've extended our influence to our blended family, a huge success. Cheers to Allston Tigue Carlson, ATC!"

Another Minnesota delegate startled Jonathan, Whinette (he always remembered to say *Lynette* to her face though it didn't fit like the office sobriquet). She wetly hissed into his eardrum, "At least he didn't say Teal Cotton, like at the first merger session. We're not a *towel*."

Allston squinted across the crowd. "I've been to the land of a Million Lakes. There's a poem about you, 'Butter and Ice.' The time has come for you new fry to leap from your little walleye pond to the big sea of belugas."

Whinette muttered "invasive carp."

The tiny mogul rose to his tiptoes and set the sound system squealing. "IT'S TIME. TIME to quit cozy advice over cups of decaf for power shots of crisis intervention. WE ARE THE NAVY SEALS OF REPUTATION MANAGEMENT!"

"I bet he goes AWOL at the first opportunity," Whinette hissed again and Jonathan turned his head before she gave him swimmer's ear. He watched Allston's young wife Charm move to the stage, her hair like a waterfall, her tight dress like a mermaid's, and her waddle like a penguin's. Jonathan and Sandy Sweetser had prepared the confidential office brief for Minneapolis attendees of the event. This was Allston's third marriage and his bride's second (her first had been to her adoptive father).

Allston held out his hand to the approaching beauty as he tortured the microphone. "Destined for me since she escaped the Romanian orphanage for the land of opportunity. There were mistakes along the way. But"—pause— "THE THIRD TIME'S THE CHARM!"

Men whistled while women clapped. Anticipating a Whinette attack, Jonathan murmured that there were pickles across the room and escaped into the flow.

The flow stopped. The burly security guard again collided with Jonathan as Chicago's mayor, swearing, was bundled out of the room. Another contingent surged into the room, and onstage Melanie reset the microphone. Allston resumed: "Welcome to a dear friend, a valued partner and client, a great philanthropist, Sam Vine!"

A man who looked like a hippo joined Allston, shook his hand, kissed Charm and Melanie on respective cheeks, waved, and caught his breath.

Jonathan had attracted an informant, a man with a boyish face and unboyish belly: "Sam Vine and the new mayor can't be in the same room. Vine and the previous mayor were toes stinking in a sock. The new politico charged Vine with overbilling the city. You *must* try the cherubs on horseback."

The cherubs were overly dry apricots stuffed with bacon, and from preparing the event brief Jonathan knew more than his informant. A decade ago, Vine had a crisis with his Minnesota business and moved to Chicago to expand his construction operations and his girth. Big as the man was, he disappeared from the podium, taking Allston down with him. That left Mrs. Charm Allston to delight the audience.

It *was* disappointing that Stephen Drexler hadn't come. Jonathan hadn't suspected that there was bad blood between Drexler and Harrington, as Denise had said. He did have suspicions about Drexler and Allston's wife. When Jonathan joined ATC, Drexler talked to him professionally about the Allston vision and confidentially about the delicate collusion of the Allston work-family and the Allston family-family. According to Drexler, Charm desired greater say in Allston's affairs, an influence going far beyond the household budget and even farther beyond her knowledge base. Drexler had been saddled, he confided, with finding things for Mrs. Allston to do. "Worth moving," Drexler maintained, "to be free of entertaining that tone-deaf Siren."

A tap from behind—a Harrington move, it couldn't be Harrington. Jonathan gagged on the cherub and dropped his tiny napkin.

"Here, I have something better." Melanie Genereux of the heart-shaped face and strawberry-blond halo offered tissues from a slim clutch. "I hear good things about you, Jonathan."

"Thank you." Had Harrington criticized him to his face only to praise behind his back? "I've been managing major clients and find the Allston expertise amazing!" Jonathan Lewis, PR Specialist, had been writing press releases and assisting with events when three weeks ago Harrington finally declared he could be the "point man" for two clients. Jonathan had felt elated until he looked up "point man," the person in front heading into battle. He had to display more presence with Melanie. He crumpled the tissues she'd handed him into one pocket and fished out a business card from the other.

"I appreciate this," Melanie said. As she handed Jonathan her card, her fingers gently brushed his, and a nerve pinged and rippled up his spine. It was a rare female who could do that. She shook her floating hair back from her face and asked, "Where's Stephen Drexler?"

Of course, she would be close to Drexler, who returned frequently to Allston's Chicago lair. "He's on a business trip to Paris, completing a project for an old client," Jonathan replied. He omitted the Minneapolis office speculation, spread by Whinette, that the divorced Drexler, who carried his beautiful self like a gift, had waiting for him *une femme*, or *deux*, or *trois*.

"I see, of course. Stephen works miracles for clients, and they're so loyal." Melanie's tone was agreeable though she scrunched her brow. She was no magazine beauty, her nose quirky, her waist short, her bust large, yet she compelled. She retrieved sparkling flutes from a tray and asked with a trace of a French accent, "The transition, it can be difficult, yes, to have someone come into your culture? You don't feel like a colony do you, Jonathan? It is going well?"

"I joined at the time of the merger." Leaving his old firm had been complicated, not to be discussed. "The older employees grumbled, a few left.

It feels, more, more professional now." He hoped that was the right thing to say.

She nodded. "Stephen Drexler is brilliant, delightful, mercurial. Let him have his moods."

That was it. Whinette called Drexler a phony. To Jonathan, Drexler's graciousness was genuine. However, when his superior switched to another train of thought, you became a blemish to blot away. The realization tied his tongue, until Melanie spoke as if she'd meant to say more all along.

"His second, Harrington. I understand he saved ATC from making serious gaffes based on bad information about clients. I don't know him well. Perhaps you can decode him." Her laugh bubbled with the champagne; then her voice lowered. "There's also .... never mind. The merger with Tigue Carlson makes me feel out of touch. Communication is everything. It's just that ... Oh, I don't want to burden you, Jonathan!" Melanie touched him again on the arm, he swore he could feel her fast pulse. She then returned to the power center of the event where Allston, his wife, and Vine were moving to an adjacent room for the dinner service.

How could Melanie be out of the loop? She had Allston's ear, didn't she? Jonathan didn't have time to dwell on that, and the alcohol had loosened up the crowd. He had a seat assignment for the dinner, he could pick up all kinds of insider information, and the evening would be a fantastic plus.

His cell phone dinged loudly, he forgotten to silence it. He pulled it from his pocket, dislodging the tissues Melanie had given him. The number was Sandy Sweetser's and a message popped up.

Niland Harrington had shared ATC digital files with Sandy, and Sandy's additions to the files were due tomorrow, Monday. The files had disappeared from the storage cloud; not only that, he couldn't reach Harrington, who never turned his phone off. Did Jonathan know what was up?

He did not, but Jonathan decided not to answer Sandy's message. Not now.

CHAPTER 3

❧

"I'm a loner," Detective Deb Metzger heard Erik Jansson say from the other desk. *Detective* Jansson, her untried new partner.

"I'm 6'2" and lesbian. What could be scarier?" Deb meant it to be a joke but it came out like a threat. When she was anxious about a new situation her jokes had an aggressive edge that she couldn't control like she wished. And the 6'2" was only in boots or if she spiked her short bleached tips straight up from their light brown roots. Her last girlfriend, very recently last, had said that it wasn't a chip on Deb's shoulder but a cement block.

"L-o-a-n-e-r." He looked up from a computer monitor. "We all are in G-Met, Greater Metro Investigative Unit for Minneapolis and St. Paul. We work with the neighboring municipalities and their forces, go between divisions, focus on linked crimes—you know, abuse and homicide, special investigations, 'intelligent policing.'"

"All policing should be 'intelligent.'" She knew he meant working with data projections to be ahead of the game. It was 8:30 Monday morning, and she and this new partner were hardly off to the races. He'd sunk back into his office chair, head inclined to the screens and printouts. Deb had moved to the Twin Cities after she and the maker of the "cement block" comment hit a metaphorical wall in the road. She had landed in this job, in a department whose multi-city jurisdiction she didn't fully comprehend, just long enough for the laser-jet ink to dry on the forms when she, with background in domestic cases and abduction (often linked to homicide) had been assigned to the new Corpse plus Photo case. Also assigned to this temporary partner.

Deb had been introduced to Erik immediately before entering this conference room slash temporary office. When shaking hands, they had been eye-to-eye, which made him 6'2" in shoes. He'd said something about coffee and re-carpeting his office and at his own expense. G-Met Chief Ibeling had prepped her for the encounter by stressing that Erik "did his job" and was a top marksman. Ibeling added with deliberation, "However, the point of our job is not to shoot people. The point of our job is to prevent the shooting of people."

Ibeling. Known as Almost Allwise Ibeling. A clerk whispered to Deb on the first day (which was like what, last Thursday?) that a reporter at a press conference attempted a nasty put-down of Ibeling by asking, "Are you Allwise?" To which Ibeling snapped, "Almost," and walked out. Deb's observations so far suggested that Almost Allwise almost always had his shirt sleeves rolled up, his forearms crossed and bulging in front of him. He didn't seem like he'd say, as did her former chief in Cannon Rapids, Iowa, that he didn't mind letting a "transgender like yourself" work in his department. Deb was a fighter but cluelessness was a target she couldn't hit. She gave up on trying to explain that "transgender" meant a shift in gender identity and that she was born a woman, would be a woman, and liked women. Then she gave up on the department as a whole. Due to an opening caused by a domestic-crime officer slipping on ice, cracking her rib, and hightailing it to Hawaii for the rest of her days, Deb had found herself at G-Met. Helped, she suspected, by a glowing recommendation from the Cannon Rapids chief that it was a great time for Miss Metzger to move on.

The pretty clerk, who admitted she too was new at G-Met, mentioned Erik as a potential partner and added that he was a Marine hero. Followed by a giggle that Erik could be on the adorable side of shy but was straightforward.

After Allmost Allwise Ibeling finished the directive not to shoot people, Deb yes-sir'd and cautiously (caution always a challenge in her own mind) mentioned Erik and the straightforward thing. She was learning fast that Ibeling was a man of few words or none. He repeated "straightforward" with a negative headshake. "Shy?" Deb ventured. "Reserved. You can draw him out, Detective Metzger. Good job for you," Ibeling answered, turned his back, and walked away.

Back to the case—the wetland grave, the Dapper Dan corpse, and the teaser photo had thrown the possibilities in all directions. The result—a stalled urgency. Like Erik, she should concentrate on her computer and its missing persons files.

Instead, she scanned the room. Standard public-funding bland with an attempt at color—puce or dead asparagus. Despite restrictions on non-police décor, a life-size cutout of a Twins baseball player stood in the corner, smiling at her as her new partner was not. She covertly studied Erik—attractive enough to be somebody's bright pretty boy. Most cops you could rough 'em up and they could be pimps and dealers. Rough up Erik and he could go undercover as what, a *conservationist*? Infiltrate the Audubon Society? A better suit, if he could wear it like it didn't itch, and he could be an SEC commissioner minus the deer-in-the-headlights daze. Don't be prejudiced, she thought, don't be a clichéd anti-male lesbo. Talk to him like he's human.

She twisted to face him. "Right, so. We have no idea if that terrible quality computer print-out-photo means anything. If you're going to take a trophy photo, at least take a decent one. I mean, we don't know if anything actually happened to a child. We're waiting for missing person updates on girls and men. We're waiting on the M.E.'s report. We're waiting on IDs. What did you say? A great suit but no wallet on this John Doe Smashed Head?"

"If the clothing labels are intact, they might provide a lead."

"White, we think he's white, right? Cases like this, they're green when you find them, guacamole. Wouldn't someone miss him? Work?"

"Maybe he didn't show up, got fired by a text message, instant rejection." Erik looked rejected, messing with that thick dark hair of his. She needed a reaction.

"So, 'Jansson,' Swedish name, isn't it? How come you're not blond?"

"Great-great-grandmother may have behaved badly on the ship coming from the Old Country."

Deb didn't know what to do with *that*. She jerked on her highlighted hair spikes. She'd draw Erik out all right. "If this guacamole guy did anything to a girl, he deserves to be compost. Yeah, neutrality, evidence—I know the spiel and so far the corpse is the only victim. But you know guys, ordinary guys, guys women think are nice ... These guys take up with girls-kids-women who don't know any better. Maybe the cads marry them, knock 'em up with a kid or two. Next thing they get fat, find they aren't living in a strip-club-fancy-panty-free-beer-sex-fantasy, and they disappear. Best case, they peaceably divorce. As if 'peaceable' and 'divorce' go together." Why was she doing this, she knew the neutral pro talk. And Erik was nodding to his computer as if it were the other consciousness in the room. "I suppose one shouldn't speak ill of the dead," she trailed off.

"Because they're not ill, they're dead," he said to the computer.

Idiot, she thought. Don't use the word idiot, it's demeaning. Divorce was not uncommon with cops. What if? Deb tried another covert look, which he caught and pretended not to. Right, I'll go into my own trance she thought and absorbed herself in a data stream. Speed finds missing children, speed in the right direction at the right time. She needed something to go on, she needed—

"Concert date's been moved."

Both detectives jerked up and swiveled to face the speaker leaning against the door jamb. An African-American man, smooth skin, smooth head, smooth voice.

"I knocked, Ricky," he winked at Erik and grinned at Deb. "Never call your partner here 'Ricky,' he hates it. Might run over you in his spike shoes, go all broody, right 'Erik'? And you, Detective, must be the newest jewel on the beltway that defines us at G-Met. I'm the black cop because you know there has to be one. Three, actually, in our unit." He strode up to her, extended his hand, and said in a thick British accent, "Bond, James Bond."

She stood up and blanked. The first name that came to mind was the nickname, not the nickname. She swallowed and came out with, "Deb, Deb Metzger."

"He goes by Jimmy, Jimmy Bond Smalls"—Erik nearly smiled. "Or James, James Bond." At which point James Bond Smalls hummed that theme song, broke it off with a big guy laugh and gave Erik a big guy hit to the shoulder. Great, just what she needed, an affirmative-action action duo.

"Ah, you wonder," Jimmy Bond Smalls turned to her, "if my father had a complex and compensated with naming me. He hated the family handle, Smalls, didn't dare change it because his own Daddy would beat him silly. Not really, Daddy was a preacher man, which makes me a son of a preacher man."

"Glad to hear pop culture's working for you." That jumped right out of Deb's mouth.

"Big time. Erik, the gospel concert's postponed, and I can't go to the gym tomorrow—long story involving the kids, the hamster, the little woman—don't tell her I said that. She's as little as you are." He clapped a hand on Deb's shoulder. "Whoa, you work out! Basketball?"

"In high school. At Iowa State I competed in discus, javelin, and shot-put." She had the trophies to show for it, housed somewhere in cardboard.

"Iowa State—that makes you a Cyclone," Smalls said. "Your partner here started at the University of Iowa—go Hawkeyes—then transferred to Minnesota because his father"—

"This story's too long," Erik interrupted.

"Your say-so." Smalls shook hands with Deb again, intoned in the British accent "a pleasure," and left.

They sat, stunned by the abrupt drop of energy.

"Can you believe him?" Deb asked and immediately realized it sounded insulting.

"When he's telling the truth."

"You don't *really* buy into that whole super-spy macho myth, do you?" Deb asked.

Erik answered like it was a question he got every day. "The idea that being great at sex, really great at sex, you can save the world—I like that."

Deb gaped at him. "Uh. Were you a Marine, for real?"

For a scant second he registered surprise. "I survived Marine Officer Training at Quantico. I did not accept a commission."

"You can do that? Not accept? Honorably?"

"As an officer *candidate*, yes. Honorably." He confronted his computer monitor.

He'd better be checking files on local missing children. Deb studied the shoe photo on her screen. She had already submitted it to national databases with state-of-the art recognition programs, without much hope of success. This image appeared to be scanned from a scan, low resolution, and laminated—to be stuck in a shoe. Five numbers on the back didn't seem to have anything to do with an address, birthdate, or phone number. The crumpled figure could have been alive when the picture was taken. No one really believed that. The photo might have been taken outdoors, but the cropped image of an adolescent girl in fetal position on a tarp or rug showed no background. The girl, somewhere between eleven and fourteen years old, wore a gray sweatshirt and jeans; standard long brown hair hid her face except for a chalk-white nose and chin. No signs of trauma. Her small left hand curled upward. Who knows how Swamp Guacamole got it. Deceased, use the appropriate, non-prejudicial language, the deceased. Maybe he wanted to save her. Maybe he was her father bent on revenge. An amateur and revenge—he could easily end up in the dirt if he'd gone down that road. The weight of the case steadied Deb. She glanced at Erik. He had in wireless earbuds.

"*What* are you listening to?" she blurted.

"Nothing." He removed them and went back to the shut face.

Nothing's going right, so she might as well take another gander at him with her athlete's eye. Oops, he started to assess her then retreated into his head. He had the lean runner thing going on. She knew he was older than he looked, in his thirties like her. He had more to his upper-body than you might guess at first, meaning strangers probably underestimated him, especially if he got that dreamy look. Being underestimated—she knew something about that. Say something *intelligent* she directed herself. Remember, *intelligent* policing.

Erik startled her with a rapid turn. "Check out these files. The first is the scarier situation, a girl from a county to the north missing three months, abductor unknown. The second is a local girl, Haley Haugen, missing a few weeks. Haley was probably taken by her father, Dwight Haugen, unemployed and separated from the mother, Lorena. Both girls are about the right age and size, similar hair." He swiveled the monitor towards her. "You know these cases. See what you think."

Deb pulled her chair closer to him, hesitated, breathed. "Are you a tolerant sort, Erik?"

He looked at her. "My sister's a poet. I can tolerate most things."

CHAPTER 4

꧁

The asthma attack felt like judgment, for what he wasn't sure. After the gala, Jonathan had spent the night at an O'Hare airport hotel. He went to bed hyper-stimulated and finally drifted off about 2:30 a.m. Then a weight—hefty as a man—squeezed down on his chest, and at 4:30 he woke, his head pounding and his heart thumping, to find no one there. At O'Hare, his first flight was cancelled. He took Tylenol with strong Styrofoam-tasting tea from a kiosk. His second flight was delayed. He finally arrived at MSP about noon and took the shuttle to the off-airport parking site by the wildlife refuge. In Chicago, the trees were leafy and flowers brimmed from tiny urban spaces. Here bare branches darkened under lowering skies. The shuttle dropped Jonathan near his Hyundai and his asthmatic wheezing stopped as he headed west on 494 to pick up 35 North into Minneapolis. He felt sophisticated to be heading from the airport straight to the office. He turned the radio to local news to re-engage with the normal.

The wheezing returned as Jonathan parked his car in the garage attached to the ATC tower, part of the castle-keep of downtown Minneapolis businesses surrounded by skywalk moats. He held his breath as he walked straight to the entrance, not looking right or left for the large man who lurked in corners. That had to have been an hallucination during the height of his fever a few weeks ago, a figment of too little sleep and too much codeine.

Jonathan exhaled and glimpsed himself in the mirror-like marble panels of the Allston Tigue Carlson office lobby. His skin looked bleached despite the freckles, his light hair in clumps. He had not suffered severe asthma since childhood. The constriction only returned when the wrong things came together. For much of the winter, he couldn't shake bronchitis; he would improve, return to work, feel the fever, and leave again. Young people shouldn't stay sick. It's a Monday in April, an ordinary day, time to move on.

The day dragged. He texted Sandy Sweetser that there was still no word from Niland Harrington. Leave it alone, Sandy, he wanted to say. Jonathan was embarrassed that he was so in the dark, and his shrunken private office had never felt so airless. He generally used his office as a retreat and worked in the shared space of tables and chairs by Harrington's enclave, with a tech guy and the third Chicago transplant, Alluring Alicia. If he were a woman, he'd want to look like Alicia Krause. Deep melting chocolate Latina eyes, thick long Latina hair, voluptuous. Only her vanilla skin evoked her German father. But three weeks ago Alicia didn't show up, she'd quit, without a goodbye to him, and Jonathan had thought they were allies under the goading reign of Harrington.

He rebooted his computer and re-entered a passcode. Wonder of wonders, Jonathan got in. There had been so many login issues the past few months that Harrington had a tech person look for a security breach and set up a constantly changing encryption. No one else had logged onto the Harrington-group network, no one else around. Jonathan's email displayed old messages about the monied widows. He'd become a hand-holder of the rich, easing them and their pet projects into an era of greater media presence and greater media scrutiny.

Usually the concept "rich" made him keen and wide-eyed, but in assigning the widows to Jonathan, Harrington had underscored that these women were "old" TeagueCarlson clients with staid public personas. Forward-bounding ATC would take on livelier clients—the disrupters and innovators with volatility in their impact and their reputations. Jonathan had the graveyard shift.

Harrington hadn't answered Friday emails, and formerly Alicia picked up the thread when Harrington had other business. At the Chicago gala, two people quietly asked after Alicia, and Jonathan replied with a pleasant nothing. Melanie Genereux never brought up her name. Just as well, he had no idea if Alicia had indeed quit, or where she had gone.

He coughed at the screen. He called the clinic to request another round of antibiotics and an inhaler. He checked voice mail. Harrington was nothing if not a nag, but he had seemed a role model, someone who was not *the* top, not where the buck stopped, yet someone with *access*. Jonathan examined his fingernails, fiddled with a pen, viewed the weather forecast on his phone app— tomorrow would be wet and wetter—and again checked his inbox. A string theory of emails from other people. He made himself open a search engine to confirm the news heard while driving from the airport: the discovery of an unidentified man's corpse in the refuge. Unthinkable. How would they *find* a body there? No reason, absolutely no reason on earth to think … Jonathan's chest ached and he fought for a breath.

CHAPTER 5

꙳

E rik passed on the information that magnets, the swallowing of them, could be fatal to Detective Deb Metzger. He had just clicked off the Monday afternoon call to Trish Gerard, the social worker handling the Haugen case. Gerard was on her way to the emergency room. Her ten-year-old son was in no immediate peril from ingesting magnets, and Trish's experience of waiting in ER's made it possible for her to tell Erik that she'd have adequate time to speak with him and his partner about Haley Haugen. She named the hospital and added, "You'll know me by my middle-class afro, red eyeglasses, and irresponsible son."

Erik had spent hours online, his partner on the phone, kicking up leads on the first missing girl. The sheriff one county north used the G-Met interest and the threat of new evidence to scare up leads of his own, and that girl materialized, held by an adult cousin. The sheriff arrested the cousin and recovered the girl, and the girl's step-mother vowed to start her on a different, less visible recovery. She was not the girl of Harrington's shoe photo.

That left Haley, Trish Gerard's case. The detectives entered the waiting area shortly after 2:00 p.m. A moan to the left set Erik on edge. He scanned the space for exits and saw the moan's source—a man in tattered tweed lifted his raw weepy eyes to Erik before aiming spit at him.

"No—over here," Deb snapped and indicated Gerard. The social worker sat across the room absorbed with her laptop, while the boy sealed himself off from the room's social mélange with ear-buds attached to a hand-held game. His thumbs flew.

"We'll need privacy," Erik said and moved to the head of the reception line.

"Hey," a woman yelled as he brushed beside her at the counter. "Hey, dude, I'm having a baby here!" Her hoodie lacked a baby bump and read, "Over Easy."

"No you're not," the young receptionist said to the woman. Her eyes never left the computer.

"Am too!"

"Only if you got lucky last night. You weren't yesterday." The receptionist skimmed the credentials Erik placed on the counter. She looked up to his eyes and swallowed honey. "Detective? I know you. You run by that Lake Nokomis cafe." She hesitated. "Don't you?"

"Uh, depends on my training schedule."

"You come in all heated up from sprinting."

"I'm more of a distance man." Erik relaxed himself over the counter and peered at her identification clip—"Patrice."

"Your form must be so important, Detective"—

"This is urgent." Deb elbowed herself between them. "A private place to talk with Ms. Gerard over there, waiting with her son."

Patrice came from behind the counter to direct them, glanced coolly at Deb and inclined uncomfortably close to Erik. The woman in line clutched his arm.

"This baby," she hiss-spit in his face, "it could be yours."

THE WHEELCHAIR-ACCESSIBLE DRESSING ROOM WITH a bench on one side and two folding chairs on the other could, theoretically, hold four people. Erik and Deb squeezed together on the bench. Gerard's son, eyes glued to the game, slid into a chair and pulled his legs up under him, as his mother settled beside him. Gerard's knees, as she arranged her bag, her coat, and her laptop, bumped into Erik's. He jostled for position, bumping into Deb's broad shoulders. She jostled back.

Gerard bumped Erik's knee again as she addressed Deb. "You have amazing cheek bones—they draw attention to those huge eyes of yours. That must be the first thing people notice about you."

"Actually, my size."

"Oh, I've seen much bigger women, behind bars. You're not from Minnesota, the way you talk?"

"I grew up in Iowa." Deb leaned back, trying to gain space. "You can tell the difference between an Iowa and Minnesota accent?"

"I'm from Iowa, too," Erik threw in. There wasn't room for both sets of shoulders.

"Your son, Ms. Gerard," his fellow Iowan spoke up as they squirmed their way back into personal spaces. "What happened?"

"It's Trish. Austin was trying to impress eighth-grade girls—ha!—with his 'magnetic appeal.' He made a tongue stud with magnets from science class and was showing it off until the girls squealed 'gross.' When he closed his mouth, the magnets went down the tubes. His teacher"—she poked Austin who removed an ear-bud. "Your science teacher's name?"

"Cheesit." The ear-bud went in again.

"Mr. Chezik said if the magnets joined when swallowed, Austin would be fine. If they separated and were drawn to each other despite intervening flesh and membrane, well"—

"Some magnets *repel*." Deb interjected as she and Erik bumped shoulders again.

Gerard leaned between them. "Mr. Cheesit, *Chezik*, explained to Austin and his non-admirers adhesion, closure, and implosion. One girl vomited, but Austin kept his cool, which was unfortunate. If the x-ray show separate magnets, it's surgery. If they're safely joined, it's prunes for Austin."

Austin glanced up, his gigabyte foe took the advantage, and an explosion jumped from the device. "Ow, I killed myself."

The boy was resurrected and absorbed in another bout before Deb passed to Gerard a copy of the mystery-girl photo.

"Tell me again, where was this found?" Gerard asked.

"In the shoe of a corpse, man died about two weeks ago, no ID yet," Erik answered. "Expensive shoes, expensive suit, expensive tie. Brown hair beginning to gray, 5' 8," late 40s, weight about 150."

"Not Dwight Haugen, for sure. Dirty—and I mean dirty—blond. Hasn't been that small since seventh grade." Gerard gently waved the photo up and down. "If you told me this was Haley Haugen, I'd say, I see that. If you told me it *wasn't* Haley, I'd say lots of girls have that look." She launched into Haley's story.

The more Erik heard, the more the scenario sounded all too common. That is, if Haley had been abducted by her father Dwight Haugen and not fallen prey to other psychopathic possibilities.

At the depth of the recession, Dwight had been furloughed from his job at the St. Paul Ford plant and did not take it well. His heavy drinking went to heavier drinking. Once a half-eaten casserole—"hot-dish" according to the police report Gerard shared—had become hood décor for Lorena's van. In a later report, both Haugens answered the cops' knock covered with a substantial amount of another hot dish, "over-salted." Haley and her little sister Sierra spent more and more nights, even during the school-week, at sleepovers. Haley's middle-school grades yo-yoed up and down; Gerard commented that her hormones were yo-yoing too.

Meanwhile, Dwight's furlough turned into a pink slip. He clung to a beer-infused hope that he'd be rehired, then the whole plant closed. Dwight got a non-union construction gig last August, to be laid off when cold weather arrived. He began complaining of back pain and spent his days on the couch, his nights at bars. After a third upended hot dish, he vanished at the end of February in his pride and joy, the battered V6 standard cab XL 4WD red Ranger, and took a family credit card, quickly maxed out. Lorena Haugen relied on her big-box store wages, the local food shelf, and a heating fuel program to get by. She refused to answer his calls after he left a message saying she could get a divorce anytime she wanted to pay for it.

Then Dwight began intercepting Haley on her way home from school (Sierra stayed for aftercare) to say he'd work things out. He gave his older daughter cash, source unknown. Back in March, Haley admitted to a teacher that the previous afternoon he drove up to her totally buzzed and pleaded through the truck window that she fetch her sister. She ran into a coffee shop while he drove over the sidewalk, crushed a woman's low hanging monster bag (*Longchamp* italicized in the incident report), shouted "squinched-butt latte liberal," and peeled off. The girl was used to him a little drunk. This was scary different.

When authorities tried to reach Dwight Haugen, his phone was out of service. Lorena swore that he went over his limit sexting a bottle-blonde, bottle-brained bimbo. Dwight's limit can be small, Lorena told Gerard, "and he reaches it fast." Two days later Haley wasn't around when Lorena and Sierra arrived home, and her phone was off. Haugen had been doing odd jobs at fishing-hunting-drinking cabins up north. His buddies there pleaded ignorance of his whereabouts, though one guy said he'd happily rat out Haugen for Haley's sake. That is, if Haugen had taken her.

Erik was absorbing this, Deb asking questions on how to best approach Lorena, and Austin announcing the number of knot-wits he'd destroyed, when an attendant arrived to say the boy would be moved to radiology "in ten." Gerard concluded with a warning, "I'd keep close tabs on Haugen's next-door buddy, Brent Nail, aka 'Bent.'"

"Bent Nail? Have they gotten into trouble?" Erik sat up.

"Nail hangs out at his house and friends' cabins building his own line of furniture. The stuff looks like logs dropped on a buzz saw and reassembled with duct tape. He and Haugen spent a night in jail together."

"Did Bent get between Lorena and her husband?" Deb asked.

"No. The boys were out drinking on Lorena's paycheck when guys at the bar invented a game, 'hit the Nail on the head.' Bent was the victim until he decided that Haugen could be Thor and he could be the hammer. Thor/ Haugen picked Nail/Hammer and threw him at the others. Anyway, Haley. These cases can be simple—parent takes kid, parent brings kid back. Good luck."

As the radiology attendant claimed Austin, Gerard's phone buzzed and she stiffened: "Speak of the devil, it's Lorena Haugen. Something's up.

CHAPTER 6

꧁

They often want final solutions. Deb stiffened in the seat of the fleet car as Erik spoke the Haugen address into the GPS system. She knew the neighborhood from college internships spent in the Twin Cities, internships which taught Deb that her temperament better suited enforcement than social work. Back in Iowa, the last case she worked involved an estranged father who, while the wife was at work, dropped in on the sitter and the two children. The man had explained that he'd take the kids for ice cream and the sitter could take a break, which after a call to the mother, she did. An hour later, the sitter returned to find the children's bodies, two shots in each, under the father's, blood and milkshakes spreading across the floor.

It had been a soul-sinking case of déjà vu. Deb had been that babysitter once, only she walked in to find the pregnant mom on the floor, half her face gone, and when the police arrived they had Deb coax the blood-spattered four-year-old out of an under-stairs hidey-hole.

Nothing in Lorena's phone call implied disaster. The woman sounded more pissed than anything as she complained that Dwight had called and blam, hung up. But the coincidence of the shoe-photo find fired in Deb's brain all sorts of horrendous outcomes. The DMV image of Dwight Haugen showed weight to throw around. Erik, having contacted potential back-up, was *humming* to himself.

"*You'd* want every lead followed." Deb's explosion on the "you" made him jump. "If it was your kid, you'd want, you know"—

Erik nodded what Deb took as agreement as he drove them through the high-crime heart of the Minneapolis Third Precinct. As they turned off East Lake Street to drive south toward Minnehaha Park, she tracked the ebb and flow of housing values. "For Sale" signs popped up along the Haugen block, a rundown section with tiny duplexes.

"If your kid was missing"—Deb caught her repetition as Erik peered ahead. Maybe his pretty-boy eyes could charm Lorena to share. Lorena had grumbled over the phone that she'd meet them before it was time to pick up little Sierra. Deb then asked, "Are you safe?" "What, sure, of course," Lorena snorted. You don't push the girl's photo into the mother's face first thing. Add to that a police sketch based on the corpse's dimensions and tailored clothes, maybe someone known to the family, though it strained Deb to think how.

Erik weaseled into a space a half block past the Haugens. Crumbling stones made a path over a mud-mat of a lawn, and a faded flag of hearts drooped from a pole and hid the door. A woman peeked out the window and withdrew. Deb signaled her partner to hang back.

She rehearsed in her head the right tone of assurance as she climbed the uneven steps. She reached out to knock—the door banged open and a man threw himself at her like a dirty Viking on a bender. She fought for balance as they grappled. He pulled back for a second—Dwight Haugen all right—and barreled his bulk at her again. *What had Lorena said to him?* Deb dodged and grabbed his bicep hard, his head-butt missed yet he was stunned—he'd smacked into the invisible cement block on her shoulder. She pivoted to throw him off—he was out of shape and whacked-out and ignoring Erik's commands. She tightened again on the arm as Dwight Haugen grabbed at the heart flag, ripping it and falling. Deb shifted her weight to keep from sliding under him and caught sight of a skinny man, moustache drooping and snow shovel held like a torch, running from next door and yowling—must be Bent Nail. He locked on her eyes for a second and without breaking stride, he boomeranged back to his house. Haugen shoved and Deb's foot slipped and she swallowed air. She dropped fifteen inches, the rough concrete scraping her shin all the way down with three hundred pounds of Dwight about to crush her, when Erik grabbed the man's matted hair, and the two of *them* fell backwards and rolled on the ground. Deb grabbed her bloody shin and blinked through tears to see Erik extricate himself as Haugen screamed "You effin' Ballerina!" Erik did a fast over-under dance wrapping Haugen's hands behind him for handcuffs and Haugen fell hard on his backside. Lorena came up from behind shouting "I got a gun"—a hair dryer—and the cord whipped Deb's face. She clamped her jaw against stinging pain and hauled herself up to secure Lorena, whose innocence or collaboration could be determined later. Deb was gasping when grinning Erik seized the credit, "Viking down, Dryer blocked, Nail bent."

"Haley!" Lorena, in Deb's arm-lock, screamed as uniformed officers ran up to them. "The bastard parks around the block"—a head twist left—"He barged in sayin' Haley needed 'woman help' when you"—a pink-eyed glare at Deb—"showed up." Deb ran-stumbled around the corner despite the wetness around her ankle, leaving Erik to deliver the adult Haugens to backup. Behind bushes trimmed by a punk rocker, a rusted Subaru sat half on a neighbor's daffodils, half on the curb. Let her be alive, let her be safe. There Haley was in the car.

CHAPTER 7

✧

Haley had heard her mother scream and then a stranger's shout, "*Police!*" A woman with spiked hair and way tall charged around the corner, strong like she could be in the Olympics. Haley slunk down and the woman slowed, held up a badge, and said, "You're safe. Safe."

The woman stopped ten feet away. Something made Haley unlock the door but she didn't move. She could hear the woman like they weren't sirens everywhere. "Detective Deb Metzger, you're safe, Haley."

Haley began sobbing, "He took my phone! He took my phone! He took my phone!"

The woman helped her out and they were at the front of the house. Police had Dad handcuffed. Mom was screaming without sound, a first. There was a man in a messed-up suit with this face that was kind of wow. Haley made herself turn toward her dad and saw him as they would see him, dirty, drunk and druggy.

In the middle of February, Dad had vamoosed, Mom went from one hissy fit to another, Sierra was clingy, and school sucked big time. All Haley had were frenemies, Sydney and her drama, Karin and her mean-girl schemes. It had gotten suckier when the boys in her group wanted the girls to post nudies on Instagram. The girls said sure, when you put *your* bits online and it had to be Jacob who put up a crotch-shot of an old grown-up, so gross. Then there was a pic that could be anyone of the guys, or a politician. Next breasts went up, with brown hair hanging down them not hiding a thing. The hair was like hers, but it wasn't her. It had to be Sydney with a wig or something. But everybody said that it was Haley's humungous honkers. On Yik-Yak nameless guys bragged about how they got her to do it and next there'd be pictures of her ass. She would have kicked their scrawny asses if she knew for sure which guys has posted the photos.

By March Haley wanted to stay home. She was sick she told Mom, who said "yeah, right," and sent her off. Her chest hurt, probably because it was getting so humongous, yeah, right again. Third day she felt dizzy. She called Dad at lunch period (the guys yucked they would never call it "period" which was a sick girl thing). The call wouldn't go through. She tried their neighbor dude, Mr. Nail, and left a message. Next day her Dad drove by in his pickup as she was going home and he said they'd take a vacation to the lake cabin. She thought that would make her feel better right away. It didn't. Dad wanted to leave after one night. So they ended up she didn't know where, a bigger cabin with three little bedrooms and a center room with this monster black stove and smoky hanging antlers. Everything was hazy. She was sicko miserable. Dad made her stay by herself and said he was going to find the hobbit. Or hobo or hermit, whatever.

She dozed, hallucinated for sure. Someone gawked in the window, there was a chin. Or it was that dumb ruffle curtain moving. At home, Mom was always closing the curtains because of peeping Toms, dirty old men who wanted to see you naked. She didn't sit around naked, and why would anybody peep when there was the internet full of stupid boys posting humongous honkers?

Dad came back, smelling of booze, with antibiotics, Tylenol, and cough medicine, the best kind, he said, with codeine. She took pills, a swig of syrup that tasted like old cherries, and crawled back onto her lumpy mattress. Something was knocking at her head, or the door. It happened again. Then Dad was yelling, "Hey, bring it back." The next morning, she woke up to use the bathroom, at least it wasn't a hole in the woods. She asked Dad about the knocking. He acted stoned and slurred, "That guy left it on the step, it's okay," then snored. "It"—her phone, which Dad had taken? She couldn't find it, it had to be on him, but no way she would search him. She took another round of drugs and returned to bed.

She slept like weeks, a real sleeping beauty except her hair wasn't washed and her face sprouted zits. Dad was gone a lot, then he was teaching her to play cards, then she hid in a bedroom when strange buddies of his showed up for poker, and when they left he rigged up the TV with a foil antenna. It was the Final Four Something. She didn't know basketball could be so great. Fast, big guys pounding and sweating. She was still sweating and beginning to feel crampy. Crampy in the stinky cabin, crampy in the gut. Dad was out of it. She wanted her mother, she wanted to go home, she cried.

So today Dad brought her home, only police got him. And Haley had Mom now, only to ride with her and the detective woman in an ambulance, away from home. She cried.

CHAPTER 8

❧

L ucky me—Deb hobbled across the ER waiting era for the second time
that day. Her first full Monday on a G-Met case and she'd landed herself
in the hospital. Haley Haugen had been checked in by Trish Gerard and her
mother for overnight observation and treatment of bronchitis. As far as Deb
could make out, Dwight Haugen had brought his daughter hundreds of miles
back for tampons. Whatever it takes. He was in overnight as well, checked
right into a guarded hospital room to sleep off substances he'd consumed.

Deb's wait for medical attention was longer since she had to submit
incident reports. So here she was again, at the very station where flirty Patrice
had oozed over her partner Erik. Pain from her encounter with Dwight set off
nausea. A little ginger ale of relief bubbled up when she saw a new shift had
replaced Patrice. An orderly insisted on wheeling her to x-ray waiting. She
pulled out her phone but hesitated over making the call—no need to panic a
panicker. Wait, hell, the panicker, the ex-girlfriend by Deb's choice, was gone
from her life. She must need serious meds.

She was abandoned in an empty room by radiology for a second round of
waiting. Her left shin and right shoulder throbbed to a god-awful techno beat
out of the speakers. She covered her ears and studied the pain poster on one
wall. Smiley Faces had met their just desserts to indicate misery on a one to
ten scale. She was deciding if her mouth was a straight line four or a Harpo-
Marx-in-need-of-narcotics nine, when her side vision caught a sweet-faced
man approaching. He bent over someone, Erik? The sweet face must have
been a delusion or it attached to the boy with him, about five years old. The
boy held out a bag greasy with fries and smelling of hot burger.

"What do you say, Ben?" Erik, blank-faced and hiding behind a child.

"Hi, I'm Ben, and Daddy said you could have this 'cause you beat up a man. I got the same." Ben looked up to his father who held another bag.

"Officer Deb defended herself," he corrected. Father and son had the same eyes. "There's also a hummus and vegie-stuffed pita."

"I can eat your fries," Ben said.

"Thank you, Ben. I'm happy to meet you." Deb smiled and took the hot food. Ben received his own fries and sat beside her to eat.

"You're okay?" Erik stood at court-martial attention.

"I've had my share of injuries. I intend to be on duty tomorrow."

"We have a lead. The medical examiner recovered finger prints from Swamp John Doe." Erik's eye followed a French fry the boy retrieved from the floor. "Hope all goes quickly from there."

The odds had flipped. Haley was alive, the holder of the photo was not. Tension eased from Deb's locked muscles, but that hint of relaxation left her faint. There was a humming around her. Oh, Ben humming between French fries.

"Do you need a ride?" Erik spoke from somewhere remote.

"I've arranged one," Deb lied to the hurty-face poster. Damned if she'd pass out in front of them. "I bet you two have to head home to bed."

"Am I staying with you tonight, Daddy?" Ben hopped up and spilled fries on her lap and the floor. "Mom said I had to be back. I don't, do I? Daddy? Do I?"

The attendant broke in with "Deb Metzger." She stood and moved fast to get a jump on the queasiness. She didn't want to know how this encounter would end.

CHAPTER 9

⧫

People clung to the walls as Erik marched through the G-Met hallways Tuesday morning, an indication he must be fuming. Last night after the hospital, he wanted to explode in super-nova anger, but being his father's son he didn't. Kristine, his former wife, burned scarlet at Ben's pleading that they overturn a custody schedule as calibrated as a space launch. When the scarlet was about to yield to tears, Erik placated Ben with ridiculous future scenarios (and hid the ketchup-stained jacket); the boy went to bed not delighted but not sobbing. To cope with divorce, he should have spent less time training in SWAT-like maneuvers and more in crisis negotiation.

This case would be over all ready, his new partner Deb on her way to another, if they had an ID for the wetland corpse. When you know *who* someone is, you generally know *why* he's dead. And this man was dead in a way that made Erik's flesh crawl as he read the M.E.'s preliminary report. The fingerprints, obtained by a Frankenstein-like inflation of decayed skin, had no match in the system. More reason for fuming. He knocked his head against his office desk three times—no luck in it, but a possible bruise.

Post encounter, Dwight Haugen and Haley were undergoing physical and psychological evaluations. No opportunity yet to ask about the photo found with the dead man. There was that crawling sensation again as Erik speculated about—what did Deb call him—Swamp Guacamole's connection to a girl. She'd left a voice message that she was taking the day off, despite what she'd said last night, to dope up on ibuprofen and dumb down on TV. Her wounds were irritating. Irritating—described herself there, though skilled in a cropped blonde Xena Warrior Princess kind of way.

It was irritating that he'd missed his morning run. Erik hated missing his run. He'd slept past his usual 6:00 a.m. rising time and had to rush to his ex-wife's house for a pre-arranged breakfast with Ben. According to routine, Kristine should be armored in her lawyer suit and on her way out. This morning Erik fixed breakfast (it had been his house too, he knew where the utensils were) while she showered. She entered the kitchen, red-eyed and buttoning her blouse, grabbed two dry pancakes, and dashed to her Subaru. Erik deduced that her "mentor" had not come over last night, no man-sock odor. A year ago, that bastard—base, duplicitous lawyer-bastard—had "mentored" her into bed. At least he stayed away on her Ben nights. The boy did ask as Erik drove him to kindergarten why Mommy had a special person but Daddy didn't. He was tempted to say, because Daddy's a two-timed fool caught between self-righteous rage and sick-puppy loyalty. Instead, he replied, "Daddy's saving all his time for you."

Almost a relief to have a relationship with a dead person. Erik should reread the ME's report on the wetland corpse but felt an urge for action. He rubbed his thighs, stood up, circled his desk, stretched his quads, stretched all over, and gazed out the filmy office window. Heavy clouds mobbed themselves into a dark threat, making midday like night. He stared down at his computer screen as if literal distance would give him perspective and reread the M.E.'s report.

Cause of death, basal skull fracture. The man would have been rendered immediately unconscious, with death occurring within minutes. The wound had traces of grit, concrete, and a composite consistent with stair-tread material; there was blood on the clothing, but not as much as the man would have lost from the injury. He may have been wearing an overcoat or been wrapped in something absorbent. The back of the head hit the edge of an immoveable object, at an angle with the head coming down and with a force indicating velocity beyond that of a normal slip. No wallet, keys, phone. Possible scenario: someone chases the man down a parking ramp stairway—plenty by the airport and there's still ice—the victim does a cartoon flip with feet flying up and head falling down, only he doesn't bounce. But a tragic fall can't be the whole plot. A man dressed like an executive would likely surrender a wallet when threatened. A stranger finding a man dying on a stairway might be the anti-Samaritan and take his belongings, but would not go to elaborate lengths to hide the body. A gang initiation? Those generally involved rivals. A perpetrator with means dumped the body and fled by plane?

The phone rang its annoying institutional PBX ring, half-bell half-siren. Erik uttered the standard response in a deep quick voice, "Detective Erik Jansson."

"It's Paul, forwarding a tip email sent to local law enforcement agencies, including us—might relate to your swamp find. I haven't traced the origin,

seems sent through proxy servers. Doing as much as I can without a warrant."
He hung up.

News from Paul in G-Met's Cyber-Tech unit always had to be taken
seriously. Erik opened the email: "Niland Harrington is missing." That was it.
He clicked into DMV computer records and his heart raced. Harrington's size,
age, hair, and blood type matched the corpse. Erik trolled for an employer,
a Minneapolis public relations firm with high-end clients, Allston Tigue
Carlson or ATC. He called: Harrington hadn't been in the office for two
weeks according to a receptionist. She tried to reach "the last of Harrington's
team," a Jonathan Lewis: no answer. Harrington's supervisor, Stephen Drexler,
was overseas. Erik left messages for all, tried the DMV phone number for
Harrington, and then a cell number provided by the receptionist. Zero
answers. The tell-tale email account was registered to Niland Harrington.

Had the man reported himself missing and anticipated his own death?
Barely credible. More credible, Harrington and his computer had been
hijacked and the murderer decided to tease officials. But why, and why now?

CHAPTER 10

❧

Five o'clock commuters and a foggy rain clogged Erik's drive to the dead man's apartment.

He had called Deb to brief her, a brief brief: Niland Harrington, forty-four, employed by Allston Tigue Carlson, no known life partner, had presumably left for vacation over two weeks ago. DNA from gloves left at Harrington's office confirmed the ID. Deb sounded pained to hear from him but said she would come back on duty.

Painful to admit, Erik had difficulty with partners. There'd been the incomprehensible floundering of his marriage, and his professional partnerships had not sailed smoothly either. The only so far at G-Met, white-haired Loften, had been a bland edification in standard detection and the perils of Type 2 Diabetes, from which the senior officer suffered. After a few cases that required Erik's input and quick legwork, Loften announced he would move on before the youngster stole his thunder. Not that Erik was sour-apple green. He had been hotly seasoned as a uniformed officer in a Minneapolis precinct.

His partner then was also an older man, Bob Uhle. For Erik the last name became "Youll" as in "you'll be sorry." Uhle, his height towering and his nose like a camel's, introduced himself as a Big Man of Few Words: the first assertion was undeniable and the second no one dared contest. Uhle had a great slap-on-your-back rapport in the precinct and union. They jawed about his high arrest rate and how his collars arrived at the station in silent compliance. Erik learned why in lessons unrecorded prior to body-cams. Uhle came across as understanding, lenient even, when people explained how their teenager must have slipped a drug trace into the Volvo, how they'd had a sip of bubbly over a colleague's promotion and were more tired than anything, how they'd pretty please like to call a lawyer before another word.

However, be down-and-out, be a woman with jaundiced skin and a waistline of despair, and Uhle would launch into a rant that was more threat than advice. He'd speak down his camel nose to the woman that those s-o-b public defenders would see her as an effing whore and pry into every filthy pore of her sucky life so they could cover their hairy butts when some a-hole prosecutor proved what a stinkin' load of crap she was. That was the cleanest example.

Erik knew about relentless persistence in interrogation. He'd received buckets of spit in the face during Marine Officer Training, where he was called Candidate Incapable (all of them were Candidates Incapable). He'd also been trained more than once about hate-speech and harassment, and knew Uhle was required to take refresher courses online. On the street, Uhle ignored the department code for interaction, and Erik's hints about the tone Uhle took with "fuckin' unfortunates" failed. So Erik explicitly told Uhle that he was harassing them.

Erik was called Officer Pussy on their rounds thereafter. When Uhle chatted up his cronies, he called his young partner "Lambkin" and set off a laugh riot. Erik opted for not responding to Pussy or Lambkin, which brought Uhle close to throttling him. The next time Uhle cornered a woman and let flow his verbal sewer, Erik interrupted with a text-book explanation of the system to her and later told Uhle he'd be forced to report him. Uhle thought this hilarious and swore he'd back off. He didn't, and in reports Uhle began including his rude phrases as coming out of Erik's mouth. Then there was an obscene shaming tirade against a girl, under eighteen, high as a kite, toddler in tow, in terrible need. Erik said nothing to Uhle but blew the whistle through the requisite forms.

Internal Affairs gave Erik a harsh and proper grilling. Uhle was put on leave. Unreliable witnesses were called in for rounds of he said/she said/he said/ yeah he said/hell no I never said. Whenever Erik left his precinct desk, he'd return to find toilet paper steeping in his coffee. He became invisible, except to a few who stopped him in the parking lot to make extraordinarily cheerful remarks about the weather.

Uhle retired early with a noisy send-off backed by the undertone of rumors—his collars were too often released, it was about time, no surprise, too bad about the others. (*Other what*, Erik wondered.) Through dealings not completely transparent, he was sent to Quantico, where he'd already endured the Marines, for a police investigation and leadership course. Boot-camp agony worsened by lectures. He landed at G-Met.

He'd arrived now at Harrington's apartment building, where the Tuesday-night gloom had triggered the street lights. Red and yellow tulips bordering the building were battered down to wet glowing rags. By the curb, a cobalt-blue BMW 3 series sat slick and gleaming . At the end of the street a beat-up van and two pickups seemed out of place, except a pickup's never out of place in Minnesota. One of the CSI team claimed a section for department vehicles. Parking was at a premium, as were the renovated penthouses that lined the eastern shore of Lake Bde Maka Ska.

Deb Metzger drove up in a hybrid and raised herself out of it like a giant school girl in a yellow slicker. Her brightness made Erik realize he'd worked himself into a funk. He fidgeted in the entryway of the building's north side and noted the lack of security cameras.

Deb reached him in a few strides. "Did the cat die?"

"I don't have a cat."

"It's an expression," she growled.

He said nothing as he opened the door and worked his jaw out of a clench.

A bug-eyed building supervisor directed them to floor five and unlocked the door. Deb behind him, Erik entered a passage that opened to a dim interior. The apartment spread out to a raised seating area with a picture window that should have a vista, but rain water hitting lake water conjured up fog. He summoned in the CSI team, led by Foster in his ubiquitous lab coat and anti-snakebite boots. After a technician checked a switch for prints, Erik flipped it to cast light into the spare modernist space. No signs of disruption or violence. The thermostat at the end of the hall indicated seventy-two degrees. Midwesterners, proudly tight, set thermostats lower for predictable absences. He directed a tech to check if the device was "smart" with memory of past settings. The tech looked dubious but had watched enough television to half-believe that eccentric detectives must be on to something.

He had progressed fourteen feet and Deb's breath scorched his neck. He rubbed his tightening forehead and signaled her to pass. To their left were bathroom and bedrooms doors, to the right a black granite counter set off the kitchen area. In the lower dining area, artful objects stood artfully displayed. Harrington could have a swanky party here, for twenty, even thirty. Yet there were no water-glass marks on the counter, no plants on the sill, no pet hairs on the chair.

Deb broke the emptiness. "This"—her voice echoed as she pointed to a large painting occupying the left wall—"comes from the school of 'Put Daisies in a Blender.'"

He bit back a smile and nodded toward a mottled painting on the right—"and that?"

"Derivative school. Barfed peonies." Deb was about to comment on a third rashy-looking canvas when Foster dramatically cleared his throat to hurry things along.

Deb headed to the side tables in the elevated section to examine photo albums for any image like the one on the corpse. Erik went to a wood-paneled office on the left. Glossy magazines' "Who's Who" photographs covered one wall. Harrington's was not the image he noticed first, though he soon picked him out. The man was as expected, his size average, his smile an unrevealing curve.

What probably mattered most was the company he kept. A jowly mogul occupied front and center in all photos. A tall refined man, maybe forty, generally stood between Harrington and the mogul—likely Harrington's superior, Stephen Drexler. In several a woman with wild strawberry-blonde hair and a heart-shaped face stood out. She beamed next to Mogul, appeared delighted by Polished Man, and wore a flat face with Harrington.

Then there was the photo that first caught his eye: between Harrington and the presumed Drexler posed a woman with large eyes and lustrous black hair. Her features were Latina, but the pale sheen of her skin was lighter than Erik's.

He directed Foster to examine the desk and file cabinet. Three shelves held books on business, biographies of the successful, and dvd's on golf. Next to the shelves a door opened to the bathroom, stocked with antacids. The other side of the bathroom opened to the bedroom. Erik stepped into the room just as Deb entered from a different door.

"Oh," she gulped and he had a sharp intake as they took in the panorama. Black and white photos of nudes—male and female—hung on every wall.

"Oh," Deb repeated. "In the category of 'I know it when I see it,' there's pornography, and then there's—this. No violence, no children. Nudes aren't exactly neutral for profiling a pedophile but"—her voice shook—"I, I've seen worse in movies."

Erik faced an enlarged pelvis shot of a fully formed adult male.

"Yeah, that's the only full frontal." Deb defensively squared her shoulders.

Erik cruised by a half a buttock, then—it could have been, it wasn't, it couldn't be, the breast, Kristine. No, of course not, his judgment was impaired in this overheated bedroom, damn thermostat not doing its job.

Deb attacked. "You *memorizing* that breast?"

He glared her into silence. In the living area, rain slapped the windows. Foster stuck his head in.

"We're discussing *art*." Erik clipped the last word. The technician ducked away.

"I mean, they're not *that* hot," Deb said. "Not *real* quality, you know, like those nudes of Georgia O'Keeffe, the ones her arty-farty old boyfriend took. *Those* have character."

"You know photography?" He didn't keep the fight from his voice and her red face was the only color in the room.

"Well, I know those. I mean, you get these to make guests think you're a sexy whatever. *If* guests are ever here. Except for your friend full-frontal, I bet law-abiding citizens in this neighborhood have racier stuff. I mean, *parents*, anybody's parents could have these."

"Parents. *Your* parents?"

"My parents? In Iowa? Hell no, *heck* no. Yours?"

"Also in Iowa." He surveyed the images again. "There'd be discussion. My mother would talk about freedom of expression and acceptance of the human body. My father would pretend to listen. A price would be mentioned—you wouldn't find these at Target. And they'd be *What? That much? Real money?* My mother would mention children in Africa, my father fishing gear. Wait, wait—that would have been *before* my sister found a job with a male professor, drawing class. Life Model."

"I'd like to meet this sis"—Deb began but Foster entered with news. "There seems to be a brother in San Francisco, a mother long dead, a father in an Illinois Alzheimer's unit. In the closet there's golf paraphernalia and a bag with his college team logo. And I need help with the desk. Drawer won't budge."

The three of them surrounded the desk in the office. Foster pointed to the middle drawer on the right.

"Sit on it," Erik said. He meant Deb, but Foster took the role of counter-weight. Deb kicked the side of the desk as Erik pulled the handle hard and saved himself from falling on his rear.

The drawer held a Kleenex box and travel brochures.

"Why was it stuck?" Erik persisted. He dropped to his knees and took a flashlight from Foster. Fallen between the bottom drawer and the front panel of the desk was a small flip notebook, the kind people kept in a pocket before cell phones vanquished them. A flip through showed "HAB Breakthrough," "Thomas," and then "S.D." linked to dates and places from seven months ago in Chicago to one month ago in Minneapolis.

"South Dakota?" Deb asked.

"More likely Stephen Drexler, Harrington's superior," Erik said. Another page appeared to be a password list.

The notebook was something, but nothing in the apartment connected to a missing girl. Deb confirmed that the main room photo albums had old images that could be a father and brother and recent ones of golf buddies to be identified. She sounded annoyed. Foster looked annoyed. Erik *was* annoyed. There was an absence. "No computer," he grumbled. What could you know of a man without his computer?"

THE SAVORY SMELL OF ROAST chicken and the spicy one of green curry drifted through the hallway, and Erik's stomach ached to reply. Niland Harrington's neighbors had gone back to fixing their dinners after revealing next to nothing. The curry, a single man, had already forgotten anything he knew about Harrington, except for the golf obsession. The roast chicken, a young couple, knew Harrington had a "top-secret" project and despised cats, particularly their white hair-factory who tried to rub herself naked against Erik's pants.

The crime scene team had left. Foster took a cashbox with a computerized lock which required dismantling in the lab, along with the bed sheets—how terrible to think a man is his sheets. Deb's face again registered pain or psychic indigestion, so she left.

Erik switched off lights to the Harrington apartment and moved toward the door, which had been left ajar. Then a flickering in the lake window, no, a reflection. His heart thumped and he spun back to the door. The rain had ceased and he could swear he heard breathing. Hand on his gun, he eased to the opening, glimpsed the shift of a shadow, and barked "Police!"

A man of medium height in a black jacket and baseball cap slipped into the elevator and hit the buttons before Erik could reach him. Wait and see if he stopped to hide on another floor or rush to the bottom? The man might cross over to the building's south side. Erik leapt the stair rails and ran down the flights.

At the first floor entry, he saw the elevator was on two. Was it slow or had the man already left and sent the elevator on an errand? Erik pushed the exterior door open, ready to run, looking from the elevator landing to down the street. The apartment door next to the elevator opened and a woman buried in a llama-sized sweater stepped out and screamed, "Who *are* you!" and he saw movement outside the south entry and took off.

He was blocked. A small man in a trench coat, earphones plugged in and minute dog in arms, stepped in front of him on the sidewalk. Erik spun him like a dancer and with a "sorry" ran to the corner. A Toyota Camry and an SUV pulled out of parking spaces at the same time and accelerated onto the cross street. The BMW was gone. *Rhhhhr*—a siren screamed and a Ford Interceptor raced up. Sweater woman by the elevator had called the cops on *him*, and the female patrols always wanted to cuff Erik.

If someone was nervous about Harrington's apartment, nervous about being seen, something in the case was very much alive.

CHAPTER 11

❧

Wired tight, Deb peered through the interview room's one-way window to study Dwight Haugen. He sure looked like a thug with secrets. He'd tested positive yesterday for oxycodone and a gross-misdemeanor level of alcohol, two strikes against him beyond the physical ones that had brought him down. It would solve everything if Haugen had rescued his little princess from a drug-dispensing pedophile dweeb, aka Harrington, and then whacked said dweeb. Plus it would put her on the fast track of her new job—she had started a case on Monday and could finish it today, Wednesday. All she needed was a fact or two.

So far the only charge against Haugen was assaulting an officer, i.e., her. The Haley situation was complicated. The parents weren't divorced, so no custody agreement violation, and Haley had wanted to go. Haugen had first taken her to their family cabin near Ely but skipped out before local authorities could catch up with him and hid in a cabin owned by Bent Nail's family two hours north of the cities.

Facts—the other "facts" kept dissolving. The photo found with Harrington's corpse confused Lorena Haugen. When asked if the girl was Haley, Lorena muttered "Dunno." She didn't recognize Niland Harrington's photo. Fact: there was no evidence that Haley had been physically abused. Unknown: psychic trauma. Fact: her dad lost/ran over her phone on the return trip. Probable fact: he said by accident but he might admit to partly on purpose. Supposition: Haugen's bad judgment hadn't become a tragedy for Haley. *If* he had killed, he could plunge into the desperation that makes a man turn on his family to put *all* the problems in the ground once and for all.

Deb bolstered herself—she knew where she stood with him, the bitch cop.

Her scraped-raw leg (damn that rotten step) fired pain as she entered the room. Haugen—hard telling where his hard head was at. Seemed like he'd done just enough head-messing recreational substances that his escape-with-Haley plan had popped, fizzed, and dribbled away. Deb set down a file, seated herself with deliberation, and started.

The first questions of the are-you-really-so-and-so kind made Haugen haul up his shoulders and roll them back. Next he snagged his upper lip to drag up to a sneer. The first move made him look like a gorilla, the second like a rabbit. Haugen had lost the lottery with his pro-bono lawyer—sharpest thing about the legal was his argyle socks and he appeared determined not to be bit by Haugen. Time to speed up the questioning.

"You picked Haley up at the coffee shop in your Ford Ranger."

"Uh," from Haugen. Attorney Argyle cleared his throat, and he amended his answer to a "yes."

"You took her phone?"

"Yeah, told her I didn't want to be tracked 'cause my license was expired. She wasn't happy. You know when she's not happy—she gets real noisy about being quiet. That was nothin' compared to her super-sized wailing when I dropped the phone and the Subaru did a number on it."

Haugen hadn't come back in his own Ranger, recognizable from its Tweety-bird mud-flaps, but in that "borrowed" Subaru: "That vehicle was last registered to your neighbor's, Mr. Nail's, grandfather. Who's been dead three years."

Haugen shrugged.

"So Bent was in on this," she said louder.

"Nail don't know a thing. The rust-bucket happened to be there when my Ranger seized up. I didn't tell him anything, he can't keep a secret. Nail, he's what they call a freakin' *extrovert*. I got nothin' more." Haugen thrust out his chest and snorted.

Deb threw her weight into a stand and smacked her hands down on the table: "Look here, 'Dwight.' You gotta say what went on with Haley *every step of the way*. Know what I think?" Deb opened the file and threw down Niland Harrington's picture. "I think this man took Haley, or tried to take her, you found him, and now he's a corpse!"

"*What?* You're *crazy*! I didn't kill nobody!" Haugen heaved himself up to hit her, she blocked the hand, and he raised the other—

And Argyle slipped between them. "*Take murder off the table!*" He pulled down his client's hand and pushed away Harrington's photo. "I can withdraw my client if you keep up this tone, Detective. Mr. Haugen, stay in your *seat*. You do not need to say anything that incriminates you. For certain 'people' that means saying nothing at all." The lawyer sat back with a thwap. He crossed his legs, resting an ankle on the opposite knee. The diamond pattern of his socks shimmered. The pulse thumped in Haugen's thick neck.

"Mr. Haugen," Deb resumed. "You put *Haley* at risk, your *daughter*, your *little girl*! How do you feel about *that*?"

Argyle sighed on cue. "Again, Detective, do not make assumptions about Mr. Haugen's feelings. His feelings for Miss Haugen are irrelevant." Haugen stared at him, and he in turn stared at a watch big enough to eat dinner on.

Deb spoke firmly to regain Haugen's attention. "We all know it's best for Haley, and you too Mr. Haugen, if we talk this through calmly."

Haugen grabbed his head and moaned. "Haley, she *wanted* to go. Awesome, she said. The poor kid needed to chill from her Mom screaming all the time. My wife's screaming—it's like a 400-pound defensive back slams you, slams you *screaming*." He vigorously rubbed his head. "What's more, Haley was sick and her mother ignored it. I kept the fire going and she stayed in bed coughing. I got her meds, she got better.

"You want to know what *happened*?"—his voice rose but not the body— "I'll tell ya. I took care of 'my little girl.' I kept her *safe*. You want to count every little step, follow me to the toilet, check out my aim? Maybe, Detective, you and your pissy-boy cop friends and sneazly court-turds don't like what I do to feel a little good about the plated green vomit with a side of pureed snot I get for trying to be a *man*!" He stopped abruptly to stare at his crotch. The lawyer interrupted with legal jargon until Haugen stared at him like he was shined shit.

Deb put on a patient face and hoped Haugen would unburden himself, if he remembered what he had to unburden. "I'm with you. You kept Haley safe. You moved. You changed from one cabin to another?"

"Up near Ely, this guy I knew—there were days this guy had money— he said, hey, hang in there with your kid—let's get a card game going, and I told him no. Then he said, 'you could make money with that kid.' Maybe he meant she could work at McDonald's, but I wasn't going to get whatcha call a clarification. We were *out* of there. Went to Nail's, uh, Nail's grandfather's place. I changed whole lakes. You know, Land O Lakes."

"Was this the man with money?" She slapped down the photo of Harrington again.

"Like I said, never seen that dweeb. A guy came to the door while we were at the Nail place to borrow my phone, ow!" The lawyer had rib-jabbed him.

"You let him in?"

"Course not."

"So he used your cell phone? I thought it wasn't working."

"My client does not need to answer irrelevant questions," Argyle said while checking his nails.

"Mr. Haugen, did you tell Haley what your 'friend' said up near Ely? Did that friend, a name would help, follow you to the Nail family cabin?"

"Look, I'm not an *idiot*. No need to work her up. Back at home, she'd work herself up with her phone, like it was an IV. Life's more than a phone. There's TV. When she was sick, I worked like the devil to get reception on a set old enough to remember the first Superbowl. We watched the Final Four tournament. We made bets—not *real* bets—and she got mooney over a player, and I thought we could stay while I fixed up a plan. The Ely guy, never knew a last name. Bob, that's it, Bob."

"So Bob's your uncle?"

"No relation. At Nail's after the Final Four, these headaches started and I wanted to take an axe to my head, and Haley needed stuff, like woman stuff."

"You had an axe!?" Deb said at scream-pitch. The lawyer started to speak but Haugen beat him to it.

"Whoa whoa whoa. I used that axe to cut wood. Made my headaches better, using that maul and splitting the log right down the middle. Stand, hit, split. Stand, hit, split." Haugen grasped his head again.

Deb lifted herself less aggressively than before. "Bob wants your daughter to make money, you change lakes, strangers come to the door, she's sick. You do something right big time, you come back."

"Haley and me were driving around the camp roads, looking for a shortcut back." Haugen paused to get his story straight. "One road looked like it headed southwest to the highway, but it twisted real close to cabins with private way signs. So, uh, not having GPS I got turned around. I kept passing a place with a guy in the driveway, a big bruiser in Carhartt, hosing out a Dodge Ram, a ton of money in that Ram. A truck, Detective, you know, a pickup?"

"I recognize a pickup when it comes at me." That didn't come out right.

"He'd been hosing it out—the snow bank was all red, like in that movie with the woman cop that talks Minnesotan and the wood-chipper. He was still at it on our loop back. Guys up there, they, uh, might *collide* with a deer. I say all friendly, 'You hosing out a dead body?' He acts like he's going to jump me. Mean sonofabitch!"

"And Haley? Did she say anything? Was she worried?"

"Uh, she had to be in the car, yeah. I gunned the Sube, it spun, we took off when it grabbed."

Haugen flopped back. Deb knew a fish tale when she heard one. Not a hook to hang a fact on. Linking him to Swamp Guacamole Harrington was a dead-end. What could've been her big G-Met trophy had become the one that got away.

An officer escorted Haugen back to holding. Deb and Attorney Argyle were shoulder to shoulder, his lower, as they reached the door. He said in an undertone, "You can't defend people like that."

She ended it: "But you can try."

IT WAS STUPID AT THE hospital. Everybody acted like Haley had been molested, like she'd let *that* happen. She could take care of herself, except for like the bronchitis part. She would've been practically dead if Dad hadn't gotten her that Z-pack. After they'd gotten her in a stupid gown like an open-flap pup tent, they put her on an IV with a creepo stick in her hand and put a creepo tube up her nose for oxygen. It did make her feel fresh and clean right away, and the IV had drugs that numbed what Dad called her "female" pains—like, was she really stuck with those for her whole stupid life? If the whole deal made her breasts humongous, then all right. Her mom, unbelievably quiet, held her unplugged hand. The beep-beep-beep monitors faded away and she fell into a pillowy dream. She woke up, had breakfast while her mom went to fetch things, and slept again. She slept to afternoon, and then they were disconnecting her, like free at last from the evil empire.

Really, they were trying. Even her mom was nice so Haley felt bad for running off. Mom slipped a replacement phone, same number so all the contacts and passwords worked, into a flowery quilted bag for her.

Now the woman detective showed up, another grownup who "meant well." The woman made a big deal out of how Haley wasn't in trouble and she wanted to hear Haley speak for herself, if that was fine with her mother, so why not, while Mom waited in the lobby.

They went to a room done up like a library for children. Haley avoided the stuffed Winnie-the-Pooh chair (*really*) and sat at a table.

"You can call me Detective Metzger," the tall woman said. There was a vocab word—*formidable*. This woman had fought her huge dad and freakin' arrested him. "Or Deb if you'd like."

"Why not Detective Deb?" Haley twisted her long horse-tail hair between her fingers.

"You can say that," the woman said. "I just don't want guys on the street calling me that."

That Haley totally got. "I left because Mom didn't believe me about feeling bad, and she wouldn't stop screaming at me because she didn't want to watch a video I brought from school."

"What video?"

Haley whacked her hair away from her face. "One about a mom screaming at her daughter, and a wimpy dork father listening to his wimpy dork son's feelings." Behind Detective Deb's right ear was a wall poster of a kitten hanging by tiny claws from a rope. It kind of stabbed her. She was hanging like the kitten. Actually, *Dad* was the kitten with its little claws about to go.

"Is my dad going to jail? I mean, he'd get drunk and yell at Mom and fall asleep snoring. But he helped me with homework, except the math, 'cause he said they reinvented it." She stuck out her chin. "*You* caught him, didn't you? Can't you let him go?"

"It looks like he'll be out on bail soon, Haley. Being away for as long as you were, no one knowing, that's serious. You handled it. The best I can do for you, for all of you, is to find out exactly what happened." Detective Deb didn't push or expect a line from Haley.

"I mean, can you have screaming depression? I think Mom has screaming depression. Dad has snoring depression."

"We can help them look into that, definitely. Can you tell me more about when you were up north?"

"We went to Ely one night. A creep came to visit Dad, but I fell asleep while they were talking. Next morning Dad takes me to this different place, belonged to Bent Nail's forbears he said. First I thought he meant bears, like some numb Goldilocks thing. I had this cough and was shivery. He got the stove going and had me breathe over steam. He went out to ... to get me medicine, and"—she stopped. She skipped over the part where her Dad had sucked down beer and took OxyContin for back pain. He was so out of it that he claimed a man came by when she was sleeping, borrowed his phone, and brought it back just fine in the morning. Dad must've dreamed that phone stuff because his Walmart burner had already run out of minutes.

Instead, she'd talk more about Dad taking care of her. "I was totally zonked for days. I kinda remember him going out and locking me in. Like, there wasn't even internet. Dad rigged up a foil antenna to a fat TV. We watched basketball. I like that Asian player. It wasn't that different from being at home sick"—she had wanted bad to go home—"then it seemed like we should go. Dad lost my phone and found it when he *crushed* it under the car."

Detective Deb nodded. "You've had to watch out for yourself. You're strong, Haley, you know how to take things, right?"

"Yeah"—strong enough not to rat on Dad.

"I'll show you photos and ask if they have any meaning to you, if that's all right. So, okay, tell me if you recognize anyone." Detective Deb laid out photos of men about her parents' age, a few dressed like bums and a couple in fancy-schmanzy suits. Haley pointed to one of the suits and Detective Deb sucked in a gasp.

"This one looks rich. I don't know people like that." Haley caught the let-down look. "For a cop, you're not good at being stone-faced. Not that being a stone-face is so great."

Detective Deb laughed. "Tell me about it. I work with one. You're doing great, Haley. I have another set of young women. Remember, you're safe. This is to help me out." She spread out photos of girls at different places—the mall, a sports field, a messy room, outdoors. Some images were sharp, some fuzzy.

"Oh, I have jeans like this." It was a fuzzy image of a sleeping girl with hair all over her face. "And our hair's the same." It was way weird, sick weird. "I mean, is she okay? Are these girls missing? Are they *taken*?" She'd seen a movie with a Hollywood Dad hero, totally outrageous, but she didn't feel so sure now. Her voice squeaked. "What's going on?"

"Haley, I try many angles with cases. If nothing looks familiar, fine. If something does strike a bell, it's important to know."

This wasn't about her dad. Something was happening near the cabin, druggies or baddies. Haley studied the men's photos again. "This one, this big monster guy. I didn't see him, but I saw like his cousin. There was this place with a monster pick-up and a man. Fugly. Big Wartface."

"Did this man see you?"

"Dunno. Maybe. He was hosing stuff out his truck, and Dad yelled to him about a dead body, you know, a joke, and this guy look liked he'd smack us down with an axe, like in that movie." Everything was like a movie, an adventure, and she'd survived.

Detective Deb clammed up for a bit. Then, "I'll put you with a police sketch artist."

Haley acted like she was done and they headed toward the lobby. It hadn't been so bad, except for the fuzzy girl photo, which was kind of pukey.

Anyway, she had stuff to tell her friends at school. She shouldn't have thought of school, with its pervs. Except she had defenses, like a six-footer with attitude. "Detective—Deb, you're on Facebook, Twitter, Instagram, right? I can friend you."

"Haley, you have to be very careful with social media."

"Stalker-net. Know that. So?"

"Haley, if you need anything, call me. I'll give you contact cards. If I can't answer right away, somebody I trust will."

"Like that man you were with at my house?"

"Detective Erik." Detective Deb squinted. "The friending thing, cops aren't good friends. We have to keep secrets, go where the trouble is, where 911 sends us. Another thing, it's not always good for people to know you're hanging out with a cop."

Uncool, carpool, cesspool, she thought to herself as the woman gave her two business cards. Haley dumped them into the black hole of her new bag.

CHAPTER 12

⁂

The media is to privacy what Satan is to salvation, Erik thought, they're agin it. He sat at his kitchen table studying online articles on Harrington's employer, Allston Tigue Carlson. He had elected to work at home all morning before he realized his refrigerator was near empty. He swallowed the last bites of a luncheon frittata made from not-so-fresh eggs and leftover green beans—enough protein to get him through the Wednesday afternoon of interviews at Harrington's workplace. Erik had no further information on the Harrington-account email that announced Harrington was missing. That irked him. Knowing nothing about the mystery man near Harrington's apartment last night irked him. More irksome yet, Deb. Deb was immersed in a day of family fun with Haugens. She had crashed into that case, and with or without a connection to the corpse, she owned it.

Satan and salvation—must be a saying from his father's hunting buddy, the "Professor." The professor, a transplant to Iowa, had kept his Alabama accent sugared and his advice consistency-free when he opined to the teenaged Erik in a chilly prairie pot-hole duck blind. Erik's father would be attuned to the horizon's morning glow and the whistle-whap of wings, while the professor steered the boy through life with "wisdom, and, if necessary, truth." Or at least keep him awake. "You know a woman's trouble," the professor once started, but then drifted into consideration of a ham-stuffed biscuit provided by his wife along with a thermos of hot coffee.

Erik's trouble was he'd lost a woman, Kristine, the tangle of wit and limbs and the surprise of each other. He picked up his mug of coffee—as cold as this case—and read online about the recent woman trouble of an ATC client.

A blog, *Hidden Muck*, had run an article, "Jail Bait to Jail Time," claiming that an executive of a local firm had seduced his partner's underage daughter. *Muck* featured a photo of the leggy girl bending over to receive a tennis serve at a match; she was mature in many ways. The partner/father discovered the indiscretion, delivered a kick to the executive's offending member and dislocated his jaw, and demanded that the seducer be arrested. The partner/father was arrested instead. ATC made statements on behalf of the injured party—the executive who could not speak for himself, not until the jaw healed. That executive had *not* been having an affair with a partner's teenage daughter. Rather, he'd been having an affair with the partner's *older* daughter from a previous marriage. A retired and much admired CEO had been called back to manage the firm temporarily. Erik's interpretation: the partnership (if not the affair) is over.

The blog, shock of all shocks, sensationalized, while ATC statements jumped from one rolling log to another: neutrality on the facts; an undertone of moral concern; a refusal to judge outsiders' opinions based on incomplete data; a withholding of its own judgment on behaviors; and a steady emphasis on company responsibility and improvement. The ATC spokesperson was Stephen Drexler.

More cases handled by Drexler: A fast-food restaurant was attacked on social media for health-code violations. With ATC's assistance, the restaurant immediately responded through Twitter, online outlets, and press releases that inspections and a video of practices disproved the accusation. The source of the attack was a fired employee. The media, however, picked up on the restaurant's dubious labor practices. Then ATC explained that restaurant management was very willing to be part of a national conversation on labor issues. Interpretation: the labor issue is being handed over to politicians for mangling.

Much harder to follow was a case that dated back to Chicago, before the merger that attached Allston groups to the local Tigue Carlson. Stephen Drexler worked for a different crisis management firm but took on the case of Theodore Allston's associate, Sam Vine. Vine, a former St. Paul developer transplanted to the Windy City, had been accused of conflicts of interests. (Conflict of interest—wasn't that the nature of human activity?) Vine's centered on road construction contracts and a shared investment with a city councilman. A journalist put a multicolor chart online so the public could trace how Vine's many interests wove together into a maze of influence accented by a red thread of corruption.

Drexler stressed that Vine had a strong sense of civic duty. Regarding the perceived conflict, Vine voluntarily withdrew contracts and paid a penalty in one situation that was really a misunderstanding. Vine's contingent of lawyers and accountants were channeling information flow so they could better detect, as Erik understood it, when their own Peters were paying Pauls and having Pauls pay back the Peters. Interpretation: in a group with so many Peters, it was perplexing. And the case apparently led to Drexler being hired by Allston.

Drexler's crisis responses were not simple whitewash jobs. He helped clients explain in appropriate tones alleged corporate malfeasance and personal misbehaviors. The statements claimed to present substantiated "facts" and not unprovable "alternate facts." But the statements' transparency did not always feel truly transparent, a light that hid shadows rather than dispel them. In addition, Drexler maintained a minimal personal profile. Except for official statements and a description of his skills on the ATC website, there was *nada* on the man.

Erik wanted action. He called ATC to confirm interview times. The receptionist explained that Drexler was arranging to leave Paris, where he'd been when Harrington was discovered. As for others at ATC, the receptionist believed Jonathan Lewis was closest to the dead man and would be available immediately. That meant a rushed shower for Erik and a quick change into the better of his two suits. He tied the first tie he grabbed and rushed out the door. Chief Ibeling had said that Erik, with a bit of effort, could pass as native in the corporate world. That was concerning.

Not until he'd hurried through the ATC parking garage and paused in the marble foyer to check himself in the reflective surfaces, did he realize what he had chosen. The tie, a gift from his son Ben, had a tiny pattern of frolicking otters. The frolicking looked like mating. Erik yanked off the tie and stuffed it in a pocket. He'd try for native another day.

CHAPTER 13

❧

Jonathan stalled at the intersection of ATC hallways. His smart phone demanded attention. A message from Drexler—the internet must work over the Atlantic—directing ATC employees to cooperate with the police investigation and to be scrupulous about guarding client confidentiality. Drexler had a law degree; Jonathan assumed his director meant reveal nothing.

"Mr. Lewis?"

Jonathan startled and glanced up to see a lean compelling man holding out his credentials.

"Mr. Lewis, I'm Detective Erik Jansson. We have an appointment?"

"Oh, yes, Jonathan Lewis. Harrington, I mean—we can, um, talk in this conference room, less claustrophobic than my cell of a workspace." He winced the second he said "cell" and gestured awkwardly toward a conference room.

The straightforward detective could be a boy scout, except his dark brown hair was unruly, the tie was missing, and he moved as if he wanted to burst out of his clothes. Jonathan should offer a seat. He opened his mouth, a wheezy cough came out, and the detective helped himself to a chair at the table.

The questions were perfunctory: where had he last seen Harrington, what was he wearing, so on and so forth. The detective established that no money was found on Harrington's corpse and that Harrington's leased Mercedes had been parked in his building's garage. However, several thousand dollars were discovered in Harrington's apartment. A robbery gone lethal seemed to be where the conversation was heading. The detective had a pleasant open face. This would be over soon.

"The cash," the detective stated. "Mr. Lewis, do you know why Mr. Harrington had so much on hand?"

"There'd been security breaches with our company credit cards. We entertain high-end clients, travel, and Harrington must have been avoiding, um, problems."

The detective mildly persisted. "Did you entertain clients with him? Where?"

Jonathan named several expensive restaurants and reception venues.

"Mr. Harrington felt comfortable taking out hundreds, thousands, of dollars to pay at a public venue? Why not a check?"

Jonathan admitted to never actually witnessing a large transaction, and checks had to be requested in precise amounts and cut on computers.

"Did you pay on occasion with cash?"

Jonathan hadn't been allowed that. "Harrington liked the feel of a fat roll in his pants"—

The detective made eye contact.

"I mean, Detective, he liked the power rush of holding—the cash, I mean. I can retract that, right?"

"This is an interview, not an interrogation. The interrogation, if you wish, comes later."

Was the detective teasing him? Jonathan rubbed his brow. "Uh, we get a per diem for time with clients, who are spread over Minnesota, the Dakotas, and Wisconsin. You get a per diem, don't you ..."

The detective reached into his pants and put two cents on the table.

Jonathan aimed for camaraderie. "Tough boss, uh?"

"I work for you, for the people. What was it like to work with Harrington? He was your mentor, correct?"

"The two of us didn't work together *all* the time. Harrington came to Tigue Carlson with the Allston merger, from Chicago. At first a real mentor, old-fashioned, my aunts would say he looked Episcopalian." Jonathan stared at the detective's tie-less neck. Harrington always dressed to the nines. "The last few weeks he was supposed to be on vacation but, um, not answering emails, that wasn't him."

"What was 'him'?" the detective asked.

Jonathan could finally say what he wanted about his boss. "Harrington had ambition which he tried to hide with a veneer of, um, helping you. He was expanding ATC's reach. I used to do press releases and plan events. He promoted me to compiling client profiles for confidential ATC use and assigned me clients to direct on charity projects."

"But you got along with Harrington. Did others?"

"That's not what I"—Jonathan fingered the knot of his tie and blinked at the detective's bare throat.

"It's a look, but if a suit without a tie bothers you"—the detective stood, yanked open his shirt collar, pulled off his jacket, and pushed up his shirt sleeves. Some men remove the constructed coat and lose substance: this one didn't. "Mr. Lewis?"

"Harrington seemed to care, and I thought I could learn from him. Then"—

"Then?"

"Breathing down your neck—that was standard," Jonathan rasped. "Harrington was a watchdog. Since we became ATC, we'd been holding extensive information on Fortune 500 types. We were to handle everything with discretion. Harrington called himself the 'the Leak Terminator.' He had this smile, a little crook at the end. Creepy as you got to know him better. Actually, as he got to know *you* better."

"What do you mean, he got to know you?"

"He'd ambush you. You'd walk around a corner and there'd be that smile and he'd ask questions before you could think. I'd be at my desk, lean back in my chair, and he'd be there, silent. He'd ask about my social life, drilling for … I should back up. I didn't connect with him on any social media, but he knew what I posted. Everybody knows … I'm gay."

The detective didn't blink. "Did Harrington have a significant other?"

"No, I don't think so."

"Did he mention family? Siblings, nephews, nieces?

"No."

"Did he like to be around puppies, kittens, women, children?"

"At first I thought he inclined toward men."

"You approached?"

"God no. He was too finicky even to be gay. The point is"—Jonathan pushed his blond hair and cowlicks popped up—"he knew more than the rest of us. We're all in the business of knowing the good and the bad. Our clients' questionable practices, unreliable colleagues, problem relatives. Stephen Drexler, director here, taught me that. Harrington oversaw the linking of information across divisions—security, information management, client searches, reputation monitoring, political activity, philanthropy. You know, so I wouldn't be set to announce a wealthy client's support of educational initiatives, only to find out that his son had been kicked out of his Dad's alma mater, and then Dad reneged on his pledge to the alma mater and threatened a lawsuit. There's protocol, though Harrington, for all his warnings"—

"For all his warnings?"

"Wasn't discreet. We all gossiped within a code, but Harrington"— Jonathan studied the back of his hands. "You know, never mind."

"A man's dead." The detective's eyes caught him. "Dead in a way that may mean others aren't safe."

"He'd find employees' 'irregularities,' and people were fired. You notice that in an office of seventy. I'm sure Human Resources has a list. That's all I have."

"Back to the cash"—the detective settled in. "How did Harrington get approval and record his expenses?"

"He must've worked something out with Stephen Drexler. We did online recording, which was messed up after the breaches, and uh, some records were corrupted. The tech consultant, Andrew Cushing, tried to recover data."

"Cushing?"

"An old scarecrow of a guy. Peculiar."

"How?"

"There's the cat. Never mind the cat. There was an ATC directive and Cushing was working on it—Broaden Communication, Tighten Privacy."

"Contradictory, but true. Security and military organizations require quick information access and an absolutely secure system."

"Wiki-leaks shot down that myth." Jonathan had the edge, the detective's sinewed forearms be damned. "If there were mistakes Harrington was ready to try people for treason. Cushing, I don't know if he violated anything. It was hard to have non-weird chit-chat with Cushing. Especially if he'd brought in his cat to keep him company. He stopped that when Whinette, *Lynette* Johnson, claimed to be allergic. Cushing would size you up like an English butler and know exactly what you needed, for technology I mean. A few weeks ago, he just wasn't here. Harrington said Cushing had a short-term contract and was no longer needed."

"Harrington's duties—mentor, supervisor, watchdog, rainmaker with clients," the detective pursued. "Wasn't that a lot of responsibility for one man?"

Jonathan hesitated. "Alicia, Alicia Krause, also transferred from Chicago, Hispanic despite the last name, acted as Harrington's second-in-command."

"Alicia Krause. Is she here today?"

"Alicia"—Jonathan might as well say it. "She quit right before Harrington disappeared."

NOTHING LIKE DEATH TO ENLIVEN the office. Jonathan felt keyed up after Detective Jansson left, though it was nice he'd been concerned about Jonathan, asking how long he'd suffered with bronchitis.

Now that the law had moved on to other employees, Jonathan went to his office cell and refreshed his email. At least he didn't blurt out a lot about Alicia. Rumor had it that she'd left Minneapolis to avoid an abusive boyfriend. It was dull without her. She told funny-sad stories of past romances and had a sexy laugh to die for. She was attuned to Harrington, but before disappearing had been skittish around him. The last email Jonathan received from her had been strange, from a non-work address. Alicia had asked about an ATC drive password. She should be able to reset her own password, and Jonathan didn't have access to that drive, which held cases carried over from Chicago. Also, he *had* tried to reach her a few days ago to ask if she was all right, the detective didn't need to know that, and never received an answer. And that drive—it was the same drive, the missing one he now realized, that Sandy Sweetser had called about the night of the ATC gala.

Jonathan experienced relief that this connection had not come to mind during the interview with the detective. He leaned back comfortably in his desk chair, only it skidded and he fell, and like that, his place at ATC seemed just as insecure.

CHAPTER 14

❧

E rik was squeezing in a pre-noon workout at the gym to relieve tension
that had been building since yesterday's interviews with ATC employees.
But some fool had set the music at heavy-metal jackhammer—yacka yacka,
bump bump bump. The fool turned out to be Drees, also a detective at G-Met.
Drees, an eager-beaver achiever and so blond and handsome he gleamed—
Erik couldn't stand him. Drees, pretending to check his free weight form in
the mirror, peered at Erik's weight settings on the biceps bar, so Erik switched
to a not-so-close lat machine.

The Harrington case—the parsimonious explanation was simple:
Harrington was robbed by a stranger(s), killed during the process, and
buried to hide the evidence. Highly unlikely the perpetrator(s) would be
apprehended.

This did not account for the picture of the girl in his shoe.

The juicy alternative: scandals at ATC led to the murder of a preening
dweeb, the European interlude of a worldly boss, the lay-off of a cat-addicted
eccentric, and the disappearance of an exotic woman.

A scandal could account for the picture of the girl in the shoe, but Erik
had no idea how.

With Harrington, familiarity bred unease, that's what Erik gathered
from his interview with a jittery Jonathan Lewis. Jitters tended to come with
murders.

Yesterday's other telling interview occurred at the end with the
Administrative Assistant in Accounting, a "Triple A." A stern and unwelcoming
woman, she wore oversized earrings in which the cameo profile was also stern
and unwelcoming. She barked at Erik that her seniority dated back to the

dawn of Tigue Carlson before Allston added his A to her list. Harrington alone of the callow office horde showed her due respect. Erik asked questions about how Harrington's cash handling could meet auditing standards, and she huffed that Stephen Drexler signed off on Harrington's expense sheets so Drexler was ultimately responsible. If a whistle were to be blown on anyone at ATC, it should be blown at Alicia Krause, and not a wolf whistle either. Alicia helped Harrington organize reports but apparently switched this task to a personal device. The Triple A had noticed Alicia's digital tablet, covered in "a loud native print" in Harrington's hand. He had to take it to straighten everything out. Alicia quit. After that, Harrington fell behind in submitting expense reports for the obvious reason of Death. With that the Triple A and her bobbing cameo earrings slammed the gates shut on Erik.

THEY RUINED A PERFECTLY GOOD place with a name. Jimmy Bond Smalls was helping Deb track down Erik and told her that this gym had been dubbed "Testosterone Zone." Because of the competition, he explained against the thud of a mindless macho beat. "So, think what estrogen can do!" she shouted. Hormones under the bridge, she and Smalls moved around a blond sweating man squinting at Erik and blocked his view. Then Erik changed the pins on his lat machine so it appeared he'd used extreme weight.

"That'll mess with Drees' head," said Smalls.

"Isn't that cheating, and who's Drees?" Deb feared Erik was going to pull up his shirt to wipe his face.

"The man staring at us," Small answered. "He and Erik"—

"Aren't you supposed to be in a psych evaluation?" Erik interrupted with a look at Deb. Jimmy Bond Smalls cleared his throat and Erik added, "with a Haugen?"

"Been there, done that, will repeat. What's your progress, and I'm not talking about your Art-project Ab-sculpting."

"My cue to leave." Smalls and the buffer he provided disappeared.

Deb cocked her head toward the treadmills behind a glass partition. She was in her standard button-down shirt and trousers, but a little walk wouldn't hurt. "How about you cool down and I get a walk that gets me nowhere, which is where this case is going." As they moved on, Drees behind them yanked at the lat machine and swore.

The music shifted from head-slamming metal to classic rock. Erik started his treadmill at a moderate walk.

Deb jabbed her machine's sensors. "I don't have a heart rate."

"Harrington's ATC minion, Jonathan Lewis, told me that because of 'compromised business accounts,' Harrington had been using cash, not credit cards."

"What about card bonus points?"

"Maybe paid himself fat folding bonus points. Simple explanation, someone saw Harrington flashing cash and violently relieved him of it. Less simple, Harrington fired four people, did not renew a tech person's contract, his boss took a vacation about the time of death, and a woman associate quit. Enough office disturbance to request warrants for his files."

"Back to the cash, maybe the Accounts Department took a stern view of it."

"Ah, the accountant assassin theory. That administrative assistant was his only fan. I spent the morning researching the Fired Four. One, a grandmother"—

"A murderous grandma, that's your best shot?" Deb's pace triggered the treadmill's sensors and it sped up. She shouldn't be perspiring.

"The grandmother"—Erik pushed up his pace—"I skyped. She's in Tucson with a great view and I asked about the hiking"—

"Hike on back to the case."

On the play list, Jumpin' Jack was flashing. "The Fired Four all landed on their feet, in better shoes. One dismissed man said that leaving Allston Tigue Carlson was like escaping solitary confinement in Marrakesh."

"He'd been in solitary?"

"He'd seen a movie." Erik's feet pounded faster.

Deb, meaning to slow the treadmill, hit hill climb. "What did people say about that shoe photo of the unknown girl?"

Erik's breathing became heavier. "I didn't show it."

"*What?*" Deb jogged on incline.

"Jonathan Lewis, like Haley Haugen, has had bronchitis"—

"Oh, let's put half the population of the Midwest on the suspect list because who *hasn't* had that crud! The photo? If it was your kid, wouldn't you want every lead followed? Wouldn't you?"

Erik gained speed. "As I was entering the ATC offices, it occurred to me—I didn't have time to discuss it with you—that we might initially hold back that information. If Harrington was in a racket—child porn or trafficking—we don't want to scare possible associates into deep hiding. The bronchitis—never mind. Harrington, intimidating others was his source of satisfaction."

"Well, I ain't got no satisfaction!"

That song pounded through from the weight area, and Erik, damn him, grinned. "Or that photo was something he had on an employee. We need to find Andrew Cushing the computer tech, and this sexy woman, Alicia Krause."

"Sexy? That's *relevan*t?" Deb's street shoes thwacked the tread material.

Erik's machine whirred up to a squealing pitch that drowned out the Rolling Stones. "She was presented"—he huffed—"as desirable."

"That's how you're going to describe her?" Sweat trickled down the inside of Deb's shirt. "Really, *really*?"

Erik stopped suddenly. "We have an appointment. You might want to clean up."

Deb tried to stop and stumbled. She could hear the lyrics to "Under My Thumb."

THEY ARRIVED LATE AT THE café. Fortunately, Lynette Johnson from ATC was later yet, arriving at 12:45 instead of noon. Erik faced Deb across a booth table and reported what Jonathan Lewis said: Lynette, aka "Whinette," had been fired from ATC and then rehired on the principle, keep your friends close and your enemies closer. His shower had done little to cool him.

"What ATC people kept coming back to," he clasped a coffee cup and resumed his comments, "is that Alicia Krause had become frantic and dependent on the tech person, Cushing, and—she's coming, Whi—Lynette Johnson."

He slid around by Deb as the woman bore down on them, looking like an upscale hippie with her bags and wraps. She dumped the load on the side he'd vacated and ordered a server to put down a kettle of chips and a mega-drink.

"I don't want everyone knowing what I do with my personal leave day." Whinette openly scanned the café. "Especially if it's job hunting. ATC's a sinking ship."

"The rats are leaving," Erik said. Deb elbowed him.

Whinette didn't blink. "You asked on the phone if I know where Alicia Krause is—probably with the next *lover*. She'd sashay in and men would drop their jaws. They'd drop something else, if they could—even that busybody Lewis. Secret, he's gay! The men ate up her slut tales." Whinette chomped down chips. "They say her father's a Nazi Argentinian and her mother an erotic dancer. Alicia was supposed to be a nun. *That* didn't take. I swear she's a drug addict—always rushing off to the bathroom, never wanted company."

"How was Alicia involved with Harrington?" Deb reached for the chips but changed her mind.

"She did Reputation Recovery. She should have recovered her own. Harrington, that tick, had her search out client references on the internet. Say you're a surgeon, and your practice suddenly declines. You want to find out what people are blogging about you. People! They haven't anything better to do than run down someone who's doing their job. To think, people trusted Alicia!" Whinette gave Erik a "not-for-you" lash flutter and inclined toward Deb. "*She slept her way to that position.*"

"Ms. Johnson, could you say more about her relationship with Harrington?" Erik redirected the subject.

She chomped thoughtfully. "Well, it was Drexler she had the hots for, 'delicious Alicia delighting Drexler.' Bet he dumped her when he heard her delights were shared with a restraining-order character. She was Harrington's errand girl, 'breasts beat brains' in that position." Whinette heaved her sizeable attributes. "Harrington had confidential work left over from the Chicago office, and she was supposed to be closing that out. She'd trot off to that creepy tech guy in charge of file security, Cushing. I call him Katmandu."

Erik joined Deb in a blank stare.

"He had this awful cat, and he's a *man*, who 'doos' techy things," Whinette brayed at her own joke.

Erik lined up napkins between himself and Whinette. "Why do you think ATC is declining?"

"Duh, a dead guy! So I heard you completely ruled out robbery"—

"No," Erik and Deb interrupted.

"Well, ATC has no clue about a person's potential. Lewis, not as adorable as he thinks." Whinette slurped her drink. "Alicia took files home, a real no-no. And that pervert Cushing. Drexler's a dream, if he can get away from his harpy intern Settina who won't let me by to give him the straight story."

"Why do you call Cushing a pervert?" Deb asked.

A legitimate question which provoked Whinette to consume all but one chip and forty-five minutes. All she revealed was a lengthy catalog of Cushing's interests in vintage magazines and dusty books. When Whinette's phone alerted her to a job interview, she leaned over, cleavage spilling into Erik's face, and dropped her business card which missed the table and fell onto his lap. Deb snatched it before Whinette could stretch a retrieve, and the woman dashed, as much as she could dash with her stuff, to the door. She turned back and trumpeted, "Oh, last time I saw Alicia, she wouldn't stop sobbing about her iPad. How could she lose it with that orange cover made by some oppressed woman? I tell ya, hot mess!" Whinette was pushed through the door by other patrons.

The iPad sounded like the one the Triple A had seen with Harrington. Erik shook his head no to Whinette's card when Deb offered it and moved opposite her again. ATC people talked with relish of Alicia as warm, generous, naïve and calculating. They tsk-tsked her distraction and bad luck with men, all with a glint in the eye. They wanted blood. Erik picked up the last chip, put it down, and muttered, "I understand the impulse behind stoning."

Deb assumed *he* was doing the stoning and came down on him like a semi-truck. "Pinning it on the vulnerable woman because she's hot and they're not. Assume she's a slut and sluts make bad things happen. That's your take-away?"

It wasn't. Erik did take away that working with Deb required a talent he had yet to discover.

CHAPTER 15

❧

Watch it—Jonathan, sequestered in his office cell, caught himself about to click on the computer mouse on a slow Thursday morning. He switched to a news site, no problem there if anyone should check his search history. He was dying to check out friends' snarky postings and party pics. He hungered for cyber contact; a hot spasm made him realize that his desire might arise from a deep bodily dissatisfaction—he'd been solitary for some time. That detective yesterday had wanted to know about Harrington's sex life (if it existed). Jonathan couldn't trust that everyone would see things like he did, his playful online presence—not after Harrington. Yes, compartmentalization was brilliant. A box over here to share, a box no one needed to poke, keep problems submerged. Bring your own device.

Jonathan felt the ease of cleared lungs. An hour ago, he'd cleared his head when the returned Drexler called from an airport, and he debriefed his director on the police progress with Harrington. Jonathan—a little stab to the heart—experienced how much more adept Drexler was than Harrington at retrieving information you didn't know you had, squeezing you dry, and you liking it the whole time. Best to learn from the masters.

Work, back to that, time to dismiss distractions, except that detective yesterday looked fabulously healthy, which seemed odd for law enforcement. Swat teams, they were buff, right, but detectives? Jonathan assumed they'd be seedy and corrupted by drink, like Sandy Sweetser on a bad day. Though Sandy wasn't much of a drinker, and his worry lines came from caring for his mother in St. Cloud and doing those low-pay freelance articles on depressing people deserving better, the bottom one percent. He hadn't seen Sandy since he'd helped prepare the briefs for the ATC gala. Jonathan had texted last night that he didn't see anything in the Harrington group folders that looked like the files Sandy couldn't retrieve about an ATC charity. Sandy texted back that if a Young Brain like Jonathan couldn't find them, it was a lost cause. Disheveled, funny Sandy.

The widow file, the top one percent. Marry hard data with enhanced intuition to satisfy client needs. That's what Drexler told Jonathan when he joined ATC, and Harrington repeated it when he'd assigned Jonathan these cases. Time to earn your new salary, the dead man—yet to be dead—said and uncharacteristically slapped Jonathan on the back.

It had been empowering to leave his glorified gopher role at Homes & Sarton. And sweet to leave for other reasons. Jonathan had tried a new avenue, a man in his mid-forties who nearly broke his heart. There had never been anything more than warmth between them, him and the boss. Maybe his boss compartmentalized, and naive Jonathan didn't. Not that he really expected anything. The man had guided Jonathan without pushing and Jonathan felt he could ask him anything, anything but what the man's real inclinations were. Then he saw his boss at the theater, a farce, with another man who looked like it wasn't warmth he was receiving but *heat*.

Jonathan's face heated as he studied the folders of the Monied Widows, Lydia Arnfelt and Teresa Stoffel. The Monied Widows wanted certain philanthropic organizations vetted by ATC before determining if they'd be anonymous donors or front-and-forward in the organizations' PR. Mrs. Stoffel *had* been a Homes & Sarton client, he was sure. He had signed a one-year non-compete clause with them when he left. That first night of drinks with Harrington, free-flowing cabernet might have led Jonathan to drop the name of Widow-Want-It-All Stoffel. *If* Harrington had seen an opportunity for poaching, it had to have come from adding up a city's worth of rumors. It was a free society, a free market.

The other widow, Mrs. Arnfelt, had come to the ATC office not long after that detective left. Mrs. Arnfelt's lined face reminded him of the great aunts who raised him after his mother disappeared into the wind (there was a surfeit of wind in North Dakota). His aunts pushed procreation on him—they didn't disapprove of sex, just of sex making you happy. Yet there was something else about Mrs. Arnfelt, the way she moved quietly in her quiet clothes. At his gentle urging, she told stories of how she and her sister (dying of cancer— Lydia wanted to honor her through a charity) were the first in the family to leave the North Dakota farm and attend college. In an era of curfews, the sisters shared a dorm room nearest the back exit and earned spending money by charging to let in the after-hours girls. "Rules can be helpful," she said to Jonathan. "They provoke the imagination."

She then reminisced about her husband. She'd met him at the college when he hit her with a snowball—"he lacked social graces." Later she did extra shifts as a nurse to support him in law school. "He paid me back," she said, "with love, with faith, with humor, with children, and"—she touched the papers outlining the largesse of her legacy, "much much more."

Today Mrs. Stoffel presented an entirely different case. Jonathan left the office after lunch and drove his screamingly cheap car to her mansion in the lake-rich western suburbs of Minneapolis. An attendant took him to a room decorated with perfectly shelved books. She entered energetic and purposeful—a glammed up fifty-five or sixty-five, hard to tell despite his gift for telling these things. She had an easy laugh, she was fun, she knew tons of people, she'd be useful. Mrs. Stoffel wanted to save the education system through private organizations. The more she talked, the more Jonathan realized that she wanted to ferret out "subversive ideologues." He became confused if the ideologues were "left-wing dingbats" or "right-wing loonies." Mrs. Stoffel licked her lips, he could swear, when she asked for background checks on a few people and murmured names in his ear. Background checks— he suspected ATC, using someone with ferreting skills like Sandy, could handle the request but hesitated to knock on that door.

Harrington had said be judicious about sharing information with clients. Maybe Harrington fatally overshared, it could be why he was dead? Jonathan mused as he left the sweetly demanding Mrs. Stoffel.

CHAPTER 16

❦

So ATC had an office slut. Somebody had to be stuck in that role to keep the talk going, Deb figured. It burned that no one knew where Alicia Krause was—as a rule, women did not disappear into better lives. Deb wanted to chew her fingernails. Erik, face set on remote, chewed a protein bar as he drove them to the Uptown apartment of unreachable Alicia. People will open the door when they're not answering phones. After the Whinette interview Deb gulped a sandwich of line-caught tuna. It hit her stomach like it still had jump in it. Erik must have swallowed his super-food pellet because he said something about passing an all-orientations-welcome bowling alley that hosted a transgender tournament. "I can bowl in any alley," she snipped. He opened his mouth, nothing. She should probably apologize.

They passed a bento-box restaurant and a vintage clothing store with a mannequin in a corset and cowboy hat. It was a neighborhood for artist/ activists, trendy young professionals, and middle-agers who believed themselves hip. Deb searched for apartments in Uptown before landing in a St. Paul sublet. It was in a building here that she realized she didn't need to acquire space for two. Why she couldn't keep her singleness in her head, she didn't know. She had been ass-backward about the break up with CeeCee back in Cannon Rapids. Deb announced her new position in the Twin Cities and then queasily said she would make the move alone. They hadn't been *that* committed to each other. They had gambled on living together, and what-the-hey, the gamble didn't pay off. They'd met at an event where community leaders drink to donors coughing up the dough for a program, in this case a women's shelter. CeeCee represented the credit union, Detective Deb the local heat. It was like that one great moment in high school—someone finally liked you! After weeks of movie-going and hands all over each other, Deb had moved in with CeeCee, who as the manager at a credit union owned the whole shebang, a house, yard, and picket fence. That they shared a bed didn't keep them from passing each other silly notes at breakfast. That was the first month. The second month they struggled to make their schedules compatible, Deb's constantly a problem with her police work and late night domestic calls. The third month, CeeCee in her manager voice said Deb shouldn't whine all the time about her department but get over it or move on already. Next CeeCee would rattle on about the financial whirl of central Iowa. The fourth month, Deb felt like CeeCee didn't get her anymore, while she didn't get CeeCee's taste for the Lifetime Channel and Spike TV, not to mention the knitting everywhere.

Relationships should go somewhere, Deb thought, but where? She and CeeCee tried heart-to-heart conversations about the meaning of life—neither of them knew. The talk declined to, "And what's your schedule, today, hon?" Deb slipped into complaining again about her police cohort—complaining, it's what people *do*. That's when CeeCee asserted that it wasn't a chip on Deb's shoulder but a concrete block. Deb moved to the cot by the shelving in the storage room. If she thrashed in her sleep, skeins of yarn tumbled down on her, like she was being bombed by sheep. Deb, under the pretense of visiting college friends, went for the G-Met interview in Minnesota. When Deb finally choked out that it was better for them both if she went off on her own, teary CeeCee was shocked. Then *she* twisted the knife and said bitterly, "How can you be so shallow."

Deb squirmed in the seat of the G-Met car—did you have to be deep to understand shallow? She glanced at her partner, divorced Erik. Did he get divorced because he was shallow? He was quiet. Did that make him deep? If she threw him in the Mississippi River, he'd be plenty deep.

A truck moved with a hydraulic spish. Erik turned the corner and did an awesome job parallel parking. As they stepped up to the building entrance, a tall man in pin-stripes and dreadlocks exited so they did not need to be buzzed in. The elevator occupied, they took the fire-exit stairs to the third floor—to hear a crash and see Krause's door ajar. In January, Alicia had had a restraining order against a man—now presumably in Tennessee.

"You armed?" Deb whispered. Her partner nodded, they sidled up to the open door, she slid in first and both yelled, "Police!"

"You're fucking joking, right?" A grungy man challenged them. A too-small blazer pinched his arms and displayed acres of a Grateful Dead t-shirt, and his pants' cargo pockets were loaded with bulky unseen possessions. "I live here!"

"Here?" Deb held out her ID. "Sure about that? This place looks tossed."

"All right, three doors down. I thought she had a cat that needed to be watered."

"You feed a cat, you water plants," Erik pointed out in a dry voice.

"Cats need water, don't they? They're not amphibrious or ambidexmous." He huffed up to Erik. "What d'ya want?"

"Your name and your connection to Alicia Krause." Erik's height increased as his voice lowered. Deb had to admit that her partner could parallel park and intimidate.

"Dicky Cox." The man grasped the labels of his tight blazer and stuck out his chest. "And we're not lovers, if that's what you mean. She must have plenty, cleavage like the Delaware Water Gap."

"Your identification," from Erik.

The man hauled a bulging wallet from one of his deep-dish pockets and handed over a license. "So Dicky Cox is not a stage name," Erik said and returned the wallet.

Dicky moved closer to Deb. He smelled and it wasn't laundry soap. "Alicia gave me a key, to take care of a cat. And get this, she borrowed money from *me*, my disability settlement. Loaned her five hundred big ones, and poof, she's gone. Never saw the cat. She's a wetback, not legal, right? From Columbia?"

"How about Peru. There's a topographical map behind your head and a gigunda llama on the floor." Deb pointed to the toy that looked like a body to be outlined in chalk.

"All right all ready," Dicky grumbled.

"Did you do this?" Erik swept his arm across the living area where cushions were strewn about, closets and cupboards open.

"Look." Dicky made eye contact with Deb. "It was no showroom when I came in. Was she having an affair with a dead guy? One of those squid-fuckers she worked with? What's his name, Herring-face?"

"Unless your name is on the lease," Deb said, "I recommend you leave."

Dicky's cargo pockets hung him up at the door. "She owes me, don't forget. And you know what? She played hard to get, but I bet she wasn't. Not … at … all." He popped out into the hallway and lumbered away.

Alicia's apartment door *had* been open, so they could take a look-see in the name of checking a missing woman's welfare, even if no one had officially reported her missing since she had apparently quit of her own free will. A lilac perfume scented the satin coverlet of the bed. A container, the size of a medical sharps container, had been ripped from the bathroom wall, the closet was a mess and the dresser half-emptied. No computers or tablets.

Erik signaled they should leave and then paused to stare at the llama. Its glass eye was clouded. "We should check the morgue," he said and Deb nodded. A woman dropping out of her life made the classic set-up for a fatality.

PEOPLE WERE SHROUDING OUTDOOR PLANTS as Erik and Deb left the apartment building. The temperature was plummeting with a freeze warning for the mid-April night. Erik drove back past the welcoming bowling alley where he took Ben sometimes. He needed to think about Alicia Krause and whether to declare her a Person of Interest. He also had to decide whether to take Interstate 94 or a surface road to the G-Met station, unpleasantly situated on a blighted block not far from St. Paul Police Headquarters. It was the hour when nothing rushed. Erik stopped and started his way through traffic. Deb occupied herself with the car computer.

"So"—her word cracked the silence. "Krause has dual citizenship, born in Peru to an American citizen, her father, from Germany and naturalized here years ago. No recent action on her passports. What was that about, Dicky Cox being a stage name?"

"Dick and Cox, two names for"—

"I get it."

Silence.

Deb's phone beeped, she answered. "No Jane Doe in the morgue," she relayed to him. "Not yet anyway. Say Alicia escaped something or someone. She had a good job. Why borrow cash from Dicky Cox?"

Erik shrugged. "Does anything about Harrington suggest an abuser?"

"More like harassment. He sounds like a vindictive bastard. There's a chance Alicia ran from him. Of course, a woman can be abused *and* be a criminal. Women also abuse men. If she needed untraceable cash and Harrington"—

Neither wanted to spell it out.

"Warrants for everything," Erik finally said.

"Yeah, apartment search, bank accounts, phone records." Deb hmmmed. "Abuse isn't always a man/woman dealy. I read an article about lesbians abusing lesbians. All it takes for potential abuse is two people."

"One suffices." That got him a look. Deb had a large stock of looks.

The drive to the station was lurch, stop, lurch stop, listen to honks, lurch stop. The G-Met parking lot was near empty. Erik turned off the engine, closed his eyes, and opened them again to an unfocused gaze on their island of concrete, ice particles forming in the cracks.

Deb rolled her head around on her shoulders and asked dully, "Do you want to get a, um, drink or something?"

Erik inhaled and she said immediately, "Never mind."

"No, uh," he started. "Sure." They stared at the parking lot.

"Another time," Deb said and got out of the car. A blast of cold air hit him.

"Another time," he replied. She didn't hear him.

CHAPTER 17

❧

Mid-morning Friday, out of the internet cosmos, Andrew Cushing showed up. Erik, in the office first, received a call from Paul, G-Met's cyber guru who claimed all his tracking was legit. Cushing, of St. Paul P.O. Box, unknown residence, and disconnected phone had been found. He was sending test emails for a university branch in Mankato, Minnesota. The way ATC people talked, Cushing could be defined as falling between a delightful eccentric and a psycho-in-waiting, the techie sort who had access to others' secrets, who had been on the outs with Harrington, who might collect young girls. Deb, with her nose for creeps, needed to arrive.

Erik was in the process of sending her a hurry-up text when his office phone rang—ATC's Stephen Drexler, back from Paris, finally making contact.

That morning Erik had left him a message that G-Met was reaching out to the media and the public for information on the death of Niland Harrington. Drexler, manager of crises, thanked Erik and read the statement ATC (i.e., Drexler) would release simultaneously: it expressed sorrow over a coworker's death and stated that an internal investigation would cooperate with law enforcement. *However*, the probability of a connection between ATC and Harrington's death was minute. As a confidential aside, Drexler told Erik when he asked about Alicia that Ms. Krause had a reputation for volatility that harmed no one but herself. Then he and Erik agreed to postpone the interview scheduled for that afternoon, for reasons both left unstated.

Another beep jarred Erik, a new email:

It is a truth universally acknowledged, that a solo cop in possession of a tough case must be in want of a partner.

The sender was younger sister, poet Sonje. In a keeping-in-touch email, he'd mentioned his new G-Met partner and the difficulty of talking to her. And Sonje emailed this literary blooey which Erik was not going to share with Deb.

And where was she? The Haugen side of things, evidently not a side of this case at all, had sucked her in. That dead-end photo matched nothing in Amber Alert. If it were his child he wouldn't want it forgotten. He dropped to the floor for pushups when with a clatter a dripping travel mug bounced his way. He twisted toward the door and scowled.

"A wonderful day to you too." Deb picked up the mug.

"Road trip!"—adrenalin took over—"Andrew Cushing's in Mankato, doesn't know we're coming. We're ahead of the game." Erik said and slammed shut his laptop on the acknowledgement of universal truth. Action time. He was ready to make it happen.

IN SECONDS THE DETECTIVES CROSSED the G-Met parking lot. Deb's turn to drive, but she wasn't familiar with western Minnesota, which inspired this exchange with her partner: "You drive, you know the road"; "Nothing to know, it's a line."

Buckled in, Deb listened to Erik explain in a jiff Cushing's whereabouts (contract work as computer trouble-shooter) and that the beneficiary of Harrington's moderate wealth, besides the father in an Alzheimer's unit, was a Scottish society for the preservation of historic golf courses. A murderous hit originating in St. Andrews-by-the-Loch seemed low on the possibility list, he posited. Deb agreed.

Their destination was over an hour away.

Silence.

Erik squirmed.

She'd start with Plan A, say anything. "So, um, what's up?"

Erik gave it some thought. "A spring polar vortex again tonight."

"Weather, that's your best shot?"

"The blackened snow clumps out here, they look like dirty glacier bits in a sea of dead grass."

Was he serious?

Deb switched to Plan B, say something else. "Okay, Erik, we investigate crimes as outstanding members of G-Met. I still don't get exactly what the Greater Metro Force *is*, other than a department that had an opening I walked into. Not to mention this *awesome* partnership."

"We resemble Minnesota's Bureau of Criminal Apprehension, the BCA. Smaller, more of a bastard child."

"Right, we're a bastard. Did G-Met happen because of Almost Allwise Ibeling being on the ins or outs with somebody?"

"It was a way to utilize Ibeling's talents, when other departments had people with influence, I mean talents. Another force is a way to get more law-enforcement revenue from each municipality. And national funding for special initiatives—then if anything goes wrong, we can blame the federal government. It's all a way to make the pie bigger."

"Pie? You hungry?" Too late—they sped past the little-Starbucks-on-the-prairie. Deb rebooted: "My"—no need to admit that her mother was her only current confidant—"a friend asked if Greater Metro meant I rode the buses to control people who go ballistic when they're so busy texting they forget to get off."

"Our region covers the Twin Cities proper and improper, the inner ring suburbs like Edina, and the outer ring like Eden Prairie and Apple Valley. Or take the intersection of Interstate 35W and 94 by the Minneapolis Convention Center as the epicenter"—

"That intersection? The epicenter from Hell," Deb inserted.

"Draw an imaginary radius of 20 miles from that point. G-Met is called when there are overloads or jurisdiction issues within that area."

"Like a person stands in Edina and shoots his buddy in Wayzata?"

"They'd have to go through St. Louis Park. Be careful about the suburbs. Their dogs don't have pedigrees, they have law degrees. G-Met quietly"—he emphasized *quietly*—"takes on sensitive"—

"Ooh, we're black ops? Do we have to worry about being outed? I should know about being outed, except I never was. I mean I was, am, a lesbian but not exactly outed." Deb peeked at her foot—nope, not in her mouth.

"On not being outed, did you present a card?" Erik asked with that unreadable straight face.

"A card! Am I the Avon Lady? Do they have Avon ladies anymore? There's that Skin-so-soft everyone wants for bug repellent. I was so big in high school that people assumed steroids and lesbo leanings. My mother had talks with me, saying just because I was 'big-boned' I didn't have to be queer. She's no little pansy herself. She left kindergarten teaching for greenhouse work because her Barry White voice terrified children. She was *happy* to marry my father. Not so happy as to *stay* married to the man. She's seeing a bass in the church choir. Where was I?"

"Jurisdiction. St. Louis Park or Minnetonka."

"I like their moccasins."

No response.

"So, Erik, not a Marine. You trained, what happened there?"

"I couldn't say 'booyah' right." He said it with accent on the *yah*.

She evinced dissatisfaction.

Erik sighed, "My wife, ex-wife, girlfriend then, had an internship in

Virginia, and I thought"—

"You thought the Marines at nearby Quantico would provide opportunity for romantic interludes? Right, cause that's what they're *known* for. What kind of hopeless romantic are you?"

"The hopeless kind."

Beep—an email alert which Deb read aloud. They had warrants for Harrington's ATC expense accounts; they were denied warrants for his case files unless they had evidence of suspicious behavior on the part of a client. In response, her partner did one head nod.

Tires droned.

Hard cases like this required persistence: "So, Erik, how did you become a police dude? Like, were you a street cop? Did you get *evaluated* as a street cop?"

He checked the car mirrors. "I was evaluated. I was *interesting*."

"Interesting?" Did Ibeling write that?"

"Ibeling says I have a gift for fraud. Someone must have evaluated you."

"My first evaluator said I was Strong Vinegar looking for a Pickle. I got pulled into crime, law enforcement I mean, through bullying issues, never mind that, and my neighbor's sister was killed, domestic violence." She left out her role as babysitter for the victim.

"I'm sorry to hear that." That sounded genuine. Erik gripped the steering wheel. He opened his mouth, he closed it. He opened his mouth, he closed it. He opened it. He spoke. "Surrounded by goodness, I ran to crime."

"*What?*" Deb stared.

"Surrounded by goodness"—

"You *ran* to crime?"

"You know, the Midwest. My father heads campus security at the University of Iowa. My mother is a school superintendent, a great-grandfather a missionary in China, one uncle a farmer, an aunt a Lutheran pastor. Everyone has eyes in the back of their heads. Talking about other people isn't gossip, it's constructive criticism."

Deb leapt at the opening: "All right, your first time, with one of those corn-fed beauties Iowa grows. I bet you fell for the preacher's daughter, the PK. The long leggy blonde type. They know what they want and they aren't going to find it at church, except in a dark closet."

Erik's mouth twitched. "No. Not exactly."

"No?"

"She was the bishop's daughter."

CUSHING HAD OVER AN HOUR start on them. The people in Mankato had given a plausible next address St. Paul. More car-togetherness, only now with a siren screaming and her head throbbing. Deb's phone eeked with an urgent signal.

"Cushing?" Erik turned off the siren.

"No, message from Haley Haugen. Mother-daughter flip-outs aren't G-Met jurisdiction are they? Oh, one now from the Haugen social worker, Trish Gerard. Someone posted all over the internet how the kid survived kidnapping with a photo of 'Haley Hero,' and Trish 'expresses concern.' Predators have a way of finding these things. It's like saying, girl got away, try again."

Another message alert. Deb didn't like it. "This one's about Alicia Krause. A woman who gave a different name but matched the ID photo stayed at a North Minneapolis shelter about the time of Harrington's death. The attendant remembers she came in out of the pouring rain after midnight, soaked and exhausted. She left the next morning without signing out."

"Someone may be after her." Erik set his jaw.

Deb rolled back her shoulders. Haley was on her own for the moment. Alicia, whatever. And Cushing—they were on a manhunt, her "interesting" partner driving toward crime.

CHAPTER 18

⁕

Cushing had given them the run-around since leaving the university. He'd been delivering items to vintage magazine collectors who all knew each other and who all reluctantly provided the next destination and finally a residential address.

The detectives crossed the threshold into the St. Paul apartment sublet of Andrew Cushing. The eerie welcome of a porcupine hissing at them made Erik wary.

Another glance and the porcupine transmogrified into a giant cat atop the armoire hissing "pffft." Erik tightened his shoulders and Deb rubbed her ungloved hands. It was freezing outside, but the chill came from the man's lack of surprise.

Andrew Cushing stood over them at a flag-pole height of 6'5." A fading pink-crocheted throw hung from his shoulders. His Illini fleece had the nap washed out of it, and his pleated trousers hung on his bony frame. Gray hair lay lank across his stony forehead. His spidery fingers cupped a mug of steamy liquid that exuded bourbon. Cushing hadn't offered his hand to shake because he was "entertaining a virus." "Please, detectives"— with a lipless smile he gestured them into the room. "You'll be delightfully surrounded by murder and mayhem."

The odor of bourbon was replaced by that of ancient dust. Cheap shelving held stacks of *Life* and *Look* magazines, gnawed newspapers, and half-packed boxes. Posters from Noir films leaned here and there. A glass case held worn paperbacks with lurid covers of sharp-jawed men with guns and women bursting from undersized dresses. Cushing cleared a space on a sagged-out sofa. Deb sat in a puff of dust while Erik remained standing. He gasped—the cat had descended to chew on his trousers.

"Mr. Cushing," he started but the cat did not desist. "We're here about a very real death, Niland Harrington, the man who terminated your position at Allston Tigue Carlson. And you knew we were coming. How?"

"Ah, I see. I left Mankato because, as you witness, I have been attacked by a respiratory infection and wanted to make my deliveries before nightfall. An IT person there called my temp phone on a follow-up question and mentioned you were coming. He was under the impression that you wanted to consult me on an urgent security matter. I see now there was a misapprehension. I only recently learned of Harrington's death, on the news. I've been, distracted." Cushing waved at a glass case. "I'm selling as many artifacts as possible and packing the remainder for my return to Illinois to be near my son. I'm soon to be a grandfather." His smile became convincing until it was wiped out by a cough.

"The usual first question. Where were you during the last week of March, at the time of Harrington's death?" Erik couldn't free his pant cuff from the chewing cat.

"I was visiting nieces in New Hampshire, in the White Mountains. They live in a town where an avalanche took out an entire family. In 1826. They can confirm that."

"The avalanche or your whereabouts?" Deb asked and received no answer.

"What was the nature of your work for ATC? Security issues, firewalls and cyber-attacks?" from Erik.

"Not exactly. Time past, I worked in government archives. As information management became digital, I freelanced. At ATC, I 'interfaced' between the technical people and the client managers and helped with online issues. That meant data mining and reputation repairs. Those matters require a consciousness quite human for judgment calls. For example, I tracked and deleted inappropriate posts on clients' websites: the silly, the obscene, and the threatening."

"You were a censor," Deb stated.

"I suppose I censored out hate speech, patently false information, and language the *New York Times* deems unfit to print."

"The data mining," Erik continued.

"Data mining is as common as orange juice for breakfast. Search algorithms are the new alchemy—there's gold in tracing people's clicks. For example, certain patterns of responses point to a coordinated effort behind a reputation attack. In other words, one person or group uses multiple and secretly coordinated sources for negative comments. Also, I was to determine if social media pages attacking clients were valid. That is, not fake accounts set up by a hostile party. Someone will pretend to be an authorized site to put out misinformation—about invasions from Mars or secret death squads. Disproving a conspiracy theory can be challenging." Cushing choked up before squeezing out, "Particularly in an era of real conspiracies."

"Niland Harrington, Alicia Krause, and you came to the Twin Cities ATC office about the same time. You were fired," Erik pointed out.

Cushing hacked up phlegm in a long *aughh* which scared the cat onto Deb's lap. "Not fired. Harrington bought out the rest of my ten-week contract after a project resolved. Among other tasks, his team had been compiling files on Sam Vine, a Chicago colleague of Theodore Allston. Harrington, I believe on orders from his superior Stephen Drexler, recommended a vacation for those involved, a permanent vacation in my case. My editorial comment, for Vine and Allston, avarice and philanthropy form a caduceus. Ah, blank-faced? Caduceus, the intertwined snakes that symbolize the Greek god Hermes, 'patron of commerce and the fat purse.'"

Erik fished: "What were relations like between Harrington and his aide-de-camp, Jonathan Lewis? Between Harrington and Alicia Krause? Do you know why she quit and disappeared?"

"Ms. Krause is gone?" Cushing set his bourbon tea on a rickety table and blew his noise operatically. "Lewis and Harrington, they seemed either the perfect business couple or the father about to cut a son from the will. Alicia Krause. We are entering questionable territory ..."

"Mr. Cushing, we need to know of activity that might put Harrington in a bad way with anyone," from Deb.

"Ms. Krause wouldn't be capable of .... Harrington had asked me to check Ms. Krause's ATC work and social media postings on a day she was absent. Since he had her ATC password, I did so. Excuse me." Cushing cleared his throat—"now that I think of it, the search record would be on the computer I used at ATC, not on Harrington's. That hard drive, by protocol, would have been wiped after I left." Cushing brought his mug to his lips and his mouth twisted as if the liquid had become repulsive.

"Go on," Erik said.

Cushing peered at them: "How long have you been investigators in the Twin Cities, Detectives?"

"Seems like forever," from Deb. "Not long," from Erik. He amended, "Over three years"; she said, "at least three days."

"Yes, of course, excuse me. Everyone looks young to me. Ms. Krause was delightful and worked with me on cross-referencing information. As for her online presence—her last postings didn't sound like her. *If* I had been viewing her page for reputation research, I would have labeled it a possible fraud."

"Why didn't you follow up?" Deb asked. The cat gave her a cat-eyed appraisal.

"Ah, the possibilities for intrigue at ATC. Harrington quietly managed opposition research. If someone attacked an ATC client, Harrington would have the attacker researched. Common in politics. Also, ATC did not want its clients surprised by forgotten skeletons, though it seems that Harrington's own skeleton is doing that."

"So ATC dug up dirt on their clients, their clients' enemies, and their own employees? That's what you did?" Deb asked.

Cushing coughed. "Excuse me, I'm losing my voice. Harrington had a person in the field check my findings. A former reporter."

"A name," Erik insisted.

Cushing's bourbony fever sweat degraded to stench. "Sweetser, Sandy Sweetser."

As the detectives prepared to leave, the enormous cat leapt from Deb's lap and pounced on something invisible.

CHAPTER 19

❦

It was Monday, a week since Detective Deb took down her dad, and Haley was back in school. Her heart did a rabbit-thump as the hall monitors walked in the other direction. She pulled out her phone to check it between classes. Some schools you had to drop your phone at storage all day. Here it was the honor system not to use it, but if you're caught it's confiscated. Head down her hair hid the phone and her face. A bunch of guys brushed by her, grunting with voices that like finally had dropped from squeaks to rumbles. She bumped hard into Brayden.

"Bully!" He pushed her gently. Those eyelashes, wow. "Don't bully me, Haley Hero!" Brayden was kind of a flirt.

During the time with her father and bronchitis, she'd missed testing and spring break. Also missed—the take-down of cyber-bullying posts and body-part pics and, what's more, the workshops on how not to be a bully. Everybody was supposed to feel good about everybody. Only now if you knocked somebody by accident or said something they thought weird, they called you "bully." Like it was kind of a joke? Haley checked her phone again. Because she had been "rescued" by "the law" from "Deadbeat Dad," she was "Haley Hero." The apps showed she was totally "in."

Except the latest video of Haley and her girlfriends, supposed to be just for them, had been removed. They made it last Saturday, Haley's first day out of bed, at Sydney's. Then Karin's mom called Haley's mom and she blew up all over the place. Mom had gone on and on about how Haley looked like a ghetto princess shaking her booty down to the floor, and Haley had screamed, *Mom, that's so offensive!* It was just twerking, a stupid dance, everybody did it. Their group was mixed, not just whitey-white girls, and dark Evie danced too. Evie taught herself French, aced math, played the flute orchestra-style, and Mr. Nail said she'd be "aspirated" to private school any day. Mom yelled that Evie was a stick and who'd look at her caboose and Haley called her mom a racist body-shamer—she couldn't even! Haley texted Detective Deb and received back a "talk to you later." Typical.

She plunked down in language arts and kind of paid attention. Their assignment was to compare a news story across different outlets—blogs, TV segments, and newspapers. The newspapers had to be online because like who read paper? They should skim the news until they found a piece they could relate to. A bully-jerk called out, were they supposed to be looking for facts or opinions? This teacher, she wasn't so bad, said facts came wrapped in context. She said that there were shades of gray between fact and interpretation, so bully-jerk asked lots of shades, like in a porn movie? He landed in detention.

Last period was a school-wide assembly in the auditorium, a woman who'd gone to this place and survived. She volunteered with a group like the Peace Corps and had to be nearly thirty. She had great wavy red hair, freckles for sure, a kelly-green sweater and long legs in skinny royal blue ankle pants, not as tall and muscle-ly as Detective Deb. The woman talked about the importance of clean water in developing countries. Did developing countries really "develop," or were they like "developing breasts" that never amounted to much? The woman showed videos of the wells, the farming, and the food which looked better than the school cafeteria slop. Lots of happy laughing kids the woman tutored, adorable! For reals, Haley thought, I should do this. Then the woman talked about how she prepared for being in the region. Her village had a much lower crime rate than parts of the Twin Cities, she said. A dorkus next to Haley muttered, "cause there's nothing to steal," and she nudged his puny ribs. "Bully," he hissed through braces. The woman talked about how to be safe with water, food, bugs, snakes, storms, and most of all, people. "Much of it holds true anywhere. If suspicious person approaches me," she said, "I have moves from training. Most of all, I'd run."

Dorkus' lizard lips snorted, "Right, that'd save ya," and like the whole school laughed.

It didn't stop the woman. "I run a mile in under five minutes, and a marathon—twenty-six miles—in under three hours. Maybe, maybe, one or two of you could catch me when you're bigger. Everyone calls me Katherine now, but my nickname here was Kiki. Go look in the trophy case."

Like wow, she was the girl who'd gotten the *national* trophies way back.

Haley was joining track.

She was psyched about that when she got home, Mom at work and Sierra at aftercare. She had the one stupid computer to herself. She emailed the track coach, who'd been after her since she ran trials in Phy-Ed. She texted Karin and Sydney, already on the team, about shopping together for the right shoes (she had already guilted Mom into extra allowance). She started on the news outlet assignment—it would be cool.

THE BASS COMING THROUGH HER earbuds throbbed in her head as Haley knocked on Mr. Nail's door. (He wanted it to be "Mr. Nail" and "Ms. Haugen" because he said she was a modern woman.) Mr. Nail was off in his "Got Chores" van, but her dad was here. He'd made bail, so her mother must have changed her mind and gotten a loan on the condition he stayed with Nail. No answer. She pulled out the earbuds and tucked them in her bag, phone attached. It wasn't bass pounding her skull, it was Dad's sonic snoring.

The door wasn't locked so she entered. Their houses had the same cramped layout, with the Nail place like a lumberjack hangout. She passed the photo shrine to Mr. Nail's wife, dead for years. The photos showed her with an elk herd, in the middle of a wolf pack, and in a tree smiling at a baby eagle while the big-beaked parent beat her with its wings. Dad said she'd been "et by bears," Mom said she died of overexposure. Like, overexposure to Mr. Nail?

Dad snored from the tiny den, flopped over the bitty plaid sofa with a blanket dragging on the floor. Everything reeked of beer.

Silent scream! Dad wasn't supposed to drink, Mr. Nail said he wouldn't allow it. He'd been charged with assaulting a police officer and with possession of drugs. They'd found OxyContin in a sandwich baggie stuffed in his pants' pocket, and empty packages of decongestants, the meth kind, in the trunk of the Subaru. Haley could save her dad, convince Detective Deb to drop charges by proving he'd done super all right by her. But now?

"Wake up, Dad!" She jostled him. He chortle-snored. "Pay attention to me!" She was too mad to cry. "Wake up! Wake the FUCK UP!"

"Haley—don't talk like that." He sat up fast, coughed, and swayed for a minute before grabbing the edge of the couch. "What I said, ya gotta be better than the screw-ups around you, me included. You and Sierra are my little punkins."

She collapsed beside him, stupid tears. He put his arm around her. He wasn't too smelly.

They sat. The TV cable box hummed. She rubbed her eyes. A table was covered with pink feathers, green tufts, and glittery bits like Barbie accessories only they were for Mr. Nail's fishing lures. She pulled a paper from her bag and held it out.

"I printed this from a news story. The man's dead, probably murdered. Detective ... the police asked me about him, his name's Niland Harrington. Have you ever seen him?"

"No, course not." He sounded woozy.

"But was he up where we were? And the police had me describe that Wartface guy?"

"Wart who?"

"That man with the truck, hosing out blood? You asked about a body or something?"

"Oh, him. This guy"—he pointed with his thick finger—"never saw him. There's always a few business fellas at the lakes, roughin' it, hanging out at the store like they belong."

That lake store had about anything, only it was like walking into a dead fish. "But, Dad, didn't somebody come to our door?"

Haley's phone buzzed. She took it out and didn't even look when she turned it off. Her dad's face rumpled up. "Is that new?" Your mother spoiling you?"

"I do chores"—she meant to—"It's totally new, new apps, new brand. It helps with homework."

He took the Harrington picture from her and held it with both hands. "Totally new? Okay, then. Yeah, a guy came, not this one. Different hair or nose."

"They showed me pictures of these girls, they kept saying I was safe, but these girls ... Is there a stalker up there? Dad, tell me? What did the man at the door want?"

"To borrow"—Dad stopped. "Look, Haley. *Nobody's going to let anything happen to you.* Hear me? Do you hear me?" He stood in a rush—he scared her friends he was that big—and lumbered around. Back in January when it was so bad, Dad ripped a door off the kitchen cabinets, he kicked a hole in the wallboard, he threw the singing fish plaque, a joke gift from her, at Mom's lasagna, which, yeah, deserved it. Mom locked him out, and Haley unlocked the door way past midnight, and he loomed over her and swore and called her "Lorena" though she weighed a hundred pounds less than Mom.

Dad was steamed but got over it quick. "I'll take care of you, and don't you have homework? Go home, Haley. *Now.*" He grabbed her rough to kiss her on the cheek.

Yeah, homework. She left the picture, she didn't want it. Dad could get mad enough to throttle a person but he'd never kill anybody, for sure he wouldn't. No, course he wouldn't.

CHAPTER 20

❧

Jonathan jolted awake at his desk—no more Super-Taco Monday lunches. He'd been having nightmares in the mid-afternoon. And they were peculiar ones—Widow Stoffel with names dribbling from her carmine mouth and Allston's Chicago confederate, huge Sam Vine, peering down on him. Alicia appeared, laughing, crying, pirouetting with a swish of her skirt. There was a giant taco. Drexler requested a headache. Jonathan's mouth opened and closed while that Jansson detective stared at him. The detective turned into a knife. And Sandy Sweetser kept calling, with the world's most obnoxious ring tone, to ask Jonathan how he, Sandy, was doing.

The phone *was* ringing, that detective's number, let it ring. He was returning to interview Drexler. Drexler that morning had insinuated that Lewis had not conveyed satisfying answers to law enforcement and had failed to progress with clients. Thank god Jonathan had a widow appointment after four o'clock with Mrs. Arnfelt.

THE LOBBY OF THE HOSPICE center aimed for mass-designed comfort, but Jonathan couldn't relax when he knew people were dying past the wall. At least he was out of the pressurized office.

Lydia Arnfelt came through double doors from the private rooms. Her face was etched and folded in on itself, while her modest clothes stayed smooth and pressed. She smiled sadly when she saw him and extended her hand. He inquired after her sister.

"Yesterday was a wonderful day," Lydia replied. "Today is a different day. We'll see about tomorrow." She strengthened her smile. "We had a lovely conversation yesterday. That is the blessing we have."

"Do the doctors keep you informed?" It would help for Jonathan's planning if he had a sense of when Mrs. Arnfelt might be preoccupied with funeral arrangements. He was sympathetic; it's just that life had to happen around such events.

"I'm old enough to remember President Reagan's polyps."

"Excuse me?"

"Oh, never mind. Ronald Reagan was treated for polyps and we heard far too much about the intestinal plumbing of the free world's leader. It's important to know that a public person has the health to carry forward, but the assault on his dignity! My sister signed releases so I can be informed of her status. I do wish I could be spared the detail of every fluid exchange."

Jonathan nodded agreement to soften the transition. "There's a coffee shop nearby that might be more—private." A glance around the lobby, though, proved it empty of people except for a receptionist wearing headphones attached to her computer system.

"The consultation room has a coffee machine with cappuccino, latte, hot chocolate." Mrs. Arnfelt moved in that direction.

Jonathan hoped his reluctance didn't show as they sat in a room tinier than his office. A fish tank took up much available space. He pulled from his briefcase a laptop and ATC draft of an event plan to unveil the Helen Nelson and Lydia Arnfelt gift to a STEM (science, technology, engineering, math) program with scholarships for middle and high school girls. Lydia pointed to the event plan. "I don't need to concern myself with that, do I? We'll turn that over to the planners? I simply come with the family, the grandchildren, correct?"

"It might require attention from you to see that the details are right." Jonathan worked up momentum as two blue fish chased each other while a yellow one sucked on the aquarium glass. "If we outsource the festivities, it leaves you free to attend to your family. However, I strongly advise that we monitor any plans. People disagree about what's appropriate and about how much to reveal about donors."

"Could you explain?" Lydia asked. "The center's purpose is outlined in the mission statement, to advance the educational and research possibilities for girls and women."

"But the event staff might simply offer sweet warm punch and Costco cookies."

"That's fine."

"You have relatives coming from California and your sister's son from London. They'll want a ritual with meaning. Without our, your, let's say ATC's professional supervision, a planner might think it's cute to show that girls can do *anything* by putting them in bikinis with snorkel masks as racy marine biologists. Or they might dress them up like doctor, lawyer, Indian chief to make jokes about how far everyone's come."

"Isn't that ludicrous?" Lydia turned her head to the side and pinned him with her left eye, so Jonathan nervously pulled forward his laptop to stream a You-tube video of exactly what he meant. Mrs. Arnfelt studied the screen and then him. "I'm sure you mean well. Perhaps ATC is creating a need? Making up problems and then offering an expensive service?"

Jonathan had to sell himself to get ahead. "We live in an age of constant exposure. A carelessly worded mention on the internet spreads like the flu to social media entries, discussion forums, and blogs. People can totally exploit that, explaining why they love or hate a cause." He didn't say out loud that publishing the amount of a large gift could backfire for the giver. On second thought, he went ahead.

"For example, a philanthropist makes a major gift to a mental health center. Maybe the philanthropist is so bold to mention that his brother struggled with illness and was homeless for a time. A blogger goes digging and finds that the philanthropist cut himself off from the brother for a while—maybe for a good reason—or the blogger claims the philanthropist is a Cain who pushed unstable Abel into the streets"—a biblical reference, good. "Trivia, political scandal, celebrities without make-up, sales on cashmere, it's hard to get attention and people do something wild like have young cancer patients dress as Korean pop stars in a wacko dance." He shouldn't have said cancer.

"You must be exaggerating! I contacted Allston, Tigue, Carlson because friends from my church had been extremely pleased with the group when it was Tigue Carlson. I did hear rumors that the new ATC used clients' information against them to manufacture 'necessary services.' It reminded me of that lobbyist, Jack Abramhoff, who worked against the Native tribes who hired him to protect their casino interests, so they would pay him more to undo the damage he caused." Mrs. Arnfelt put one hand over the other to calm a tremor. "My friends love to go to casinos after church on a Sunday afternoon. I don't see it, myself."

"Mrs. Arnfelt, our business is based on trust and performance on our clients' behalf."

"Pretty words. Usually I dismiss the smell of conspiracy. People like the intrigue and don't want to face that serious problems are often *not* the result of an elaborate conspiracy. Problems occur when people are not as right as they think they are. Of course, ATC has a man dead, but according to the news it seems he was robbed. I'm sorry, you didn't know him, did you?"

Jonathan calmed his panic by studying the fish tank. The largest fish, with a head too narrow for a brain, faced him, opening and closing its mouth.

"Lydia," he started. "Mrs. Arnfelt, I apologize if my speculations upset you.

We can arrange a respectful ceremony."

Mrs. Arnfelt crossed her arms so each hand held a thin wrist.

"I can look into the rumors," he fiddled with papers, "to clear the air."

"I certainly don't want anyone looking into other people's business on my behalf."

"Reputation is our business. Therefore, our own reputation must be safeguarded." The surfacing bubbles of the fish gave Jonathan an idea. "Mrs. Arnfelt, feel free to forward this contact information to those with a grievance about ATC." He handed cards for himself and Drexler; with luck, Mrs. Arnfelt would never use them. He helped her from the chair and they turned to leave the room. For a second he thought he saw Sandy Sweetser's face in the aquarium.

Sandy had called on his mother's phone just before noon and the arrival of the taco order. Sandy's mother, like Mrs. Arnfelt's sister, had a short definable future. Still fussing over unfinished tasks for Harrington, Sandy asked if Jonathan had chanced across the "lost cause missing files," and did he know how to reach Alicia Krause? No, Jonathan said and begged off the call "to prepare for a meeting." He *had* tried to reach Alicia to see if she was all right—both phone number and email were discontinued. Then Melanie Genereux from ATC's Chicago office had emailed with a blanket request, "keep me in the loop on changes in Minneapolis." Jonathan had replied with a quick "happy to help out" and then fell into the nightmarish sleep.

Their requests were like a nagging conscience. Andrew Cushing several weeks back had given Jonathan a slip of paper (very un-electronic of him) with his private email. Cushing, who understood government surveillance and warned that all should fear the hacking capability of foreign powers, could track down the files and Alicia if anyone could. Jonathan wondered if he dared involve himself in ATC quicksand.

And Sandy, with his research into Chicago mogul Sam Vine, may know more than he realized. He had also asked Jonathan if a large man had come to the ATC office looking for him. A man whose name Sandy couldn't remember and whose face he couldn't describe.

CHAPTER 21

꧁

The Tuesday morning sun formed a large happy "O." Even the G-Met parking detritus Deb had to dodge didn't bother her. The day itself was caffeinated enough so that she had barely touched her take-out coffee. The temperatures had warmed, and Deb was high on her new position. She entered the building, a place where people could think independently, and coasted down the hall on the possibility of being the You you were meant to be.

She almost plowed down petite dark-haired Naomi, a near repeat of yesterday when she'd charged around to corner to hear Erik saying to Naomi, "Deb's a force field." Unpredictable Erik smiled and introduced her to "Naomi, forensic accountant extraordinaire." Pretty Naomi nearly gagged and Erik continued, "who's expecting," and she answered in "in seven months, my first baby," before fleeing to the restroom. Erik called after, advising water crackers and flat cola.

Today Naomi looked less frog-colored and said a nice "hello." With one hand holding a cola and the other protectively on her baby bump, she moved on. Damn. Married. To a Man.

Deb was meeting people at tortoise speed, not so bad. Sharing an office, as decreed by budget, wasn't so bad. The desks were angled into a V to avoid constant face-to-face confrontation. The angle provided a view through the window, only the insulating sealant between the double panes had failed, creating an advancing film.

Erik was vacantly staring through the film when Deb walked in. He was totally down.

"I brought you coffee!" She spontaneously held out the cup which Erik took.

They both saw it at the same time, the gloss stain on the rim. Deb felt like she was in third grade.

"It's half-empty. Are you in third grade?"

"It's not lipstick!"

"Then what is it?"

"Deb, Erik." Ibeling ambushed them from behind. Deb stepped back and Erik stood, so their heights flanked their midsize leader. "I have a meeting with Smalls' gang task force in a few minutes—this is quick. Erik"—Ibeling spread on the desk updated files on Harrington, Krause, and Cushing—"I submitted your warrant requests for ATC case files connected with these three and Harrington's phone records. If they go through, be prepared for an avalanche. Deb—Haley Haugen, decide if we pursue charges against Dwight Haugen for attacking you, it's been over a week. The two of you need to progress with the Harrington case." His hand skimmed over the photos to stop on the mystery girl. "I put a rush on this case, putting you at the head of the line with forensics, because of this murky photo. Dubious as evidence at best. You have work. Do it. Another thing."

She and Erik hung on his word.

"You're not third graders." Ibeling and his soft shoes left.

They sat. Erik took a sip of coffee from the non-glossed side and announced it good. That emboldened Deb.

"So, Erik, I studied Minnesota statutes for this job. But there're more than ten state commandments, and they're not short. Say I have a little legal uncertainty. This Haugen thing—no divorce, no custody agreement. People like us on occasion want to ask a legal question a la mode, you know."

"You want free advice from a lawyer."

"I wouldn't *put* it that way. You must have a short list, maybe civil types, not the guys you have to confront in criminal court."

"We can request legal advice, the procedure"—

"Not procedure," Deb wheedled. "I'm new. I haven't met the local 'resources.' Best way out of a maze, ask for directions. *I'm* not hung up on doing things all by myself."

Erik didn't respond for several seconds, then an angry flush took over his face. Another few seconds, the flush died down, and delighted he said, "Jot down your question. I'll make a call."

Deb wrote a note about the legal definition of "estranged."

Erik put his hand on his phone. "Don't you have to … powder your nose?"

"Women don't powder their noses anymore." Come to think of it, the lips needed re-glossing. "Back in ten." Deb walked out and wished she had a James Smalls to find, someone she could begin to understand.

When she returned, her partner gave her an all-business reply. "I left a message." She sat. He stood. "I need to adjust my suspenders." He wasn't wearing any.

"Men's room is closed for cleaning," she called after him. His phone rang and, assuming it was the lawyer he'd called, she answered it by hitting the speaker button. A woman's low voice said hello, Deb introduced herself, asked the question.

And Erik was back, grabbing the phone. He fell across Deb as he apologized to the mystery woman for the business nature of the call. He was stopped, open-mouthed, mid-sentence as Deb ducked out from under him. She couldn't make out the woman's words but sensed their sub-zero chill.

"It was a misunderstanding, Kristine," Erik insisted. He was stopped again. He rubbed his forehead, turned his back on Deb, and mumbled about the same schedule except not tomorrow morning, and then "love to Ben." He placed phone in its cradle and turned toward her.

"You called your *ex-wife*?" Deb blinked. "Your *ex*? You, uh, never got to my question."

Erik lit up like a little boy. "Sorry about that, but she called back, didn't she?"

CHAPTER 22

❦

Finally, Tuesday, a week after the identification of the corpse, Erik could meet ATC director Stephen Drexler. Last week he'd reached a traveling Drexler by phone: Drexler's comments about Harrington's duties aligned with what others said, only the lower status employees criticized Harrington's attitude while Drexler praised his attentiveness to clients. Since then, the Cushing interview raised a mosquito-thicket of questions about ATC, and Erik had spent the weekend and yesterday researching Allston and his groups. He showed credentials to a guard at one o'clock sharp and was then met at the reception desk by a velvet-skinned emissary.

"I'm Settina, Mr. Drexler's intern," she introduced herself. "Please follow me, Detective, to the conference room."

Erik had been subjected to Allston Carlson Tigue's first floor security, the card-only elevator, the fifth-floor security, this intern, and he would still not be "received" in Drexler's personal office. Settina was highly distracting. Erik couldn't help but think of her as an African icon with her stature and glow. She was svelte in a strict suit, and her swinging walk made muted thunks on the carpet. Her shoes were lady-lawyer heels except the soles seemed glued to pieces of two-by-four so that her derriere rose embarrassingly high and close. So close he almost bumped into Settina as she swiveled to open the door.

He gave a start. Stephen Drexler's presence demanded admiration—six-three or four, sleek features, a Cary Grant composure. The exception to the composure were dark hollows under his eyes. Drexler held a folder in one hand and offered the other to Erik with a fresh smile.

"Very good to meet you, Detective, I wish it could be under happier circumstances, which as I think about it, you must hear every day of your life. Please take a seat." Drexler indicated the leather chairs around the oval table made of fine wood. A counter ran along one side, and a striking abstract painting, which Erik rather liked, hung on the far wall. But the transparency of the room, its perfect emptiness, bothered him.

"The Niland Harrington case," Erik started. Drexler, who did not sit, took over without it seeming like an interruption.

"Harrington's death with the, the unusual displacement of his body is a terrible tragedy. I am, we all are, in shock. We thought well of him." Drexler had the hurt look of a child. "I believe his death had nothing to do with his position at Allston Tigue Carlson. I don't see how it could." When Erik opened his mouth, Drexler held up a hand. "However, as you said in our phone conversation, it is a striking coincidence that a co-worker can't be found. I understand you've been sent Harrington's schedule for what turned out to be his last week. Also, I'm pulling together several of Harrington's cases."

"Thank you. Will you pass on those files in paper or digital form?"

"Oh, I'm so sorry, Detective, you misunderstood. The judge who denied your warrants for such files was quite right. I can't release that material any more than you can give me confidential police documents. It is ATC's responsibility to determine any impact on clients, and I'm looking into all possibilities. Uncovering anything is unlikely, but of course I'll immediately forward pertinent information. Frustrating for you I realize." Drexler sounded entirely empathetic.

"Harrington was handling large amounts of cash."

"We had seriously compromised expense accounts after the credit card company we used was hacked. Also, with our most promising clients, it's not unusual to have generous expenses. Harrington went too far recently, he would have been reprimanded, but I fear some low-life followed him and he paid for his carelessness."

"Harrington also acted as internal police in spying on the activities of your own employees and he was involved with opposition"—

"'Opposition Research' has connotations that have nothing to do with our service to clients." Drexler put one hand on the table and casually leaned into it. "Our clients—business leaders, philanthropists, politicians, judges— come to us with complete faith that we will help them realize their vision and shape their legacy. They can't be bothered by what an ex-wife or ex-husband blabbered when drunk. They need protection from 'alternate facts,' slurs invented by anyone who envies their success. It's better for their friends—our firm—to know what there is to know. Obviously, that knowledge is carefully guarded."

"Your clients are buying privacy."

"If anyone wants to be left alone, truly alone, they're best off, I'm sorry to say, being old and poor." Drexler assessed Erik's suit. "You, Detective, with your salary on public record, with a business account, personal credit cards, email, a smartphone, do you think you have privacy? I certainly have no privacy. Not with my hours, not with the demands. My interns—they realize they have to do all kinds of tasks when they sign on—know my contact list. They know when I go the dentist, when I must cancel a private dinner engagement. They might pick up a meal, the dry cleaning, a small item." He laughed lightly. "They probably know the brand of my boxer shorts."

Erik's cheeks and his hair follicles prickled. Let Drexler have the pissing contest. "When your clients get into trouble—a mismanagement of funds, an inappropriate affair, you doctor their public image."

"We advise on *clarifications* of their circumstances. The kind of advice that would benefit the police on many occasions. Didn't one of your labs make mistakes recently? Wasn't there a questionable 'discharge of police firearms' in one officer's stiff phrasing? The media is hungry, a hunger you must know well, Detective."

"Mr. Drexler, do these dates mean anything to you? We found a list in Harrington's apartment." Erik slid over a piece of paper: four dates he'd randomly selected; two were from Harrington's mysterious little notebook.

"Nothing comes to mind. In fact, I was out of town for two of these dates."

"Our forensic accountants have not completed an examination of Mr. Harrington's accounts, but it seems you had to sign off on the largest expenses."

Drexler's composure was unflinching. "That is news to me, and I'll alert our auditors. I computer sign many documents, 'batch signing,' the way the head of a medical unit signs orders for all residents in a unit, which creates the faulty impression that one doctor takes on an excessive number of procedures. I have to trust my teams."

"Speaking of teams, Mr. Harrington, Alicia Krause, and Andrew Cushing were organizing files involving a Chicago client Sam Vine."

Drexler's mouth tightened. "You know about that? Of course, you're the police. You do your own opposition research. Alicia Krause? I am worried for her. She sent me an email about three weeks ago, quitting without notice or explanation, and apparently changed her personal phone number because Human Resources has been unable to reach her about a few details. If Alicia—Krause—behaved inappropriately, we must act. Whatever information you can share will benefit us both. Must I remind you that our clients' material is proprietary and sensitive?"

Drexler was dangerous. Not because he was sharp and arrogant or because he seemed phony. He didn't seem phony. That was the scary thing, that he transcended categories like sincere and insincere. Every word and gesture came from a core, but a core of what? To shake off a rapidly constricting tension, Erik stood and coughed, a trick borrowed from Cushing. "Excuse me, I could use something to drink."

"Coffee? Yes, coffee. I'll summon Settina." Drexler pressed a button on a device that had been in his pocket. Erik moved toward the abstract painting, angling himself to keep Drexler and the door in his field of vision. In seconds, Settina entered with soft thunks.

Drexler swooped in and whispered something French-sounding near her ear. Settina silently pulled back and left. Drexler sat in the chair Erik had vacated and crossed his legs. This meant Drexler faced the painting and Erik the door, which had not completely closed.

"I like this." Erik nodded back toward the painting.

"A gift from a Chicago client. The artist exhibits in the same galleries that have Gerhard Richters. Do you follow contemporary art?"

Erik did not share that for an anniversary he gave his wife, ex, a weekend at the Chicago Art Institute. She was supposed to reciprocate with a fishing trip, which never materialized. "Do your interns work for a year or more? That's how Ms. Krause started, isn't it?"

"Usually less. They're college grads seeking experience before moving on to a law, MBA, or a finance program. Alicia Krause started at assistant level, I believe."

"Settina, her experience and background?"

"One of those liberal arts degrees, perhaps in international relations. There's the usual story, refugee family." Drexler was losing interest and graciousness.

"She's not from the Cities or Chicago?"

"Oh, a place where they kill each other, Rwanda, Somalia." Drexler stopped at the sound of movement near the door. Settina entered with a tray of sculpted sweets, porcelain demitasse, and a steaming urn. The aroma was what God meant when He said "Coffee."

Settina set the tray on the table and glanced at Erik before sliding around Drexler and out the door, which she closed firmly. Erik tentatively touched the urn.

"I assure you"—Drexler tilted his head back—"It's the perfect temperature."

Drexler would not reveal anything more. Erik decided to lose the battle and drink the coffee.

SETTINA RETURNED TO SHOW ERIK out. Her eyes shifted focus as if she was scrutinizing him while pretending not to. Nothing ventured, no clues gained.

"If you don't mind my asking, Ms.—

"Settina, I was named after an aide worker, back in Sudan." She started to move ahead of him down the hallway.

"Settina, did you come to the Twin Cities for college?"

"I graduated last May from Macalester."

"My younger sister Sonje graduated from there, before your time, and went back to Iowa for a poetry writing program."

Settina slowed and gave him a side glance. "Back to Iowa?"

"Iowa City's my hometown."

"Ohh." Settina looked him in the face. "A church there sponsored my family when we arrived as refugees. I was six and beside myself with wonder. I remember the airports—glass doors opened themselves by magic! Once in Iowa, food and clothes were waiting for us." She named the church.

"My aunt was an interim pastor there, again before your time."

Settina stopped and laughed. "Well, Detective, I have never felt so 'Midwest'—'this person knows that person who made the worst tuna and cracker casserole.'"

They arrived at fifth floor security, where Settina asked Erik to wait. The young guard (third day on the job, he cheerfully admitted) watched as she stepped into a small office, and when she gracefully returned, the guard confessed, "Gee, Settina, you should be in the movies or something."

"There are days here when I feel like I'm in a TV drama," she smiled and offered Erik her hand. He shook it, carefully pulling away the card hidden in her palm. Apparently, Settina had learned something from television.

CHAPTER 23

⤳

Erik put a hand on his G-Met desk drawer to pull it open. Deb had texted him as he was leaving the ATC offices that she had to rush to the Nail family cabin. He would be alone for hours. He opened the drawer, put his hand on a picture frame, didn't take it out. He closed the drawer, frowned, removed his suit jacket and hung it on the chair. He picked up the jacket again and took from a pocket the card Settina had slipped him. He went to the window to decipher her minute script by its light. The sun felt close, the warmth almost drawing him through the glass. He pulled himself back to the two lines of writing. The first was a phone number beginning with the country code for Peru, "Alicia's father." The second read "Blog begins with E, strong, friend Ellen."

With the first contact, the current Mrs. Krause screamed at him from a continent away. "My husband's being put under for surgery, an emergency stent replacement, and you call about that parasite!" The woman insisted she had no information, Alicia's mother was long dead, and if that hussy was in trouble, she deserved it.

Ears ringing, he trawled the internet. Ellen and E. What did the strong mean? Entitled? Enraged? If I were friends with Ellen, he considered, what would I want? Depends upon Ellen. A woman like Alicia, issues with men, issues at work: he keyed in Empowered By Ellen and found Empowered With Ellen. The entries were aimed at single women with children (men, couples and the childless also welcome) and dealt with surviving daily challenges—a sick kid and no child care, a tantrum in a grocery store, surviving a boss, being the boss. Working out childcare schedules with divorced spouses—he could follow that blog post. He had breakfast and chauffeuring duties with Ben on

Tuesdays and Fridays, then custody every other weekend. Though with his job and Kristine's as a lawyer, disruption was not the exception but the rule. Back to Ellen's blog—links to domestic violence resources and an answering-service number for urgent requests. Erik left a message and, through the usual channels, obtained the blogger's full name, Ellen McCormick, and address.

After that, he paced through the pit of the afternoon with his refilled coffee cup, until 3:15 when the phone went off like an alarm. He nearly dropped the mug, half caught it twice, muttered to the new carpet, "You should thank me," and answered to hear Ellen McCormick ask about Alicia.

"What happened? She's supposed to be on her way here!"

He could practically hear her heart pounding. "Ms. McCormick, I'm trying to reach her in connection with the death investigation of her co-worker, Niland Harrington."

"Oh, I thought her ex-boyfriend … she called this morning, asking if she could come by my house when I got off work at 3:00. She said she didn't have her old phone. She hasn't shown up, and I'm worried."

"If she comes, get her to stay. Don't tell her police are coming, and I'm Greater Metro Police, a detective, we're different." Erik didn't know what he meant by that but received a confused agreement. He could go straight from Ellen McCormick's to pick up Ben, so he left at once in his road-worn Highlander.

He exited at Xerxes (every city should have a street name Xerxes), checked the nearest public transit stop on the chance Alicia Krause might show up, and cruised the neighborhood of modest single-family homes. He parked at the end of the block, facing McCormick's house, and opened the driver's side window. The chocolate aroma from a neighborhood bakery was mouth-watering. He held up his phone as if taking a call.

Alicia came from across the street. She had swaddled her shoulders with an enormous scarf, but her skirt floated with a slight breeze and she wore petite ankle boots. Earbuds channeled music to her, an excuse to spin about and observe. Swaying and pirouetting, lips silently moving, she mesmerized.

She saw him. Don't move, look past her, control the heart rate. She walked directly to McCormick's, Erik slid from his seat, closing the Highlander door as Alicia rang the bell, and loped up behind her. A pleasant-looking woman of about forty with a wedge-y haircut opened the door and gasped "Oh!" Alicia turned, blanched at seeing him.

"You're safe. I am Detective Erik Jansson. This is about you being safe" He held out credentials and announced their own names as if they were so shocked they'd forgotten them, "Ms. Alicia Krause, Ms. Ellen McCormick,"

Alicia turned on her friend—"What did you do!"—and to Erik—"You were in that SUV. What do *you* want?"

"He's a detective on the murder case of that man you worked with," Ellen said and drew Alicia into the house.

Erik followed without asking permission. Alicia kept her eyes on him. "Credentials can be *faked*," she said.

Ellen touched Alicia's arm. "I'm sorry, honey, I thought I was helping, I called him back—oh, it was a direct number, I didn't go through the exchange." Alicia backed toward the kitchen where a cat clock swung its tail.

"Ms. Krause," Erik said slowly. "Your safety is first. I'm not undercover, and you can check my identity online." Erik nodded toward a tablet on a side table. "Google 'Three Police Departments Run for It.'"

Askance, the women looked at him askance yet trusted the internet. Ellen tapped to read a posting from the fall: "St. Paul, Minneapolis, and the Greater Metro Departments joined forces in a fundraising field day for affordable housing." She showed Alicia. "In the 10K, G-Met's Erik Jansson and Logan Drees tied for first.' Is this you, the blue spandex? You're right—you're not undercover at *all*!" She spread her fingers across the screen. Alicia smiled.

Then took it back. "Why are you following me I wasn't Harrington's girlfriend nothing like that I don't know anything. I mean, I know the numbers to call. I can take care of myself. Harrington"—she floundered.

"I can tell you what I know," Erik said. "But that needs to be done at the Greater Metro station. You'll be safe there."

"No one is ever really safe." Alicia looked away from him.

"Alicia, you should go, settle everything," Ellen said softly. "And I should be going to my sons' soccer practice. Wait a minute, I need their snacks from the kitchen." She disappeared for a moment.

"Did you come by bus?" Erik asked and received an affirmative nod. "We can take my vehicle to the station."

"Oh, here," Ellen interrupted and in an unexpected gesture handed them both energy bars. Erik slipped his into a pocket while Alicia studied the wrapper. "Alicia, I really need to go." Ellen ushered them outside and went to her garage. She soon passed them with a wave.

Alicia walked wordlessly with Erik to his Highlander. He was opening the door for her, when she blurted out, "Are you a Lone Wolf?"

"What?" Erik had no idea what she was getting at. She was spooked so he had to wing it. "Oh, lone wolf—lone tiger or lone spider would be a better saying. Wolves are sociable animals—young males wander until they find a new pack where they can be the breeding Alpha."

Alicia opened her mouth in surprise.

"After that," Erik continued, "the Alpha male helps nurture the weaned pups and—I wanted to be a wildlife ranger once."

"Yes, I see." Alicia indulged him with another smile and took his hand to climb into the Highlander.

Late afternoon traffic created time for Erik to hear Alicia's story. She started by saying she'd made the mistake of leaving her apartment key with a louse, Dicky Cox, who'd probably cleaned her out by now. Erik asked why she'd left in the first place, and she said, "You'll hear."

Then she digressed into deep history. She told her story compulsively, with a touching awareness of her lapses in judgment. Her father was born in Germany, moved to the U.S. and became a citizen, then worked in international finance which took him to Peru. He married her mother, he divorced her mother, her mother died of cancer. He moved back to the U.S. with adolescent Alicia and a new wife who ignored Alicia. She loved dance lessons but friends and boys distracted her from schoolwork. She disappointed her father by being admitted to a mediocre college near Chicago, where she met the love of her life. She quit college to cocktail waitress and be a translator at a clinic, in support of her love's desire to be a jazz musician. Then the love of her life deserted her. At the encouragement of another "boyfriend," she finished school but he became controlling. A few years, a few jobs, and a few men later (Erik added up the gist of it in his head), Alicia had the skill set to be hired by the Chicago ATC office.

It was after 4:30 when they arrived at the G-Met station. Erik situated Alicia in an interview room and briefly excused himself. He texted Deb, who hadn't returned from the cabin, that he had Alicia. Then he contacted the on-call babysitter who picked up Ben when he couldn't. By the time he re-entered the interview room, Alicia's mood had chilled.

"Is what I say being recorded?" she asked as he sat across from her at a small table.

"Yes. This is for information. If you want a lawyer's services"—

"Lawyers serve themselves," she retorted so quietly that the recorder probably didn't catch it. She didn't keep the hurt out of her eyes. She was beautiful, her hair a rich mink color and her lips deeply red. Her skin was markedly pale.

"Ms. Krause, first I'd like your current contact information."

"You might as well call me Alicia, you've heard my life story," she said without emotion. She wrote down an address and numbers on a pad he provided.

He repeated what he'd asked the other ATC employees about Harrington's death and received similar unhelpful answers. Then he hit a nerve.

"Ms. Krause, Alicia, people at ATC said you lost your iPad before you left."

She reacted. "You found it? No? I did everything on it, you know, personal accounts, I had to change everything."

"Niland Harrington was seen with an iPad people said was yours. And then you quit."

"It looks suspicious, I know. I was getting anonymous phone calls, saying I'd better watch myself, related I think to that old restraining order. Harrington made noises about firing me. Then I lose my iPad with all my ID and login information, and, um," she stalled.

"Let me put it this way. Harrington's dead. Is there any reason for further investigation at ATC? Evidence of misconduct? Are you in danger? Might others be in danger?"

"Others?" Alicia took the snack bar from Ellen out of her bag and held it.

"How did you end up working in the Twin Cities with Harrington?"

"It began wonderfully in Chicago and I—I met a man who loved and honored his mother, only it, it"—

Erik loved his mother, he wanted to say.

"Harrington. He may have shared information with clients." Alicia said and put down the snack bar. "He did have this obsessive admiration for Stephen Drexler—you've met him? He tracked Drexler's every move. The cash reimbursements—Harrington had receipts, most he said Drexler incurred, only they didn't seem to line up with appointments. Receipts can be forged. Without a credit card statement, you'd have to check against the accounts of the restaurant or travel service. If I were paranoid"—she bit her lip—"I'd think Harrington was embezzling. Because I was organizing his forms, I'd be an accomplice. If I asked questions or was upset by his bluntness, Harrington would scream at me, 'you're half-*German*, act it! *Think*, don't *feel*,' and I wanted to scream back, Beethoven was German, blood and riot, *sturm und drang*, my *father*, his passions!" Alicia rose, her eyes flooding.

Erik's pulse raced with her anxiety. He stood and offered a handkerchief, which Ibeling said could be as crucial as a weapon. She took it and her cool hand brushed his warm one.

After she sat down, Erik took a different direction. "The investigation is being discreet about one matter. There was a photo of an adolescent girl found with Harrington's corpse."

Alicia showed no comprehension. He was about to speak again when she asked, "You mean, like a public relations image, for a brochure?"

"Not that benign."

"I don't know where Harrington … There was something with him and Drexler. Like Harrington's admiration had turned to stalking and … I've been distracted by so much lately, including my father's health. He has chronic heart problems!"—her laugh was caustic. "His family disowned him when he left his first wife for my mother. He paid my mother's medical bills when she was dying, despite their divorce, and sobbed when she passed. He said he'd care for me forever and then devoted himself solely to wife number three.

Current wife, number four, loves his account numbers."

"I reached her, trying to you," Erik said. "She told me about his stent surgery."

"*What?*"

"Isn't that what you were referring to? His surgery in Lima?" Erik blundered.

"I didn't know surgery was scheduled. *YOU KNEW AND YOU DIDN'T TELL ME FIRST THING!*"

"I'm trying"—

"I know what you're trying to do and it has nothing to do with helping *me*." She stood again. "We're *done!*"

Erik escorted Alicia out of the room. She squeezed the snack bar in her hand. He quietly reminded her that her safety was a prime concern. She was, however, a person of interest, and the department would work with her if her father needed her.

At the station exit, Erik offered to call a cab.

"No," she said, ripped open the bar, and walked out of his sight.

CHAPTER 24

❧

Pine branches whapped the windshield as Deb revved the police van through the camp-road rut. Tuesday afternoon, and the Cushing side of things was mired in background checks in case his collections had a pornographic flavor. The ATC side of things was expertly stonewalled by Harrington's boss Drexler, according to a text from Erik. The Alicia Krause side of things offered hope, because Erik had a lead to pursue while Deb was up north. It was the Haugen side of things that had thrown her into this rut and made her crazy mad.

Just when there was the possibility of charges being dropped, Dwight had jumped bail and lit out on the Yamaha bike he was supposed to be fixing for Bent Nail. Bent had reported this by calling Deb's cellphone. She wondered if Nail had gotten the number from Lorena because she sure hadn't given it to him.

Why was Dwight running? It didn't seem like there was a chance in hell, though hell may have opportunities Deb was unaware of, that Dwight had anything to do with the ATC lot. Local authorities had already checked out the Nail cabin, but Deb wanted to see the place for herself. Bent had said over the phone, "You need a guide, and that would be me."

Deb requisitioned a four-wheel drive vehicle for the lake trip and was issued a K-9 van. She was tempted to move Bent Nail from shot-gun to behind the restraint bars. For the two-and-a-half-hour trip north of the Twin Cities, Nail did a running commentary on Northwoods culture.

He started with a miracle: "An albino deer at Mille Lacs, what we drove by—seen her twice! Beautiful. Big pink ears like a rabbit."

"Can people who haven't been imbibing see it?" Deb asked.

He looked at her aghast. "She was *awesome*, leaping around all white and pure in Father Hennepin State Park. You should know about Father Hennepin, Frenchy explorer priest. He was a Recollect."

"Then I recollect I should know him," Deb punned.

"Recollects are *sacred*, like San Fransisquin. Okay, we're gettin' close to my Grandpa's cabin. You know, I put up Dwight's bail by hocking my antique fishing lures. Dwight didn't mean nothing—he can be three peas shy of a casserole. That place there with the ostentatious gate, yeah, I said 'ostentatious,' it's doctors. All men, the wives don't come up much. The women got the same face, don't get any older, 'cause they're chemicalized. I think it's the stuff that killed bugs in the 1950s, before my time, my mother swears up-and-down I warn't exposed to nothing like that. She swears. The doctors come up later in the season, when I'm up here. Afternoons I deliver tons of ice and they sit on the dock in boxer shorts with their gin and tonics."

He directed her down a dirt driveway. The key for the Nail family cabin was hidden in the retired outhouse, which didn't smell that retired. Dwight Haugen's account of time passed remained sketchy. Deb wondered if a guest, invited or not, had taken advantage of the groggy Haugens, Haley zonked out on cough-medicine and Dwight on his chosen substance of the day. When Deb had shown the shoe photo to Dwight, he declared no way that was Haley, no way in three hells anyone could have gotten to them. He spoke from the gut, not from a rational organ.

In the outdoors trash bin, Deb found empty antibiotic packs, cough syrup bottles, beer cans and food wrappers. She was being over-zealous. People (particularly a self-satisfied mayor from her last job) had accused her of casting women and girls as victims. In their view, Deb made up slights, exaggerated horrors, and re-enforced negative stereotypes. She responded (with a bullying roll of her shoulders) that she was all for strong women and that men and boys were victims, too. Then she'd hand over a card of statistics, bursting to say, "read the news, you twit." All right, she may have said that out loud, another reason for the move to the Twin Cities.

Nail jostled open the cabin door. Deb entered to be hit in the head by a low-swinging chandelier of antlers. No signs of foul play or forced entry, just more beer-can litter and surreal chairs made of warped rusted iron and birch saplings. She sealed her ears to Nail's furniture sales pitch.

Back in the van, Deb decided to find the place of the big man who had scared the Haugens. She bounced around a bend and a doe danced out. Nail grabbed Deb's arm, making her twist the front wheels into the ditch and the van stalled. A sucking sound followed as a wheel sunk deeper. The doe twitched her ears and walked away, la-di-da.

"I *hate* the woods! Damn!" Deb half fell from the van. The whole bug-repellent, scratchy plaid jackets, and compost-smelly boots deal was for the birds. Of which there were scads. The trees rattled with little things chirping and bopping.

"We're lucky it weren't a moose." Nail patted her arm. "I can haul the van out with that old truck back at my Gramp's. Ya know, moose are sufferin' here because of friggin' ticks and friggin' global warming. Whoa, that's the cabin just up the road. The Sorenson place." Nail pointed to a sign with a number on it.

"Why didn't Haugen say so? We can simply call the Sorensons"—

"Sorensons built it, sold it to the Dahlens, who sold it to some other feller."

"But it's called the Sorenson place?"

"Yup."

Deb walked to the Sorenson place empty of Sorensons and pulled out binoculars. She could see past the cabin to receding ice and a rust-red shore. "There, the color," she yelled to Nail, who pulled his own larger binoculars out of his stained Ranger Rick vest.

"Yeah, rusted fishing boat. Iron in the water, you know, like 'the iron range.'"

"Oh." Wartface could have been washing a rusty truck with rusty water or hosing out deer innards. This trip was a waste. Nail was sniffing around with his big snozzle. She'd been with him for *hours*, missing lunch, and he hadn't imbibed anything except the caramel-mocha-whipped-cream latte that she bought him, like he was her kid. She realized how to stop him from snooping.

"Hey, Nail, hungry? I'll buy something to tide us over." Deb's stomach whined, and Nail improvised a pine bough ramp to get the van back on the road.

The whine in Deb's stomach was silenced when they reached the unappetizing destination Nail had selected—a gas station/convenience store/ fishing supplies combo. The gas pumps displayed a hand-printed sign—"Due to high drive-offs, pay inside first!" The soft-drink machine by the door, its picture-front displaying fish, had a bigger sign than the pumps: "OUT OF ORDER DUE TO VANDALS!"

"Guess we won't get a drink here," she grumbled to Nail.

"As an investigator for the law, you should notice details. I can train you on details." Nail nodded for emphasis.

She looked again. The machine was a live bait dispenser.

Inside, she and Nail walked passed an empty cooler advertising leeches by the pound and half-pound. Between fishing seasons, he explained. The proprietor behind the counter looked like an ex-football player smushing down into doughnut dough. His head, widest where most people had necks, sank into the barrel of his midsection. The Wartface person Haley described wasn't so squished. He squinted at Nail. "This your girl?"

"Girl" sounded repellant. "I'm a detective with the G-Met Investigative Force," Deb announced. Shoot, she'd taken the butch-stance.

"You got credentials?" The man's eyes double-checked his place. She placed her ID on the counter. He sneered at it. "Detective? Deb? Little Debbie? You don't look like any cupcake to me."

Crap. She planted both hands on the counter. "Look, Doughnut Dough"—

"Neck," Nail interrupted. "Neck, among friends."

"Okay, Neck, I'm not here to check code violations, but I could find some. Or I could buy enough cupcakes to fatten up my assistant here if you help out. See these pictures?" She put a photo of Harrington on the counter and a sketch of a hulky Wartface. A shot in the dark, absolutely no reason for a connection.

"The suit guy, maybe. Execs come here for their manly-man adventures. The big guy, lots of big guys around here. Now help yourself to the free sushi." Neck pointed to the Live Bait tank.

If necessary Deb could vault the counter and choke that neck.

"Yo, Nail, ya didn't tell me there's a party going on!" A Native-American man walked in. He was wearing a Green Bay Packer jacket in purple Viking country.

"Detective Deb, this is Frank. Frank, this is Detective Deb"—Nail caught the look—"Detective Deb Metzger."

"Pleased to meet ya. Hey, I know those guys." Frank leaned over the images on the counter.

"You do?" Deb and Nail spoke together.

"Well, the suit and the warty guy here wanted a boat to be ready for fishing season. There was a third man they were meeting. Saw him aways away, talking with them by the big one's truck."

"The third man, was he tall and thin, Ichabod Crane-like?" Deb wondered if it was Andrew Cushing.

"Uh, no, size of this guy"—Frank indicated Harrington—"nothing stood out about him. Didn't catch any names. Bet at least one's on the tax roll. Somebody bought the Sorenson place from Peter Tigue, Sue Dahlen's hubby."

"Tigue?" Deb caught one name. The "T" in Allston Tigue Carlson. Had the retiring Tigue sold the place to Harrington? "You sure you didn't catch names, the third man?"

"The third man's Orson Welles in the movie," Nail chipped in.

"The big fella, a mob-type in Patagonia, wanted a fast boat and had a name like a gun." Frank peered at a product display as if the name would pop out of the coyote urine scent package.

"Glock, Colt?" Deb asked.

"Nooo," Frank mused. "Maybe a W or Y in there?"

"Gwock," Nail guessed. "Walther, Walther PPK? No, I got it—Wemington."

"A name, not a lisp," Frank said.

"Wesson," Deb tried.

"Nah, he wasn't a cooking oil."

"This is a frickin' business, not trivial pursuit," Neck groused.

Deb recorded what Frank knew, mostly the make of speedboats Wartface wanted. What a strange coincidence, Haugens and Harrington in the same place at the same time. Deb shivered as she and Nail left Neck's emporium for the van—had Harrington come north to scheme? A menacing thought. At least Dwight kept Haley safe, but he needed to reappear for his own good.

"Dwight Haugen, what a Huge Problemo." Deb turned the ignition. "And I forgot lunch."

"Not to worry. I bought stuff while you were interrogatin'." Nail pulled a box of Little Debbie Nutty Buddies from a plastic bag and waved it by her nose. "These are way cool! Like, were you named after a snack cake?"

CHAPTER 25

꒰ꞏꝏꞏ꒱

Wednesday morning began with an accident. Deb and Erik knocked elbows as she pulled her chair up to his computer screen, and his pet cup of coffee sloshed—if only he'd drink the stuff instead of carrying it around half-full. He had paper towels in his bottom drawer, and she sopped up the spill.

"Sorry about that," Deb apologized as she re-watched a segment of Erik's interview with Alicia Krause. Her discovery about Wartface, Harrington, and a "third man" could wait until it made sense. "So, Erik, you asked what I see. A familiar domestic-incidents pattern. Ms. Krause here distrusts law enforcement. Say she was involved in incidents that led to the restraining order—the police may have botched it, been nicey-nice to the man. Add to that, she's dual citizenship, U.S. and Peru, looks Hispanic. She's harassed by government agents every time she's at a border. Harrington taking her iPad—a bully trying to get a woman under control. You say she never explained why she left her apartment in a hurry. Could be Restraining-order Man—she's vague about him. She might also be hoping he shows up in a 'safe place' and this time it'll be different, it'll work out. Fat chance. Maybe she two-timed him and hopes Man Option B—Drexler?—shows up to rescue her. She doesn't want our ATC investigation to get in the way of a reunion and arrest her dreamboat."

Erik rolled a pen back and forth on the desk. "Hmm. I wasn't thinking that way. I admit she's romantic."

"And that matters because?"

"She feels intensely and hopes a man will change her life. She told stories of rearranging her life to please some man, to be together"—

"Duh, of course. If you love someone you, male or female, rearrange your life for them. Otherwise, boom! It's splitsville."

Erik shot her a look. His divorce.

"Not that I know how to stay in a relationship," Deb said by way of another apology.

"Don't you think"—Erik shifted his look to the screen—"there's an ATC conspiracy, trouble between Harrington and Drexler and her freezing when I mention the unknown girl's photograph. I didn't have a chance to show it to Alicia before she"—

"Lost it with you."—Deb fast-forwarded the video. "Her father's surgery. You should've mentioned first thing that you'd heard about it, you know, start with an empathy moment."

"Give me a break, it wasn't easy to keep her focus on ATC, and I thought she knew about the surgery." Erik's face heated up to angry red. "Blame her father's wife for not updating her."

"Okay, I just blew it with you, need to work on my own empathy moments. I get that you're good with details and twisty minds. With Alicia, it could also be a shock that her former boss was more awful than she imagined."

"I have her contact information. Maybe you could talk with her, in a neutral place. You're good with adolescent girls like Haley."

"That's because I totally get their need to belong and be like everyone else, when simultaneously they want to automatically despise everybody and be different. What? Don't raise your eyebrows at me—I'm past adolescence at least in years."

A loud chirp startled them. "Your phone," said Erik.

Deb checked it. "Hope for Dwight Haugen! Text from Haley—'in class, Dad sent a message that he's doing me a favor, home soon.' He shows up and I can close"—

"Detectives."

Ibeling stood behind them, arms crossed. "Jansson, to my office. Metzger, check out the emailed link."

THE MEN GONE, DEB ROLLED her chair back to her computer. A department-wide message called attention to the website "Cops on the Dumb" and directed everyone to say 'no comment' should the press call. Deb clicked to see the worst.

Her gut flipped. The piece was "Erik Jansson, Little Rat Lambkin." An anonymous source (Anonymous was due for a long stretch in purgatory) had resurrected old allegations and obtained "new" information on Erik and his former partner, Bob Uhle. Reportedly Erik had accused his partner of harassment, forcing poor Uhle into retirement. The website claimed Erik did the harassing and proof was a video clip. In the video, a woman wearing a drug store's worth of makeup said that Erik told her she looked like a tatty street ho. Cops on the Dumb warned there was nothing sheepish about that sly fox Erik.

Deb's five-count exhale turned into a splutter. Yeah, these websites hold truth like a sieve holds ice—for a little while then not at all. During that little while, police are censored, taken off cases, bothered at home. This was not the time to sit and take it. She set off to prowl the hallway on the pretense of getting coffee.

And collided with James Bond Smalls. She asked what Ibeling would do about Erik; Smalls said, "The right thing," and turned away. She caught clerks by the breakroom coffee machine and started to ask but they didn't let her finish—"Don't believe it." Naomi brushed by her without a smile. Bad mood all around. Deb returned to the office.

Erik stood by the window looking liked he'd been struck by lightning and was about to strike back.

Deb sucked in air. "You're fighting all these 'allegations,' right? You got to. That video?"

"I said every word."

Deb blinked. "Whoa, my irony meter is off. Come again?"

"The woman had a court date. She asked me if she looked fine or like a tatty street ho, and I assented to the latter."

"You ascended a ladder? You're fighting this? You're the department golden boy, everyone will back you." Deb could wring his neck for not responding.

Erik absent-mindedly picked up her coffee took a swig. "I'm going to go see Paul."

"Cyber Paul?"

"It's important to stay on Paul's good side. "Except"—

"Except what?"

"Paul only has a good side. He's the real Golden Boy here."

"Wait, like literally golden? I've seen this shy guy in the hallway, skin and hair the same tone, kinda glows."

"Paul's Danish and Dutch-Polynesian. Maybe I'm being followed."

"You're being paranoid."

"Even paranoids have enemies." Erik ditched her coffee in the trash and sat at his desk.

She sat to release the tightness in her chest. "You know, these internet things die down. Good news—we have more to go on with the Harrington case. Paul should have the background checks on the tech guy Cushing soon. And Alicia Krause might know Harrington's associates, the guys he met at the lake. I can show her the Wartface sketch. Her contact info's in the file now, right? I'll call."

"Good." Erik was pleased.

Deb put the phone in speaker mode and punched in the number. An elderly man answered. He had never heard of Alicia Krause.

"Oh god, we're nowhere," Deb said, and Erik lost the pleasant look.

CHAPTER 26

❦

Jonathan didn't know what self to be with her.

People assumed that because he was gay, tears would not distress him. They forgot he came from North Dakota. Besides, Melanie Genereux with her strawberry electric hair did not habitually draw people to her with moist eyes. More the opposite. Minutes ago, she had charged into his office, *lasered* him with those bright gray eyes, and spit out, "Are you comatose here? Where's Stephen Drexler?" Rumor was Drexler had not only left the office but left town after his interview with the detective, and Jonathan couldn't get that out of his mouth. When he stuttered an "I'm sorry," she softened and cried. She was upset, and who wouldn't be at the Harrington fiasco?

Not only was the man dead, but gone with him or because of him a treasure-trove of data on clients and projects that dated back to Harrington's time in Chicago. Jonathan felt caught in a web of unknowns when Melanie arrived.

A nearby restaurant off the skywalk network offered more privacy than the ATC office with its Whinette ears and sharp-eyed interns. Jonathan hurried Melanie there for an early lunch, and the food arrived with a rare promptness.

"Don't worry about me." Melanie dabbed at her eyes before twisting her fork into a pink slab of Ahi tuna. In her white blouse and that not-a-dress thing called a jumper, and black tights with flat shoes, she looked like a child. A busty French school-girl child. Jonathan envied how Melanie, like Drexler, could both exude sexuality and contain it. Alicia, he realized, exuded sexuality but couldn't contain it.

Melanie took another bite and surveyed the plush décor. "It's a wonderful opportunity for the two of us to lunch together. Stephen Drexler and I have been—ships in the night. I did drop in unannounced, hoping to consult with Stephen, and you, on several matters." She put him on the same level as Drexler. "I shouldn't be surprised that no one has immediate answers for me."

"I wasn't part of the research for, what did you call it, the Daria?"

"Denisha, the Denisha Circle. Niland Harrington didn't involve you? Before his transfer here, Harrington had a team scanning materials from interviews, court cases, and news articles to determine what would be effective materials for approaching agencies and donors. I believed, in this digital era, that he could complete the task from any location."

"The Denisha Circle is a support program for abused women and children, right? Alicia talked about something like that, a project for Allston?"

"Alicia?"

"Alicia Krause." Jonathan's throat pickled. "Drexler's Girl Fri—assistant when they arrived and, uh, she ended up under Harrington."

"Under Harrington."

"I mean—never mind. Alicia left." Jonathan hadn't meant to reveal that.

"I see." Melanie's brow creased. Alicia had the perfect skin, but Melanie had the forceful voice. "The Denisha Circle, I advised Allston to take on that group pro bono. His other philanthropic interests, which I oversee, are essentially rehab programs for the addicted rich." She paused with a sly smile. "Allston's no angel, fought his way up in the world, but his aspirations are 'maturing.' Confidentially, he's become competitive about philanthropy, though I haven't convinced him yet to be the Andrew Carnegie of his generation."

"Build libraries? Cyber-libraries?"

"I hadn't thought of that"—another smile from Melanie—"Allston does love to control the information. There is much about the ATC vision that you *should* have absorbed from Drexler and Harrington. The culture they were supposed to bring from Chicago was apparently left behind in baggage claim."

"If Allston's such a fighter, is he supporting women's issues to, uh, make up for his past?"

"No, no, no. Allston's wife, 'Charm,' had a rough time growing up, that's what got him started. Her response to the exploitation was to become a gold-digger. It can be difficult to empathize with *that*. Then I heard from"—a hesitation—"girls who experience chronic abuse can become hyper-sexualized. They learn too early they're valuable *only* for their sexuality. They avoid worse treatment by responding sexually—it becomes habit."

The woman of the laser eyes was back looking at him. "You have to understand, Jonathan, that once Allston takes on a person—like you or me—or a cause like the Denisha Circle, the opportunities are amazing. Commitment, loyalty—ATC has your back. The caveat: you, the group, everything, must be worth it. That brings us back to the problem."

Which problem, Jonathan wondered. The corpse problem? The Alicia disappearing act? Drexler?

Melanie sensed his confusion. "The missing Denisha files. With a serious endowment, we can offer women whose lives have been derailed, or were never *on* a rail, counseling, education, job placement. That takes deep pockets, and for Allston, or colleagues like Sam Vine, to make that commitment, everything must be vetted."

"Is this where Sandy Sweetser comes in?" Jonathan asked.

"Sweetser?" Melanie went blank.

"Researcher." The pickled feeling returned. "Sandy—Robert Sweetser. Harrington out-sourced to him background data. Sandy lives here but does freelance work in the Chicago area." Jonathan didn't know if he should go further. For all her silk-steel talk of commitment and unity, Melanie may have become a lone ranger whose horse had bolted from the ATC stable. "Sandy delivered reports to Harrington; if Harrington was busy, they went … somewhere." Jonathan assumed they went to Alicia, but maybe not, maybe to a tech person, like Andrew Cushing, an uncomfortable realization that made him look down to his plate and stuff something in his mouth.

After a silent minute, Melanie asked, "Should we order dessert?"

"The crème brûlée is good here." He signaled the waiter.

"A reliable standby, I like that." Melanie studied him; he didn't like the scrutiny. "Those missing Denisha files Harrington was supposed to send me"—she cracked the crust of the crème brûlée set before her. "Perhaps those files are on the hard drives here in Minneapolis or stored in the cloud, in a work-group cluster like Google docs. You could check that."

"The police are going through Harrington's files due to his untimely death." Jonathan wished he knew what the warrant covered regarding the files. Certain files weren't open to him anyway. About six weeks ago, several files he did have access to were "lost" when Harrington reset a master password. Jonathan couldn't be sure that had anything do to with Melanie's concerns.

She was staring at the restaurant exit. "The missing files might have been forwarded to Stephen Drexler." Her focus returned to him. "Jonathan, if you can reach Alicia Krause, let me know, would you?"

HE SHOULDN'T HAVE HAD THE crème. To shake the afternoon logy-ness, Jonathan walked the halls. Maybe it wasn't the slick richness topped by golden crunch that did him in. Maybe it was information overload. Melanie believed in the Denisha mission. She told him that everything had to be researched and vetted. The clients were women and girls who suffered from abuse, addictions, and lack of schooling, and they couldn't always provide clear accounts of their circumstances. Yet to open doors and bank accounts, Melanie emphasized, their stories had to be heard, with identifying characteristics altered. People shut out so much; they had to be shocked into action. Hence the need for background data *and* for checks on donor integrity. She sounded annoyed by Drexler's "antagonism" of the police—serve him right, she'd said under her breath so Jonathan barely heard.

He delivered Melanie to a conference room where she could make calls about her other duties and took the elevator to the seventh floor.

When he stepped off the elevator, Drexler materialized as if he'd been transported. "I heard you lunched with Melanie Genereux," his superior said. "Wonderful! I do have time so I *will* meet with her." Drexler entered the elevator and firmly pushed the button.

Jonathan's shoulders drooped with relief. A lust triangle, that's all this was. Whinette had insisted, and Jonathan believed her on this, that Drexler and Alicia had a winter fling which ended when a bad boyfriend from Alicia's past returned. Or Drexler felt pulled back toward Melanie—they must have been close in Chicago—and she'd shown up in tears when Drexler hadn't been there to secretly embrace her in his office.

Jonathan leaned on the wall by the elevator and took deep grateful un-asthmatic breaths. He took out his phone and forwarded Sandy's number to Melanie. It sounded like Melanie wanted the same files that Sandy couldn't find. Jonathan hoped Melanie wouldn't draw obliging Sandy into an ATC squabble. Jonathan had lost client files, too, information that would be very time-consuming to reconstruct. Jonathan's chest constricted as he recalled something he'd withheld from Melanie. He had asked Cushing, through private emails, to come discreetly to his office about seven a.m. that morning to attempt file recovery. Cushing arrived before Jonathan and talked security into letting him. Jonathan arrived to be greeted by Whinette hissing that she'd seen Cushing at her computer *and* Jonathan's, and he'd slipped away from her. Whinette's sighting was bad. Worse, Cushing did not leave him one tiny byte of information.

CHAPTER 27

❧

Erik hung about the office. Deb had dispatched herself to get sandwiches, though Erik's appetite was suppressed by Alicia's lack of compliance and by the morning session with Ibeling over "Cops on the Dumb." The chief wanted to know if Erik had done anything beyond the Uhle situation that could be construed as "dumb." He warned Erik to stick with "no comment" because wit would be wasted on the press. Erik muttered "like dry wine on bad duck," which led Ibeling to say in a voice like truck gears shifting, "*ERIK*," which meant the chief had slipped into the mode of *in loco parentis* or loosely translated, *crazy parent*. Ibeling had asked him about Deb's adaptation and Erik said something appropriate rather than what was on his mind, which was that certain detective pairings could be maladaptive.

And she was back. She tossed him a wrapped wrap and took off. "News on Cushing! I ran into Paul. Paul's a *really* nice guy, easy to talk to, though he doesn't actually talk much. Get this, Cushing's wife died in mysterious circumstances."

"A bashed skull like Harrington?" Erik's energy surged.

"No, not that neat. Not neat at all. Car accident. Sunny day, middle of the day, car rolls over and she's dead."

"How did Cushing survive?"

"No one was with her. Diana Saunders Cushing died in a car crash seventeen years ago south of Rockford, Illinois. The insurance payoff was generous, and an investigation of financials shows that Cushing used a chunk of it to get out of debt. The debt goes back to a hospitalization before he met Diana, when he was unemployed and uninsured."

"Why was the car crash suspicious?"

"At 2:00 p.m. on a clear day Diana crashed into a utility pole and rolled down a bank. She was driving about 80 mph in a 55 zone to a dentist appointment, but this was a quiet road out of her way. No alcohol in her bloodstream. Why a forty-two-year-old woman would lose control under those circumstances is a mystery. She was survived by her twelve-year old son from a previous marriage—she and Cushing had been married six years. The cremation and funeral occurred quickly." Deb dropped a printed news archive on Erik's desk.

"A cousin of Diana's," she continued, "wouldn't stop harping on Cushing's many 'skills.' He took care of the cars, he retrieved Diana's prescriptions, he killed the lawn weeds. He liked true crime stories, classic mysteries and classic cars. He recommended a book to everyone at a Thanksgiving dinner, which he cooked, called *The Poisoner's Handbook*. A little Red Hen of evil intent. The cousin complained about the inheritance—the insurance, the retirement fund, social security, antiques—and asked loudly in front of the press, if Cushing got it all or if anything went to the boy."

"We saw the books Cushing collected."

"Well, the cousin and reporters pressured the police, but it was too late for a thorough re-investigation. The cousin hired a private investigator to follow Cushing. That stopped when Cushing, who had custody of his wife's son, claimed harassment."

"What do you learn about the son?"

"Grown, a caterer in Bloomington, Indiana. Attended the university there. Stayed with Cushing until college. Married. End of story. Oh, no it isn't! The police found a pile of cash in the Cushing household after the wife's death. Cousin claimed Cushing squirreled it away. I had noticed photos in his apartment of kids in bathing suits. Maybe family, but you put together his smarts, his desire to collect, the *access* he had, the incredible access to data about clients, who have children, who work with children"—

"Time to visit Cushing and see what exactly is in his collection. Got warrants?"

"There!" Deb flung her arm back toward the open door. Ibeling appeared.

"Detectives, I expedited your requests," Ibeling announced. "And when you return, we have another matter to discuss."

The two looked hangdog.

"A party." Ibeling said "party" the way most people say 'dead' and walked away.

Erik and Deb grabbed their gear. Everything else could wait. Cushing had history.

IT WAS THE SOUND OF a child in pain. On the stoop of Cushing's building, Erik and Deb froze, both holding their breath then taking simultaneous inhales before rushing inside. The wail echoed in the stairwell and ascended to a vein-scraping screech. They banged open the unlocked apartment door, guns in hand. It fled between their legs. The cat.

It looked like a straight-line wind had razed the apartment, blowing old newspapers into the corners and kicking up moldy dust. They listened. Nothing. An odor seeped into the room, strong and fresh. Together they uttered, "Blood."

Erik eased forward as Deb watched for anything and anyone. He edged into a tight hallway and saw the open bathroom door, where a long foot in a split leather slipper protruded.

The body did not move. Erik kneeled and slipped his hand under the bone-thin wrist. "A pulse," he said to Deb who already had her phone in hand.

CHAPTER 28

⚓

Someone liked bashing heads, Erik thought as he drove the fleet car southeast from St. Paul. Deb rode shotgun and complained that they'd spent this entire Thursday going "Nowheresville" on who slammed Andrew Cushing into a tiled bathroom wall. He might have died but for their arrival. Deb sighed and went on with her list of issues—Cushing remained unhelpfully unconscious and was being stabilized for surgery, the son had been contacted but was too upset to provide information over the phone. The only neighbor around at the mid-afternoon time of Cushing's attack was deaf, and random fingerprints could be traced to delivery drivers who were not plausible suspects. He reminded Deb that they were tracking down a lead on the Harrington side, Sandy Sweetser. She braced a hand on the dashboard as he accelerated out of the conversation and toward a casino along the Mississippi River.

The landscape unsettled Erik. Scrubby flats framed by power lines cut off the view of irregular pools spawned when the Army Engineer Corps built locks and dams on the river in the 1930s. A backwater gain for wildlife—trumpeter swans graced the lake-like widenings near dams. Those widenings had flooded the lands of a Native American community which sought to recover its loss with the Buried Treasure Casino. The casino spread its glittery profile between river habitat and the fat twin cylinders of the nuclear power station.

"Look, your mirror!" Deb broke his mood. He glanced from the mist in front of him to see in reflection a brightening sky of marbleized golds, lavenders, and yellows, like the lining papers of an old Bible. A glance back to the road and the sky in front dimmed to dusk.

"Maybe we're finally getting somewhere," he said. "If we find Sandy Sweetser and his ATC 'research.'" His words didn't counter the suspicion that he was driving into darkness. The police motto—protect and serve. He damned well wasn't protecting Alicia Krause, and they damned well hadn't protected Andrew Cushing, not even his cat which had fled. Law enforcement agencies had been alerted to her as a missing person of interest, but he didn't send her image to the media in case she had an active stalker. She had an Illinois driver's license, but no car in her name, which didn't mean she lacked one to drive. Erik had called Ellen McCormick again, who asked angrily, had he exposed Alicia to danger? He said no but wasn't believed. What good then was he serving?

Deb again interrupted his reflections, this time with a message update. "Casino security knows we're coming. They're not going to do anything about Sandy Sweetser until we arrive." Erik's calls to Sweetser had all gone to voice-mail. Two times Sweetser returned calls, not to the detective's dedicated line but to the G-Met station. Sweetser said the message was non-urgent and it was recorded rather than forwarded immediately. Patrols had been alerted to Sweetser's license plate, and a cruiser by Buried Treasure Casino spotted it. Sweetser might be hard to pick out in the crowd because the DMV photo showed someone who wouldn't stand out—forty-four, average height and weight, brown eyes and sandy-brown hair.

Erik parked across from Sweetser's Camry, and he and Deb entered by the Bingo area. The game machine lights flared in the haze of cigarette smoke. They should have come in on the non-smoking, clean air side.

Deb startled him. "You a gamblin' man?"

"I vote in general elections." Erik tightened his inhale against the fumes. "I thought casinos pumped in oxygen, like in Vegas."

"What, your virgin lungs can't take the heat?" Deb coughed. "We could borrow air from her."

A woman at a slot machine, oxygen tank by her side, made a chair leap and congratulated herself. "Double social security—take that, Congress!" Erik scanned the crowd—retirees, a cluster of middle-aged women chatting, single men of a variety of ages. Not the room for high rollers, with most occupying the lower rungs of the middle class. Their chatter and the smoke compounded in Erik's ears and sinuses. Rows of Golden Goddess, Wolf Pack, Happy Fruit, and Fan Dancer zzringed and popped and whirred.

Again, Deb caught him off guard. "Spike up that wolverine mat you call hair. Make it easier to see you over these giant kids' games."

He ran his fingers through his hair.

"Higher than that. I've seen it come to a natural point." Deb licked her fingers and came at him. "Here, like Mom spit"—

"If you think," Erik batted her hands, she batted *his* hands and—

"Can I help you folks? You look new here." A big man with a friendly grin extended his hand. "Virgil." He wasn't dressed like an employee in his Carhartt jacket and baseball cap with a brim that looked clawed by raccoons. "I'll show you how to get started. Me and the wife come here once a week and invest ten bucks in a Diamond card—you get points besides what you win. I've been on a streak tonight. This girl's been good to me." He slid his card, attached like a security badge to a cord and his coat, into one of the many Golden Goddesses. She lit up, and a box displayed that Virgil had 2740 points or, he explained, twenty-seven dollars and forty cents, beating the house so far. Virgil had Deb punch the bet buttons. She lost him thirty-six cents.

"Demonstration over," Virgil laughed. "Got to get back to the wife in Bingo." He ejected the card and paused before them. "You know, it's relaxing here for me and my wife, *relaxing*. Away from the worries, the job, the old bad habits. A getaway. The two of us, the two of *you*, we have to keep it all in perspective."

Erik clasped Deb's hand; she wrung his like a towel. "Thank you, so much," he squeezed through his teeth. "Blackjack and poker are where?" His guide pointed and disappeared into the thickening maze.

Erik shook his hand free. "Seriously. We need a strategy."

"I'm beginning to get your kind of 'serious.'" Deb looked past him but listened to his strategy—basically, split up—as they moved around a double-sized machine separating sections, the "Wizard of Oz."

On the other side of Oz, Erik gasped as if he'd stepped on a curling witch. "We've been in *non*-smoking all this time!"

"Now entering," his partner confirmed, "second-hand hell."

Higher stakes and heavier smoke. Deb deserted Erik for the poker rooms, and croupiers scanned him for intent. A man losing at Blackjack pushed back his chair in disgust and knocked into Erik, who twisted to regain balance and saw Sweetser—Sweetser showed no signs of being seen. Sweetser, brows raised in expectation, cruised the far end of the Black-jack tables. Erik registered that Sweetser was a man about the size of the one hanging around Harrington's apartment the night of the search, only that man appeared to have dark hair. Erik moved casually in that direction. Sweetser didn't seem to see Erik, shouldn't know the detective if he saw him, yet he began to saunter away, a saunter about as natural as the detective's. Sweetser sauntered to the right. Erik sauntered to the left. A player claimed the winning hand and stood to woo-hoo, and Sweetser slipped behind him and through the crowd lining up for the buffet. Erik excused himself through it, as a couple spit "line-jumper," and pushed a button on his phone for Deb. She did not appear like a genie— the computerized gadgets at casinos could block cell reception. Sweetser reappeared in a thicket of machines, and Erik rushed around a corner only to be blocked by the game Stinkin' Rich. Where the hell was Deb? Sweetser was slipping around another Golden Goddess and coming out by Virgil. Erik waved high, badge in hand, and Virgil waved back, inadvertently clunking Sweetser. That slowed Sweetser enough so a security guard could stop him.

At Erik's approach, Virgil cheerfully tipped his raccoon-clawed cap. "Look at you, first time out and you won a whole man!"

CHAPTER 29

❧

"I'm an incurable romantic." Sandy Sweetser whitened his coffee with a shaking hand. The coffee became the same washed-out brown as his hair, and the G-Met station's lighting gave his face a neon cast as he sagged in the metal chair. Erik was alone with him in the interview room. Deb thought she saw a man pushing through the casino crowd who resembled the sketch of Haley Haugen's mystery man Wartface, so she had taken copies of casino security camera footage to peruse. This left Sweetser to Erik.

"And how did being incurably romantic lead you to the casino?" Erik asked.

"Well"—Sweetser swirled his muddied coffee—"that's where I met my girlfriend, ex-girlfriend. Girlfriend—of course she's an adult woman, likes to have a good time—you know, damn the dirty dishes, screw the job. Thought she might be there blowing off steam. And no, she wasn't there."

"Mr. Sweetser, we've been trying to reach you"—

"About dead Harrington. And it's Sandy. Mr. Sweetser's the alcoholic spirit of my father. That's why I feel mournful every time a bottle of whiskey is opened. I was in St. Cloud, staying in a room at my mother's memory care unit and using her cell phone to call her excessive list of medical providers. My mother's barely seventy, and it's like her circuit breaker took such a hit it melted."

"She had a stroke?" Erik saw that despite his easy talk Sweetser was genuinely distressed.

"Yeah, and Alzheimer's. The stroke happened when things were going great with my girlfriend. Next thing my girlfriend says, 'When the going gets tough, I get going.'" Sweetser drank his coffee like a mournful shot of whiskey.

Erik took in the man's aging baby face—wiry brows, wry smile, lined forehead, and apple cheeks. His shirt was a tired gray-green. "Why did you run at the casino?"

"I wasn't exactly running, and how could I tell you were 'the law'? I *won* at poker a few days ago. Now you can appreciate this. Being in the right can go against you. When I won, I was as happy as a fat man on a motorcycle. Then these lowlifes at my table got steamed about losing. I thought one of them was gunning for me. With Harrington dead, and I heard about the Cushing attack, it spooks you. And I know you're going to ask—I don't know Cushing, only that he worked at ATC."

Erik switched to Harrington, first asking when Sweetser last saw him. A dull plausible answer. Erik went on to where-were-you-whens. More dull plausible answers involving the mother, the casino, and movies which Sweetser claimed distracted him from the lost love of the girlfriend. A milky odor hung in the air, though the coffee was gone. Erik leaned in and his words bounced off the bare walls.

"You used to get awards for regional investigative journalism. Now you do opposition research. Dirt-digging. That's what you did for Harrington, getting dirt ATC could use to scare clients into buying reputation services, 'cyber-protection.'"

"Whoa, you're jumping way ahead. Here's what I did for Harring—wait, let me explain opposition research. It's not some bastard in a trench coat following lost women to lonely bars and politicians to sleazy motels. I'm a fact finder, like you. Sure, I started in newspaper work. Here's a sob story. I was married then, my wife and I had a kid, a great boy, oh a great boy, Noel, and he got one of those rare and deadly diseases that make for high-rated TV specials and a horrible life for anyone it touches. I quit the newspaper— my wife made more money working with computer servers—and became his nurse." Sweetser rubbed his eyes then tented his white-green hands around his nose and mouth.

Tragic, the story of the boy. Erik should check it out, and the failing mother. At this rate he'd miss his Friday breakfast with Ben. He needed to speed this up.

Then Sweetser spoke without prompting. "Noel died, the marriage died. So I sold my soul—that's a joke—and worked for political organizations. More recently for private firms that outsource data collection. Want to know how I spend my days? Researching stuff so dry your nose bleeds. Screw the internet, a lot of information's a bitch to find. Older records, public records buried in government depositories. Did a certain mayor forget to pay property taxes three years running? Was there a conflict of interest in a real estate deal? How often does a council woman show up to vote? Relations are complicated—

whether it's public or private intercourse. Complicated even when legal. Ask any lobbyist, and what lobbyists do makes my work look like angel droppings."

Erik worked his jaw. "What did Harrington tell you to do?"

"Charities. ATC clients wanted info on charities that approached them for support." Sweetser's next words rolled out like filler for a deadline. He droned on about non-profits where he trawled public records and interviewed staff to check organizations' integrity. A sample finding: a "charity" that was a one-man show for pet projects. Despite the ardent spiel the director presented to a potential donor, an ATC client, the charity was a daydream not a vision. A daydream with seed money that got the "director" a new car. Sweetser interrupted his numbing narration with a yawn. That did it.

"Stand up," Erik ordered. He took off his jacket and pushed up his sleeves.

"What?" Sweetser put his hand on the back of his chair but didn't get up.

"Stand up. Ten jumping jacks."

"Is this *pre-school*?"

"Okay. Push-ups, it's the Marines. I'm *done* with useless stuff."

Sweetser forced out a laugh and a single push-up. Erik's expression made him struggle through three more until he flopped back in his chair and panted, "An unorthodox technique, Detective, almost refreshing, but I can't think of anything else."

"Does this photo mean anything to you?" Erik slapped the photo from Harrington's shoe, the Haley Haugen look-alike, on the table.

The exercise-induced flush vanished from Sweetser's face. "Uh, no, who, what is it? What's wrong with her?"

"A step at a time. Have you seen this picture before?"

"No."

"Did you ever see anything like this in Harrington's possession?"

"No, what are you saying?"

"It's for you to say. Did Harrington show any interest of any kind in girls this age?"

"How should I know? What's going on?"

"You would swear under oath you've never seen this image."

"Easy enough to do. I mean yes, no. Yes, I'd swear that I've never seen it. Well, wait a minute."

"Wait a minute *what*?"

"I never saw that image but I saw nasty ones of abused women and children when I researched the case histories of Denisha Circle clients, that's an Allston-sponsored charity. I do freelance work in the Chicago area, and Harrington hired me before he transferred here. I collected the data and he and his assistant, Alicia … Krause, that's it, would tailor it to suit their PR model. The final product would be passed on to Allston's right-hand woman, Melanie

Genereux, who directs his philanthropic foundation. This Melanie wouldn't know me, though I've seen her presentations. She's sharp, good sharp, better than Drexler any day. Have you met Drexler, Allston's 'reputation' expert? He doesn't want a stain on his starched shirts. Anyway, in my draft write-ups, I included success photos for brochures. I copied to Harrington links to grim documentation. He might have found that photo"—Sweetser started to touch the shoe photo but didn't—"on his own."

"You must have copies of these reports."

"Notes, which I can copy for you."

"I also heard digital files went missing the same time Harrington did."

"Yeah, that set me back." Sweetser peered into his empty coffee cup.

Erik kept at him. "Maybe files were hacked, personal information leaked."

"Identifying details were altered."

"I heard from Jonathan Lewis that you had multiple projects. You must remember."

Sweetser shrugged. "Vaguely, a little stuff here, a little for Chicago."

"Saying vague things to a police officer is like saying vague things to an opposition researcher. You encourage digging. What else for Harrington?"

"I'm tired."

"Is that why your hands are trembling?"

"*Exhaustion*, Detective." Sweetser threw his cup hard in the waste basket. "This PR, reputation business attracts a few rotten ones who want a high gloss finish. Harrington had me do a background check on a local blundering idiot, runs a payroll and collection agency that has issues. Like hiring a thug named Wuger to 'encourage' prompt payment in full. Harrington declined to take on the payroll idiot as a client, but he *liked* the thug and kept his phone number."

"Is this man Wuger?" It took Erik a few minutes to retrieve on his phone the sketch of Haley's Wartface.

Sweetser's complexion matched his green shirt. "Gosh, that dude's somebody's primal fear. I can't say that I can make an ID. Saw a man's back in a parking lot and later Harrington said he'd hired 'protection.' The scariest thing ATC had me do was research one of Allston's Chicago cronies, Sam Vine. Harrington passed on to me an assignment from Melanie Genereux. She wanted to vet him as a Denisha donor. Vine could give away enough moola to support a small socialist country, aid kids so they don't end up in photos like—yours. Vine's a tricky guy to research. He's always looking for a tax break, charitable deductions provide a legal one. There was nasty business in the past over Vine's government construction contracts, boilerplate corruption. Currently everything looks on the up-and-up, though the people Vine hires can make everything perfect on paper. I wouldn't put it past him to hire the kind of people who can make everything perfect in a dark alley.

How can a guy like him *not* have mob connections? I interviewed him on his support for Melanie's project, and he *took* to me. He wanted to hire me as a private dick—an ex-wife had disappeared with an oversize chunk of money. Who came up with that term 'private dick' for the likes of us?"

"There is no 'us.'"

Sweetser heated up. "To get to the point and *get out of here*, I reported—don't know if the report got past Harrington—that Sam Vine was an acceptable donor."

"And your research for Vine?"

"I discovered that his ex-wife was running an eco-resort in Costa Rica. That's it. I'm done." Sweetser slid down in the chair, a pod stripped of its peas.

CHAPTER 30

❧

Deb charged between two scratched G-Met vehicles, hit the brakes, and parked the car with as much fury as you could park a hybrid. It was close to noon on a rainy Friday, and Dwight Haugen was still at large. Trish Gerard, the social worker, kept her updated so she knew Haley had joined track and already messed up a knee. Deb got out of her car, slammed the door, opened it to release her now black-marked trench coat, and slammed it again.

The email had infuriated her. Deb was having a Patty Melt at Ricky's Railcar Diner, when her phone beeped with the message from Ibeling: she needed to sign up for an anger management seminar asap. She bit down hard on her sandwich and instead of gooey cheese hit her tongue.

The early morning hadn't started badly, given that Haley texted repeatedly R U OK Find Dad (Deb texted back, will be in touch), and that Erik complicated the Harrington case with an email mentioning a Chicago player, Sam Vine. He wrote that Ibeling was putting him on a mid-afternoon flight to Chicago to follow up that lead. Erik added that post-op, Andrew Cushing remained in a medically-induced coma, his son at his side. The crime scene team reported that Cushing's apartment had been half-sacked, only a few boxes and drawers disturbed. Either the attacker found what he/she wanted or fled in panic. Cushing's son also called Erik from the hospital to say that his father had e-bay rivals who were fanatic about certain items in his collection. Erik, she hoped, had spent the morning investigating those e-bay crazies while she had been busy with a meeting of a new multi-agency task force on crimes against women and children.

The woman heading that task force, Lola Scheers, was an attractive fifty in a sharp black trouser suit with a vivid white shirt. That decisive appearance was offset by her heavy-hooded eyes and full crimson lips. The woman said she and Ibeling went way back, before he was all-wise, almost. She had been the bait in a prostitution sting. When her twin daughters wanted to borrow her work outfits, she retired from that role. She wanted her girls to aspire to more than being fake hookers.

Deb left that meeting with an invitation to coffee with Lola sometime. She was finally connecting with an ordinary person. Ordinary by police-world standards, meaning an ex-fake hooker qualified. Deb was feeling encouraged about life, until that anger management seminar email. Erik must've complained about her.

She strode down the hallway, jerked the office door open, saw Erik origamied into her chair, James Bond Smalls in Erik's, and blasted, "What the … *what!*"

Dead air. A muscle in Smalls' jaw jumped before he spoke. "Children killing children. A little boy killed in a walk-by. A teen full of himself, thinking he's the man with the gun, thinking that's the way if you're black. Teen's so scared he's convinced himself the feeling inside isn't sick, it's tough, it already feels like you've been shot everywhere it matters, so why not let off a round." The jaw muscle spasmed.

"That's awful. I'm so sorry, I hadn't checked the blotter." Deb swallowed dry and closed the door. Erik fingered her keyboard, tapping a rhythm, tapping it again. Her words just flew right out. "I've been ordered to attend anger management classes."

The men exploded with laughter. She involuntarily put a hand on a hip in a caricature of herself. Smalls wiped his cheek and started howling again.

"Like, is that a need written all over my face?" Deb shifted weight to the other hip and clamped her mouth shut to force down giggles.

"You have Officer Smalls to thank for that," Erik answered and moved to lean against the window. She claimed her desk.

"Oh, I put the blame squarely on our fine chief," Smalls said. "Everyone's required to take it. After an incident in which I 'raised my voice' with an offender there was a complaint of excessive vocal force, later dismissed. Almost Allwise suggested, his suggestions are orders, that I take an anger management course. It is now SOP, standard operating procedures to take the class."

"Everyone can get heated," Deb said.

"Oh, no, no, no, don't go that way." Smalls wagged his finger at her. "There's a *perception*, according to Almost Allwise, that because I'm big and African American I'd lose it, I might *scare* people. There's a *perception*, I answered, that I was being singled out. So Bright Boy"—he indicated Erik, engaged in a stare-down with a crow on the window ledge—"recommends the course be required for *everybody*. Of course, Bright Boy ends up being the high-scorer."

"On what, making people lose it?" she asked.

Another explosion of laughter from Smalls. "Ain't nothing infuriates people like white-boy dimples." He addressed Erik and the heaviness returned. "Workout tonight, my basement, around the family. In my 'safe' white house in my 'safe' white neighborhood." He left the room.

And Deb was alone with her partner. A partner who stared at crows. They were saved from small talk, from talk of any size, by a call from the receptionist: Cushing's son had arrived for his interview.

DEB ADMIRED HOW CLAM-MOUTHED ERIK got Cushing's son Rich to open up. Erik had snitched home-baked cookies from the G-Met lounge (made by Ibeling's wife, Greta, rumored to be ex-CIA, baking has become her least secret talent). He offered the cookies then waited quietly with an innocent look that probably dated back to his childhood.

Rich resembled a chubby Disney hero with wavy hair, rosy cheeks, and a sweetness that found its outlet in his profession of pastry chef. He praised the cookies' butter content and admitted to being terrified when at the age of eight his mother, Diana, introduced him to Andrew Cushing. Rather, he was terrified of Cushing's black cats, a female Satan and her spawn Sin. Cushing's dog, Mark Twain, had died. When Cushing married Diana, he gave Rich his own kitten, Angel. When Diana died—Rich blamed the accident on her mysterious headaches—Cushing adopted him and directed every resource to his well-being. He taught Rich how to make chunky apple pie—at this point the man broke down sobbing.

"I see why you became a baker." Erik sounded gentle. "You said you should have protected him. From what?"

Rich took a bite of cookie and considered. "The office. Dad called it the ATC plague. There was a Lynette or Whinette to be avoided like Typhoid Mary; a young Mr. Lewis of unformed character; a boss who believed himself a fox but was really a tick; a superior who was either the very best man for the job or a spoiled prince trapped in the prison of his self-regard. A woman or women who were twisted serpents beneath lovely raiment."

"Had your father seen under their, uh, clothes?" Deb had to ask.

"A figure of speech. Look, I've got to call my wife—she's expecting and can no longer tolerate the smell of butter cream, so we need to hire a frosting man. And I really must get back to Dad." Rich was about to crash from his sugar high. "Look, when Dad started at ATC six weeks ago, he couldn't access certain files. He asked The Tick and was brushed off. A woman helped him, I can't remember if she was serpentine or not. She was upset that bizarre things had been done to the system. Dad told me he suspected his predecessor."

"A *predecessor*?" Deb gaped. Erik was gaping too. Then it hit her like a flame-thrower. A vanished predecessor who worked with Harrington, what the f—no one had mentioned a stinkin' predecessor.

They should jump on that immediately. Except Erik had a ticket to Chicago and Deb had already promised to see Haley, and if she lost Haley's trust, it wouldn't come back.

So MUCH FOR BEING HALEY Hero. First week of track and Haley hurt her knee, what the bomb! (Dad didn't like her to drop the f-bomb, so she changed it up to "bomb.") For sure the knee wasn't terrible. Another girl had run like movie-werewolf insane and ended up in a stiff knee brace for *weeks*. Haley was prescribed a flexible wrap along with ice and rest. Yeah, like, you put your knee to sleep while the rest of you is busy? So here she was in math class, leg stuck out with a pack on her knee and expected to understand y2 minus y1 equals the slope of who cares.

Okay, she got slope, but the teacher, Cheesit, was repeating the whole lesson. (He was really Cheesit 2 since his brother, Cheesit 1, was the science teacher and had hair.) She doodled on practice paper. They couldn't find Dad and Mom was weird. Maybe they'd started Mom on anti-screaming drugs. She was foggy, but Detective Deb said worry could do that. Like her mom was actually afraid something would happen to Dad. Detective Deb said she'd see Haley soon. Like when soon?

Haley couldn't stand it, her stupid knee. She raised her hand, answered the question, and asked to go the school nurse.

"That's incorrect, Haley." Cheesit retrieved from a cooler hidden under his desk a fresh ice pack and brought it to her. She wanted to splot it on her face which must be a stupid *purple*. Brayden was *staring* at her through those eyelashes, along with that new quiet guy, Ian. She could do math.

She spoke up and worked through the problem with Cheesit. Then he had to start in about a lawnmower on a slope, and it was only the knee that kept her from bolting. Sydney in the next seat peeked at her phone and like that Cheesit came up, took it, and returned to the board while droning about at what slope does the lawnmower careen (come on, *careen*?) into his neighbor's fence. Yeah, he'd be fenced out.

Cheesit gave out the homework. It'd be online, but he always made them chant it three times so there'd be no excuses about "not knowing What to Do and When to Do It." The guys, not Brayden or Ian, sniggered over the "do it" part. Cheesit returned Sydney's phone which she grabbed like an *addict* and helped Haley stand. "Haley, go to the principal's office," he said in a quiet voice. Like, he *had* a quiet voice?

"But I was paying"—

"It's not about schoolwork, Haley. If you need anything"—

It had to be Dad.

IT WASN'T. SHE SLUMPED, LEG up and pointing at Detective Deb so she'd know whose fault everything was. They were stuck in a school office painted the colors bird egg blah and orange peel rot.

And like Detective Deb was all cheery. It sounded phony. "You're in track, Haley? Great. A minor sprain will heal soon. You must be disappointed that we don't know more about your father. We have a lead in Mankato, so if you can think of anyone he might know there, speak up. Chances are he's hiding and everything will be all right."

"All right for who? For *whom*?" Haley wasn't an idiot even though she often acted like she was not as smart as she was.

"My main concern is that you and your sister are in the best situation. Right now, I have a favor to ask. Do any of these men look familiar? Don't worry about why I'm asking."

More photos of creepos. "You already know I don't know anything about that dead man, um, Mr. Harrington."

"This may be totally separate, but investigation requires repetition and following leads, any lead, which I can tell is obvious to you."

"Kind of like math homework, trying all the angles," Haley said to be encouraging because it sounded like Detective Deb needed encouraging. She scanned the photos. What the bomb! One *was* familiar, she pointed. "That guy, one of the old ones."

Like why was he familiar? Detective Deb asked loads of questions until Haley felt her bum leg was so numb it would fall off.

"Forget the pictures." Detective Deb had that teacher-y "I'm not getting annoyed" tone. "How about the name, 'Andrew Cushing?'"

"Nooo. Can I look again?" Haley twisted the familiar photo around like a science specimen. "*OH!* I get it now. This guy? Put a long grey beard on him and he's just like the evil wizard in *Lord of the Rings*, you know, Saruman. The actor died."

Detective Deb looked like she wanted to drop a bomb, a big bomb-de-bomb. She gave it up and fooled with her phone. She showed Haley the screen and asked, "You mean this one?"

Saruman before the Eye of Sauron. "Sorry, my answer—lame, just like me."

Detective Deb laughed and explained it was important to know that Haley didn't know this man, which was like saying knowing what you don't know is, whatever. The interview made her miss her last class, fine by her. Before leaving, Detective Deb said she felt an "obligation" to "inform" Haley about the investigation. Not only because it would be on the news anyway, but for her own safety, not that she was in danger. The shaved-wizard man was Andrew Cushing. He'd been attacked and was in a coma. He had worked with the dead man Niland Harrington, no connection to Haley any one could see.

If all this was supposed to make Haley feel cozy safe, it flunked. Like, what would the Eye of Sauron see? Detective Deb offered her a ride home. Mom had another hour of work and would be picking up Sierra at aftercare. Haley wasn't sure about being seen with the law, but she wouldn't have to clumber up on the bus like a gimpy elephant.

It wasn't until after three chocolate chip cookies microwaved to be melty that Haley had a brain attack. Back at the cabin, when she'd been sick, Dad had loaned a phone to a stranger. But his phone was already dead. It *had* to be her old phone, a hand-me-down from her mother, which didn't have a passcode.

The stranger used that phone with everything on it. Haley didn't feel so good.

She limped from the kitchen, avoided the bedroom she shared with Sierra, and kind of stopped dead in the family room. Her phone bleeped with incoming texts. She didn't look. She should call Detective Deb. And say what? That her dad had done something stupid? Without her around, Dad wouldn't take care of himself. He drank, he rushed into things. Rushing to be on top in track screwed up her knee. She should take her time, that's what Cheesit always said, take your time and it'll all make sense.

Haley plopped in Dad's saggy chair and lifted her bum leg over the armrest. She tossed her phone up and down. She had to be serious, like Detective Deb that first time when Haley described Wartface. Dead serious. The dude at the cabin needed to make a call, that's all. Then Dad destroyed that old phone. It been like *weeks* before she got this new one. Yeah, she used the same number and same-old same-old passwords on a couple of apps, but like she could change it up right now. And that cabin dude wasn't even with it enough to have his own phone. Like Dad, he probably didn't get cyber-anything. What the bomb, it couldn't matter at all.

Chapter 31

꩜

Spring rain obscured Erik's view on the Minneapolis-Chicago flight. Nearly two weeks on the Harrington case, not an unusual amount of time, and Erik had to screw up his patience to stick with methodical collection of information. He let advice from his father drift through his mind. His father, who as campus security witnessed a shocking range of behavior, had told Erik this: Help people say what they don't know they know, and help them say what they don't want you to know. People confessed to his reticent farm-raised father.

ATC executives like Drexler could be reluctant to face any possible wrongdoing on Harrington's part. When Erik entered the Allston Groups building, he found the atmosphere tense as driven Type A's tried to pass as easygoing Type B's. Five o'clock on a Friday and while most Chicago Allston Group employees had left, others remained at their tasks. They directed Erik with a professional courtesy that imitated warmth.

The air literally warmed when he entered the suite for Melanie Genereux, vice-president of the Allston Philanthropic Foundation. She stood by a reception desk consulting with an older woman and a young man all ears for what she had to say. Genereux wore a fine tailored skirt and jacket. Her vibrant halo of light reddish hair brushed against his shoulder with a static snap as she extended a hand and said in a nearly imperceptible French accent, "Call me Melanie, please."

She ushered him into her office. Standing lamps dispersed soft lighting against the gray exterior view. Melanie gestured to two leather chairs by a small round table.

"Thank you for agreeing to see me so late in the day," he started.

"I'm so sorry it's a man's death that brings you to the center of my world." Melanie swept her hand around the room. "Can I get you coffee? There's a one-cup maker down the hall. No? Ah, I see, you've noticed the photographs." Event photos, like those in Harrington's apartment, covered one wall. The anomalies were of a helmeted man positioning himself on a motorcycle, in aviator sunglasses climbing into a glider, and—face obscured again by the angle—launching a heavy canoe into an Amazon-like river. "My husband. I fell in love with his sense of adventure." Her voice dropped in describing the husband, but the lilt returned when she faced Erik. "Do you have family? You must. How are they?"

"Happy families are all alike," he said. Melanie's features tightened oddly. "A saying of my mother's," he added. "She also has one about unhappy families being different. I don't have personal photographs displayed in my office." True for the past month. Post re-carpeting, he had yet to reinstate one of Ben, and he still had one of Kristine in his drawer, not knowing what else to do with it, not wanting to do anything else with it.

"My husband travels constantly." Again, Melanie's tone was noncommittal. "I keep that life separate. I wouldn't want to expose it to corruption." Her smile returned as she pointed to her photo with a former governor currently abiding in prison.

Erik took the opening: "You're satisfied with the Allston Groups' take on corruption?"

Melanie was amused. "That's a loaded question. I thought you'd be subtle. We're back to the death of Niland Harrington, aren't we?"

This close he could see circles under her eyes, not unusual for a thirty-something woman whose make-up consisted of a natural shimmer and lip gloss. "Yes. Harrington's co-worker, Andrew Cushing, was also attacked and is in a coma." Melanie interrupted with an 'oh dear' as Erik continued speaking: "Stephen Drexler has provided minimal information about Harrington's ATC projects."

"First, Detective, I've been 'instructed' that questions about files *must* be handled by our legal counsel." Melanie's slight accent trembled. "Your case would fall apart if I'm accused of violating client privacy. I've passed on my concerns about file irregularities. Allston and his advisers are not being transparent on the matter. It makes me anxious—I told myself Harrington's death was random but you—know best."

"The best I can do is pursue answers. Did you know Andrew Cushing at the Twin Cities office?" he asked.

"No." She recovered her calm.

"Did you know his predecessor, hired for IT work in Chicago, transferred to Minneapolis—Harold Burnham?" Erik had received that name from the

Minneapolis ATC office as he was boarding the airplane.

"No. You realize, Detective, I would know the people who work at the level of Allston's cabinet, not the individuals who work on their teams."

"Does that include Harrington?"

"Harrington was, to use one of Allston's favorite words, proactive. Very attentive."

"Did he get along with employees who answered to him?"

"Since we did not work together on specific projects, I can't say. I apologize for talking like an executive, but that's what I had, professional contact."

"In what ways was he attentive? To clients, to personal details?"

"His clients respected him. He handled their cases thoroughly, received their respect, and yes he did chat them up, made them comfortable about sharing 'personal details.'"

"Is that why Harrington was chosen for transfer to the Twin Cities?"

Melanie touched her necklace. "Harrington was good at assessing clients' vulnerabilities. The move was a slight promotion and raise for him. It would have been a huge promotion and raise if he had gone as head of that office as originally planned. At the last minute, Allston tapped Stephen Drexler."

"Harrington was meant to be head of the Twin Cities group?" His tone must have sharpened, the way she looked at him.

"It was confidential here in Chicago. And what I'm saying now is confidential. Harrington put up a fight. One can't fight against Allston. I sensed Harrington buried rage beneath his—his acquiescence. Stephen intrigues clients. Much more than Harrington, he's gifted at engaging people, they'll share much about their lives, though Stephen never says much about his own. They feel the allure of being so much more through him, they're drawn to him." She flushed and her fingers went from her necklace to her throat. "Then it's like a split personality. He withdraws"—

"Though you've stayed close," Erik interrupted, feeling flushed himself.

"Erik—Detective, I sense your innuendo." Melanie smiled and strands of her hair floated free. "I admit to having a crush on Stephen. He charms women and a fair number of men. I met the ex-wife once. He's well rid of that harpy, vain, self-involved. Stephen can give the impression that he's those things too, which brings us to the unspoken reason for his transfer. Allston's wife, Charm—I know, what a name—was quite taken by Stephen. Any spark and there'd be fire. They're both charmers. But real charm—no, I'll rephrase it—real authenticity comes from the heart."

Erik kept himself from saying that by definition authenticity is real. "Did Mr. Drexler and Mrs. Allston have an affair?"

Melanie crossed her legs. "Drexler is smart, also wary around power, secretive—a reason he's not more of a leader. He wouldn't make the mistake of going after the boss's wife."

"Arrogance is blind."

"The phrase is 'love is blind.' Ah, you're being clever. Take-away message: Harrington lost a very significant promotion to Stephen's sex appeal."

Erik was close enough to feel her breath. "The charity, The Denisha circle. Harrington, Alicia Krause, Andrew Cushing, Sandy Sweetser, Jonathan Lewis were all compiling reports for you, some have gone missing."

"Directing Allston's potential"— she surged with the inspiration—"has become my life. Supporting women and children who've been abused must be a priority for society. Many communities don't have services, and government agencies—their funding's a politician's whim. I don't know how closely the people you mentioned worked together. Lewis, I hardly know him but I've reached out."

"Alicia Krause?" Erik didn't reveal that she kept disappearing.

The legs re-crossed. "Alicia struck me as a lovely, if directionless, person. I gave her a chance in nonprofit fundraising, and a potential widowed donor confided that she tried to collect *him* for herself." Melanie ran a finger back and forth under her necklace again. "You asked about corruption. It's worrying. Alicia was picked up for speeding, I heard, but the ticket was dismissed. Next thing, an officer who had access to Alicia's DMV records asked her out. Then"—she lost her train of thought. "So many botched investigations. What can we believe?"

Erik didn't argue. "What did you expect to learn from the Denisha reports?"

"Oh, yes, the missing reports. We vet their accounts to present a substantiated case, personal details changed, for the supporters. I can't imagine anything in them would put people in danger."

"Sam Vine is a supporter?"

"Yes, we vet our supporters too. Vine attracts rumor mongers, but I can't imagine him involved with Harrington's death." She searched Erik's eyes and then dropped her look to the table that separated them. "The helplessness"—

"Do you feel you're in any danger?"

"I, I see no reason, to be. Is there something I should know?" She was clearly shaken and Erik regretted asking. Before he could respond, she stood to show him out.

At the door, Melanie was still, except for a finger twisting a curlicue of hair. "You're very sincere, Erik, I should say Detective, and I need to put my faith somewhere. You're originally from Ohio—it must have been a wonderful small-town boyhood."

"Iowa."

"Excuse me?"

"I'm from Iowa, the Great Vowel State. Pigs and People. Not Idaho. Not Ohio. Iowa."

She darkened—then laughed. "If you say so! I wish I could offer more help, and if I think of anything about Stephen Drexler, I'll be in touch."

AFTER A NIGHT IN WHAT had to be the noisiest of the Midway airport hotels, Erik boarded an early afternoon return flight to MSP. Yesterday's rain had given way to a hot bright sky. Erik tried to settle his knees and elbows into the confines of his seat, last row by the toilet. He looked up the G-Met website on his phone and checked his official bio—no personal or familial details, but it noted that he came from Iowa, so was probably the source of Melanie's information on him. He pulled out notes from his morning interview with Harold Burnham's ex-wife at her Orland Park home. She was clueless as to Burnham's whereabouts; they had divorced a year before his transfer to the Minneapolis ATC office. Burnham was not much for talking, she complained. Never had a chance, Erik guessed. She ranted that Burnham loved Xbox and PlayStation more than he loved her, that on weekends he went to sports bars, alone, and brought her back beer coasters. He liked to bird watch—stupid activity, you'd never catch her doing that. He didn't mind taking her shopping for clothes because he could sit and play with his phone. He never talked of his parents, assumed dead. As for her parents, Burnham didn't like them, but neither did she.

Before the devices-off announcement, he checked his phone again: Harold Burnham was not at his last-known address and the phone number was out of service. It's as if ATC trained people to be hard to find. Erik wondered if Burnham shared Harrington's fate, if they were men who knew too much, if Burnham was another dead body to be found.

Erik shut his eyes for take-off. Good to know that Melanie Genereux was helpful yet something about their interaction felt off. She had revealed motives for a Harrington and Drexler rivalry. Setting aside Harrington's shoe photo as a peccadillo—Erik's mind jumped tracks. He and Deb had talked over the photo's oddity, that nothing else pointed to Harrington having such "tastes." Harrington, who lost rank to Drexler and embezzled under his name, may have snitched this nasty item from his secretive boss for blackmail, confronted him—then Drexler would have motive for murder. Harrington hired a thug as protection, which failed. Time to go after Drexler, hard.

The plane landing jarred Erik. The light blinded and his head ached. He was back in the Twin Cities and needed to pivot his mood. First step in that direction before getting Ben—the acquisition of a smoked turkey wrap with avocado, lettuce, aioli, and shavings of piquant cheese. The last step, once Ben was in bed, would be a 37-degree icy-bottle beer.

CHAPTER 32

ఎఠ

Entering Bar SuzyBill on Saturday night, Deb felt in limbo, not stuporous flat beer limbo, but the limbo of not knowing if she could connect. After a six-day work week, it'd be great to hang with somebody, anybody, Suzy or Bill. Most G-Met sorts were boringly mature with parental duties or Netflix addictions. Drees, Erik's G-Met rival, had said SuzyBill was a precinct police fave and he'd come with her. Until a "situation arose" (hot hetero date, she figured), and Drees abandoned her. That, after she'd chucked her blazer and femmed up the hair.

Erik had spent the past twenty-four hours chasing the case in Chicago, leaving Deb to her own devices. Her devices sucked. The morning was Mankato. Yeah, Dwight Haugen had been there for a few days with a crony from the old Ford plant. That crony had moved off the grid and shook his head over Dwight becoming *ob*-sessed with those brain-parasite cell phones and how they worked. "Came to the wrong place for that," Crony said, pointing to his windmill and chickens. "Took off to the North, maybe the South," he added. "How about East or West?" she asked. "Could be," he replied.

Next she'd done the homework on the name Wuger from the Sweetser interview. Wuger sounded like Luger, a firearm, so possibly Haley Haugen's Wartface, Harrington's companion up north. Nothing on the Minnesota DMV system, but Wisconsin's popped up an Alvin Wuger, huge with the mug of a Rottweiler. She caught Haley at home and showed her Wuger's photo. Haley asked over and over why Deb couldn't find her dad; and after mis-identifying Cushing as a Lord of the Rings wizard, she would not be definite about Wuger as the Northwoods Wartface. "Could be," she replied.

Could be Deb needed a drink. SuzyBill's was hopping, people lit up and on their way to paradise. At a large table, women celebrated the third marriage, or third divorce, for one of them. Past them, three TV screens tuned to different sports hung suspended over a large glossy black oval that caged pink-shirted bartenders.

At a bend in the bar a group hooted about the damned court system and administrators who screwed them. Nothing like attacking the boss to bring people together. The group—police retirees, a few muscled young men, fewer women—huddled around a big guy with huge nose and white hair raked back from his dome. He stared up at Twins spring training on a muted screen and howled at an outrageous error. "You're right about him, Uhle!" a sixtyish woman in fancy-pocket jeans laughed. She grabbed Uhle's thick arm. "He won't stay in the majors for long!"

Deb played remora attaching to a shark. After the "Cops on the Dumb" blog on Erik undoing his partner Bob Uhle, G-Met had issued a wishy-washy statement that those charges had no validity. She needed to gather her own intel. She moved in and told the nearest bartender "more of the same," which turned out to be whiskey with a beer back, a boilermaker. Who was she, Marlon Brando? She pushed the whiskey shot down the bar where sure enough somebody gulped it.

The laughing woman noticed her and slurred, "Your precinct, hun?"

The answer, "G-Met," received an f-bomb from the woman, who leaned into Uhle's paunch. "Isn't that where, where"—

"They corralled Lambkin! Well look at you"—Uhle was damn jovial and offered Deb a drink-damp hand. She shook it and tilted her head in a way she thought made her look straight. (Go figure, tilting makes you straight.) She wasn't *hiding* her orientation, just keeping that cement-block-of-a-chip off her shoulder. She said hey, good to meet you, ordered another boilermaker, this time slugging back the whiskey.

A nice buzz was curling Deb's toes when Uhle started up on "Lambkin Jansson." Most of the crowd had never seen him, so Uhle got them belly-laughing with an imitation of Jansson's's little-boy look and hangdog stare. Uhle's buds wanted more and he gave them more. Then Uhle was drunk-serious, moaning that Lambkin Jansson was a devious snob big on the silent treatment. Deb could kind of see that, but a young police dude near her said "he's reserved" and left without a good-bye. Then Uhle claimed that Lambkin always belly-ached that Chief Ibeling had an "a-hole for a mouth."

Deb caught herself, hands on hip.

"Whoa, you a dyke?" Uhle boomed. "S'all right." He started to clap Deb on the shoulder, she flinched, and he nearly fell on her. "If you can live with it, guess I'll have to!" The laughing woman became a sea gull that wouldn't stop cackling as she supported Uhle. "Come back, Dev, Bev, what's'r name"—Uhle waved and gull-woman's squawk hit a new decibel.

Deb stumbled over the group of women celebrating the third marital incident. They asked her to take their picture with a phone. She wasn't familiar with the model and ended up viewing a slide show of pics already taken in the bar.

So she felt Marlon-Brando boiled and would have to call a cab—she swore she saw in the background of one of the earlier pictures a different lout checking out the bar. Wartface Wuger. Nowhere in sight now, but Suzy-Bill's gave Deb a place to start her manhunt.

Chapter 33

❧

Sunday afternoon, sunny but in the 50s thanks to Minnesota's bipolar climate, had been welcome time off for Erik. He'd taken Ben to Como Park Zoo. Erik now drove the two of them to his apartment building's sunken parking area in the back (he'd rented in Linden Hills near Kristine to make transferring Ben easier). They were climbing the steps to the back entrance when Erik saw that the door latch hadn't caught properly. It had happened before and he should have fixed it himself. Ben, fiddling with a one-eyed monster doll and humming a tuneless tune, didn't notice the hesitation. Once they were through the door he'd leave Ben with a first-floor neighbor, an established arrangement, and check the hallways. Err on the side of caution.

He opened the door and Alicia Krause came out of the shadows.

"Why am I being bothered?" Her black moon eyes were wet. "I can't find my iPad—I told you. I don't dare reach out to Stephen Drexler, he used to love me. I haven't been well, Andrew Cushing—my intuition said I could trust him, he was searching for files Harrington had hid, I think, and that's why he"—

Erik interrupted her incoherence. "Ms. Krause, Alicia, you need to wait *outside*."

"Why are you being mean, Daddy?" Ben asked and Alicia startled at noticing him. He held up his doll to her. "He's a Minion, he has only one eye, and I have a Woody doll, too."

"Ben!" Erik scolded and then wished he hadn't said his son's name out loud. He grabbed the boy's arm with one hand, Alicia's with the other, and pulled them around so Alicia was outside and Ben inside. "Stay here," he ordered Alicia and locked the door between them. He'd wanted to explode at her—

Why are you hiding? What are you hiding? He rushed Ben to the neighbor and dialed 911. By the time he returned to the door, Alicia was gone. A patrol car siren screamed, but Erik knew that by the time it arrived and he explained the situation, Alicia would have lost herself in the shadows.

ERIK DROVE TO WORK MONDAY morning in one of his funks. He thought he'd be delighted if a beautiful woman burst into his life, but not like yesterday. He walked into Greater Metro to be told by the receptionist that a woman was waiting for him in an interview room. Before he could ask, "Alicia Krause?" she said, "Melanie Genereux, from Chicago." He texted that information to Deb, who usually arrived a half hour after he did.

He stopped to get a cup of coffee in the breakroom. Back in the hallway, he realized he should have grabbed two cups, one for himself and one for Melanie. He stepped into the room and she stood. Her suit looked silken while the static in her hair and eyes signaled distress.

"Erik, Detective Jansson, such a relief to see you. Oh, is this for me? How kind."

She took the coffee and sat. Erik told her the session would be recorded, which surprised her, and picked up one of the available pads.

"Are you safe?" he asked.

"I think so. I hate playing the damsel-in-distress, barging in like this. I'd thought my husband was going to accompany me, but he informed me, long distance, that I'm no longer part of his adventure." She sniffed back a sob. "After our talk Friday, I couldn't stop thinking about Stephen Drexler. He couldn't be intentionally involved in anything … I called him, we arranged to meet, and I flew out yesterday, Sunday. I've traveled here on short notice before, Harrington's request—he simply wished me to pass on to Allston how well he'd assumed his new duties. I'm running on—Stephen and I were to meet for dinner last night, but he never appeared."

"Take your time," Erik said. He wondered if Alicia and Drexler had disappeared together.

Melanie sipped coffee and explained that she was to meet Drexler at a Linden Hills bistro. She parked her rental car in the dark lot behind the building, where a big man watched every step she took into the restaurant. A half hour later, she called no-show Drexler and then texted. Nothing.

When she decided to leave, the man from the parking lot was waiting on the sidewalk. She returned to the bistro bar for fifteen minutes, he was gone, and she headed to her car—to see him standing on the other side of it. That scared her and she fell in behind a group of carousing teens and texted a ride service.

Melanie paused for a slow breath. Her hand was on the table, close to

Erik's.

"What did you hope to learn from Drexler?" he asked.

"I never received the research that Harrington's group completed for me. I told you as much in Chicago. Much of it was background on Allston's old time crony, Sam Vine. I feared I was missing something or Stephen was failing to see something. He's incredibly astute but can be blind to what's nearest him."

Erik considered that the blindness might be to Melanie's feelings for Drexler.

"Stephen is so private, I thought I could appeal to his—entrepreneurial instinct." Melanie's wistfulness begged for a soothing touch.

"Harrington was seen with a large man like the one you describe," he said, Deb's Wartface Wuger. "Have you reached out to other ATC employees here, Jonathan Lewis or the freelancer Sandy Sweetser?"

"Oh. Lewis. He's sweet, and I wouldn't want to … jeopardize him." She hesitated. "I hadn't thought of Sweetser. That man in a coma, the tech fellow, I remember now that Harrington assigned file organization to him and Alicia Krause. So maybe he or Alicia has the files. Where's my mind, I shouldn't be so rattled. When I was so upset last night, I was going to call you from the street, run to your place if I had to, then the ride service arrived. I was in your neighborhood, right?"

He caught his breath. "How would you know my home address?"

Her eyes widened. "The ATC system. That information would have been entered by the Minneapolis office when you started the Harrington investigation, as part of your official contact information."

"My 'official information' does not include my home address."

"Drexler, a person who answers to him, must have found it."

Melanie's ignorance might be protection and Erik hated to break it but he had to. "A picture of an adolescent girl—unconscious or dead—was found with Niland Harrington's body." Erik couldn't sit still. He had to stand.

And she stood. "*What?*" Then she was sobbing on his shoulder.

He was gently reseating her when there was a knock on the door. It opened—Deb.

"Hey there! I'm the partner, Detective Deb Metzger." She nodded to Melanie who was dabbing a tissue at her eyes.

Deb, using a loudly pleasant tone new to Erik, took over the rest of the interview. They learned nothing. Melanie said the girls served by the Denisha Circle had suffered abuse and a photo like the one found with Harrington might come from police records and possibly be in a research file. However, an image like that never reached her.

To close out the interview, Deb made sure Melanie Genereux had emergency numbers on speed dial. In return, Melanie would forward sample

Denisha files from the past. Melanie thanked them both and wished them a speedy resolution to the case. To Erik, the resolution didn't seem any closer, but the list of vulnerable people—unknown girls, Alicia, Melanie—was growing longer.

CHAPTER 34

꘎

"D rexler," Erik said. Back in their office after the Melanie interview, he plonked down in his office chair. "Before the Cushing attack, before these women showing up, I was ready to believe that Harrington had been murdered in a robbery, and that coincidentally there were intrigues at ATC, because intrigues aren't uncommon in high-powered places. Now"—

Erik realized he was talking to a wall. Deb had stopped off somewhere. His phone dinged with a message, a friend from the Minneapolis force. He wanted to train together for an upcoming 10 K and by the way, he'd seen a G-Met investigator, Deb, at SuzyBill's Bar. Having a drink with Bob Uhle. He didn't have a chance to respond before Deb strode in with coffee.

"Alicia," she said and sat down. "I could believe she was simply a woman terrified by a stalker, until I saw the notes you sent about her 'visit.' She's messing with you"—

"Hey!"

"How are you 'bothering' her? Did she show up dressed for seduction? And Melanie—she's great, but I watched the first part of your interview with her through the mirror. Aah, she likes you, and you don't think she's so bad either. That damsel-in-distress act"—

"I tried to finesse"—

"Right. Police Academy Lesson One: how to unlock the safety on your Finesse."

"At least I know what that means. As for 'bothering' Alicia, she probably learned from friends unhelpful to us that we're searching for her and that her apartment's under surveillance. Drexler's ignoring her. Her intuition led her to trust Cushing who"—

"Her intuition sucks. Sounds like a story to me, feeding you lines until you reveal what you *know*."

"Can you lighten up?" Erik stood and paced. "And, by the way, how was it having a drink with Bob Uhle?"

"Okay, I get ahead of myself. I get anxious when beautiful women throw themselves at full-blooded male colleagues—I've known a fair share who think below the belt. I mean, sometime a beautiful woman could throw herself at *me*! I'd like that challenge. And Uhle, I know what body part he thinks with— it's below the belt and not in front."

Erik burst into a laugh but before Deb could catch a breath was serious again. "Both women pointed to Drexler holding on to secrets. Harrington had something on him, related to the missing files, which might be on that iPad he took from Alicia."

"You know, women like her get pushed around. Maybe Drexler coopted the thug, tentatively identified as Wartface Wuger, had him kill Harrington and 'persuade' Alicia to distract you. And, oh god, what about this gangster-guy, Sam Vine?"

Erik returned to his chair. "I pray on my knees a Chicago mobster has nothing to do with anything. Enough complications already."

"Like missing Dwight Haugen. Maybe he did us a favor, leading us up north to Wuger. In fact, I have an appointment with the manager at Suzy-Bill's. They may know where to find him."

"Hmmm," Erik muttered.

"Hmmm, yourself." Deb left him her half-finished coffee before going out the door. He didn't appreciate the gesture.

Alicia's noncompliance gave Erik grounds to request warrants for her personal records. Did she want him to act on her behalf, but not as an officer of the law—is that why she'd asked earlier if he was a lone wolf? Was she a Delilah playing him as a Samson? Drexler was another matter. Erik couldn't go after a person that savvy and privileged on sheer conjecture. If he could bring in Alicia, have Deb's hyperbolic presence shake her up, maybe she'd reveal more about her former lover.

There had been the outline of a sharps container in Alicia's apartment, she said she'd been unwell—her health issues could provide means of tracking her. Sharps—the thought of needles, injections, punctures, skewers unmanned him all right. If only he could speed up the process and access her medical records without a warrant. He could also try brokering peace in the Middle East.

He remembered how Kristine, new girlfriend and new law student at the time, had been incensed when studying the Patriot Act. Privacy protections could be leap-frogged in the name of national security. To rivet her interest, he explained that police could access medical records without resort to warrants. He quoted the American Civil Liberties Union: "law enforcement is entitled to your records simply by asserting that you are a suspect or the victim of a crime." Her eyes narrowed at him as if he were to blame for the whole system. He back-pedaled to add that except for a life-or-death emergency, the privacy assurances of HIPAA (which should stand for a dance style and not for the Health Insurance Portability and Accountability Act) ruled. At G-Met, Ibeling said that it would take "an act of Congress" to get medical information without a warrant.

Erik uploaded the warrant requests. He then opened his desk drawer and took out one of the lapses in his power-driven diet, a chocolate bar. He tore into it.

The phone, as always, startled him—the warrants were being processed, and staffers would handle the tedious job of contacting medical providers. Erik's first G-Met partner, Loften had diabetes. Maybe Alicia had diabetes, though why hide that? She was an unlikely candidate for Type 2 since she was under thirty-five, curvy but not overweight. Type 1, which used to be called "juvenile onset," acted like an autoimmune disorder in which the body's ability to make insulin was destroyed. Type 1 seemed more probable and more dangerous.

Erik's computer dinged with new messages.

The first from Cyber Paul read "note tagging" over photos from local online running sites. Erik's name appeared under his finish at a charity race. Another image showed the back of a man in running gear and a small boy next to him, ERIK JANSSON AND SON. A cold pain seized him. Someone not only knew a great deal about him *and* his family but was spreading that knowledge across the internet.

THE SUZYBILL BARKEEPER WAS A little guy and a big flirt, overlooking Deb's stature and the mannerisms she beefed up to keep him at a distance. She knew from Wisconsin DMV that Wuger's permanent residence was in Hudson on the St. Croix River, but he hadn't been seen there for months. The barkeep informed her that Wuger had moved to the Twin Cities. He'd worked, on legal and illegal grounds, for collection agencies and was known to break bones. Wuger had also bragged lately about "up-scaling to an e-lite employer."

To escape the barkeep's futile advances, Deb didn't stay at SuzyBill's for lunch. She came across an Asian place on her way back to G-Met. Scarfing Pad Thai, she checked her phone. Her sources in domestic-crime prevention reported that Melanie Genereux's charity, The Denisha Circle, had an excellent reputation. Melanie had also forwarded background files, names redacted. A quick look suggested nothing out of the ordinary.

She stood to leave and noticed escapee noodles on her pants. She dashed to her nearby St. Paul sublet to change clothes. She chose her trimmest skirt suit to recover a feeling of professionalism that the spilled lunch had undone. She returned to G-Met and confronted her computer, alone. Erik was gone, no message about his return. Their partnership was one of quiet interludes with spontaneous combustion, mostly from her. Best way to get out of the awkwardness would be to solve the damn case.

Deb went back to the case beginning, the dead body. Harrington—pedophile, blackmailer, or murderer? Maybe the original owner of the photo—Harrington or Drexler—got off on images of vulnerable children, that's all. If he was a molester or a blackmailer, he took precautions about his methods, his trail, his mementos. There had to be more than a girl in a shoe. Deb spread across both desks the apparently harmless photo albums taken from Harrington's apartment. The night of the nudes, the racy bedroom images. The guy couldn't decide between men and women. It could all be a screen—he wanted other people to read his sexuality as best suited them. Maybe Harrington, Drexler, and this tech guy, the unfindable Burnham, had been in cahoots on collecting images of passive girls.

People's obsessions—why couldn't they be harmless? Like collecting airstream trailers, gnome dolls, duck stamps, references to duck stamps in movies. Deb rolled her head and stretched her triceps. She would love to go golfing, and most local courses had finally dried enough after spring run-off to open for the season.

Golf. Harrington was obsessed with golf, yet the golf bag at his apartment dated back nearly thirty years. It showed up in album photos of Harrington's college golf team. He had to have more clubs, he had to belong to a club, maybe several, though no payments appeared on the financial report. There had to be a locker.

There was, at the third and priciest club she called. The noodle spill had been fate—Deb's suit could pass the dress code. Last summer she learned the embarrassing way that these fancy clubs have dress codes. (You'd think cargo pants would be useful in golf.) When she arrived at Loch Inverness, the manager Bob Fetterly, evenly tanned despite cancer warnings and Minnesota winters, was suspicious despite her credentials and the fact that Harrington was quite thoroughly dead. As Fetterly explained the club layout, Deb inserted questions about the holes and about the long-past Tiger Woods-Lindsay Vonn pairing and split. True Love gone wrong? She really did know her sports, she thought to herself as he laughed and warmed to her. Harrington had been referred by one of ATC's Minneapolis clients, grandson of a club founder, and Fetterly had waived the fee for six months. In return, he assumed

Harrington would schedule expensive private events. Deb showed him photos of Harrington and his ATC colleagues. The manager recognized Harrington, and Drexler as an occasional guest of other members. Jonathan Lewis was a maybe. Fetterly paused over Sweetser—"looks more like a guy who'd work here, and I don't mean as the Pro." Haley Haugen got a negative, her father and Andrew Cushing a "no way." The former tech guy, Burnham, Fetterly hesitated—maybe, he came a few times with Harrington, the two looked a bit alike.

Another photo and Fetterly stiffened. Alicia Krause.

"Hey," Fetterly spoke to man walking by in a turquoise polo shirt. "Purnell, isn't this your new girlfriend?"

Purnell strolled over like someone accustomed to taking his handsome time and glanced at the image. "Alicia? Alicia Corazella? Disappeared on me."

Deb's pulse sped. She asked about their relationship. Old-fashioned dates, no significant action, Purnell said with disapproval. She nodded as if agreeing he was right to scorn a woman for holding out. Purnell had met Alicia when she came by to talk to Harrington and later to find him—post Harrington's death, Deb computed. Soon after, Purnell heard his last from Alicia. She called to say her mother was hospitalized in Nicaragua and she had to leave. (A father in Peru, a deceased mother with the surname Corazella.) Not much to go on except Alicia Krause aka Corazella was into deceit.

Purnell dismissed, Fetterly found the key for Harrington's locker and left Deb alone. Shoes and clothes to check for DNA, a score pad, toiletries in a vanity kit. A hefty golf bag. Side pockets held balls, sunglasses , score cards. The zipper stuck on the largest pocket, and she was reluctant to stain her suit with lubricating grease. The locker room was generously supplied with mouthwash, soaps, lotions, and sunscreen. She opted for SPF 30 and spread a little along the zipper. It loosened.

What a rush—a towel wrapped around a rectangular edge. She eased towel and contents from the bag. An iPad with a distinctive cover, Alicia Krause's. Deb had done it. Thirteen days since the body was identified, and she was about to solve her first G-Met case.

CHAPTER 35

❧

After his Monday afternoon appointment with the dentist, Erik wanted to avoid G-Met so he went back to his apartment. The dentist had explained that Erik didn't need a root canal because the pain he was experiencing came from grinding his teeth at night. The dentist recommended a mouth guard and calming meditation then said other than that, Erik had great teeth. Erik didn't want to be known for his teeth. Couldn't he be known for effective action, for doing the right thing for people, in a not boring, not always straight-arrow way?

He could escape the office, but not the internet, not the case.

Erik checked for the Uhle allegations on "Cops on the Dumb"—dropped, the site had switched to State Trooper blunders. Then Ellen McCormick, the blogging soccer mom who knew Alicia, called his cell in a fury. She had heard nothing from Alicia until yesterday, when Alicia left two words on voice mail, "Please help." Erik revised the timeline in his head. Sunday, Alicia surprises him and then avoids the patrol he called; later she reaches out to Ellen. When Ellen tried the number, it was dead. (About the same time, Melanie was a few miles away fleeing from a man presumed to be Wuger.) Then near midnight, someone threw a rock through Ellen's window and she called 911. "You've set a stalker on me," she shouted at Erik. He replied that he could request a uniformed officer—he should have simply listened because Ellen cut off the call. He called back. She snipped, "I called them last night! Don't you have a clue to what's happening?" For the second time, he was cut off.

The afternoon was turning into a root canal after all. He needed a run hard enough to pound out the headache, but short enough that he could shower and swing by a grocery before picking up Ben. He rarely had his son for a weeknight, but Kristine remained out of town at a west-coast legal conference. He and Ben could eat an organic vegie pizza while watching a movie. Ben would probably pick his favorite, the animation about a fish searching for someone.

Instead the boy chose the book about a lonely toy rabbit that became real. Erik had to read it ten times and it added to the exhausting day. At last Ben fell into an immovable sleep on the big bed, clutching a stuffed bunny like the one in the story. Erik eased himself off the bed, tossed his new mouth guard in his sock drawer, and sprawled on the couch in his t-shirt and boxers. The story looped through his head, a rabbit, alone in a cupboard, alone.

A *whack* seemed to split his skull open. Ben screamed. Erik banged his head against the couch arm and Ben ran crying to him. Erik scooped him up while grabbing his phone. A window had broken, a wrench and glass on the floor, and wind gusting in through the jagged hole. He put Ben on the couch, and ordered "STAY!" like the child was a dog. He slid up to the window. Nothing, too dim to see. He checked his phone, 4 a.m. He had a second floor apartment. That throw required power.

He called 911 and organized himself. Retrieving his gun might frighten Ben. Retrieving his pants was a better move. Ben whimpered, "You scared me, Daddy!"

He picked up the boy and sat with him. "The window broke, that's all." He should call Kristine. Wait, she was scheduled to be on a red-eye flight returning from San Francisco. Deb. What could Deb do if he called her?

The officers, city not G-met, arrived. In this situation, he was the citizen and they were the investigators. Erik focused on getting Ben out of the apartment.

He called Jimmy Bond Smalls, who understood the police life and the need for a haven.

CHAPTER 36

❦

There's nothing quite like explaining to your wife, ex-wife, how you put your shared son in harm's way. Tuesday morning in Kristine's office, that den of lawyers, had been the worst way to begin the day. Kristine's eyes were already red from her demanding schedule of night flight directly to work. When she did look at him, Erik lost his concentration and lost whatever consoling thing he thought he had to say. He lingered, thinking it would come to him, it didn't, and the arrival of her client forced him out. But Kristine had relented enough to call him mid-afternoon. Could he do her and really Ben, a favor? Ben had hidden his Woody doll in her briefcase before her trip, and when she pulled out a brief during a business lunch at the Cities Club, Woody came along and splatted in the pasta salad. Woody had been set aside and forgotten. She had just picked up Ben at preschool and he was asking for Woody at fifteen minute intervals. She called the club and they'd found the toy, but she had to take Ben to a birthday party at a god-awful fast food place. Could Erik retrieve the doll when he was done for the day, and drop it by the—her house?

Erik said yes and clicked off to avoid blurting out that she was rubbing it in, that she met wealthy clients for divine food at exclusive places. She didn't intend that. He had meant to support her career in labor law with clients minimum-wage and corporate. Before Ben screamed his way into being, she had argued one nonprofit do-gooder in the family was enough. It took Erik an uncharacteristically long time to realize she meant *him*. If his parents heard him termed a do-gooder, he said, they'd laugh out loud, meaning make a nearly discernible noise. They were Scandinavians after all. As for nonprofit, that sounded lifeless. "I'm a Knight Erring," he countered. She laughed that he meant knight-errant. He'd said what he intended, Knight Erring, and at that point, clothes were off, most definitely clothes were off, though she whispered something about a red Mountie uniform.

THE BANQUETTE SEATING OF THE Cities Club dining room curved around Jonathan, Mrs. Stoffel, and Stephen Drexler. It felt more like Anxiety Hour than Happy Hour. Jonathan was relieved that Mrs. Stoffel provided a generous buffer and that the angle of the seat meant he wasn't confronting Drexler eye-to-eye. Jonathan fidgeted and Mrs. Stoffel put her hand on his. Hers was almost hot, and soft except for the iron hardness of rings and bracelet. Jonathan expected her to launch into intrigues linked with ATC. He knew she had been chatty with Harrington to the point of calling him "Niland."

Instead she commanded Drexler to tell her about himself, and he launched into his obsession with Scotch. Mrs. Stoffel liked the full-bodied Aberlour. Drexler preferred the tang of Glenfarclas and that it was thoroughly "Scot." One of the few distilleries, he said, operated not by an international conglomerate but by a family. The Glenfarclas family? Jonathan had asked. No, the Grants, had been Drexler's answer; glens are valleys, like an Irish dingle. On hearing "dingle," Mrs. Stoffel squeezed Jonathan's thigh. The Dingle talk stopped when the two Scotches arrived, along with the Mendota Springs water Jonathan had ordered.

Mrs. Stoffel began dropping names that had no meaning for anyone but her. "Jim Cullen sticks to the standard glossy-ad Glenfiddich. Jim reminds me of you, Stephen, though I doubt he has your education," she started.

"Glenfiddich is owned by a different Grant, the William Grant family, who grasped marketing to save themselves," Drexler said. "Speyside in Scotland is a wonderful visit. Sometime I should go from there to St. Andrews, but I'm not the golfer that Harrington"—Drexler's suave confidence stalled.

"Don't you think Jim likes his Glenfiddich a little too much?" Mrs. Stoffel sweetened her voice with the Aberlour. "Didn't you inherit him as a client, Stephen, from poor unlucky Niland?" She nodded toward Jonathan as Harrington's factotum. "Jim gallantly orders for me when we're together, which could explain why he's running into trouble with his investment agency. Something there's about to boil, don't you agree, Stephen?"

"We don't have that account anymore. None of us can take our position for granted." Drexler was transfixed by the oily swirl in his glass.

Miniature quiches—the *amuse-bouche*—arrived on tiny plates. Mrs. Stoffel swallowed hers between words. "Cynthia Kovak, a dear friend, needs guidance. A witless employee made a mistake, and now her company's reputation is under fire. She would love to have you help her, Stephen. I imagine that women"—she halted. Jonathan was relieved until he saw why.

The sharp-angled detective stood over them. He drew himself up in a well-cut suit that looked like he'd run in it. He had a sniper's stare.

"It appears ATC's media savvy has been extended to me and those connected with me," the detective spoke harshly. He was gripping a cowboy doll.

"Detective—what was the name?" Drexler stood. He was taller by an inch, he used that inch. He had forgotten he was holding a bitty quiche fork.

"Erik Jansson, it's all over the internet. My running routine, my son, false allegations." Club members arriving for happy hour stalled behind the detective. "You and your agency, Mr. Drexler, are very clever at employing available media to get the word out. The wrong word. Clever at keeping your own dealings—buried."

"Ooh, a pun?" Mrs. Stoffel cooed and offered her sparkly ringed hand. "Teresa Stoffel."

"Ma'am," he answered. A policeman actually saying "ma'am" gave Jonathan an embarrassing thrill. Erik placed a card in Teresa's hand. "All knowledge matters."

"You're not 'private,' Detective?" She hadn't given up, but he ignored her question and locked eyes on Lewis. Evince outrage, Jonathan directed himself. He couldn't.

But Drexler did. "There is no *reason* for you to interrupt our evening and distress Mrs. Stoffel," Drexler said as Mrs. Stoffel put on her engagingly-distressed face. "No *reason* for you to rudely intrude."

"No *reason* for you, Mr. Drexler, not to answer *reasonable* questions and act *reasonably* toward anyone who has a life, lives, to protect." Red points like needle jabs appeared on the detective's cheekbones.

"Do you have a subpoena, Detective, well I forgot your name again." Drexler and the detective stood so close that they breathed each other's carbon dioxide. The doll flopped forlornly from the detective's pocket.

"*Gentlemen*, is there a problem?" A strong-voiced man came up behind the detective. Tall as the two standing men, with a trim gray beard, double-breasted suit and cane, he had the air of a person who settled things and whose questions became statements. "As chair of the club's board, can I help."

"It's all right, Tom." Drexler sat. "The officer is frustrated that he can't do his job."

"He seems to be doing fine to me." Mrs. Stoffel's shark teeth glittered.

Erik stated his name as he gave the bearded man his card, moved to leave, and then turned back. His tone mocked Drexler's—"Lovely club, sense of community. It is frustrating that concern is missing"—the detective's directness returned—"about a co-worker in a coma, a man dead, an unidentified young girl possibly murdered, a woman missing." He walked out, cowboy doll stashed somewhere. The man with the cane frowned at Drexler before moving on. Drexler looked shaken, which heightened Jonathan's anxiety. And what had the detective said about a girl murdered?

Mrs. Stoffel opened her fuchsia mouth but Drexler spoke first and stood again. "Let's meet again, soon, Teresa. I have urgent business—nothing to do with this incident of course."

She grasped Jonathan's arm like she was pulling him into a deal and looked to Drexler. "Let me add, Stephen, people often find a need to talk with me. Oh, and I used to know your Chicago boss's—don't look at me like I mean 'gangster'—I knew 'Ted Allston's' new best friend quite well when he lived here, Sam Vine. Sam, a good man to know in a crisis." Mrs. Stoffel downed the rest of her Scotch like a sailor, took Drexler's hand to rise, winked at Jonathan, and swiveled her hips past them both.

CHAPTER 37

❧

With a practiced maneuver, Erik kicked open his office door—mail in one hand, coffee in the other, cinnamon roll in his mouth. Deb sat rigid while Ibeling rapped his knuckle against their window. The roll made it to Erik's desk, dropping next to case materials.

"How long as it been like this?" Ibeling indicated the window's encroaching film.

"Since just before you came in, sir," Erik said.

"The two of you should have clear vision. It's Wednesday, closing in on three weeks since the discovery of the Harrington corpse. Our average closing for rush cases is a month, just to remind you. That domestic incident with the Haugens." Ibeling fixed on Deb. "Have you made progress?"

"The Task Force is narrowing in on a distributor of child pornography who uses a public library branch. I was briefed on that yesterday."

"Not the case I asked about."

"Haley Haugen," Deb tried again, "is not a victim of abuse. But some *idiot* posts her activities on social media, can't trace the source. Ummm, Dwight Haugen is playing hide'n'seek."

"A game he's winning, Deb. Erik, what evidence have you recovered in the Niland Harrington case?"

"His work accounts show minor embezzling suggesting that Stephen Drexler"—

"Leave Mr. Drexler alone," Ibeling snapped, "until you have evidence. He called to report that you accosted him in a public place when he was with a client. I had to talk him out of a restraining order"—

"That PR cutout!" Erik snapped.

"If you're going to have a personal emotion, Detective, do not have it with a person of interest. Or I might have an unpleasant personal emotion, starting now. Physical evidence in the Andrew Cushing attack?"

Deb stepped in. "Fingerprints traced back to various delivery men who aren't suspects. The cat is missing."

"We're not going to subpoena a feline."

Erik took a turn. "Deb recovered an iPad in Harrington's golf bag. Waiting for the tech unit"—

Deb jumped in. "Harrington's coworker, Alicia Krause, is at large. Erik last"—

"Also missing, Cushing's ATC predecessor, Harold Burnham," Erik spoke over her.

Ibeling slapped his hand on Erik's desk, causing the pastry to fling itself into the wastebasket. He frowned at the DMV photos of Dwight Haugen and Alicia Krause, at the ATC photo ID of Burnham. "They are not needles. That"—pointing out the blurred window—"is not a haystack." He walked back to the window and thwapped it with a knuckle. A crow barked. "Regular people have pigeons on their window sills."

He was gone.

"It's dead," Deb announced.

"The bird?"

"Your roll. Fell apart in the trash, roll no more."

"Detectives!"

They jumped at the return of Ibeling. "Check your email for the evite to the upcoming office party. Deb, Erik reminded you, of course, about your presentation to the Anger Management seminar?"

He left again. They sat.

"What's the difference between the anger management seminar and the party? Aren't they—redundant?" Deb stared at the ceiling as she asked.

"One has too little coffee, the other too much alcohol."

"That sounds about right," Deb agreed. She put her head down on her file-littered desk and asked a muffled question—"What are we going to do next?"

Erik studied the cinnamon roll in the waste basket. "You could … come up with a past domestic situation you defused to talk about at the seminar. Doesn't have to have a perfect resolution"—

"Because perfect resolutions don't exist," she mumbled.

"And I'll … play fireman and rescue a cat."

Deb did not lift her head but gave him the A-OK sign.

IT HAD BEEN TWELVE DAYS since the attack on Andrew Cushing. Erik drove to the man's apartment through a drizzle—there had been more than enough

April showers. He stopped on the way to eat a breakfast sandwich, which cleared his mind, and called Deb back at the office. Her gruff voice indicated she had fallen asleep on the job, but since the job was constant, when else would you sleep? Erik had interviewed people at the ATC office about Harrington's predilections and more recently about Harold Burnham's and had learned that Harrington got high on influence and that Burnham was a nondescript man increasingly stricken by debilitating headaches. He suggested that Deb go to ATC with the indistinct photograph from Harrington's shoe. He gathered that his partner had a gift for giving voice—a loud voice—to the voiceless, and she might stir up something.

Sun broke through in streaks, gleaming trees and puddles. Cushing's newly arrived relatives had called to ask if anyone had found the cat. Erik signaled to parallel park, but an oblivious truck tailgated him. He moved on and feared that the cat, nine lives notwithstanding, had been flattened by a likeminded oblivious truck.

He parked behind the building—since the cat could not return to the locked apartment, it might go to a food source, the garbage cans housed in a rickety attachment. Erik jiggled the latch open to see that many people hauled garbage as far as the cans but not actually into the cans, management too cheap to acquire dumpsters. With sun hitting the rain-soaked piles, a fetid odor intensified. Nothing would come of this—he kicked a can and there was a scrawny cry. He wrestled the overflowing can aside and there in a dark corner, a green glint. "Kitty kitty"—his falsetto worked. A soaked stringy thing crawled to him. The cat looked half its original size, except for the saucer eyes with an expression not unlike Deb's on hearing her anger-management assignment. Erik picked up the cat, smelly and mewling, and it snuggled into his fleece. He would take the cat to a local shelter for care and inform the Cushing family. He had at last saved a life.

CHAPTER 38

✥

The ATC office buzz over Harrington had been subsiding until a big-shouldered woman showed up late Wednesday morning. Jonathan felt certain that Detective Deb Metzger was lesbian, and while he was content to be quietly out as gay, she was loudly out about everything. She bluntly repeated questions the other detective had asked and nagged them about the Harrington group portable laptops. The investigation already had many of Harrington's work files from ATC servers. What had happened to Alicia Krause's computer, Alexander Cushing's, or Harold Burnham's, she wanted to know. When someone leaves ATC employ, the hard drives are wiped. Usually the unit tech person does that, and Cushing hadn't been replaced so Jonathan didn't know, maybe his director Drexler did. She grilled him about Burnham—he had hardly any contact with the tech person, who left ATC while Jonathan was absent with bronchitis. She showed him a DMV image of a big man—he thought he'd seen a person that size, but couldn't think where. Then she showed him a blurry photograph of a collapsed girl.

The photo stunned him, and Detective Metzger spoke up about the vulnerable, how they were exploited, how they were erased, how others had to act on their behalf. Jonathan was confounded: he had seen nothing of this side of Harrington and could think of nothing to say. Detective Metzger left him with his mouth open and her card in his hand.

Jonathan started to work through lunch on the Widow Arnfelt project: her sister had died and he needed to handle all the STEM initiative preparation, but his concentration was shot. He phoned the hospital to check on Cushing—only family members were allowed information and access. He left his name and number, and a nephew with an east-coast accent called back to say yup,

Uncle Andy doing pretty good for comatose, and, say, they'd found the cat.

Jonathan felt a need to restore his vigor. That male detective, Jansson, could take him easily. This female one, Metzger, not only looked like she could take him but just as soon snap him in half.

He told the receptionist where he was going "in case of emergency," though it seemed like the life-and-death emergencies had already happened, and left for the Lake Isles Beach and Racquet Club.

The club was near dead Harrington's apartment—Jonathan wouldn't think about that. He also wouldn't think about the romance that never was with the work-out buddy he'd lost. In January, that buddy had been transferred to his firm's London branch for a year, leaving Jonathan with his car, an Acura, to tend, and with a deflated sense of what might have been. Jonathan's locker had been untouched for months, but the items in it smelled clean enough. He changed and headed for a warmup on an elliptical machine.

After fifteen minutes of stationary exertion, Jonathan headed toward the weight area and a tall man pulling a shirt over his head elbowed him in passing and stopped to say excuse me.

Drexler. Fit and handsome except for blue hollows beneath his eyes.

"Lewis," he said without surprise. "Do you play racquetball?"

"Yes." That came out too fast. If Drexler wanted to play, it could only mean one thing.

His boss wanted to beat him.

Drexler acquired racquets and a court. They entered the narrow room with a glass wall so people could observe the give and take, Drexler saying something Jonathan missed so like a numb-nut he said, "Huh?"

"I was remarking that the police aren't getting anywhere with the Harrington investigation. He apparently had side interests none of us knew about." Drexler whammed a practice ball so hard that ricocheted off two walls and Jonathan ducked. "Another warm-up shot." Again Drexler hit the ball too hard, shrugged, and said. "Lewis, you serve first."

That meant Jonathan would face the wall, with Drexler behind him holding a racquet.

Jonathan had to focus or he'd be a victim of head trauma. The feel of the game came back to him, and Drexler, despite the ferocity of his first shots, seemed preoccupied. After a missed ball, Drexler resumed conversation.

I wouldn't be surprised if we were served more unproductive warrants." He hit a wild serve. "I need to get my game back. A week ago, when Melanie Genereux dropped in on you, I couldn't see her after all. Allston calls, she answers. Did she talk about Sam Vine, Allston's crony?" He hit an easy serve and the point played out in Jonathan's favor.

"I believe so, no substance to it."

"What else did you discuss?"

"She talked about loyalty." Jonathan missed an easy ball.

"Tied to advancement or as a general virtue?" Drexler lunged to catch Jonathan's best shot.

"Um, that Allston valued it and that it could make things happen. She told me about his charity to aid abused women and children"—Jonathan didn't swing and the ball dribbled itself to a stop.

"That's just occurring to you now?" Drexler coldly said. He retrieved the ball and tossed it up and down in one hand. "It occurred to me after the detective left—a possible pedophile involved with such an organization. Of course the charity files wouldn't have photos of that sort. Merely a disturbing coincidence." Drexler slammed a serve.

Jonathan lost the point and put his shaking hands down on his thighs. His lungs labored for breath.

"I worry about Alicia," Drexler spoke without inflection. "Do you know how to contact her, Lewis? You shake your head no. I wonder if Alicia knew, knows, something, and if she passed it on to Cushing. Perhaps a pornography ring? Nothing to do with ATC." Drexler, very sweat-soaked for the amount of play, paddled the ball against the floor. "Did the detective show you a picture of an ugly thug? Cushing might recover, but I'm not sure he'll be the same." Drexler hit a serve and Jonathan surprised himself with his strong return.

"Good point, Lewis, I'm done." Drexler's posture was upright but his face exhausted as he offered a hand to shake. "By the way, there isn't anything you're 'unintentionally' holding back, is there? If so, someone should be told. Oh, that thug, it's come back to me. I've seen him in the parking garage next to our offices. Watch out."

Drexler headed for the lockers while Jonathan wiped his red face with a towel. He had come to suspect that Harrington was embezzling under Drexler's name, and Lydia Arnfelt had suspected that ATC fabricated threats against its own clients. These things fell away next to the vague threat Jonathan now experienced. It wasn't exhaustion he saw in Drexler's face, it was fear. And fear led to desperate acts.

JONATHAN DID NOT EXPECT A rush hour at this library branch. Adults picked up materials on their way home from work. Teens faked studying. A hawk-nosed boy with the flushed gorgeousness of youth gave Jonathan a look-over. A high school girl peered at him over her Clark Kent glasses. When Jonathan was sixteen, he'd ridden a wave of androgynous mystique and both sexes noticed. He envied Drexler's universal attractiveness, though how it was deployed beyond the office remained unknown. And Drexler's performance on the racquetball court—was he warning Jonathan off, directing Jonathan to dig deeper (into what?), implying that if Jonathan found anything, he should take it to Drexler and no one else?

In contrast, Melanie Genereux's email, which he saw on his phone after showering and dressing at the club, was outright. Any news on the Harrington investigation, any sign of missing files, what was Drexler up to? She had used a personal email account, and Jonathan intended to reply from his private address on a public terminal.

A hunched man, weedy stubble over a terrain of wrinkles, ambled past Jonathan toward a terminal dedicated to genealogy research. He was intercepted by a young woman with mocha skin and fuchsia cat-eye glasses, who spoke firmly: "We're always happy to see you, Mr. Olson. Please remember the time limit, so other patrons can also have access."

The regular terminals were occupied and the circulation desk busy. When Jonathan was a bare twelve, his aunts would check out devout and inspirational reading—then send him back to the library for steamy romances and gossip magazines. Which started town rumors that Jonathan's reading was to blame for his "inclination toward sin."

Maybe Cushing, as much as Jonathan liked him, had a dark interest in illicit materials. In their last contact, Cushing had instructed Jonathan on how to retrieve emails from spam. Harrington had set up a broad filter that swept up legitimate messages from clients who'd complained by phone that they never received a reply. Cushing had supplied Harrington's access codes. Once a terminal opened—

"Lewis, hey!"

Sweetser—act pleased. "Hey, Sandy." About forty branches in the Hennepin County system and Sandy happened on this one.

"Haven't seen you in a long time. You look good." Sweetser was the same. "Researching your ancestors? Finding Daddy and Mummy's secrets?"

"The *last* thing I would do." Jonathan reached to grab the back of a chair, only there wasn't one.

"Whoa, you okay? Has someone been pushing you around? Those close-minded cousins of yours?"

Jonathan needed to explain his presence—Lydia Arnfelt, that's it. "Research for a client who wants to promote STEM programs—science, technology, engineering, math—for girls. I wanted to see what materials the library had. You?"

Sweetser tracked the young librarian. Besides the cat-eye glasses, she wore a short fringed skirt, a fitted top, and a necklace on loan from a pharaoh. "Me? Looking for Marian the Librarian."

"That's her name?"

"You know, Marian, sexy saucy libra—rian. Balzac in Iowa? T that rhymes with P and that's Pool right here in River City? *The Music Man*? Mar——ian," Sweetser intoned until people looked. "Never mind. This branch has a great selection of large-print books, though my ailing mother rarely finishes a book or remembers she started one. Her care, what a burden, not that I should complain. You know, it's great to see you, to see *anyone* not stuck on grilling you about poor Harrington. You'd think Mr. Self-Entitled Drexler could convince the police it has nothing to do with ATC. I'm thinking it had to be robbery."

"Well," Jonathan dragged the word out. He couldn't contact Melanie Genereux, not with sociable Sweetser hanging on. One of Melanie's requests was bizarre: did Drexler hang diplomas hang in his office? "Harrington liked carrying cash. And, um, I'm worried about Alicia. Maybe that old boyfriend, Mr. Restraining Order, has returned."

"Yeah, Alicia liked you. You've heard nothing?"

"No, but a huge man, maybe that ex-boyfriend, hangs around the ATC parking area. Didn't Harrington hire a security person for himself, or was it you, when you went to Chicago to interview Sam Vine?" Jonathan fished and found he liked fishing when it didn't involve slimy aquatic creatures.

"You know about that?" Sweetser squeaked. "How did you"—

"Harrington told me," Jonathan lied.

"Alicia—I wouldn't want that security guy after her, name like Wombat or Wotan. I almost think the guy was hired to *keep* me from finding anything."

"Did you find out something you shouldn't have about Vine, Allston?"

"Nothing compromising, so ignorance is bliss." Sweetser sounded relieved.

"It's not what you know. It's what they *suspect* you know."

"Make me paranoid, Jonathan! I, why, no one wants me! I wish Marian here did." Sweetser looked sickly.

Had to be the library lighting, not yet LED but a dizzying dying fluorescent. Jonathan's head buzzed, he shouldn't have spooked his friend. They were distracted by the entrance of a swanky woman—sleepy eyes, white shirt that glared under the pulsing light. She walked right to The Marian. An older man, another librarian from his ID badge, joined them and the woman disappeared with him.

Sweetser looked human again and poked him. "And good for you! This STEM philanthropic project sounds exactly like what you should be doing. Great info, I'm sure, on the data-bases here. A terminal is free." Sweetser maneuvered Jonathan past the Genealogy hog. "Go ahead, log in with your library card number."

"My card?" Jonathan acted distracted.

"I'll use mine." Sweetser pulled his from a worn wallet. "See EBSCOhost and enter here, 'STEM'"—

The Marian Librarian touched Sweetser's arm. "Could the two of you please move over there? We're having a serious issue." She directed them away, and her male colleague returned to announce a Star Wars/Dr. Who confab one level down with free refreshments. The teens auto-herded to the stairs and elevator.

As if on cue a middle-aged man came through the entry. His cheeks seemed stuffed with lumpy acorns, and his hair was a dirty reddish-brown. His expression shut out everyone and reminded Jonathan of the tech consultant before Cushing, Burnham. No one stopped chipmunk-man from going to a terminal.

The buzzing worsened.

Sweetser leaned into Jonathan. "Melanie Genereux, Chicago office, know her? She raised an interesting point, that for a show-off Drexler didn't hang proof of that so-called U. Michigan law degree in his office. You ever see anything like that? Are you all right? You're white as a sheet."

"A-asthma," he stuttered. So he wasn't the favored one, but, and the but made him feel worse—if Melanie was secretly reaching out to him *and* to Sweetser, she must be trapped between the lions and hyenas of Ted Allston's world.

"Here, let's get you seated. Hey, what's going on?" Sweetser swiveled around.

The swanky woman reappeared with police officers and they surrounded the chipmunk-man hunched over a terminal. When she spoke, he jumped up and grabbed at her. The officers intercepted. The man talked loudly to the pulsing lights. Jonathan should never have come.

"A hacker?" Sweetser asked as the man was escorted out. The Marian Librarian calmed a shaking Mr. Olson. "Wait—I've seen that woman in the suit, her picture, in an article about crimes against children. Authorities must have traced the IP address. Oh god, It's kiddie porn."

"I, um, nature calls." Jonathan put his hand to his temple. Sweat trickled down Sweetser's face. He moved to a terminal while Jonathan found the men's room.

The sink water stunk of sulfur. Jonathan knew he was thinking like Scooby Doo, but he bet Melanie was on the verge of discovering an awful truth—that Drexler wasn't what he seemed.

None of us are what we seem, a preacher had preached back when Jonathan's voice was changing. It gave him the willies, like the preacher saw into his pimply hormonally-tortured soul. He stepped out of the library men's room, Sweetser gone and a terminal available. Jonathan opened his private email.

A new message from a new address. Alicia Krause. She begged Jonathan for help. If he couldn't save Melanie from Allston's terrifying beasts, he could save Alicia.

CHAPTER 39

༄

Fed up with department forms and smelling like the cat he'd rescued, Erik was about to flee for the day when Paul chased him down the hallway. Deb, who'd been on the phone with the crimes-against-woman-and-children task force, caught up with them in Paul's computer warren, a narrow space supra-heated by electronics. Paul had decoded the iPad found in Niland Harrington's golf bag. His reserve struggled with his excitement and lost.

"The initial code to unlock the tablet was simple," he said to Erik on one side of him. To Deb on the other, "Alicia Krause's birthday reversed. The Gmail account is hers. That user name and birth code also opened her Cloud account." Paul linked the iPad to a large monitor. "One deleted folder I recovered is a medical log."

"Does it look like a plan for a diabetic?" Erik asked, whapping a pen against his thigh.

"Could be—symbols for glucose. The tablet's office program has folders on resources for people escaping domestic violence. A few are labelled 'off record.'"

"There is an underground network of safe houses that will have nothing to do with law enforcement," Deb said. "Due to lack of trust, criminal activity of their own—police are the enemy."

Paul ran his finger down the screen. "Most files appear to be downloads from a work computer. The question—why transfer so much to her personal tablet? Why not work from a cloud account? Or, conspiracy theory"—

"Yes?" from Erik.

"Alicia Krause thought her work computer wasn't secure. On a peer-to-peer network, co-workers have access. Also, someone could have installed a keylogger to catch all key strokes. It's like a wiretap on internet searches to obtain passwords, phone numbers, credit card information," Paul said. "A keylogger can be as simple as USB thumb drive attached to a computer stuck under a desk. Installing and retrieving it could be easy in an office where people share space. Or a 'peer' could download malware which captures key strokes and sends intel to a remote location. Anti-virus programs usually detect that activity, unless those programs were deliberately disabled."

"Keyloggers are how abusers can figure out their partner's searching for ways to leave," from Deb.

"Here's what we have," Paul continued. "A folder labelled 'Think Twice,' which is a collection of reports from news media and interest groups. The shared theme is police incompetence and corruption. In several instances police failed to follow up on reports of domestic incidents and women died, or police were complicit in the violence. Here's an example"—he pointed to the screen. "A man released for lack of evidence goes home and beats his pregnant girlfriend to death."

All three twitched.

"It gets worse," Paul said. "The last dated document in that folder concerns a cover-up. It appears to be a draft report on Twin Cities police involvement with a prostitution and pornography ring."

The three heads nearly touched the screen to skim the file. No recipient was designated, no departmental heading, only the DRAFT stamp. The report appeared destined for the head of a clandestine investigative unit. The authors were identified as A, B, and C: a law enforcement officer, a departmental researcher, and an independent investigator.

The ringleader was identified as a corrupt high-ranking police officer, code name Stabber. The involved businessmen included Blunderbuss, who operated a payroll service. The group started operations after a police investigation of a prostitution ring. Stabber decided money could be made from the hotel room surveillance tapes, and with Blunderbuss branched out into sharing child pornography images from investigation files. A police colleague suspected Stabber, but they had been in the military together and Stabber had his friend transferred to a different division and the matter was dropped—

Until a whistle-blower in Stabber's unit became suspicious about the disappearance of surveillance tapes and she was dismissed. Her dismissal led to this investigation. There the report ended.

Deb looked tasered. "So, uh, shoot me—not really—doesn't Stabber's friend sound like Ibeling?"

"You can take Ibeling at his word." Erik wanted to douse his hot face. "You can take him at his word unless … unless that word is about a fish he's caught. It's all vaguely familiar. 'Blunderbuss' sounds like a person in Harrington's files, someone he did NOT take on as a client."

"We can't dismiss it, the police corruption bit." Deb gave the monitor a hate-stare.

"Yes, but," Erik started.

"Yes, but?" Deb echoed, not nicely.

"If I were Alicia Krause and reading this, I wouldn't trust law enforcement," Erik said. "But it's off, somehow."

"Detectives." Paul clenched and unclenched his fingers and opened another file. "This section of the 'note to self' application could be immediately useful."

"What, a guide to meditation"—Deb stopped her growl, and Erik pulled in to the screen.

Names. William Thomas, Peter Martindale, Michael Stanwood, Joseph Reed, and Stephen Drexler.

"Business associates?" Deb asked.

Erik snapped his pen. "I don't remember those names from any ATC list of employees or clients. Associates, but not for legal enterprises?"

"We need to get on this, and the police corruption angle"—Deb was angry and she would damn well show it.

"That report doesn't sound right." Erik snapped his pen harder.

"I'm mortal," Paul interrupted.

"Huh?" from Deb. "You're not omniscient?" from Erik.

"I need to eat and sleep," Paul said. "This stuff—it will still be bad in the morning."

"That's right!"—Deb sounded surprised. "We can get a good night's sleep"—

"And it will still be bad," Erik finished. "If it's bad, it will keep."

They had tangibles to investigate and could end on a point of agreement.

CHAPTER 40

⚓

Haley balanced, reached back to grab her left heel, and pulled it to her behind. She zipped up her warm-up jacket and made her phone in the inside pocket secure. At least running in Minnehaha Park was pretty, and sometimes she saw Detective Deb's partner, Detective J., on the trails and he would talk to her. This Wednesday she didn't have to be home until 7:00 p.m. when Mom returned from her shift.

It sucked that a couple of meets had been canceled because of spring heave damage to the track (like always), one school having a budget crisis (ditto like always) and another school violating eligibility rules (ditto ditto like always). The girls with her, led by Sydney, Karin's BFF (yeah, right), were arguing that Karin had been lying about her phone being screwed up as an excuse for missing so much. (Karin had taken her big mouth to the orthodontist for wire tightening, hope it hurt.) Sydney blabbed about online catfishing, and smart Evie said Karin wasn't Karin, at least not on Twitter and Snapchat, what-the-bomb. Evie said that Karin's dad had called Evie's mom last night and said they should all change everything because it was Karin's name on the account but it wasn't Karin and that fake Karin had all their contact info. Karin's identity had been stolen, he said. Haley stretched her other quad—not Karin's *complete* identity which could use a makeover, her being a pill so much of the time.

Haley so did not want to change anything on her phone because how would Dad reach her? He didn't have a regular number, picking up a tracphone whenever, or she'd be calling him all the time. *Why* was he gone so long? Maybe he'd gotten a job out of state and was going to come back with money just to show everyone. Haley didn't know if she could live with Mom much longer, gone from screaming to moping. "Worse than a teen," Mr. Nail had said of Mom. He helped Haley and Sierra with school work. He had strange ideas about math but fantastic ideas for projects. He wanted Haley to do a history diorama that would use invasive mussel shells and his stuffed white squirrel. Which would have been great except it was Cold War history. Maybe he had a toy nuke and the squirrel could be radiated.

Her friends yakked. Haley took the stretch band off her hair so it could fly and called "Eat my dust!" She took off fast, only tiny Evie following and she couldn't keep up. Haley ran so hard it gave her cramps before she looped round to the south end of the park. She jogged onto the grass and doubled up, a stabbing pain in her side. She was being stared at, creepy old people on benches, especially that woman with gross lipstick who dressed like it was the Depression or something. Haley knew history.

She straightened and pulled her phone out. A cramp made her want to vomit. She doubled up again. She shook it off, gave up on the workout, and walked home. On the way, she called Detective Deb, busy. Trying not to be a cry baby, she left a message that her dad wouldn't forget her. And that a friend's phone had been hacked and, if it made any difference, a stranger had borrowed her phone when she and Dad were hanging out at the Nail cabin.

When Haley got out of the shower, she heard her mom pull up in the van, but no one came in. In a towel, she slipped out by the front window and peeked. Mom was talking to people in another van. A van labelled "Cyber Crime Unit."

DEB WAS PUTTING POSSIBLE CORRUPTION at G-Met out of her mind by tackling microwaved lasagna when Haley Haugen called. The girl unloaded over "Mom's old landline" and wanted to know why the Cyber Unit was at her house and what the geeks were finding. "They're right there, you could ask them." Deb realized she sounded short and told Haley to go on.

"I *know* what happened!" Haley insisted. "My phone's fine now, but I'm positive plus that Dad's gone back to Mr. Nail's grandpa's cabin. Dad's after that man who took my phone when I was sick. See, this man did *whatever* with the SIM card and passwords and I'm *super positive* plus he infiltrated my friend network and turned into a fake Karin, and I'm like *pluperfect* positive plus that this creepazoid hung with that Harrington guy that's dead, not when he was dead, before. Wartface was, uh, busy with his truck, and Creepazoid killed that Harrington because Harrington didn't like him taking girls' phones. Maybe Wartface didn't like it but hid the body back here because, you figure that out, anyway, I think the phone guy's scared of Wartface cause he's just bad but Dad will find him, the creepazoid I mean. He shouldn't have taken my phone."

Deb, rubbery lasagna in her mouth, mumbled, "I'm chewing it over." She should be very worried, and she was. Haley's data was a commodity to be sold online or a treasure trove for a solitary pervert.

The girl ran on fumes. "It explains *everything*. Like think—Dad's kind of slow, especially if he drinks, but he promised me he wouldn't, so he figured it out and he doesn't want that man to find him, so nobody can find him, Dad I mean. Wait, the cyber geeks are talking to Mom about IP addresses. You can't like kill someone through an IP address, like that's a horror movie made-up thing, right? Really, it explains everything! You get it, right?"

"It's, um, possible, Haley, but I'd keep quiet about it"—because it would confuse everybody. "Definitely I'll go to the cabins tomorrow." She repeated this until Haley finally understood what she was not to do. Wonder of wonders if Haley was onto something, and the trip had already been set. Deb would do a second warranted search of the area where Harrington, Wartface, and this third man, Haley's creepazoid, had been seen.

The alarm didn't buzz Deb awake next morning, Haley did. She called at 5:47 a.m. to repeat her Theory of Everything. She sounded strung out like she'd dreamed terrors all night. Deb calmed her down by listening to her one more time. Deb slugged coffee and called Erik to jolt him awake—he croaked that he was already up but begged off the trip because this Thursday he was attending a play put on by the children at Ben's preschool. He had an idea about the source of the Alicia iPad report on police corruption—Deb could hear him making coffee in the background. Meanwhile, she could forward the report to Lola Scheers, the person in charge of the women-children crimes task force. Erik between coffee gulps assured Deb that Ibeling had done, would do, the right thing—not always the thing that made you happy—but the right thing. The burden of modern life, he said to end the call, is vindication by procedure.

When Deb arrived at the office, she dispatched the report as Erik suggested and then received a call from Paul. He'd put together one name from the notepad found in Harrington's apartment, "Thomas"—too generic to have meaning at the time—with "William Thomas" from Alicia's iPad. William Thomas had a new gas station card with enough credit to keep a soul in sweatshirts, doughnuts and beer. The card had been used at Neck's store about the time Harrington was there, used in South St. Paul after the body was found, used two days ago in Eden Prairie. If William Thomas, whoever he was, was hanging around the cities, Dwight Haugen wouldn't be finding him up north. Deb as part of her road trip could ask if anyone knew of this Thomas. Problem fact: William Thomas died three years ago, yet someone assumed enough of his identity to have a viable self at Buy-N-Run.

In the G-Met lot, Deb switched to a fleet Scout 4x4 and stocked it with a small coffee, granola bars, a boiled egg, and chocolate so decadent she didn't dare speak its name. She headed north into the blustery day. After an hour, she was dying for another cup of coffee but her gut clenched, her intuitive organ. Something bad was about to happen.

Her cell rang.

"Detective Deb, c'est moi!"

Bent Nail, who else.

CHAPTER 41

❧

Ben's play, held at 10:00 a.m. for no reason Erik understood, was the minor
disaster that such events usually are. Ben had the role of Father Hennepin,
or "Father Nenpin" as the boy pronounced it, discovering St. Anthony Falls,
birthplace of Minneapolis. Ben had gestured broadly in announcing the
discovery and thus knocked over the cardboard cutout of the falls. This led to
a fight—as much giggling as wrestling—with a boy playing a Dakota Sioux,
and the break-up of the fight constituted the final act. Erik congratulated
Ben for going on with the show, and then in the parking lot was cornered by
Winky Mom, a divorcee who winked at him every time their paths crossed.
Her real name slipped Erik's mind, and his pause gave her the opening to say,
"Let's go to a real play together, Saturday night," and he was committed to a
date he didn't want.

He tried to force women from his thoughts as he merged his Highlander
onto the crosstown expressway. Winky Mom was attractive, despite or because
of blouses cut low and snug. She lacked Kristine's vitality, and there'd been
Alicia's heart visibly pounding, Melanie's hair wisping across his chin. Erik
turned on the radio as a distraction, only to hear a man sing and moan about
how he lost her, how they had been destined, how in his dreams she slipped
into the shadows.

He had just shut off the radio when he got a call—Ibeling's ring. A rusted
Crown Victoria nearly rammed Erik as he signaled and pulled over.

"The note reads, 'Detective Jansson, if you don't watch out, you'll be
hurtin'. Your boy will be hurtin' real bad.' It's being investigated as we speak.
Precautions are being put in place," Ibeling explained. "And the Uhle mess is
online again."

Erik should have had dry toast drenched with Maalox for breakfast. Ibeling would already be contacting Ben's school. A process for every kind of threat. Another email ding—a message from the animal shelter: "Drop by, your cat has issues!"

Erik wished he could surrender feline responsibility and prayed Andrew Cushing would recover. He hadn't solved even that part of the case. Who knew Cushing best at ATC? Jonathan Lewis—Lewis also close to Alicia, to Harrington, closer than he wanted to admit. Lewis, maybe not so innocent.

JONATHAN KNEW HOW TO WORK a funeral. He arrived shortly before the 11:00 service for Mrs. Arnfelt's sister. He was blessedly relieved to have a break from his clandestine morning tasks. At the office first thing, he'd learned that Drexler had taken a day's leave without explanation. Jonathan talked his way past the security guard, intending to search Drexler's computer for the possible aliases listed in Harrington's spam notes. He was about to try the computer when Settina walked in. Jonathan mumbled something about emailing Drexler an attachment that he could no longer find in his own files. She said, "check your sent mail." Jonathan blushed his way out and returned to his apartment to change for the funeral. There on his personal computer he retrieved documents from a Harrington cloud account accessed through a "spam" link, as Andrew Cushing had suspected. Harrington, what a sneak, had sent himself adhoc notes under a heading which he tagged as spam, and that spam was not automatically trashed but required manual deletion. Jonathan barely had time to deal with it.

Outside the church, Jonathan shook hands with businessmen he claimed to have met and gave them his card. He explained how he came to Mrs. Arnfelt's aid with a memorial for her sister Helen. From Harrington and Drexler, he'd learned the lines and understated gestures, but he had advantages they didn't. He was native. He could gather clients and information by expressing a familiar sympathy.

He entered the sanctuary and had to sit immediately or be forced to stand the entire the service. He positioned himself as far as possible from the lilies which lined the aisles: their heavy odor choked him up. He expected the Scandinavian heritage in aging flesh, and it was present. An elderly couple in front appeared frail enough to join Helen Johnson before the hour was up. But he had expected the event to be more *white*. The grandchildren walked by him, college-aged and younger, whose hair ranged from white-blond mist to saturated black sheets.

He didn't expect Settina. She was with a tall young man, maybe Chinese, who had his arm around her shoulders until they reached Mrs. Arnfelt. The young man hugged her like family and then introduced Settina. Settina saw him. That sharp-eyed sphinx.

Jonathan wanted to leave. The dead were dead. It didn't matter, the details, how you died and who showed up in a pretense of care. He couldn't make himself stay for the luncheon. There was work, there was always undone work.

Back at the office, Jonathan felt sucked into a reality where you walked on a rusted screen over an abyss and any second you would plunge—into what he couldn't imagine except for the ceaseless nausea of a nightmare fall. He thought of his great-aunts' cooking.

A message from an unknown number turned out to be Melanie Genereux. She feared that Drexler was covering up an event in his past. He appeared in Chicago last night and wanted her to meet him at a "private" hotel room. "I've been too trusting of Drexler, everyone, Allston, my husband who's left me. I'm trying not to panic," Melanie whispered in the message. "I said yes to Drexler but went to a friend's instead." She begged Jonathan's discretion and please, please keep her informed.

It was too late for discretion. He'd already sent an anonymous tip to the detectives, felt like he was having a heart attack in the process. He'd formatted and printed off Harrington's spam items in a way that *if* the information seemed to come from ATC, it would be traced to Whinette. He used mustard yellow kitchen gloves to place the information in an anonymous tip box at a police station on the way to the funeral. The sheet included contact details for an AW and a list of payments to that AW, references to HAB, and a list of names that ended with Stephen Drexler's.

He didn't share everything. Jonathan left out he argument he'd overheard in the garage the week before Alicia Krause left ATC. He had been heading to his car when his path was blocked by an idling pickup truck. On the other side a man was screaming, Harrington, screaming that stupid Alicia needed to get her fucking big butt out of the way. Sweet Alicia had to be the victim. If she lashed out against Harrington, it was because she had to. Maybe that stalker boyfriend had been around, and who knows what a dangerous guy like that would do if a tick like Harrington interrupted a fight between him and Alicia.

It was only early afternoon, but Jonathan couldn't accomplish a thing He headed to the parking garage, where he'd taken to parking by a security camera. A hueep hueep noise unlocked his Hyundai and he slid in. Alicia had emailed him that morning through an alias. Could you help, she begged, send your personal email. I'll be in touch.

A woman started the Audi next to Jonathan, shot him a why-are-you-sitting-there look, and zoomed out of her space. He pushed the ignition. If Alicia didn't get him killed, Drexler would.

CHAPTER 42

꧁꧂

Some people make death threats like others write letters to the editor.
"It doesn't say *die*," Ibeling said and handed Erik a printout of the full email message.

Erik's right leg jiggled like it was pumping him up to be shot through the ceiling of Ibeling's office. Paul stood in a penitent posture, eyes downcast to his tablet screen. Erik faced Ibeling. "No 'die' statement, but a 'you'll be hurtin'' and 'stop you permanent.' What am I to do with *that*?"—a beat of a few seconds—"Sir."

"I'm checking past files for regulars who prefer bad grammar," Paul said.

"So it's a giveaway that this person says, 'Don't think I don't know where you live.' I'll be killed by a person who 'prefers' double negatives. He'll not leave me not dead." Erik beat the palms of his hands against his forehead. "I'm sorry, Paul. If anyone can find this pig bladder"—

"Erik," Ibeling took over. "You know most threats remain just that, threats. And you and Uhle"—he frowned—"is an internet brush fire we're dousing. Meanwhile, a detail will be around your apartment and your son's school. What *you* need to do, Detective, is make progress on the Harrington case."

"You're assuming that my ATC investigation inspired this?" Erik's leg jiggled harder.

"When you 'assume'"—Paul's voice went up—"you make an 'ass' out of 'u' and 'me.'"

No one coughed out a laugh. Erik stood and put a hand on Paul's shoulder. As the two walked out, Paul heading one way, Erik the other, Ibeling called into the corridor, "You'll hear more when I know more."

Routine platitudes. One of the mail room's two Julia's caught up with him, the nosier one, with an anonymous tip letter. She whispered to him, despite the secure surroundings, that the letter showed no evidence of fingerprints or anthrax. He put on his "that's fantastic—got to go" smile to cut short her quizzing, ducked in his office, closed the door.

Small favors—Deb was off to the lake cabin. He could settle down with the letter. Erik gloved his hands and removed the internal sheet. Heading: "Harrington Spam," below that "Drexler Identities." The aliases were familiar from Alicia's notes, only this time several were followed by dates, addresses, and question marks.

ALL AFTERNOON, G-MET CYBER TECHS were on the virtual trail of the Drexler aliases to turn the tip's question marks into answers. They were searching the "dark net," the mapless internet catacombs of search engines dedicated to untrace-ability and anonymity. "Everyone in government security hates these engines for what they can hide," Paul said. "Then say it's what they use in their private lives, wouldn't catch them on any ordinary server."

Erik acted on another of the day's messages, the one about feline issues. He drove to the animal shelter where he'd left the cat, labeled "an extremely large coon." At reception, a kitten whizzed by, to be scooped up by a green-haired woman. She crossed her arms over her chest with a kitten head popping out, and eyed him up and down like he was cherry pie.

"Hello, Detective Erik Jansson, I wanted to check on"—

"Oh, Pisser." She disappeared into a kennel area with tiny kitten, returned with large beast, and plopped him into Erik's arms, thus exposing the text of her t-shirt: "Don't Be A Dick." Beneath that, small letters spelled out "Spay and Neuter," followed by a stick- man, "Dick"; a stick dog, "Dick's Dog"; and a winding trail of stick puppies across her torso. At the end of the trail, the woman had stuck her name tag, BARB. She rubbed the cat's round face as Erik held on to the mass.

"Yo, Pisser. Great guy. *Super* friendly. Pissed all over the place last night. Milton was the name on the collar, but he sure answered fast to Pisser. Piss, that's all he did. Uncontrolled diabetes. You call yourself a detective. Couldn't you detect diabetes?"

"You sent me an email, the owner's in the hospital, and I wanted to see if she, he"—

"HE, with a name like Milton, *Pisser* Milton. WAS a he anyway. This old guy's got the fathead of a tom, was all grown up before he went under the knife." Barb stretched up to Erik's face. "Males, you don't take care of their nuts early, they get a swelled head!" Her cackle startled Pisser Milton who dug his claws into Erik's arms. His "ow" escaped as Barb stated, "Money."

"Money?" Pisser Milton took that as an endearment and rubbed his fat tom head against Erik's cheek.

"Yeah. People catnip, money, drives 'em crazy. We have to charge you for meds. You could save a bunch if Pisser has the right stuff at his do-mi-cile. Bring 'em in and I'll give you a discount on a pet adoption." When Erik didn't react, she threw her head back—"or nut removal!" Pisser Milton flexed his penetrating claws until Erik unhitched him for the transfer to the bosom of "don't-be-a-dick" Barb.

When Erik entered Cushing's building, a passing neighbor said a woman, Latina, had come by to ask about Cushing, she'd been around before. No, she didn't leave a name. This was not welcome information to Erik—if it was Alicia, what did she want? The police tape on Cushing's door remained untouched. Erik undid it, unlocked the door, and unwillingly employed his nostrils. Pisser Milton's aura was layered under the lingering odors of blood, chemicals, and police plastic. He edged around the incident tape in the bathroom and headed to the medicine cabinet. No pet pills, but the ibuprofen tempted since the pungent smells tightened a band around his head. On to a narrow closet—its door had been ajar when they discovered Cushing, presumably because it contained the kitty-litter box.

The band around Erik's head ratcheted tighter as he considered the paper work the cat would condemn him to if he took anything. He photographed the shelf before removing Pisser's meds with a gloved hand. He prepared himself for a new onslaught of odor as he leaned over the litter box. There was the slight sharp bite of urine and there was odorless poop—unexpected rectangular poop. It was a thumb drive.

CHAPTER 43

꩜

It was the same damn deer—Deb skidded into the ditch—the same deer that spooked her during that first lake trip. She'd already had one scare minutes earlier, nearly spinning off a narrow bridge into a stream gully. Earlier, Bent Nail had called to apologize for his French and his absence, like he'd been invited. He warned her the roads were slick enough for naked mud wrestling. Maybe her problem was that she had an eye out for wrestlers, not deer. She eased out of the Scout to fall on her butt. Muddy but not naked. She tried Bent Nail's trick of working branches under the ditched wheel and spun the Scout back on the road. No fear in the doe's eyes when she looked at Deb as if to say, it's not hunting season, why worry?

Deb wished to hell she could feel that much at ease. Activity at the mystery camp, Nail had told her, tire tracks. She wondered if Alvin Wuger was hiding there.

The wind hit Deb as she arrived at the Sorenson/Harrington cabin. No one visible. The Scout had local radio dispatch while her phone—barely a reception bar—might as well be dead. The ditch delay meant she missed the locksmith who had opened the door. She focused on the warranted task: examining the cabin where Harrington was seen with Wuger, aka Wartface, and the third man, likely the ATC tech person Harold Burnham. The going theory: Harrington, with Wuger's backup, was convincing Burnham to hack into Stephen Drexler's ATC accounts. Alicia—maybe she interfered or maybe she was in on it. There were APB bulletins out in a tri-state area for Wuger, Burnham, and Alicia Krause, but Deb was holding off on reaching out to public media. It could scare them deeper in hiding, and the woods here, she couldn't remember the quote, were whatever dark and deep.

In the cabin, she didn't see much: decent furnishings and speed-boat brochures. Garbage removed. Foster's CSI team, bogged down in a separate bloody case, was coming in tomorrow to check surfaces for prints. She gloved her hands and searched for papers, bills, tech devices—nothing but an abandoned VHS player and tube TV. With a flashlight, she could see vintage issues of *Playboy* stuffed under one bed, nothing to arrest anybody about, and a rolled-up poster in the dust bunnies against the back. She pulled it out, a yellowed girly pin-up dating back to an older generation of backwoods fishermen.

A howl and the door banged. She whipped around with her gun. Nothing. She thought she'd shut the warped door, and there was no Bent Nail around to theorize about phantom sounds. Deb gathered a few *Playboys* and the poster (*not* for her personal entertainment) to check for prints, though they'd probably be ancient.

Rising gusts grabbed her as she returned to the Scout and opened the door against the force. Huge black birds gurgled and flapped heavily around her as she eased onto the road. The bridge was ahead with its washed-out edge. Deb saw from this angle that yellow sawhorses meant to mark the damage had tumbled down the bank. The wind roared louder.

Not the wind—a blue pickup shot out from a side road and barreled down on her. She twisted her wheel toward the bank, saw the sawhorses, and instinctively corrected left. She heard the roar, couldn't see the truck, her blind spot, she'd be hit—she gasped and invoked the god of Airbags. No impact, a blur—the truck squealed and veered past, gunned over the bridge, and vanished. No time to catch the license.

And her wheels were slipping on mud—don't slide, don't slide, don't slide. The Scout slid sideways and halted on the bank's edge. In the rearview mirror, Deb saw the doe with eyes like hockey pucks. The animal must have jumped in front of the truck, making the driver swerve left instead of ramming Deb to his right. (If the driver was a he.) The trembling doe stared back. Okay, Doe-eyes, Deb exhaled, we're even—no, I owe you. The deer flipped her white tail and leapt down the bank.

Where the doe disappeared, there was a glint. Deb slid out of the car. She lacked the deer's hooved agility and had to clamber around the broken sawhorses. Hidden by brushy undergrowth was a Yamaha motorcycle and under it, she bit her cheek, the body of Dwight Haugen.

CHAPTER 44

❧

Running in circles, that's all Erik was doing, running round and round the Linden Hills neighborhood on a Thursday evening. He'd delivered the kitty-litter thumb drive to Paul and delivered Ben to safety. He'd been caught in traffic over an hour when returning from his ex-in-laws, in St. Louis Park, and he had to move, move, move. He'd left Ben, popping up and down with the grandparents, and Kristine whose moods pin-balled so fast he couldn't catch them, and the security detail. A security officer distracted the boy while Erik, outlined the procedures. When it was time to leave, Ben hugged him, and Erik was surprised when the adults hugged him as well. Kristine smelled wonderful but she wouldn't meet his eyes, just as well because they were brimming.

Three more half-mile loops and he'd call it quits. Before setting out for his run, he'd received a text from Deb that Dwight Haugen was dead, she'd call on return. The Dwight news was tragic, Erik could barely absorb that events were becoming fatal.

He should call his parents in Iowa to alert them about Ben. At least his father wouldn't judge Erik's endangering career choice. Erik had wanted to go into crime since he was scarcely older than Ben, though his father made his former police work and his security job sound, in Iowa speak, as plain as buttons on underwear. No talk of special gear until that family reunion dull enough to bore paint when his father declared that he reserved the handcuffs for his mother. Little Erik was promptly sent to bed as if *he'd* done something wrong. Soon after, a security detail spent nights at their house. There had been a threat, and Erik never knew more than that until later.

His school administrator mother and his campus security father made decisions that upset people—a person fired, a scandal revealed, a rumor squelched, a student expelled. Revenge was often petty—the burnt pie left on his mother's desk, broken beer bottles strewn around his father's work jeep, a cat head in the family mailbox. That first night of the detail, his mother cried in front of everyone, and Erik wanted to protect her and echoed his father's "everything will be fine." Then his father's professor hunting buddy Pfeiffer kept Erik company while his dad made phone calls and his mom fussed over his older sister and the colicky baby destined for poetry. Pfeiffer told Erik that his father "Sven" usually dealt with profs off their meds, "like herding cats," and college students overdosing on fun, "like herding drunk cats." Then the woman arrived.

She had long hair, half tossed up the way women did on TV, and was tricked out in a snug suit and spiky shoes. Women little Erik knew didn't look like that. She volunteered to show his father, and he could come too, the van outside. Parked next to it was her Ferrari. The van held all kinds of security gadgetry and two men with guns. She showed him the police scanner, cameras on the house, and night goggles. She showed him how to hold a flashlight so it could be flipped to hit a bad person on the head. From the mini-fridge she took a sandwich and a glass bottle of Coke for him. He only got Coke on the fourth of July, and then half a can. Everyone paid him attention. After that she spun off in her red car. The van and men stayed. Several weeks later the van and the sandwiches stopped coming and nothing had happened.

Erik dreamed of the Ferrari as he slowed by the Better Bean coffee shop, roasting dark blends for the morning brews. At the intersection fifty feet away, a man held a steaming cup and spoke to someone in a dark pickup, which roared off when Erik shouted. The pedestrian turned and waved—Sandy Sweetser, a hundred yards from Erik's building.

THE FLUORESCENT OVERHEADS IN THE G-Met interview room had been switched out to LEDs. Instead of seeming green, Sweetser was whited out. Deb looked punched under the eyes on her return from delivering terrible news to the Haugens. Nearly eleven p.m., and Erik was fuming about Sweetser loitering in his neighborhood.

Sweetser acted as if *he* were the one sorely tried. "Officers, you took away my coffee and you're depriving me of sleep. I have to attend an early morning meeting about my mother, who sure as hell needs an advocate. She has moments of sweet clarity when she wants all her signing privileges back. Then she requests a 'do-not-resuscitate' order if her eyelid twitches, and five minutes later demands to be kept alive until the Second Coming. And the Third, and the Fourth."

"What were you doing near Better Bean?" Erik had already asked that question, and Sweetser sighed dramatically and renamed an acquaintance in the area. "And that man in the pick-up looked suspicious."

"Suspicious? You're conditioned to think *everything* is suspicious." Sweetser shrugged at Deb as if wondering how she put up with such a prick.

"We don't want to harass a man devoted to his mother," Deb said. "However, in my experience, devotion and violent impulses can go hand-in-fist. Mr. Sweetser, a man in a truck is wanted in connection to Harrington's death, the endangerment of minors, and the death of a man named Dwight Haugen."

"*What?* Who's he? What could that have to do with"—

"With Harrington's death, with Alicia Krause's disappearance, you tell us." Erik leaned back in his chair. "We've learned that you were on the same Chicago flight as Alvin Wuger six weeks ago. Wuger owns a pickup truck." He didn't go into the pickup was black and Deb had recently seen a blue one. "Wuger was seen up north with Harrington and another ATC disappearing act, Harold Burnham, a week before Harrington was last seen." His chair legs hit the floor with a bang. "Our first interview—you never said you and Wuger worked *together!*"

"Look, he's that memory you repress to survive. Yeah, Harrington had Wuger go with me to Chicago when I was researching Sam Vine for this whole charity deal. Didn't find anything, as I already told you, though Vine—there's a guy who knows where bodies are buried." Sweetser rubbed his hands on his pant legs. "Wuger. I can't think of a reason for him to do in Harrington. Harrington fed him fresh cash. Wuger treated me like I was a terrorist mole. Like he'd protect me as long as I delivered, then kill me just for having seen him. Wasn't him tonight. Believe me, I have no desire to protect Wuger."

Erik was livid. "And Alicia Krause, do you have a desire to protect her? We've learned she visited Cushing's apartment the day before he was attacked and again recently. Do you know why?"

"No. What could she want from Cushing?"

"Mr. Sweetser, *answer* questions, don't ask them." Erik wanted to shake him. "You said you and Harrington's team were gathering background on Denisha circle donors and clients. You were seen helping Ms. Krause with her ATC computer several times. Had she discovered something? You research people, what do you know of her personal habits, where she shops, what doctor she sees"—

"Hold it," Deb interrupted. "Mr. Sweetser, your ATC dealings have 'cover-up' written all over them."

Sweetser pressed his hands into the table and stood, chair clattering back. "*You want cover-up? I'll give you cover-up!* Stephen Drexler doesn't have a past. Magically self-generated. That's *suspicious.* That's what I got. I came willingly,

I'm *done.*"

Erik worked his jaw and nodded that yes, they were done, and Sweetser stalked out the door. They had made no progress except to shift the weight of suspicion more heavily onto Wuger, Drexler, and Vine. Deb seethed, ready for a fight. He didn't know it would be with him.

"*Erik, what are you doing!*" She grabbed her hair. "Making a vulnerable woman more vulnerable! Putting all kinds of ideas in this man's head about Alicia Krause."

"First I'm too soft on Alicia and"—

"*Alicia*, first name basis? You'd have gotten more from this harmless dweeb if you'd hadn't looked ready to twist him like a pretzel."

"He was in my neighborhood. With the threat, with Ben"—

"What threat?"

"Don't look gob-smacked. You're supposed to read the G-Met alerts."

"I could barely get a signal to call about Haugen."

"Well, if a murderer drops by tonight, I'll make sure he leaves enough clues so you can solve my case like this." He snapped his fingers and stamped out.

Back in his apartment, a patrol outside, Erik knew he should apologize to Deb. He felt like a clawed animal was trapped in his head. When he collapsed on the bed and yanked up the covers, it scrabbled beneath his skull, down his neck to his spine, to settle in for a long pained stay.

CHAPTER 45

⚜

The G-Met parking lot, cracked blight and all, was kind of comforting on a Friday morning. Deb sat in her car half-dozing in the sunlight. She couldn't sleep last night, not with Haley's refrain circling her brain, *you waited until Dad was dead to find him!*

She stirred herself to check her phone. A message from Erik saying "sorry about my tone and please check reports."

Deb spent time digesting reports from Forensic Accounting (Naomi) and Cyber-Tech (Paul). Their teams were piecing together the tip sent by Anonymous (Erik's theory, Jonathan Lewis pretending to be Whinette), the notepad found in Harrington's apartment, and the dead man's ATC financials. It clarified that Harrington wanted to get Stephen Drexler one way or another: embezzling under Drexler's name, hacking into his passwords, and tracking down his past identities.

"HAB" in Harrington's notes seemed to be Harold Allen Burnham. Harrington discovered HAB's "secret stash" in January. New speculation: the stash was pictures of adolescent girls, and Harrington used that intel to force Burnham into hacking Drexler.

Information obtained through warrants: the financials for Alicia Corazella Krause showed she had debt the American way, over $100,000 owed to credit card companies. A settlement report indicated that Alicia blamed the debt on a former boyfriend and she'd worked out a payment system. All seemed in order until Alicia quit ATC. She immediately withdrew a thousand dollars. Then three days after Niland Harrington's corpse had been identified, $15,000 ballooned in her account. A small amount for blackmail, but the source was disturbing—virtually untraceable offshore accounts. This transaction was followed by cash deposits in the thousands, which were shuffled to a new account at a different bank under the name Alicia Corazella. There were a few debit purchases, including one this week at a local pharmacy for contraception.

Deb did some deep breathing before leaving the womb of her hybrid.

He had a gift for surprise. Deb entered the office to find Erik humming at his desk and flipping over and over a long triangular piece fashioned like an executive's name plate. His white shirt looked crisp, though the sleeves were pushed up. The name plate threw her—"Passive" etched on one side, "Aggressive" on another. Erik flipped it again, and Deb could see that someone had hand-written on the base, "Hazardous."

"So Partner, all safe on the home front? And what's *that*? Your Academy graduation plaque?"

"No commotion anywhere, Ben's fine, thanks. This?" He flipped the plaque to "passive. "It's bestowed weekly on a worthy recipient. You want it?"

"When I earn it. Wait, maybe that's already happened."

"I have questions." Erik contemplated their clouded window. "When you're dealing with abused women, or women under threat, do they frustrate you? Do you tell them what to do?"

"Yeah, sure. Sometimes the intervention by officials, therapists, and doctors needs to be extensive. The scariest thing is when a woman leaves and then returns to a jerk who kills her. The point is to get these women in control of their own lives. You know that. They're not perfect. *I'm* not perfect. Who is?"

"Women aren't crying on my shoulder because I'm perfect?—Wait, incoming email from Melanie Genereux, Drexler's ATC counterpart in Chicago. She says Drexler is failing to communicate with the Mother Ship." Erik yanked his desk drawer open, peeked in, pushed it back. He slung his suit coat over the cry-on-able shoulder, said, "I'm thirsty," and disappeared down the hallway.

Deb wasn't thirsty but her stomach gnawed on itself. She had no appetite last night, after the Haugen misery—*You waited until Dad was dead to find him.* Erik's desk—the drawer hadn't closed completely. She went over, did a test pull, saw color, another tiny pull. The drawer jammed. She jerked and— phlumph—the drawer let go and bounced in her lap as she fell back in Erik's chair.

Candy bars lay here and there, but the colorful thing was a photo of Erik, happy like you wouldn't believe, with a bright-faced woman.

"*What are you doing?*" Paul stood in the door.

"I wanted a granola bar, that's all. Please don't tell him, don't tell him."

"I came back for that." Paul pointed to "Aggressive/Passive/Hazardous. "I put it in here when, umm, when an FBI agent was coming to my office."

"They have their own. It says Fully Bonded Idiots. What happened with Erik and her? I mean, he's not happy"—she replaced the photo in the drawer but couldn't get the drawer into its slot.

Paul eyed her like she was armed and dangerous and retrieved the plaque. "It was sudden. Rumor is, she took up with someone, Erik—you couldn't talk to him, and Ibeling was overheard lecturing him."

"Who started the rumor?"

"I guess I did. I heard Ibeling arguing that they—Erik and she—were too much alike, quick, stubborn, extreme expectations. Practically the next day the divorce was over and done."

"*AGAIN?*" Erik startled them and loomed over the desk in two steps. "It sticks." He slammed the drawer shut.

"I'm so sorry. It won't happen again. It's my fault," Deb backed around to her side of things. "I was starved, hungry."

He threw three Kit-Kat bars which slid across her desk onto the floor. "I'm the one who gets to be hungry here"—a smile flickered and died. "I run. I have a father who fish fear and women worship. I have a mother who believes in dedication, accountability, and the BBC. I have a son who is under a death threat. I'm divorced. Is that enough?" He seized the plaque from Paul and slapped it on Deb's desk, "Aggressive" displayed. He grabbed the door in leaving but didn't slam it.

Deb was trembling. Being famished made it worse. She unwrapped the chocolate and bit. Paul slipped away. Hell, her eyes were watering. She wanted nothing like this. She threw away the uneaten part of the bar and fled to the women's room.

She slapped herself with cold water, studied her nose in the mirror. She used to measure it daily before she grew into it. It didn't look stuck on. It wasn't a nose that inclined to one side so she always appeared to head stage left. It didn't appear borrowed from her aunt or brother or Gerard Depardieu.

In middle school they called her Horse, and she owned it. She had the long legs, she had the hair, long and naturally blond then. Palomino, Greg the basketball center called her. But a different guy started in with Horse Chompers, Rubber Lips, and Nag Nose. She called him Splot. Then in the cafeteria line, Greg and Carly, brilliant Carly, destined for TV anchor-hood, talked to her. Until Splot shoved Deb, Deb spilt milk on Carly, no crying over that, and Splot hooted Nag Nose, and she pushed his nose stage right. That was the first time she went to the principal's office.

Erik—she dreaded what they'd become. Him, quick to feel betrayed, her quick to feel slighted. They accidently set traps for each other. Or was it the case, Deb considered—women seeking Erik's attention, threats distracting him and undermining the investigation, her being run off the road. Someone might be baiting them, waiting for the next victim to fall into a trap.

CHAPTER 46

❧

All things dry in time. Paul forced a reconciliation by telling Deb that the kitty-litter thumb drive was ready to try. She waited in his cyber-suite, head in hands, as Paul pulled in Erik, who had been running laps around the building. *Do your job*, she chanted to herself, *do your job*. She was on one side of the computer, Erik, steaming from running, on the other. Paul played Switzerland in the middle.

Paul lifted his eyes upward, brought the drive yoga-style to his heart, and slipped it into the USB port.

"Cushing downloaded in a hurry, no official author or document titles," was all he had for a few minutes.

Erik scowled at the monitor. "Sandy Sweetser compiled a report on domestic abuse cases that paralleled snippets on websites about resources for women. The fleshed-out report, names altered, was supposed to inspire donors. Look, this one claims to profile the most vulnerable"—

"Chronic abusers sense the most vulnerable, the girls who don't have a support system, who are too broken to resist." Deb interrupted.

Erik checked his notes. "Sweetser's draft Denisha reports went missing after he sent them to Harrington. We did not receive any files of that type through the ATC warrants. What about that numbered file?"

Paul did computer stuff. "It lists links to encrypted cloud files, but looking at the document info it seems that before Cushing was attacked, he broke the encryption, lucky for us."

Paul began opening the files—Deb was buzzed from holding her breath. Again, background reports on Allston group clients, this time in the Chicago area. The biggest file did not name the subject of the report, but it read like an undercover investigation of a heavy-weight mover and shaker. Highlighted in another were the names of clients' daughters. Another document provided links to news articles on missing children in Illinois, Wisconsin, and Minnesota.

"These files don't look like Sweetser's work," from Erik.

Paul clicked away, muttering that several files were corrupted.

The thirteenth file opened with a photo series: three adolescent girls talking in a park, an image of the same girls walking to or from school, judging by the backpacks, and then a single girl, a girl resembling Haley Haugen.

Only she looked more like the girl curled and still in another photo. The photo found in Harrington's shoe. The photo had a number on the back, and it corresponded with the file.

"No shi-it," Deb whistled between her teeth.

Paul was motionless. Erik broke their trance: "Find embedded timestamps. See if the images pair with the victim stories. See if the promotional stories pair with crime stories. See if a crime *follows* a promotional story."

"So you think," Paul started.

Deb shut her eyes. "Allston Groups provided a means to find victims."

CHAPTER 47

❧

Erik felt like he was swimming through the air as he exited G-Met for a late lunch. Adding to the unreality was the sight of a vintage Porsche in a bold magenta hue next to his Highlander. A woman leaned against it, box-shaped, to go with the Boxster she drove. She dressed like a Secretary of State. For face, a comparison to Winston Churchill was not unthinkable.

She beckoned him with her business card. "I scratched this Boxster, my brother's, last time I visited. Rather, a goat-eyed Louie gouged it in a parking lot. My brother wanted me to have the Boxster repainted, I did, this nice custom color. Not like he did a thing last year when he crunched my Porsche Cayenne. Sibling rivalry aside, I'm Gail Ellenbecker, Sam Vine's attorney. I know you're Detective Erik Jansson. That was an intriguing email you sent me. Most investigators would prefer sticking their arm down an alligator's throat to reaching out to Mr. Vine. Call me Gail, and I'll take you for a ride."

He took the passenger seat and involuntarily caressed the wood trimmings. She started the ignition. "I know. It smells more like a Bentley. You must have a gift, Detective, for knowing a highway where the patrols are scarce and little Boxster can open up."

"Everything's patrolled," he said before suggesting a route. They remained silent as Gail adeptly wove through traffic. Once on South 52, she sped out of his jurisdiction.

She began. "I won't ask how you got my name and contact information."

"I called Vine's office."

"Ah, the direct method. And you left your number in the traditional way, though I did additional research, Detective. You're featured most unpleasantly in a variety of websites. I'll assume skewed information out of context. You should hire ATC's Stephen Drexler to shore up your reputation, if you don't incarcerate him. Not my official business to know that, which is why you didn't hear me say anything. You want to know if my client, Mr. Vine, has sensed any intrusions into his private information. By the way, I only recently joined the phalanx of lawyers at his service. No one lawyer has access, for lack of a more guarded phrase, to all his secrets. I happened to oppose his interest in the courtroom once. After that, he decided I was a diamond in the rough. I said I stay rough." She pressed down the gas, jolting Erik. "What could a nice Iowa boy like you possibly want from me?"

"The body of Allston Teague Carlson employee Niland Harrington, formerly of Chicago, was discovered decomposing in a wetland," he answered. "Harrington and his group had been continuing work on a Chicago-based project, the Denisha Circle." Erik stopped himself from checking her speedometer. "About fifteen years ago Vine was in St. Paul with construction and trucking interests, and on the verge of investigations, he shut down those interests. It seems Vine moved to Chicago to become an honest man."

Gail stared at him. "Don't we all." She sped past refineries surrounded by military-level security. She accelerated again as the scenery changed to farmland and Erik grabbed his knees. She smiled. "It feels much more comfortable when you're the one in control."

"It's planting season. They find bodies then."

She laughed and zipped off at the next exit. She braked next to stripped acres of corn. "Tell me your timeline."

He did, dropping the Alicia and Cushing subplots, and described the photo found in Harrington's shoe.

"We're off record here, Detective." Gail watched a hawk swoop from a power-line to grasp a fuzzy blur rustling in the stalks. "I'll attend to Mr. Vine in Chicago—you don't want to crowd him. He referred to me two pro bono clients, domestic violence cases from the Denisha Circle. One client last summer, a mess of bad choices, complained that she and her twelve-year old daughter were being watched and followed. We filed a restraining order against the ex-boyfriend. She also sobered up, which made a few lurking shadows disappear, but the daughter remained spooked by "a mystery man" until January, when Allston moved a group of people here." She restarted the Boxster's purr.

They drove back to the Cities a mere fifteen mph over limit. Gail chatted about her niece in Medina, who would receive a service award the next day. Her talk drifted to her college-age sons. "After reading an article in the *Wall Street Journal* about the expense of child-raising, we refer to them as Cost Centers A and B."

"You've managed a family and demanding career?" Ouch, girly question.

"Worst thing to ask a woman. Default assumption—because of her, people suffer."

"Worst question to ask a man, how does he keep from being a jerk. You can drive over the median and there's a detour. Anyone asks I'll show my credentials."

"You didn't say your credentials would prevent ticketing. For me, the second time around was better. He fathered the Cost Centers and he's stuck with me. He took reduced time, I took reduced time, when the boys were small. Yeah, I loved being with them and hated hated hated time away from the office. Lawyers," she faced Erik, "fight each other and later go for drinks together. You never know which side you'll be on in the morning."

"My high profile client Vine," she continued, "wants low-profile in the courts. Let's shift attention to his 'friend' Ted Allston. He's a moldy old cheese, tendrils everywhere. Compulsively loyal to his people when they're loyal to him. My client Vine found the Denisha cause extremely compelling, or found Allston's frizz-haired lieutenant, Melanie something, extremely compelling, and Vine's not often compelled by anything but his own wants. The Denisha Circle was presented as a pilot project that would be controlled and monitored so his vast sums would not be wasted."

"Controlled and monitored."

"Are you going to parrot everything? No, I see you can be an eloquent non-talker." And Erik did not speak the rest of the ride back into congestion.

Gail Ellenbacker declared she was more than ready for one of her brother's watery cocktails when they pulled into the parking lot and she deposited Erik by his Highlander.

"One more question"—Erik put his hand on her open car window. "You went to University of Chicago Law School. Do you have contacts there? I'm curious about a, uh, an alleged graduate."

She handed him a different card than before. "Maybe." She hit the accelerator, leaving Erik to cough on exhaust and wonder how much gangster still lived in Sam Vine.

CHAPTER 48

꩜

Andrew Cushing had risen from the dead. The skull fracture, the pneumonia, and what had looked like MRSA but was an ordinary bedsore, had made for a dire prognosis.

He'd regained occasional consciousness, and the east-coast nephews had come and gone, leaving the son Rich in attendance. Erik decided his next-to-last task on this endless Friday should be a visit. The hospital resisted allowing an interview, but Rich had a helpful change of heart if certain conditions of timing were followed. After all, Erik had saved his father's cat. The staff put Erik through a pre-surgical scrub procedure and outfitted him from paper hat to booties. The final touch was a plastic-feeling over-layer. The doctor, an acerbic woman, briefed Erik outside the room. Rich had disappeared like the Scarlet Pimpernel.

"Mr. Cushing is healing wonderfully, but being fully cognizant is another matter. Your expectations should be minimal, Detective. He might never remember the trauma." With that she escorted him into the room, pointed out the emergency button, and departed as if she had far better things to do, which she did.

The saran wrap Erik wore made him feverish and faint, and he immediately sat in a chair and put his head between his knees. A skeleton, brittle-thin and gray, lay in the bed. Tubes in the nose, an IV inserted in the blackened hand, tubes under the sheet, a catheter somewhere. The eyes fluttered. Erik had faced gunfire, hand-to-hand combat, the press, an IRS agent. Time to woman-up and face sickness.

"Mr. Cushing, it's wonderful," he repeated the doctor's word, "to see you recovering. If there's anything we can do." What could he do? Find the attacker.

"I'm Detective Jansson. My partner Detective Deb Metzger and I interviewed you in your apartment."

"In book?" Cushing asked faintly.

"Could you say that again, please?"

"Detective in book?"

"No, ah, I'm a real detective. You were attacked. Can you tell me anything?"

"Wanted poster," Cushing murmured. "Head." His mouth froze open though the monitors showed no change. The man was exhausted in seconds.

"If you want to talk later." Erik was unsure if Cushing wanted a poster or had seen his attacker on a Wanted Poster. He stood just as Cushing's son entered the room dressed like a giant antiseptic Smurf and lugging a duffle bag.

"Did he say anything?" Rich Cushing whispered, nervous.

"He mentioned a poster, that's it."

"Please," Rich implored. "Watch the door, and, uh, everything's triple-washed in disinfectant."

Erik scanned the hallway, no one coming, and turned back toward the Cushings.

On the bed was the giant cat wrapped in blue hospital pads. The broad head was uncovered, and the son gently took his father's hand and helped him stroke Pisser Milton.

It was an area of rebirth after tragedy. From the hospital, Erik drove over the new I-35W bridge. He'd been out of the state when the previous bridge cracked apart, and like everyone else he had stared in numbed disbelief at the TV image of buckled lanes, dashed cars, and sheer collapse.

He drove past the Guthrie Theater (and winced at the thought of Winky Mom who wanted to attend a play together the following weekend.) According to the ATC office, Stephen Drexler was working from home, "home" being the North Loop neighborhood. Drexler had rented rather than bought, and he could have afforded more. Erik cruised past the building, reminding himself that he knew how to stay safe. Drexler likely loved culture, strolling along the river, shopping at Askov Finlayson, and eating at the Bachelor Farmer. Drexler was no farmer, but a bachelor. His ex-wife, when Erik called her, had been astoundingly uncurious about Drexler's past. The more they talked, the more she inclined toward would he have to surrender possessions, would there be a windfall in all this for her?

More restaurants. This raised the question: the night Melanie said Drexler wanted to meet her at a restaurant but never arrived, why had Drexler made reservations at a place that required him to drive?

Drexler had a BMW and had acquired a Minnesota driver's license within a week of arriving in the state. The man's ATC financials indicated short business trips to Chicago and New York. Within the year he'd also traveled to Scotland, Paris, Arizona, and Nevada. Drexler had means. His earnings were siphoned off into retirement vehicles, an offshore account, and an opaque trust fund. Curiously, he donated not to the Denisha Circle but to a different organization, as "anonymous," for victims of domestic violence.

The police radio bleeped, and Erik zipped the car into the loading zone of a building. If this was the call he expected, he would need back-up before approaching Drexler. One name on the alias list was Peter Martindale, a lawyer and a vanished suspect in a Pennsylvania murder case from seven years back.

Erik stared at a dumpster as the Pennsylvania officer gave him the gist: "Young hotshot lawyer Martindale allegedly had an affair with his assistant. The assistant may have discovered the lawyer's participation in money-laundering schemes. There's an anonymous tip to us, but she disappears. She's found off a remote roadside, beaten to death. Martindale's never seen again."

"Can you transmit photos?" Erik asked. It was like being in a duck blind, fingers burning at the tips, waiting. Martindale's image came across on the car computer—a plausible resemblance, if the nose had been altered. "This Martindale is six-feet-one," he observed. Drexler was six-three.

"That's not right," the officer replied, and Erik tightened. "Vain guy, exaggerated filling out the DMV forms. Left-behind clothes suggest closer to five-ten."

A garbage truck bee-lined for the dumpster, about to pin Erik. "I have to go. Do you have voice files?"

"Sure do. I'll transmit all the stuff like that. Is this a live lead?"

As Erik backed out, the truck angled in and drove over a dead pigeon. "No."

And Drexler was not "at home."

CHAPTER 49

❧

Deb sipped black coffee, a lousy acid-attack substitute for Monday morning breakfast. Since finding Dwight Haugen, she'd either had no appetite or was starving. And how mortifying to fall out with Erik last week over a Kit-Kat bar, a treat so easily split for two. The phone rang, for him, and she took the message. She had beaten Erik to the office and was determined to, she wasn't sure, be less of herself? Be more of her good self when she figured out what that was? It was the first day of May, good time for a fresh start, and maybe it'd be a month of less rain and more clues.

Erik entered with a not-quite convincing smile. "Sorry I'm late, complicated arrangements with Ben. How was your weekend?"

A lot of words for him. "Not bad. I went golfing with old friends. I have old friends, it's new ones I have trouble finding. The problem with golf, I kept thinking about Harrington and ruining my par. You?"

"Canoeing with Ben, my father, and my ex-father-in-law."

"Wasn't that awkward?" This was a family dynamic Deb hadn't expected.

"Apparently only for me. They indulged Ben, let him splash water into the canoe and collect worms for 'bait' in their travel mugs.'"

"Of course they did. Speaking of places with bait, surveillance video from that lakeside store, 'Neck's Place,' showed Wuger in a black truck about the time the Haugens were in the area." Deb sloshed coffee on her notepad. "Oh, A woman just called you"—

"Virtue's model, the paragon of animals"—

"A piece of work all right. She said that she can't get together with you this weekend." She dabbed at the spill with a kleenex. "It's okay, you can look relieved."

He looked relieved.

"Her husband's in town then."

"What?"

"I made that part up." Deb waited until relief had re-established itself in his face. "No I didn't. There is a husband. She said it's complicated."

"Then people do get back together?"

"*That's* your take-away?"

He ignored her as a mailroom Julia came to the door with a letter. He took it and said "thank you" firmly so she would leave. He studied the envelope then flipped it to her—"for you."

Deb was taken aback by the familiar name, CeeCee's in the upper corner. She moaned, "how 'bout *not* getting back together." Erik must have heard, so she said, "An old flame that won't die out."

He peered out the door and said, "Mail is reading pleasure for many. What's a little federal offense among friends?"

Her letter didn't look steamed. She shook it and a thin express letter unstuck itself from hers and fell to the desk: addressed to Erik, a P.O Box return address in Missouri, and a Chicago postage cancellation. She held it to out him.

"Cable bill." Calm voice, chili-red cheekbones.

He needed space, Deb got the message, and she needed sustenance to offset the coffee sloshing in her stomach. "Getting food," she said and left her silent partner to his private correspondence.

ERIK OPENED THE ENVELOPE, A single sheet of paper. On top three phone numbers. A computer check showed they were in the University of Chicago exchange. Below those, the sheet read, "Check these links to Chicago area news articles, hadn't made connections before," and then a closing with the name Portia. He knew that name. His mother had insisted in her indirect way of insisting that he take Shakespeare in college as his father muttered from behind a newspaper, "Sure you want him exposed to all that sex and violence?" Portia was the brilliant lawyer who defended the bigoted and entitled. Also a make of German car. If only all clues could be this easy.

He entered the details into his computer.

A story from last fall was about women, former victims of abuse, who suspected that they, not the alleged abusers, were under police surveillance. The police denied that, but there was evidence of phones being hacked.

A story from a previous year reported on an adolescent girl who had been moved from a violent situation to foster care. Then she disappeared without a trace. The case recalled one on the kitty-litter thumb drive.

Erik's teeth were on edge as he began the final set of stories, dated this past

October before the ATC people arrived in the Twin Cities. Elise McAuliffe, the twelve-year old daughter of a wealthy Chicago couple, had disappeared, and the first story published photographs of the girl. Days later, her body was found in a ditch between a park near her school and a major highway. Culvert work had disturbed the corpse, and the police were extremely hopeful that they had evidence to trace an apparent serial killer. For years, a killer had drugged girls into unconsciousness and cardiac arrest in the tri-state area of Illinois, Indiana, and Michigan. This was the first time the body had been found before external DNA evidence had disintegrated; there were fibers and hand marks. That optimism deflated when police were unable to track down a suspect. The parents released a statement, thanking the many who had given their all to find Elise. They added a plea: "This brings violence against women and children home to us, into our broken hearts. Help us end that violence." The reporter noted that the McAuliffes were major donors to a Ted Allston charity, the Denisha Circle.

Erik stood, paced, stared out the window, circled his desk, sat, shook out his arms, and copied the media links into a file to share with Paul and Deb. He shredded the letter from "Portia."

He reread the last story and checked it against other websites.

The girl in Harrington's shoe was Elise McAuliffe.

CHAPTER 50

There's no one you can trust all time—except the dog that won't steal your lunch. There's some you trust can none of the time—Stephen Drexler high on that list. There are some that circumstances demand you trust—your partner in investigation. There are those where you must redefine the trust—his ex-wife as devoted parent to Ben. Then there are those you can trust nearly all the time—Erik's mother. She'd sent him a package of white shirts. He didn't dwell on the origin of that behavior but, while Deb was out-of-office on Haugen matters, changed into one. He had to convince Settina at ATC he was trustworthy by being devious.

Failing to reach her by phone, he connected with Jonathan Lewis who believed Settina was going that evening to a bistro, *Le Chat Francaise*. Lewis elaborated that he knew this because he made the recommendation. Lewis fell on the trust continuum around "some of the time."

Erik talked the parking valet out of the restaurant's fee but tipped him. He left his suit jacket in the car and entered the bistro through the service entrance, flashing his ID. He tucked the ID in his pants' pocket and his tie between the third and fourth buttonholes of the new shirt. Through the kitchen door's oval window, he saw Settina in profile at a table. She appeared delicately young in a wispy frock, like Joan of Arc before her judges. She brought protection, a young man with Asian features whose open countenance and attire said total Minnesotan: Gophers sweatshirt, Twins baseball hat, jeans, and gray cross-training shoes with bright orange laces. His hands on hers, they slipped into their own ardent dimension.

Erik intercepted a server and took his drinks tray, swerved around tables, and stopped by theirs.

"Settina, quick, the oddest thing about Drexler." Erik set the wine glasses down.

"The degree thing, the number—wait, what are you doing here?" Settina pulled her hands away from her escort's and put them to her face.

"Detective Erik Jansson." He offered the boyfriend a hand to shake and pulled up a chair to join them.

"Um, sure, I'm Daniel and I'm trying to keep up," Daniel replied. "Not that I'm dumb, I'm in a Ph.D. program at the U, biomass"—

"Even here you can't trust police." Settina's voice nearly froze the wine. "And anything you tell me, Detective, I'll tell Daniel. He stays."

"Can't you take our order?" the man at the next table interrupted and tilted back toward Erik. "You do take orders?"

"All the time, sir." He held up his ID. "What kind of court order would you like?"

The couple sulked back. The ambient noise increased to thwart their eavesdropping.

Erik continued: "We suspect Drexler, and Andrew Cushing's predecessor, Harold Burnham, had something to fear from Harrington—blackmail, extortion. Alicia Krause may have been coerced into the scheme. Have you heard from her, Settina?"

She sipped the wine and grimaced, apparently not what she'd ordered. "I know she was frightened, and not because of that ex-boyfriend who used to stalk her. That's it. You can leave now." She wouldn't face him.

"There's a report circulating about a sex-trafficking ring involving corrupt police. I have reason to believe Ms. Krause saw it. That report is fraudulent. It borrows details from the 'Minnesota Nice Guys' case several years back and the plot from a Swedish crime novel made famous by a BBC actor."

She gasped, and Daniel said, "Cool, I mean not cool," then signaled a bonafide server to bring more wine and another water because, Erik realized, he had drunk Daniel's.

Settina still wouldn't look at him but spoke so low Erik had to lean close. "I tried to know as little as possible of Harrington. Burnham I barely knew, but Harrington began trailing him constantly, and this poor man, maybe not so poor, wanted to be left alone. Burnham—everybody in the office thought he had OCD, obsessive-compulsive disorder, which was worsening, maybe schizophrenia. Everyone—Whinette I mean—said he left for medical reasons."

"Settina, please explain what you meant about Drexler's degree, the number."

"It's silly, nothing." Settina spoke lightly but reached for Daniel's hand.

"Remember there was a photo of an adolescent girl found in Harrington's shoe. My partner said you were out of the office when she came by with it. The girl was maybe unconscious, more likely dead."

"Ohhh." Settina's pupils became depthless. Daniel would have slugged Erik except Settina had his hand.

"Take a moment. Someone at ATC has put women and children in danger. Drexler is not the one who needs protection."

Settina steadied herself. "Drexler. He, he could draw a moth to a flame"— she squeezed Daniel's hand—"if you let him. He and Alicia had an affair right after the transfer, but in February it fell apart. Everyone believes Drexler's a womanizer. He has this enormous photo in his office, a glamorous woman, like in that Hitchcock film"—her eyes beseeched Daniel.

"*Rear Window*, Grace Kelly," he filled in.

"People went wild that it was a sign, Drexler's a pervert fixated on a fantasy. I joked it was ancestor worship. Even stranger, everyone said he went to University of Michigan law school. In one of his enchanting moments, he told me Chicago, then had me swear not to tell anyone. And he switched computers the first of March."

Generous baskets of salty hot *les frites* appeared. Settina put her hands in her lap and Daniel ate as he spoke, "easy as pie to hack a co-worker. Drexler could request a file, and it would come with embedded spy-ware. Harrington or your other guy"—

"Burnham," Erik said. "That number, you mentioned Settina."

Settina hesitated. "A phone number, not Alicia's. If it ever showed up on caller ID, I was not to answer but tell Drexler asap."

She'd been holding this back. Erik scribbled his anger out on a napkin. The napkin was cloth. "If you or Alicia are in danger, here's contact information for my partner—wait, besides this napkin I have her card, Detective Deb Metzger. Believe me, she has no truck with bad behavior toward women."

Daniel fidgeted and took the napkin, desperate to move in a way that protected Settina. She barely murmured. "The phone number I mentioned—I, umm, forgot the instructions and picked up once. An older woman said 'Stephen?' and when I started to speak she hung up." She glanced at Erik's pen, he gave it to her, she wrote on the back of Deb's card, and returned it.

He drew in a deep breath. "Anything else?"

"Uh, yeah"—Daniel acted quickly on his worry and eagerness. "First, the bistro manager's heading over to fire you. Second, where'd you get that great shirt?"

CHAPTER 51

❧

When Drexler did not return to his apartment that evening, Erik put out a call on the man's BMW, parked his fleet vehicle in the dead pigeon alley, and directed his jumpiness into ongoing computer searches of the man's identities. Going backward from Drexler on the alias list, G-Met research recovered additional names. One Steven Liddell in Pennsylvania had a juvenile record, sealed. Erik studied newspaper archives for hints—a domestic and a beating. Jackie Rosen had matriculated at the University of Michigan but never graduated. Michael Stanwood graduated from University of Michigan without apparently having matriculated. Peter Martindale had distinguished himself at University of Chicago Law School. A few Joseph Reeds had bad credit; one was on the no-fly list; and one in Ohio (not Iowa) received numerous awards for anti-poverty initiatives.

He switched to articles on Melanie Genereux. One gushed over Allston Foundation's championing of the abused: it called Melanie a "petite powerhouse," a cringe-worthy label. A much sharper article in an airline magazine published over two years ago praised Genereux's possession of the cause; she raised significant funds in a flash; she had an unflinching straight-ahead vision.

The author, Sandy Sweetser. The article must have impressed Melanie or her Allston Group associates because, according to Erik's notes, after that date Sweetser was hired as a contract researcher. Sweetser, though he knew all about Melanie and her causes, had claimed that she wouldn't know him. Possible, since Human Resources and Harrington would have handled the details. Sweetser might also consider himself forgettable or—by playing forgettable hoped he'd be forgotten by people like Vine and Wuger. Erik felt uneasy, and hungry.

He was chewing a protein bar he'd found under the car seat when the patrol cops called. Drexler's BMW had entered the ATC parking garage. He was about to try Drexler's office phone when he remembered the number he'd learned from Settina. He traced it: an Arizona area code, an account billed to "Joseph Reed." The account had a second mobile number. Erik called and asked for Joseph Reed.

THE OFFICE TOWERS WENT DEAD at night. A security guard on the lobby level scrutinized Erik as if he were up to no good. The elevator made a muffled whoosh, and when Erik stepped out on ATC's dimly lit seventh floor he imagined more than heard the death drone of the last vacuum cleaner. People knew he was here (their voicemails anyway); people (their voicemails) knew Drexler was here, nothing to be concerned about, unknot the stomach.

Drexler appeared. It was his voice that answered the Reed call. He had offered no explanation but agreed it would be prudent to meet with Erik. No point in dragging Drexler to the station without charges—in an official setting, he would use his law training to talk his way out of any corner.

Drexler/Reed wordlessly unlocked the door to his ATC suite and Erik followed. Drexler entered his private office and flipped on a desk lamp which cast noir-ish shadows on the walls. Erik sat on the other side of the desk and faced a large portrait that hung over the man's head. The blonde woman looked as if she had departed the ingénue years for the disappointment of marriage. She poised on the cliff edge of her chair, long pedicured hands one over the other on the curved angle of her knee.

Drexler unlocked a desk drawer. "I have no bourbon to pull out," he said sourly. No gun either, Erik prayed. Drexler placed a folder, old-fashioned paper, on his desk. He put his hand to his computer and stopped. Every touch was logged. Paper, burnable, shreddable, dissolvable, digestible, had advantages.

"Do you mind turning on more lights?" Erik asked.

Drexler adjusted the blinds to prevent a leak of light. He flipped a switch under his desk and spot lighting sizzled over the woman's image. The long slash of Drexler's mouth compressed as he silently read through the folder. Erik stared at the unnatural blonde in the photograph and then presented a photograph of his own.

"Mr. Drexler, this image of a girl was found with Harrington's corpse. I've said that before. If you know anything, say it. Now."

Drexler placed his thumb and second finger on the outside edges of the photo and drew it closer. He focused on it for a long minute. He took his hand from the photo and pushed back in his chair. The woman coolly smiled over his head.

"There's nothing, nothing to indicate Harrington had any interest in girls, little girls. He was distasteful, but not in that way." Drexler transferred his repugnance to Erik. "Harrington channeled his minor energies into golf, his major energies into manipulating the hierarchy. Sidling up to women, to men, for information. The powerless"—he tapped the photo's edge—"were invisible to him. Ancillaries to power he would leverage. This, this 'child,' nothing I know of Niland Harrington leads to this." If doubt crossed Drexler's face for a second, he conquered it. "Harrington wanted to be more than he was. No, he wanted to be *what* he was but with more. He couldn't see that to lead he had to be more than a smirking, conniving, memory-perfect snitch. Iago causes things to happen. It's still Othello's play. Harrington wasn't even an Iago."

Erik remained quiet. He knew what Drexler meant but hoped his appearing not as smart would make Drexler talk more. He was about to find out if that strategy would work.

"If that's too highbrow," Drexler filled the gap, "he wasn't Jason Bourne. He's the suit killed in the first movie and forgotten."

"There's a woman in the play, in the movie. The woman dies," Erik said.

"Woman, man, a person had to have *value* to attract Harrington."

"Harrington might not want the girl for himself. Maybe she was leverage. Maybe he was setting you up to be strangled."

"No, no, no. I won't be a victim. No. No," Drexler answered.

Erik felt like the Wolf in Red Riding Hood, talking smooth when he wanted to snap his jaws tight. Only it was another wolf across from him. "First, the accounts we're examining, Harrington took out excessive cash, signed your name, made you responsible."

"Do not think there aren't other investigations." Drexler's eyes gleamed yellow in the dim light. "That questionable behavior started back in Chicago. He may have learned that in the past I recommended Melanie, rather than him, for head of Allston's philanthropy branch, and he was not happy about the transfer here. When the cash withdrawals started here in Minneapolis, I suspected Harrington was forging authorizations under my name. However, I was, shall we say, preoccupied. The FBI has a deep interest in Ted Allston. I had been working closely with Allston and found it unsavory, so I requested this transfer. Not long after, the FBI contacted me about what I might have observed. They are remaining discreetly in touch, shall we say."

"Harrington's group investigated donors linked with a Chicago support group for women, particularly Sam Vine. Harrington could have stumbled across compromising information," Erik said.

Drexler licked his lips, which for a wolf signaled not appetite but anxiety. "Possible. Sam Vine was being pursued by Melanie Genereux. Harrington answered to her, not me, on that project. What Melanie wants, she always, almost always, gets."

"Can you think of anything she didn't get?"

No answer.

Erik studied the woman in the photograph, took a tight inhale, and spoke, "Your mother was, is, striking."

The wolf vanished into a smile. "She worked as a model in Chicago, lingerie, when other models starved themselves into stick figures. Later she had a position in an art gallery."

"Your father?"

"Not worth mentioning." The smile died.

"Oh, I think he's worth mentioning, Mr. Drexler," Erik said. "If he's the reason you kept changing identities. At times legally, at times not. It's not easy to have more than one social security number. Maybe you learned tricks from your father, Martin Day Liddell, a financial con-artist. He's being released from prison in a few weeks. You heard about his release the first of February, and you stopped paying attention to ATC"—

Drexler stood. "I'm not to be cornered. Mr. Liddell, no doubt, expanded his circle of avaricious Fortune 500 types in that federally funded hotel. He probably can't wait to use those contacts on the outside. Mr. Liddell—never call him my father, I should have done more than break his smug jaw those years ago."

"Your mother"—Erik stood so they snarled face to face.

"*Stays out of this.* You called the phone *she* calls, Detective. She doesn't like my 'hiding games,' as she calls them. All to keep Mr. Liddell from finding her. Despite the divorce, he would try, as he did successfully before, to seduce away her life's savings. She's become accustomed to the new names. She knows not to be found. I shudder to think you called *her.*"

"There's no reason for your mother to have anything to do with this."

"Is that a threat, Detective?" The men were close enough to strangle each other.

"No, it's a statement." Erik sat down firmly.

Drexler remained standing.

"And I assume your mother's phone number will soon be changed," Erik said.

Drexler's smile returned but it chilled. "Before you're even out of the building, Detective."

"Mr. Liddell tried to steal your previous identity."

"He'd consider that a compliment to me, the only sincere one he ever paid." Drexler sat and picked up a sheet of paper and tore it into strips. "When we were young, he would take me and my little sister to banks, office parties, meetings with prominent corporate friends. He would adore us in front of a 'mark,' show what a decent family man he was. We mistook his interest for something real. My mother loved us, but her vanity, his ability to win every argument, prevented her from protecting us. By the time I was a senior in high school, I'd became too stubborn for him, so he displayed my lovely sister. He wanted to take her to dinners with business associates to teach her 'finance.' He wasn't whoring her out, not yet, but he was addicted to the con. One night my sister locked herself in her room, and my mother finally put her foot down. That's when he hit Mother. I hit back harder."

Erik said nothing for several minutes, then—"You escaped him, you survived. Your sister?"

"Ran away from home the day she turned eighteen. Five years ago I was in the Atlanta airport, and I caught this woman staring at me. In terror that she might be found out, it might get back to *him*. Not that I would ever—but she wouldn't risk any contact. She moved into a crowd when she sensed me staring back, a child with her, a beautiful child. I like to think she has a good life somewhere, but I will never try to know. Let her have the power of choice. The only way that man can find me, her, my mother, is if someone like you"—

"Or Harrington. Or Alicia Krause. Maybe you talk in your sleep. Maybe they put you, your family, at risk."

Drexler rolled a pencil back and forth over a file. "I am not being blackmailed. Alicia is more enthusiastic than wise. After we ... before Harrington disappeared, she'd been distraught about a former boyfriend. I may have suggested an alternative. The value of disappearing so even the people that you fancy love you are without a clue."

"She's in danger. What does she know? What do *you* know?"

Drexler kept his silence.

Then in an unexpected move he pushed across the file. "An account of Harrington's ATC indiscretions, which were coming to an end weeks before he disappeared. He may have sensed my increased attention."

"Or he found another, 'better' way to—

"It's moot at this juncture, Detective. If there's anything I can do about that child in the photo, it will happen. But I can think of nothing."

If Drexler had stopped before that last statement, Erik would have trusted him more. Not that he really trusted him at all. Drexler turned the light out on his mother.

Out of the dark Erik heard, "Alicia trusted Jonathan Lewis."

CHAPTER 52

❦

Swollen Minnehaha Creek surged over the falls at ominous whitewater speed. With a drop of more than fifty feet, the falls were the dramatic center of the Minneapolis park and divided the terrain into the groomed street-level plateau and the gorge which fell further through the lower glen. Erik, outfitted in his warm-weather running clothes and a baseball hat, slowed from a jog to a walk. It was hot, an omen of July in May, and he couldn't run the waterside path, not with the protruding tree roots, depressions of muck, and slippery steel decking over swampy growth. Spring's heavy rains had not given way to flowers so much as transformed the creek into a frothy overflow.

Erik was ostensibly watching Haley Haugen, due to arrive soon. He had done this a few times before at Deb's offhand request that if he was running, he might as well run with teens, and he'd half-joked, why not, and it became a thing. This was not an official detail, like the one assigned to Kristine and Ben, but a gesture to help Haley feel safer. Deb had told Erik that morning that when she showed up at the park late yesterday afternoon, Haley wouldn't look at her—"she despises me because of her Dad." Dead Dwight Haugen, found by chance. If Niland Harrington had been dumped here in the buffer of plants down the gorge, he would still be rotting in the soil.

A wild rank odor and the creek's roaring crept inside Erik's head. The late afternoon air hung a gray steaming weight.

HALEY'S FRIENDS WERE YAKKING AS they showed up near the head of the falls. Track had turned into a bust, so she ran after school with random guys and girls. Everybody invited her to everything since her dad's death, then avoided her when she showed. They jogged in place to warm up, except the sticky air made you feel trapped in plastic. She'd gone back to classes yesterday, Monday, where she felt trapped in an envelope of skin, all empty air inside. An adult would call it grief, like that would help. Yesterday she ran hard and her legs surged ahead all muscle-tough just to show Detective Deb how strong she was—*but why didn't she find Dad before he was dead?*

Detective Deb's partner, Detective J., might be around. He'd spoken to her one time when she was off by herself. When she joined her girlfriends, they asked like who's the dream scene, and she came up with he was a college running coach giving her tips. Sydney wouldn't let it go, so Haley went on that years ago, in an ice storm, when nobody's phone worked, this man's wife and twin baby girls went off in the car to the doctor. And he was like *horrified* when he realized the ice was too bad and ran after them and slipped and couldn't get to them and they died in a crash, which was why he ran all the time now, it was too sad. The girls bought it. She was good at making up stories to fit their nosy minds.

The dumb guys leaned over the falls bridge and babbled louder than the creek.

"If I push you in," Dorkus bragged to Ian, the new quiet guy, "you'd end up so drowned by the time ya float all the way south to New Orleans, dead, dead, dead."

"Shhh—Haley's father!" Sydney hissed so *everyone* heard.

Haley knew what they all said, that Dad was drunk when he skidded off the bridge into high water. Like that hacker-stalker phone man, that guy Dad was after, didn't drive him off the road. Detective Deb had told her mother they were examining these chips from vehicle lights and Haley—the phone in her shorts hip pocket making her look deformed—could call Detective Deb right now to straighten them out, and she was dying to drop f-bombs full of shit all over the guys, except she had hardly any air. She took a gulp and bolted.

TIME TO RUN BACK UP to the falls. Erik ascended the stone stairway, fouled with graffiti, to the upper plateau. As he loped beneath the pergolas at the park's upper end, he saw Haley's group hanging around the falls bridge. One might be the traitor who continued to post Haley-items online—he doubted that she did it herself.

A high-school couple, a bean-pole boy and string-bean girl, played a game of Frisbee behind him. He'd never seen anyone resembling a stalker or Harold Burnham, yet a pattern he couldn't quite grasp nagged at him. It could be awareness of park regulars, like two retired women in matching pink trainers or the man with a fir-tree beard and a Rottweiler. That reclusive bird-watching woman in the frowsy coat was missing; she was practically unnoticeable except for her big hair like a wig.

Like a wig.

An inkling made him shudder, and his clinging Under Armour failed to wick dampness. Everything was about to change. Massing blue-black clouds depopulated the park as Haley's group did inadequate warm-ups around the statue of Hiawatha and his love. Erik tugged his sweaty baseball cap to the bridge of his nose and felt weirdly awkward. The point of running is life becoming peripheral to movement. Not head static that made mind and limb jerk out of sync under darkening gloom.

The static crackled and popped when he leaned against a pergola to stretch his quads. What box had he opened with Vine's lawyer? He checked his phone. A message from Deb—Wuger was playing a winning game of hard to catch. No word of Alicia Krause's whereabouts. Information obtained with the warrants indicated her prescription for an insulin analog was due for a refill. Erik's stomach knotted as Haley passed him. Maybe slippery Drexler had joined Alicia, maybe a new man altogether.

Then Haley bolted from her group, tripping down the steps by the falls, what was she thinking. Erik ran after but didn't see her—she must have run downstream into the glen. He rushed past a guy from Haley's group staring into roaring water and shouted, "watch out."

FUCKING FUCK THEM ALL, FUCKITY fuckity fuck. Haley practically fell down the steps, she didn't care, before she hit the wet path. She crunched down slippery rocks fast until it was her and the trees thick with blowing leaves and the twisting stream and a throbbing ankle and she couldn't see, her eyes so wet.

A man had her arm and she froze.

"It's not safe here, people have been seen." He dressed like a ranger, his voice was flat tin and his eyes vibrated. "Come with me, Haley." Her name, oh god, oh god—she hit the phone on her hip. It screamed, she screamed, he was forcing something sick into her mouth. She pushed and kicked and it was dizzy and black. Water in her nostrils, ears, no grip, then a grip so hard on her arm she breathed in water.

ERIK SKIDDED PAST TURNS AND foot bridges and saw the back of a park uniform, the wrong uniform. The man struggled, it had to be with Haley, he had a holster, and there were screams, an off-key doubling. Erik punched his phone's 911 button, shouted, the girl fell into the creek, and the man crashed into the dense brush. Erik lost his balance, knee scraping against a rock, and then stumbled forward as he saw the ranger appear way ahead on the path. Thunder cracked and echoed with a loud *brumm* and lightning snagged the tree tops. Haley's head rose and fell in water. He thrashed in and pulled her on the bank where she gasped, awareness coming and going from her eyes. That bean-pole boy ran up, Erik shouted over thunder, "Police, help her," and bolted up the fouled steps of the lower glen, heart trying to throb outside his chest, while the man closed in on a van in the parking lot. Erik caught the eye of the teen's girlfriend.

Thwack—the Frisbee hit the ranger's face and he crashed down. Erik jumped him. The man had panic's strength, and they wrestled as Erik reached again and again for the man's flailing hands, the two of them sucking for air and they were being doused, a downpour. Erik caught the wiry hands and straddled the man. Water running into his eyes, his mouth, he disarmed the holster of a jerry-rigged canister. The man tried to kick off Erik, but he was winded, and the girlfriend threw her string-bean weight across his legs. Rain pounded them, saturating everything. A cruiser and an ambulance spun into the parking lot, and the teen with water dripping from her nose retrieved the Frisbee and with a grin announced "Score."

CHAPTER 53

H aley's attacker was as talkative as granite. He had not even said the
word "lawyer." Erik entered the viewing room with the one-way mirror,
a place that felt fake with its TV-set image. He gingerly adjusted the jeans
he'd pulled over his bloody legs back at the park and pulled at the sleeves of
another of the white button-downs stored in his office for such contingencies.
He was dreaming of a hot shower when his partner arrived.

"Haley's not in shock anymore," Deb said. "Dazed, but real pleased about
her screaming phone siren. She'll stay in the hospital overnight. I'll check on
her again, give her a break from her mother's wailing, and then you could to
see if she has more to say." She surveyed the man through the mirror.

"Do you have anything for pain?" he asked.

"To cause or prevent? Does it matter if it's gender-specific?"

Erik didn't answer. She dug in her bag, pulled out two bottles and handed
him the one labeled "ibuprofen." He swallowed the pills dry and fiddled with
the bottle. "Thanks. This 'ranger' has a van registered to William Thomas.
Several William Thomas's are in the DMV system but none with the post
office box and apartment address listed on the registration. A uniform called
ten minutes ago to say that the apartment building exists, but there's no
apartment 607 B. The van contained wigs, women's clothing, chloroform in a
rigged-up dispenser, a Taser, an unloaded gun, shells, twist-tie restraints, and
duct tape."

"The kidnapper's kit," she confirmed.

"Do you recognize him?" Thomas was average height, brown eyes, and
a head shaved several weeks back with hair re-growing in motley colors
suggesting nightly experimentation with different dyes.

Deb rubbed a knotted neck muscle. "We thought William Thomas was a Drexler alias. Harrington was intending to frame Drexler, blackmailing Harold Burnham into helping him, so this must be"—Deb took the pain pills from Erik and popped a double dose.

"Let's get someone from ATC to confirm the ID," he said. They had Burnham at last, hacker of Denisha Files. And murderer of Niland Harrington.

Unless it was Wuger.

SCAB'S WASN'T THE WORST BAR in the Cities, Smalls told Erik in the 11 p.m. call, despite its train-yard location. Smalls had been pursuing an informant hiding from hip-hop enemies in Scab's, a country-western joint, where he saw a Wuger look-a-like going out the door. Smalls couldn't stay to question the Scab's clientele because he received another tip that his informant had entered the Mythic Club in the Warehouse District.

Erik was officially off duty, unofficially exhausted, and too keyed up to sleep. He'd returned to G-Met to fill out forms, but he couldn't make the filling happen. After Burnham had been taken to a cell, he'd gone home to shower, put his bloodied clothes in the laundry, and taken care of his injuries. Then he'd checked on Haley in the hospital: she'd been ghost white with hyper-bright eyes yet thrilled to talk about a book with an interstellar love triangle that sounded disconcerting familiar. He might as well drop by Scabs before calling it quits for the night.

The joint was not familiar. Often such establishments hired off-duty cops as outside security. Not here. Erik regretted wearing the fleece with the national park logo, but rallied his defenses and pushed through the heavy door. The nasal music would make anyone weep into their beer. He squeezed through a crowd—men with hanging guts, women with leathery cleavage—to be stopped dead by a terrifying vision. Wartface Wuger.

Wuger had returned. He wore a wrinkled suit and a striped shirt open at the hairy throat. He held a phone, and shot glasses staggered in a row on the bar that supported his mass. Wuger turned to stare—a pig eye had more expression—and hefted himself up, a hundred-fifty pounds on Erik. Best defense—run.

He didn't: "Detective Erik Jansson with Greater Metro. Are you Alvin Wuger?"

"Get called other names but can't repeat them in this fine company," Wuger slurred. "Did you miss the exit to Dinky Town? No college-student strippers here"—he upped his volume—"Or lookin' for that girlfriend, Alicia, the one you harass?" That caught the attention of the nearby drinkers. A man with ham arms pressed against Erik's left and flexed the muscles beneath his U.S. Marines *semper fidelis* tattoo. A woman, thick gray braid trailing down her biker vest, crowded his right. A mouth-breather angled up behind him. Wuger picked up a fresh whiskey and swayed. "Senorita, what was it, Krause, Corazella? Hiding so you can't hurt her. What's her condition, blood pressure, blood sugar, battered woman?" He knew what Erik knew. "Ya know, ya kinda remind me of Ted Bundy."

"You remind me of a pork sandwich three days old." Erik squared his shoulders, laced his hands behind his back —let it be the right move. Ham-arm squinted at him as the bartender reached under the bar. "We can discuss this at the G-Met station."

"What, the fucking transit station?" Wuger slammed his whiskey glass on the counter. "Got a warrant, Stalker boy?"

"If any of you can identify a young girl's stalker, caught in the act, check the news. We need to find where he lived." Erik released his hands as he scanned the crowd. A sodden crew to hear long sentences—"That stalker and Mr. Wuger here worked for a man found dead a few weeks back, Niland Harrington. On the dead man was a photo of a similar girl."

Wuger reached in his coat but Erik caught the thick wrist and jammed close so Wuger's other arm was pushed against the bar. The ogre's breath could drop a horse. The barflies tightened in, slugged drinks, and made bets while the sound system throbbed out a bass-line and a singer wailed up to a needling pitch.

Ham-Arm flexed his tattoo again and grabbed Erik's shoulder. He shouted in his ear, "Trained reflexes. You military, son?"

"Trained with Marines."

Ham-Arm let him go and the crowd edged back, thirsting for liquor and action. Gray Braid glared at Wuger. "I don't think Butt-Model here's the stalker, Squirrel-Dick."

"Was just getting my hankie," Wuger sneered, unsteady on his feet. There was no gun in his coat pocket. Erik released his hand, and Wuger grumbled, "I swear I'll be in tomorrow. What I could tell ya about that Herringfish." The next words landed like a sledge hammer—"Course, he couldn't boss Alicia. She plays a good victim and for a hot little thing knows enough 'bout computers to get us all in deep shit. You texting her pics of that limp asparagus you call a"—

The crowd leaned in again. Ham-Arm stood solid as he exhaled a flammable breath on Erik. "You went to Quantico?"

"And Sunday School."

Ham-Arm bellowed and Erik desperately needed a next move—

When a code came across his phone.

"Mythic Nightclub, an officer down," he said low to Ham-Arm, who blocked interference as Erik rushed out. Erik didn't believe Wuger would voluntarily come to the station, he couldn't bring him in alone, so back in his Highlander he called a patrol to pick up Wuger and left to see if the officer down was Smalls.

ERIK DIDN'T PULL INTO HIS sub-building parking garage until 2:00 a.m.

Wuger had anticipated Erik in the bar. Holding that phone.

He leaned on the steering wheel and closed his eyes. At the Mythic, Smalls was fine, another officer took a gunshot to the arm, and the meth-high shooter was captured. Back at Scabs, Wuger had pulled a gun from a drunk and dodged the patrol Erik had called.

The phone. Erik pulled a flashlight from the glove compartment, jumped from his Highlander, and crawled under it. He bumped his head on rough concrete. He saw a device on the muffler and bumped his head again. He'd been tracked. Screw him.

He hauled himself out from under and rubbed his face with blackened hands. Who could get to his Highlander? He parked on public streets, by Ben's school—

Alicia had been to his apartment, distracting him. What if she and Wuger were accomplices, by choice or force, what if someone smart, like Drexler, coordinated it all?

What ifs could devour him—he should go to bed. If only sleep would come.

CHAPTER 54

❧

Fourteen hours after his capture, Burnham had not broken yet, but being the smarty-type psychopath he might correct Deb if she baited him enough. That kind did not appreciate being linked to crimes they considered amateur.

The morning office was lifeless without Erik pacing around. He was having a powwow with Paul, who'd traced the IP address of the threat against Erik and his son. She'd been copied on the emailed update: a woman who hooked up with Wuger (hard to understand female attraction) owned the computer. She claimed Wuger dumped her quick, and if she had known what a mean s-o-b he was she never would have done—Deb skipped over the sex act descriptions.

Back to Burnham, the lead suspect for Harrington's death and the source of the shoe photo. She stalled over the photo. Erik believed he had identified the girl from a news story, Elise McAuliffe. (He never said how he knew about the story.) She was not eager to approach bereaved parents, slice open a wound, and slide into it the picture that might be a stranger's daughter. She had a standard line that anything the parents could say would prevent future losses and advance justice. Her comments could be flung back at her like gravel. Where were the police when my child was taken, why wasn't the killer found sooner, were you deaf, dumb, and blind? Grief seminars had taught her about PGD, prolonged grief disorder. Some of the grieved became trapped in a cycle of pain and reasonless guilt; others ate with insatiable hunger every gross detail as if that provided a truth that could shut the door on the whole thing. In any number of heartbreaking cases, the family wanted to find in the void a purpose. She needed to make calls to investigators in Naperville, Calumet

Heights, and South Holland on cold cases involving missing or murdered adolescents that resembled Haley. Yeah, she should call the McAuliffes as well.

They had missed a lot with Burnham. About the time Harrington disappeared, Burnham had deserted the apartment listed on his employment forms. All the tips about residences coming in were unhelpful. Traffic cams showed Burnham's van in the Minnehaha park area repeatedly after Haley's return from the cabin. Yet the stalker had escaped notice—because everyone was looking for a man. Time to photo-shop onto Burnham's image the women's clothes and wigs found in the van.

Women's clothes—Deb thought about Alicia Krause. Could she disguise herself as a man? Doubtful, but if *she* were Alicia with Harrington dead, Burnham captured, Wuger free, and she were complicit in their cover-ups, she'd run.

Which Deb desperately wanted to do because this afternoon was the anger-management seminar and the after-work office party. Run like wild.

CHAPTER 55

❧

The G-Met party was scheduled for Wednesday evening for two reasons. First—those with Saturday and Sunday duty did not want to spoil the bit of weekend they had to themselves. Second—those with the weekend off most definitely did not want to spoil their freedom with official togetherness. The party, Deb overheard in the G-Met women's room, was Drees' idea— Drees, Erik's nemesis from the gym. And Erik had emailed that at the party they could catch each other up on new developments in the case. Great, an evening of shop-talk. Could be worse, it could be an evening of total sincerity with strangers. Deb raised herself out of the cab with serious drinking on her to-do list and pulled down her tough-fem skirt in leather-like black satin. No animals suffered in the making of that skirt; she just suffered in the wearing of it.

Deb rang the doorbell. Ibeling had a pleasant neighborhood near Grand Avenue in St. Paul for his two-story bungalow. No answer. She rolled her shoulders and thought *flee* before pregnant Naomi opened the door and welcomed her into the dark wood foyer. "Greta Ibeling is busy in the kitchen, and Almost Allwise—he can't hear me—is trapped in conversation. Drinks stronger than my ginger-ale are on the sideboard in the dining room."

It took a while to move on from the entry. Naomi introduced Deb to an arriving toxicologist and his wife, a study in contrasts since he was Scandinavian pale and she was Hispanic dark. Jimmy Bond Smalls drew Deb into the living room crowd. He introduced his wife, a tall black-skinned violist who, unlike Jimmy, had a real British accent. Deb was jostled out of a conversation about the London Underground versus Light Rail and nearly fell into an older man's lap. "Zywieck," he introduced himself, half rising from the depths of upholstery. He patted the Labs flanking his chair. "This pair used to work for me, Butch and Sundance. I remember the first body part they found." Ibeling interrupted to take her drink order, a scotch. He brought it to her in time to save her from another Zywieck story starting with "this guy finds a head."

A man bumped into her back, an investigator she had met once in passing. He said "excuse me" in frigid tones and moved away. Don't even think it, she ordered herself, not the time to imagine bias. She didn't see Erik. Paul was at a conference in an undisclosed location on a confidential topic. Food—the spread on the table had been devastated by a swat team, the real swat team, who left behind a few broken crackers. People wandered in and out of the kitchen, so Deb made her way. While everything else about the house said Arts & Crafts restored, the kitchen Viking appliances and refrigerator wall said pro. Greta Ibeling, maybe ex-CIA, maybe not, pulled a sheet of spanakopita from one of the ovens and then took Deb's hands with her own, warm from the oven mitts. She smiled like the Midwestern grandmother she was. As they became acquainted over reloading serving platters, a man broke into the conversation.

Drees.

He shook Deb's hand with an extrovert's vigor before quizzing Greta on what she thought of government surveillance of citizens. "The NSA knows us better than our own sweethearts," he said with a wink at Deb.

Greta slid tender shrimp under a broiler. "Governments, corporations, will always want information, it's power and money. Bureaucracy can be an expanding octopus"—Greta shut the oven door—"Does that octopus gobble the little krill or protect them from outer-space death rays? I've been watching sci-fi movies with my grandsons." She checked the broiling shrimp and heat blasted the three of them. "National Security—the devils and angels crowd each other in the details." She pulled out the shrimp and bare-handedly tossed the sizzling bites with a citrus and cilantro dressing, and added, "Drees, could you take this platter to the dining table?" He obeyed.

"You should go out and mingle," she said to Deb while dealing with a garlicky mushroom-olive tapenade. "We're having this event because Erik said you were so absorbed with cases that you've been isolated from the Greater Metro crowd."

"Erik?" Deb halted the progress of a snitched shrimp toward her mouth.

"Yes, according to Allwise—of course I know that name. After these dishes come out, I'd love to chat more. I'd love to hear about your special skills." She trained her spy vision on Deb.

"I've never assassinated anyone."

"None of us have, dear. Is it too early to bring out the tiramisu?"

Deb wandered back to the mass of the party. The food was fabulous, her scotch off.

CSI Foster, jabbering at a newly arrived Erik, saw his own glass was empty and moved to the makeshift bar. Deb's partner held a fragile stemmed glass of white wine.

"*That's* your swill?" She startled him.

"Pouilly-Fuisse. I always think that if I whisper 'Pouilly-Fuisse' in a woman's ear, she'll slap me in French."

"I can slap you, and it won't be in French. I know you knew I would say that."

Erik's eyes slid by her. He wanted to aim his quips at a gorgeous hetero, and she at a gorgeous non-hetero. His eyes came back. "How's the drink?"

"Meh," she shrugged.

Smalls joined them, one hand on Deb's shoulder, the other holding his glass of ruby red. "When Ibeling buys hard liquor for these events," he said into her ear, "the operative word is"—

"Discount," Erik completed.

"If we're blessed," Smalls resumed, "Mrs. I. pulls out 'odds and ends' of wine she just happens to have around."

"Smuggled," from Erik.

"Totally smuggled," Smalls agreed.

"Can I have a taste?" She inclined toward Erik who recoiled.

Smalls intervened. "It's liquid platinum. I'll get you a glass." He worked his way toward the sideboard.

A clunking silence, which surprise, Erik broke. "So how was the seminar, anger management?

"Postponed at the last minute."

"I imagine that made the organizers furious."

"So, Erik, in G-Met world, does 'indefinitely postponed' mean never or the day after tomorrow?"

"Every day is anger management day. Hello, Drees," he said flatly.

"Good to catch up with you again, Deborah." Drees turned to Erik. "And Ricky, you should get out more, you shouldn't hole up alone. You used to tell these crazy funny stories and leave the pitch-perfect punch line to the wife, ah, her name?"

"Your wine," Smalls interrupted, handed Deb the glass, and left. Deb sipped—it *was* liquid platinum—and realized she'd missed Erik's reply.

"I understand you went through a breakup recently." Drees to her, his hand on her arm.

"What? I, uh, um." Damn NSA, damn mail-room Julias, nothing private.

"Being dumped is rough." Drees sounded absolutely sympathetically genuine. She could kill him. "I'm sure she didn't deserve you, but it still puts you in a pit of despair."

"Deb," Erik butted in, "can shot-put a twenty-pound weight into a pit." Drees removed his hand from her. "She can wrestle a pit-bull then eat dinner with him. People can seem sweet and peachy but they have a pit instead of a heart, right, *Drees*?"

"Clearly, I need to drink what you're drinking. There's Ibeling, I need to speak to him." Drees made for the chief.

Deb raised her glass as a toast to Erik. "Great news, in a bad way. The Chicago authorities followed up on your tip, about Elise. They linked Burnham's DNA to that murder. Burnham took photos, altered them to erase embedded identifiers, and filed them as trophies. Possibly sold copies online to sickos. So we know the tragic tale of the girl in the shoe photo and we got her killer."

"At last!"—Erik clinked glasses with Deb. "But nothing yet to prove he killed Harrington, who may have been blackmailing him?"

"No. This Wuger guy who's 'at large,' seems Harrington hired him as protection. Wuger sure failed at that job, but he must know what Harrington had on Burnham. Maybe knows if Harrington was blackmailing Drexler over 'allowing' a predator access to ATC files. And there's Andrew Cushing, maybe he witnessed something. He's improving by leaps and bounds."

"The power of pet dander."

A male screeched across the room. Pot-bellied Naomi perched on her husband's lap and he groaned about the weight to the hoots of the light/dark couple from the entry. The woman with lovely brown eyes and shining hair reminded Deb of someone she'd never met, and she turned back to Erik. "So what's with Alicia Krause? Has she 'appealed' to you again?—Let me rephrase that question, how is your family doing?"

"Still under watch. As for Alicia 'Corazella,' she's booked on a flight tomorrow night to New Mexico, maybe to slip across the border. Bus, train, and airports are being monitored."

"Okay, uh, just one more question." Deb feared if Erik left, Drees might return. "That helpful woman in Chicago, you texted that she called you, Melanie?"

"She called because of the Burnham capture." Erik was deadpan. "She said, 'It's wonderful to know you're fine, to know you're on the case. Burnham, who knew? How terrible, exclamation point. Take care of yourself.' Then she shared information on Drexler's use of private jets."

"That sounds kind of sweet, whoa!" Deb was being goosed by one dog while the other one licked Erik's free hand. "Don't look so shocked, it's just Butch, or Sundance. What's with your face? Were you invisibly slapped?"

"I've been a Labrador retriever, pointed in a direction. I need to go."

"Of all the"—

He was gone, Drees heading her way. Deb rushed in the bathroom and turned on the faucet. She should sic Drees on Wartface Wuger or vice-versa. She had forgotten to tell Erik that an informant at Scab's Bar called the tip line to say that Wuger had sold a black pickup to a bartender there and recently had bodywork done on a blue pickup. On top of that, Foster had told her tonight that the girly poster she'd found in the lake cabin had a drop of Cushing's blood, a memento from that attack.

And sure they had a presumed murderer in custody, but the fear that Burnham might talk could have Wartface Wuger dangerously upset, upset enough to kill anyone involved.

She'd locked herself in the bathroom long enough. She dodged Drees and got to the porch before realizing she hadn't called a cab.

"I've called one already."

Deb jumped at the voice. Greta Ibeling, the real all-wise.

CHAPTER 56

❧

Jonathan held the pill bottle wondering how many. His head felt cracked to shards. He shook Tylenol into an unsteady hand under the glow of the nightlight. It wasn't late, but he'd drawn the shades and turned off all lights to trick his body into believing this was the hour for deepest sleep.

He threw back the tablets. Alcohol was the probable culprit, although lately celibacy wore on him, making him twist the sheets into rags. Or was he blaming lust for all the unrecognizable feelings let loose by the Harrington investigation? The headache, though not the ache of the body, could be blamed on his new reading and viewing habits. Jonathan used to skim the *StarTribune* and *Pioneer Press*, and Sunday's *New York Times* entertainment section; he'd flip through news channels. His expanded role at ATC called for greater worldliness. He added to his online newsstand the publications his high-level clients might read: *Wall Street Journal*, *Huffington Post*, *Washington Post*, *The Economist*, *The Weekly Standard*, and *Bloomberg News*. This exposure thoroughly convinced him the world was a perilous place. Very wise to construct one's own turret of safety.

He'd missed this evening's news. Mrs. Stoffel's after-work cocktail gathering metastasized into an endless evening of—words failed him. The alcoholic content of the drinks could disinfect a plague ward. A beetle-faced payroll manager who was rich beyond legal explanation, along with his terrifying sausage of a wife, entered to set the room abuzz. They talked about how Harrington had hired away one of their "payment enforcers." Jonathan took an embarrassingly long bathroom break to avoid the honor of meeting them.

After emerging, Jonathan saw that Sandy Sweetser, surprisingly unrumpled in dress pants, had arrived. Sweetser's presence mystified him until he realized that Sweetser had contacts with regional magazines, and Mrs. Stoffel was tight with local publishers. He didn't dare ask Sweetser if he had any ideas about Alicia. Jonathan had twice received messages from her, the second this morning from yet another alias. Keep it a secret, she pleaded, I'm in danger, police can't help. He sent a reply and a few hours later a follow-up. By then her number was "no longer in service."

He had to get out of his head. Jonathan tried to converse with an older business-weary man and a woman with a knowing smile. Nothing clicked until Sweetser joined them, claiming he'd fled a conversation about how a woman's cats saved her. "This saves me," the older man announced and raised his glass. "Downward dog for me," the woman added, and Jonathan nudged Sweetser before he let loose a remark about doggy-style.

"What saved you, Jonathan?" Sweetser happily turned on him.

"Bible camp" came out before he could think. "Got me out of my great aunts' house. It was fun—friends, swimming, late night fooling the counselors pretended not to see. Except the session with the Damnation theme. We were so terrified of hellfire that we broke into the office to call home. Oh, yeah, and the food poisoning. After that, I bribed my aunts—for every week of bible camp, one of sports camp, or even math camp—I was no good at those." Not until his aunts died did he realize that they had borrowed money, sold heirloom jewelry, took out a second mortgage, so he could attend the camps and later a university far from home. Their sacrifice stirred in Jonathan deep guilt and deeper gratitude, their unexpressed love, especially since they lectured him that being "different" would cause him problems. Different— unlike his horrible cousins they never said "gay" or "fruity" or "faggot." The women had no idea what to do with him and hoped someone somewhere would, which brought Jonathan back into the conversation. "My favorite was theater camp."

"I bet that's been a help in PR work," the woman laughed.

"Especially at a place like ATC," the older man ha-ha'ed while Sweetser rubbed his temples. "Your dead man, Harrington"—the man took a big swig—"hired a heavy from what's-his-name over there to protect himself. Is it true that Harrington's gorgeous assistant seduced the thug, and then had the thug kill her boss? You're damned quiet, Lewis. Harrington's practices. That must have been a hell of an elephant in the room."

Sweetser stupified them: *"You want to know why people don't talk about the elephant in the room! Because it will shit all over you. A ton of shit. Buried in shit. It's so big if it moves it kills you."*

They numbly stared as Sweetser took a big swallow of his drink. "You want an elephant, there's"—he stalled with another swallow. "Alvin Wuger, that's the heavy. There's a rogue bull for you."

"Rogue Bull, that's my fragrance," Jonathan quipped, and the group howled. The man and woman, both drunk enough to wave like wheat in the wind, moved on. Sweetser admitted that the party folk were *très sophistiqué* for his simple self and he was going home.

By that point the room was spinning and Mrs. Stoffel had whirled into multiple Mrs. Stoffels. Jonathan decided then and there to take tomorrow off. He had come by cab, he would leave by cab. He was no fool.

Barely inside his apartment, on a straight path to the bathroom, he received the call from Melanie Genereux. Stephen Drexler was fired. Jonathan was to arrive by 7:30 a.m. to see that Drexler's office lock was changed. Drexler was not to remove any of his things. Jonathan should prepare himself for a showdown.

CHAPTER 57

❦

The morning light went black. Jonathan was picked up and slammed against the wall like a ragdoll.

Seconds before he had been worrying about Drexler—would his boss show up to be fired? Drexler was a paradox, oblivious to the immediate yet with a prairie pronghorn's sense of danger. Jonathan closed his eyes to the imagined scene of Drexler's head on an antelope as he pushed open his building's back exit into the parking area.

Now with them open he could barely see through tears of pain.

"Where's Alicia?" A huge man grabbed his neck and slammed him again against the wall behind the dumpster. This giant must be the man Sweeter railed against, Wuger. His right hand wielded a broken bottle and he hissed about Alicia blackmailing, Alicia knowing too much, Alicia having it in for everyone, Jonathan included.

Jonathan's lungs seized up. He whispered he didn't know. Another slam and his teeth came down on his tongue.

"What a shame"—The giant didn't keep his voice to a whisper—"to slip on a step and break your back, cut your face." The bottle etched Jonathan's neck.

He told. She had wanted a car and he left one for her. He wheezed out a location.

A glass edge drew blood bubbles and then the giant released him and he slid down the wall. The giant wasn't done. "I can come back, anytime, if you tell the wrong story. Let's rehearse. What just happened?"

"I, I slipped, on trash."

"Go to the emergency room." The giant named one notorious for its long wait. "If you go to the police—trust me, don't. Who knows, you might slip again and hit your head, hard."

He was gone. Jonathan hazed over for lack of oxygen. He pulled himself up from the alley concrete and hobbled to his Hyundai, next to the open space where he used to park the Acura. Alicia knew Jonathan's former work-out buddy had deserted him for London, leaving him to tend bitter regrets and the Acura. When she messaged yesterday that she needed transportation, Jonathan did not hesitate to offer the car. Yesterday he cautiously dropped it in the St. Paul neighborhood she'd indicated. He taped the key to the muffler and walked a mile before catching a cab to that awful Mrs. Stoffel's.

Jonathan eased his raw back against the seat and started the Hyundai. His middle-school Taekwondo lessons had proved a waste. He pulled an inhaler from the glove compartment and took a deep singeing breath. The giant had a hard face to identify, except to say it was an oversize wart stuck on a pricey suit that had been packed in a toiletry kit.

Relying on the arm that didn't feel broken, he steered onto the Crosstown, eastbound. Jonathan passed the exit for the falls where Burnham had been caught. It felt too late for the police, it couldn't be too late. He crossed the Mississippi, was caught in a slowdown, turned on news radio, turned it off, turned on easy rock, turned it off, turned on Money Matters, turned it off. He wrangled out of traffic—he followed memorized directions through Mendota Heights for a neighborhood enclave he had never heard of until meeting his widow client, Lydia Arnfelt. Lydia who could bear responsibilities, Lydia who had resources. People were all wrong if they believed wealth was no protection. He exited and drove past new housing developments and a school named "Friendly Village." The new construction disappeared. He drove over a hill.

It was like entering old growth forest. The trees spread tall and dense. Driveways followed long curves into unseen environs. Here and there he glimpsed a spacious porch or massive brick front, a dream of a house, the address.

He couldn't be alone. Lydia had to be there.

THE CALL CAME FROM A woman, no time to double-check the tip. Erik reached Deb on her way to work, telling her to go to Settina's apartment, find if she'd heard anything about Alicia Krause's plans. He drummed his fingers on his G-Met desk. A Thursday morning public-place abduction was madness unless a concealed weapon or a hostage elsewhere kept Alicia in line. It could be a ruse—she could be in control. Wuger (who else) wanted the iPad (which she didn't have), the thumb drive (which she didn't have), and anything she knew about Drexler, money-laundering, Burnham, victims. To talk, she had to be conscious. To stay conscious, diabetic Alicia needed meds.

Deb called back and Erik ran to the G-Met lot—a time frame and location. He grabbed the Kevlar vest from his Highlander, adjusted his gun, and took a duffle bag and flung it into the passenger seat of the unmarked Interceptor—a Taurus on testosterone. At a traffic stop he pulled from the duffle a pocketed khaki jacket and wriggled it over the vest, put on a matching floppy hat, and prescription-less glasses. He could be on the track of the Rufous-sided stool pigeon.

Time was against him, but to avoid attention Erik slowed in the drugstore parking lot. Few cars in this family neighborhood, a neighborhood with quick access to Snelling and I-35. The graphite Acura ZDX described in the call was parked in the row nearest the building. He drove past the empty Acura and a blue Dodge pickup parked head out and away from the sole security camera. Erik circled to the row behind those vehicles, backed into a space, and glanced down as if texting. He was—backup. The bulky Kevlar vest heated like an oven.

Alicia emerged, her white face surrounded by black tangles. Wuger had an arm wrapped around her, a plastic bag dangling from the thick wrist, and his opposite hand stuck into his Patagonia fleece pocket. Alicia shook violently as he shoved her into the truck and rushed to the driver's seat.

Erik jammed the accelerator to the floor—the Taurus hit the Dodge at an angle, spun the truck's backside around, and his airbag exploded against him with a force beyond anticipation. He heard shouts and car doors. He jerked his seat to recline and squirmed out as a furious Wuger—his airbag hadn't functioned—stumbled from the truck to grab Alicia. Wuger held a .38 but would have to re-angle to fire. He yelped—Alicia must have pinched a tender part. An alarm sounded from the building. Erik, his nine millimeter in hand, slipped behind the Acura and peered around to see Wuger pushing Alicia back into the truck. She screamed but the scream had no volume. An audience of staff and retirees emerged from the door, saw the guns, and pulled back inside. Wuger saw Erik and aimed but Alicia bit his earlobe, a yowl. Erik ducked behind the truck, his view Alicia's tiny flats and Wuger's ogre boots. He fired at the boots and heard another yowl. Alicia fell to the sidewalk and a shot from Wuger ricocheted from the pavement to graze Erik's arm. She struggled up, Erik catching her before Wuger, who jumped in the truck. Erik and Alicia lost balance, and he twisted so his skull wouldn't hit first and his Kevlar was between her and Wuger. Alicia hoarsely cried "Roll" and they did as the truck swerved toward them and was gone. Erik grabbed her wrists. She was trembling with shock and breathed unevenly against his cheek. He was hot and sore and angry and he sure wasn't going to roll on top of her. They lay pressed together on their sides as sirens wailed from opposite directions.

CHAPTER 58

❧

"Officer down" came across her phone and Deb ran to her car. Next the notice of a pursuit—a Dodge pickup spotted around Lexington and Randolph. No one coming toward the women she'd just left, Settina and Ellen, though she ordered a patrol to that address in case. (Alicia had sworn to the women that once she reached a safe distance she would contact authorities.) Deb pulled her car over to catch a breath, and the call came from Erik—in an ambulance with Alicia—Wuger armed and on the run. State Troopers and city forces blocking I-35 E, he said ending the call. It wasn't hard to become lost in St. Paul. There was a grid congested with narrow streets and stop signs; then the grid was whacked out of line by the river, and interstate exits weren't paralleled by entrances, and finally the core of the city shifted from foursquare to diagonals. She pulled over for a second and put up the portable siren, and a blind fury surged through her. When it came to trouble, Wuger had always kept above water, until now, when he was desperate enough to kidnap women in broad daylight and shoot police. She *had* to get him. Above water—the talk back at Neck's lake store, Wuger liked boats—she hit the accelerator and wailed the car to the river marina off Lexington.

There she jumped out to see Wuger limping on a dock and tumbling into a fishing boat on the Mississippi River. She shouted as he started the motor.

She was commandeering a faster boat from the dock master when a St. Paul police car rushed in, and one of the officers, Jakes, joined her and started the engine.

A hundred yards ahead of them downstream, Wuger wriggled into a life vest, shifting the thirty-eight from one hand to the other. He zoomed toward the confluence with the Minnesota River. He could have a vehicle parked at another dock downstream. Deb's boat nearly tipped over catching up to him. Wuger glanced over his shoulder, one hand on the wheel and the other aiming his gun at her. She ducked, nearly tipping the boat again, and heard shouts. Wuger failed to see a barge. Awesome fail—his boat ricocheted off the barge like a pool ball and Wuger somersaulted into the river. Deb pulled out her gun. Wuger couldn't swim and hold his weapon above water for long, but that realization did nothing to slow her pulse.

It became a show. Barge guys watched from the back of their tug; Deb waved her badge at them. Two signaled V's and the third flashed Deb his hairy chest while the barge steadily moved downstream. Deb and Jakes followed Wuger at a distance.

He was going to swim for it.

Wuger fired a wild shot that skewed toward the bank and another that like a flat stone skipped across the surface as the kickback sent him underwater. The gun was gone when he popped up, choking, spitting, and splashing.

"Police! Give it up," she yelled and Jakes put-putted closer. The blind fury threatened her again, and nausea from the wave-jumping. She un-gritted her teeth: "We haven't been properly introduced. I'm Detective Deb Metzger and I've heard so many bad things about you that it's a real displeasure to meet you."

Scary unbelievable. Wuger floundered for a few seconds, pulling off his boots underwater, then pulled downstream with a powerful stroke. Deb didn't know if by an incredible long shot he had a waterproof grenade on him, so Jakes kept a distance, angling the boat between man and shore.

"He's got the blubber and ballast to last a while," Jakes observed.

"Blubber all right. He'll be a challenge to pull into the boat," she said to Jakes and then louder, "Wuger, how much you weigh? 330, 350? Help us out."

He paddled.

"I should have brought a book 'cause this is taking time." Deb looked to her pilot. "Wait, Jakes. Weren't you first on the scene with the Harrington body?"

"That was my twin. On the Bloomington Force."

"That's confusing"

"It hasn't confused our girlfriends yet."

Deb didn't pursue that one; she stuck with the man bobbing toward the Gulf of Mexico. "Hey, Wuger! What's in this water, anyway?"

Jakes answered for him. "Used to be pollutants. Around the bend is Pig's Eye Island, the city dump for decades. Today it's a heron rookery."

"No shit. Do birds shit in the water? I guess they do if they're water birds. You listening Wuger? You're not being talkative. I've heard drowning people don't talk. They're busy drowning. What? Did I hear the f-bomb? So no drowning yet? I heard that one, too. Are we going for a record here, Wuger?"

"There already is one set at a lake near Bemidji. Last July, a two-hour stand-off, or float-off," Jakes said.

"Two hours in July? Hear that, Wuger? How fast could this water chill beer? Thirsty, Wuger? Wait, you've already swallowed liquid refreshment. What's that green stuff floating over there? You're not answering my questions, and I'm holding that against you. Legally, it's not waterboarding if it's an elective swim. We have something like a harpoon here. Ready to pull in a whale, Jakes?"

Wuger gasped, Deb held out a pole, he grabbed it, and his Moby Dick weight threatened to pull the three of them under. Then the county sheriff's patrol boat motored up to them. It would take official hoists and restraints to transport Haley's Wartface to a nice dry jail cell.

WHITE FLASHING NOVAS BURNED HALEY'S eyelids when she closed them. When she opened them there were black holes, a black hole instead of a person, a black hole instead of the TV. Mr. Nail nudged her and she saw her math text again. At his kitchen table, he talked Haley through tangents. "You gotta read instructions step-by-step, Haley," he lectured. "You gotta memorize the rules and *then* be intuitive. Like I am when I design furniture." He slapped his table which made Haley's notebook slide into her lap because the table angles must've been intuitive.

Mom was like addicted to work because she said scanning prices (*boring!*) held her together. She fussed over Sierra but would sigh at Haley all drama-like, "I don't know what do to with you," cry, hug her, and put on a nicotine patch.

At school everyone called her Haley Hero again. Only Dad was the fallen hero. He must've scared Wartface and that Burnham-stalker-man out of hiding. She blinked away a black hole. Detective Deb made her furious by saying that Haley wouldn't have to testify in court, when Haley needed to tell everybody how *awful* those men were. Detective J., in this nice super-white shirt, had visited her in the hospital after the attack. He said that DNA and witnesses would be enough and people wanted to shield minors from court. At first she thought he said "miners" and was confused. He let Brayden drop by for a minute, and Brayden didn't say much except "you did good" and she felt like floating off the bed to the ceiling. When she came home yesterday, Ian from math class came to talk over the assignments. Smart. Teachers encouraged Ian, said he was coming out of his shell like a snail or clam. Ian told her to keep this secret—he'd lost a father, to prison. His father was alive, but not in a way that mattered to Ian. She blurted that must be why everyone worried Ian could be a school shooter. He looked so hurt and she said, "duh, my pain meds," and he laughed, like the best laugh ever—not to worry, his father was a nonviolent conman, a charmer. That's why Ian avoided being charming he said in a warm way that made her tingle. "Charm for the good," she said, and they bumped fists.

Brayden was Brayden but she should help Ian with his charm issues. She was dying—not dying, that word made her puke—she was *desperate* to talk to people and couldn't. Back in the hospital, after her Mom left to pick up Sierra, she'd cried to Detective Deb and didn't want her to leave. When Detective J. replaced her, and after Brayden left, Detective J. noticed a book her mom brought in with a hologram cover that showed different faces depending how you looked. A sci-fi love story, she explained to Detective J., and this girl was so much in love with a guy who didn't know she existed (because she existed on a different plane) that she went blind, literally. But another guy on her plane was obsessed with her and she had the power to make him do things but she knew she shouldn't, except maybe he could cure her from being blind if she did. If Haley were writing the book, the guy on the higher plane would wake up and see outside himself, you know?

Detective J. seemed into the plot, then for a sec angry, and after that sad. She said she bet it had a happy ending and he laughed, like Ian, and said that at her age he read books about dogs.

Haley woke up from time travel and was back in Mr. Nail's kitchen and he had a snack for her, a mini-cake he called a "Detective Debbie." The tracphone on the table buzzed—Mom. Haley answered, then told Mr. Nail, "Mom and Sierra will be late. I got to go home and do my job, the meds and all." Detective Deb had given her a job, because when you had a job you had to pay attention and not see holes.

Haley and Mr. Nail—his legs like nervous noodles—walked across the little yard to her house. She used a fob to disarm the alarm system that her mom's store had donated. When she opened the door, Mr. Nail jumped at the siren-sound and high glint of green.

"He's just a cat." Haley made puckering sounds at the beast on top of the refrigerator. "Mil—ton. Come down, little Miltie." She said to Mr. Nail, "His owner Mr. Cushing is recovering from a really bad attack, and he found evidence, so I'm doing him a favor. I met him in the hospital. He can barely talk but you can tell he's super smart like a good wizard. Milton, pretty please come down or I'll call you Pisser!"

Pisser Milton jumped to the counter while Mr. Nail backed up against the cabinets. Haley scooped up the cat, who covered her whole front and purred.

CHAPTER 59

꧁꧂

Long, procedure-filled hours after Deb's waterworld adventure, she found Erik leaning against the hospital corridor wall, his eyes closed. His left arm hung in a sling and that hand was wrapped. The blood had not been perfectly cleaned from his temple.

"Hey," she touched his good arm.

He opened his eyes but didn't snap to attention.

"I brought a sandwich and an apple." She handed over a bag. "Wuger's being treated for hypothermia, a bullet-grazed foot, and a fat head."

A nurse smiled her way up to Erik and set down a chair. Seeing Deb, she said coldly, "I suppose you'll want one." She departed on her errand, planting annoyance into every step. Erik signaled Deb to sit. She shook her head, and he slumped into the chair and placed the bag of food on the floor.

"Thanks." His voice was cracker-dry. "What about Wuger's foot?"

"He gets to keep it. If you'd shot him in the brain, information might have leaked out." Deb watched as the nurse slammed down a chair for her.

Erik picked up the food bag. "I saved Alicia's life with an energy bar. Her blood sugar was crashing. In the ambulance, she cursed me seven ways to damnation in Spanish. She swore it was all my fault."

"Did you charge her with anything?"

"Obstructing an investigation to keep her in place. I don't usually drink this chemical stuff"—he pulled an icy Coke can from the bag and cracked the tab—"except when it tastes so good." He gulped down half. "They're stabilizing her insulin levels and putting her on an IV for hydration. She's in bad shape and doesn't want to talk to me."

"I fully understand."

A glance at her before he started glumly on the sandwich. He'd never seemed glum around food before. He took a bite, chewed, then asked, "How did you get her friends to give over the information about the pharmacist who gamed the record-keeping system for her?"

Deb spiked her hair, stood up, and spread her arms to prepare the scene. "So. Found Ellen McCormick and Settina together while you were playing gun-tag with Wuger. Alicia had called them yesterday, out of the blue to get money for meds. She'd spent the night in Settina's apartment, like they could protect each other with high heels and boho scarves. Daniel, Settina's boyfriend, was out this morning taking a master-of-the-universe exam at the U. So, imagine me talking really fast, really loud."

"Easily done."

"Moving on, they 'enunciated' in a fancy way that talking to 'that Erik' brought on deep shit. I *could* have gone on agreeing with them for a loooong time. Instead, I say, got news for you kiddos. *That* was good cop. You want bad cop, you got bad cop. You don't want to know my nickname, you don't want to even say it! Next I talk cable-TV jive, puff up my feathers, swagger a cock walk—which blows the socks right off the guys, but they ate it up! Not that I want to discuss the erotics of the moment. Anyway, I changed tactics."

"What's your nickname?"

"Don't go there. I got serious. I *considered* my audience—an advocate and a refugee. Asked them to remember what they'd seen before, the atrocities done to women, their bodies, their faces, and like that Settina told me." Deb caught her breath. "How did the tip come in?"

"A Lydia Arnfelt called me about Wuger beating Jonathan Lewis for what he knew about Alicia."

"Is Arnfelt his lawyer?"

"A philanthropist. Lewis fled under her wing."

"Oh, interesting thing at G-Met just before I left. Flower guy wandering in the hallway with a bouquet for 'the running detective.' Drees claimed it for his office, no signature, just a strange message—'For the Knight Erring, do well.' Drees said it should be knight-errant, and like what do I know, but you have that poet-sister"—

"The only way to know for sure," Erik said in an intense whisper, "is for you to switch the passive-aggressive plaque for the bouquet. Do it."

She shushed him. A police officer had arrived to stand guard over Alicia. Time to go home.

CHAPTER 60

❦

A licia was lovely, even in an interview room blind to the gorgeous day outside. But when she turned to Deb, her eyes were heartbreaking: "I began to see myself in these women who deluded themselves about relationships that were possessive, manipulative." The charges had been dropped, but whenever those eyes slipped to Erik, Alicia reddened and her gaze fell to the table.

She took in a deep breath. "In Chicago, I worked half-time with Drexler. The other half I compiled case histories for the Denisha project headed by Melanie Genereux, which helped so many women. Continued with that after the transfer here. This nice man, Sweetser, did much of the research. He totally believed in Melanie and the cause. Drexler—it felt real—but he'd never read past chapter one of a love story. There was no 'next,' no 'ever after.'" She let go of a sigh.

Erik had his mineral gaze on Alicia and she flinched. Deb interceded. "Tell me more about the Twin Cities ATC group. What about Jonathan Lewis?"

"He was a lamb Harrington tried to turn into a barracuda. Jonathan and Sweetser would pull me aside, saying Harrington was messing with accounts and files."

"What was Sweetser's role at that point?" Deb asked.

"During February and March, Harrington wanted me to pull together a big cache of data from client profiles, Chicago donor profiles, and the Denisha materials. This included these terrible news stories about crimes against women and children. Harrington said, 'you can organize it even if you don't understand it.' The intrusiveness made me anxious and I asked the tech support Harold Burnham about ATC's privacy policy, and why we had kept all the background information and why we were dragging on forwarding the promotional information to Chicago. He *screamed* at me, 'None of your business!' The next day he was gone. Andrew Cushing came in." Alicia choked a little and covered her mouth with a trembling hand. Erik offered her water. She didn't touch it.

"Cushing had trouble accessing files, so I gave him—passwords—I'd obtained. Cushing said there were additional encryptions. He cracked one code and he asked me, privately, if the Denisha research included 'disturbing images' and child pornography sites. I was shocked. I felt betrayed by everyone, except Cushing. And Jonathan. I overheard him defending me to, um"—

"Whinette," Deb said.

"Yes, though I don't think that's her legal name. I was scared. I brought in my iPad and started to transfer files. But I hadn't been tracking my insulin and felt incredibly faint. I went to the bathroom, came back, and the iPad was gone. I panicked. I went into hiding."

"But you kept in touch with Cushing," Deb said.

"He 'hid' the files and was going to download the rest of the encrypted ones onto a thumb drive for me to take to a person I trusted, Melanie in Chicago."

"Why not the police, I have to ask," Erik said.

"I need to get up." Alicia stood unsteadily. She was pale.

Erik stood and responded before Deb could. "Ms. Krause, do you need to check your blood levels? Stress can"—

"I understand my blood," she snapped at him. "What I don't understand is why you, 'Detective,' froze my bank accounts and sent nasty personal emails—and I don't know how you found that email address which I closed—saying I was the chief suspect in Harrington's death. I knew I had to get that evidence myself. Before the iPad was taken, Sweetser forwarded me that report on local police corruption."

"I never acted on your accounts. I didn't know that email address and never send personal messages to persons of interest."

"*What?*" Tears ran down Alicia's cheeks and she rubbed them away violently and turned as if to leave, Erik reached out, and Deb got between them.

"Sit down, both of you," she commanded. "That corruption report is—corrupt. It seems a Corazella account was fabricated and your regular account was hijacked by"—

"Burnham?" Alicia put her head in her hands and her hair fell forward. "I heard in the news about the attack on Cushing. I hoped against hope the thumb drive might be in Cushing's apartment, but I'm afraid Burnham took it."

"Actually," Erik said. "Wuger, who grabbed you, attacked Cushing. The thumb drive—Cushing's cat saved it for us. We have it."

"*Then what do you want with me!* Is this *fun* for you?"—Alicia was shaking and her anger embraced both detectives. "Yes, I do need to check my blood. At least mine runs red and warm."

A uniformed woman escorted Alicia out. Erik tapped his pen loudly against the table while Deb used hers to etch into a notepad, ALICIA'S BANK ACCOUNT HACKED, ALICIA'S BANK ACCOUNT HACKED, ALICIA'S BANK ACCOUNT HACKED.

CHAPTER 61

❧

Jonathan counted to five on his inhale, held for five, and released his breath at the same pace. Pain meds for his back, a few online yoga classes, and he felt in control for the interview. He had come to peace with his Huck-Finn hair. He was not his old eager-to-please self; he could claim authority. He'd never worn his three-hundred-dollar suit so well. He walked into the interview room.

The woman and man stood at the same tall height and he had a stab of déjà vu. The woman began.

"We want you to take a personality assessment, common in these hiring situations. The news has created awful chatter around your circumstances. Since we last talked, Allston Tigue Carlson has foundered under these terrible, terrible allegations. Misuse of client information, money laundering, murder!"

Jonathan cleared his throat. "You're right, Lisa. It is terrible. I had only the slightest awareness of how warped the culture had become, obviously enough awareness to realize I should leave. If you're interested in me for this position—I am definitely interested—the court may demand time from me for testimony." As Lisa nodded and the man frowned, Jonathan recalled going to Drexler for a recommendation. He had been anxious about asking for one back in March, after such a short time at ATC, and worried about skipping over Harrington to secretly approach his superior. Drexler, however, had been gracious. "It will be a good move for you," he said shaking hands with Jonathan. Then he turned sardonic: "Meanwhile, learn from our successes and pay particular attention to our failures."

As Lisa discussed the importance of knowing a new employee's strengths and weaknesses, Jonathan saw that the man, Greg, continued to scowl.

"I can't comment on the investigation," Jonathan said. "But let me say this, when it's your watch, you have to watch, otherwise it's on your watch." Klutzy. "Another way to think of it, Stephen Drexler should be convicted for failing to follow his own advice." That elicited subdued laughter. Jonathan was glad he stole the line from the fit detective. "In risk management, we tell our clients that during a crisis they must confront the worst. Denial is gas on a fire. They must put aside emotional self-justification for honest self-evaluation. Problems do not vanish when you turn your back on them. They, they become a cancer." It was delivered with confidence. Jonathan would face in the future whether he could follow his own creed.

CHAPTER 62

❧

Sandy Sweetser contracted in front of the detectives, receding into a shell. He had perversely dismissed his lawyer.

Deb started. "Your friend Wuger is not a talker. But on one event, he was very forthcoming."

"*Friend*—any dealings I had with him were forced on me and then he threatened my ex-wife. You're right—he's not a talker. He's a blunt instrument. Who'd believe him?"

"You underestimate his narrative capability," Erik said.

"I bet there's no end of secrets Wuger is hiding. And don't you have enough ticks and weasels with the whole ATC lot to sort out their conniving pretenses? Hiding behind attorneys."

"Power-of-attorney, you have that." Deb jabbed a pencil at files on the table between them. "Your mother's bare-bones insurance doesn't begin to cover the level of care you've arranged for her. I'd want the same for someone I love. Your mother's bank account which you control has been swollen with lump-sum deposits since January, five thousand, ten thousand dollars, more. The early transactions line up with Harrington's embezzled funds. He was paying you and Wuger to get everything you could on Drexler and Burnham."

"Drexler. Harrington discovered Burnham's 'hobbies' on his own."

"Not quite the truth, Mr. Sweetser," Deb said. "The rest of the transactions— you tell us. Half the recent ones match those in the Alicia Krause account you hijacked and the Alicia Corazella one you invented to throw us off."

"Lawyer," Sweetser's word faded and he sagged like a man with no fight in him.

Until Erik stated: "You said you didn't want one for this round, but you can have one—still waving it off? There were mystery deposits after Harrington died, from offshore accounts. Someone had means. By the way, she's not coming to your rescue."

"*Hey!*" Sweetser barked. "Alicia may seem to mean well"—

"You know I'm not talking about Ms. Krause," Erik said. "And I doubt Melanie Genereux returns your love."

"*Melanie?* Won't this all fall on *Drexler*?"

"Because you, or was it Melanie, thought Drexler would make a perfect fall guy—slick, powerful, arrogant. Who'd sympathize with that?" Erik drilled on. "Drexler had his match in Melanie Genereux. The compassionate Ms. Genereux who protected children by letting stalkers collect information on them. Do you think she's going to admit knowing you, step up and praise your loyalty, your"—

"*Come off it!* Melanie *really* wanted to make a difference. Maybe she had a morbid fascination with pet cases, but she wanted to help, she was driven. That's why she started investigations."

"And she paid you to investigate, as a contract employee, and later, secretly, off the books. Begin with Chicago," Deb said.

"Starting two years ago, Melanie had me collect information on women and children served by the Denisha Circle, tales to bring tears to donors' eyes and suction the money from their bulging wallets. The tech guy, Burnham, helped correlate data. He was certainly excellent at tracking things down, which should have been a red light. Mind you, I was an outsider, going back and forth to the Twin Cities. But I got the sense that a precious infrastructure of unmet desires was overheated in Chicago. Next Allston dispatched Drexler to the Twin Cities. Melanie he kept close. Drexler"—

"Ignore Drexler," Erik advised. "Everything you know on the charity."

"Last year, two girls helped by the Denisha project disappeared. These— victims—had terrible histories, no shortage of suspects. I didn't know anything about the daughter of donors, the McAuliffes. Melanie was suspicious of Sam Vine's pushiness to be involved with the girls, maybe not the way for a gangster to redeem himself. End of February Melanie met with us—Harrington, me, Alicia—here in the cities. Drexler, who knows where he was. Melanie said the victims didn't receive help soon enough, all the more reason to push for the Denisha Group. Then someone"—

"Alicia."

"Alicia worried that a donor, maybe Vine, had a deadly hobby, using *us* to find victims. We were stunned. Melanie lost it, she started screaming. I swear her hair was on *fire*. Snapped in our faces, 'You have to make this right!' Over and over, 'you have to make this right!'"

"Perfect time to call the police," from Deb.

"Melanie *insisted* we had no legal right to turn over trusted clients and donors to incompetent police because one of us was a ghoul imagining things. She gave us marching orders—search for leaks, research donor backgrounds."

"In other words, sit on it," Erik again.

"There was no proof! Better than letting the police scare everybody into deep cover. You're all about violation of privacy, don't you watch the news?"

Erik let loose the anger. "*Want a violation of privacy? Start with a crime.* A crime that seizes account numbers, a crime that invades the body to take a life. I'm guessing you shredded receipts for keyloggers and auto-trackers, tossed a few computers into the river. You could have come forward when Burnham disappeared."

"We knew nothing for sure! And our focus was on donors, not one of our own. Harrington said he was on top of it—now I see he was planning to blame it all on Drexler. Then Cushing showed up, said Burnham had done peculiar things. Harrington told Melanie that Cushing was unstable, and Melanie—Melanie believed we could figure everything out and *then* take proper evidence to the police. She calls me from Chicago. She's sobbing that Harrington has turned on her and forced Alicia into his plan. Melanie wants me to get all Denisha files to her, which had disappeared. For the women and children, she said. She knew about my son, his death, and so I"—

"Butter up Jonathan Lewis," Deb finished the sentence. "See how close he could get to Alicia, unwittingly distract her, Alicia by now labeled as a paranoid liar. You fool around at her desk, install a keylogger, hack her computer."

Sweetser chewed his lip. "Look, I *like* Jonathan. Harrington, what a bastard, turns Wuger into his personal Hulk of a body guard, and tells me that Alicia's an unstable blackmailer, and Drexler's a pervert. I-I thought passing on information to Melanie would get to the bottom of everything. Wuger was an ugly means to a good end, and then after the—incident—a fucking deadly inescapable means."

"I can't believe it, *a means to an end*?" Erik resonated with disgust. Deb would kick him for it, but she was restraining herself from strangling Sweetser, who went on talking as if inflamed.

"*I'm* the good guy. Alicia disappears and Cushing's dismissed. That Burnham— deteriorating mentally—Harrington and Wuger took him up north, hoping to use him to get to Drexler, only Burnham gives them the slip."

"By borrowing a phone from Dwight Haugen, his daughter's phone," Deb said. "Get to the point—how did Harrington die?"

Sweetser shut his eyes. "Wuger, playing chauffeur, takes me and Harrington to a restaurant in Edina, where Harrington says Alicia has files that could put us all in jail and I had to keep track of her and yeah I had her passwords. The threats to me *and* my ex-wife don't start until we're outside heading up the parking ramp stairs. Wuger had parked us on the deserted roof, should have been a warning. Nasty wind and soaking rain. Harrington says he's never seen Melanie trust anyone the way she trusts me. Then he lets it slip that he discovered in February that Burnham had something for kids, that he'd found a suspicious photo in Burnham's desk. Harrington was going for blackmail, Melanie, the whole of ATC. He says, 'looks like kiddie porn, maybe more, so incredibly useful.' It hit me, the missing girls—*Harrington knew Burnham was the one.*"

Sweetser's frame trembled in tiny spasms. "That bastard. I run, man, I run. I run down the stairs and they're after me. I turn. I grab Harrington's foot and pull. Hell I pull so damn hard. And he fell, he fell damn hard." Sweetser stopped.

Erik spoke slowly, "Wuger helped you dump the body. He had plenty of reasons for avoiding investigation. You took it to a place you knew, a place where you'd go to escape from the ATC swamp, where you'd walk alone and stare at the water. Just you and the bird watchers who stopped to ask what you'd seen and you told them. A ghost."

CHAPTER 63

❧

H e was between states.

The sun was rising on Saturday morning as Erik drove his Highlander, kayak strapped on top, over the St. Croix River where it converged with the Mississippi. Pre-dawn he'd gone to the G-Met office to see that Deb had snitched the "Knight Erring" bouquet from Drees' office, replacing it with limp tulips. She kept the passive/aggressive plaque. With that behind him, he pulled into a gas station on the Wisconsin side. He needed escape from the clutter in his head.

It was nearly a month to the day when the corpse of Niland Harrington had been unearthed. The case had become so tangled with people's desires and ambitions that no one had a clear eye on the fact that a man was killing children.

There was nothing online now about Erik or his son, thanks to Cyber-Paul. Bob Uhle had moved to the Florida panhandle. The threats to Ben were all Wuger, his idea of fun. Wuger's blue truck had also encountered Dwight Haugen's Yamaha, but it was impossible to prove intent. Sweetser, with his talent for erasing an internet trail, admitted to tracking Erik and reposting negative comments "to buy helpful time." Stephen Drexler, that player of complicated games, never arrived at the ATC office the morning of the attack on Jonathan Lewis. He was traced to Scottsdale, Arizona, where yesterday on G-Met's behalf, local police raced their squad car across a golf course to bring him in for questioning. Drexler explained that he'd been attending to his mother and was soon whisked away by the FBI. Erik imagined that the name "Drexler" would be abandoned for a new one provided by Witness Protection. Ibeling also received a prompt call from the golf club about paying for "damage to the greens." "You're Scottsdale," he barked. "Suck it up."

Erik was unscrewing the fuel cap when a man called out, "Detective!" Who would know him here?

"Detective Deb's partner!"

Bent Nail. He grinned his way over. "Hey, fishing opener so I'm headin' downriver with my brother Rusty. Great job catching that girl-killer guy, and that big guy, and that other screwed-up guy. Me and my girlfriend were wonderin'"—Nail's eyes drooped with earnestness—"if Detective Deb would like to double-date. I know a guy, and a not-guy, her choice, and, uh, weekend, she's not answering her work phone."

Erik explained that he could not give out her personal information but would gladly forward Nail's, which he did on his phone, as "urgent."

Nail hauled away his fishing boat, and Erik caught up on his messages as his tank filled. When authorities approached Melanie Genereux, she insisted they were in error and admitted to nothing. Allston was disinclined to confront wrongdoing by one of his own, until he might decide Melanie had become inconvenient. That mystifying first email sent in Harrington's name, the one that announced the dead man was missing—no one admitted sending it. Possibly a burdened Sandy Sweetser. Sweetser had lawyered up, and one question he never answered was what did he tell Melanie after he killed Harrington. Did he say that Alicia had been right, that someone—and he had Burnham's name then—had used ATC to murder children? Or did he shield her with ambiguity? Sad sad Sweetser, facing obstruction and manslaughter charges at the very least.

Alicia Krause had flown to Peru to attend to her father. She would return for further testimony and asked if the detectives knew the anonymous source paying for her excellent lawyer. She vowed to make the next year man-free, her last words to Deb. Her last words to Erik were none.

He wasn't as bad as she thought, but he wasn't as good as she'd hoped.

Erik wondered for a second which woman he was really thinking about.

He checked his last message about picking up Ben later from his maternal grandparents, home of prodigious spoiling. Not that his own parents were any better with the boy. Dauntingly practical they had loomed in Erik's boyhood— denying any adventure that might lead to a tree three stories high, a sling-shot system in the car, seven boys giving themselves haircuts, or an animal in their bedroom. Suspicious of squirming that might hide mischief, his mother would slyly say, "Oh, the agitated heart 'till someone really find us out." Skinned-flint or flint-skinned, he'd thought his parents then. Never, though, the pinched and high-nosed who looked down on him as irretrievably damaged. "*You're* a spoiled boy," they'd say, "Do you think the world's your oyster?" Just because of a face that says, used to say, all things welcome. Spoiled or lucky, lucky or loved? What would his boy be?

Phone turned off and stowed under the seat, Erik drove north to find a launch. His black gloves made him feel deployed on a secret mission, but without them chilly water could trickle down the paddle onto his sore arm. He parked and leveraged down the kayak, resting it on a patch of startling violets and pristine white blossoms. Chickadees and jays chided him as he studied the sun. He decided on optimism. The gloves came off, and he changed the wetsuit jacket for a sleek hydro-skin shirt and pushed off.

The paddle slipped into a cloud. He followed through the motion, sliding the other end into the deep reflection of a tree. The constant current ran buried beneath calm; the morning water of the St. Croix lay placid and glass flat. The move upstream would be smooth pivots and surges.

He was alone.

The detective put maximum muscle into his paddling for a while and then drifted to observe the bank with its trees in tender leaf. No bodies here today, except the many, infinitesimal and large, through attrition and violence, always returning to earth.

He stiffened. Shadows crossed over him. They fell on the water before him; behind him an unidentifiable sound. He twisted to look up and back.

White pelicans. Fifty, sixty, sweeping down to the water and curving upward. Broader than he was tall, white wings bordered with black primaries. They swooped close enough that Erik could see the knob on the upper pink-yellow bill, signal of the spring desire to mate. They lifted and banked again. In the rhythm of their migration they were enormous and elegant. For another moment the pelicans circled and arced in the warmth of an updraft.

They straightened and moved forward, heading north into summer, and he followed.

Priscilla Paton grew up on a dairy farm in Maine. She received a B.A. from Bowdoin College and a Ph.D. in English Literature from Boston College. A former college professor, she has taught in Kansas, Texas, Florida, Ohio, and Minnesota. She has previously published a children's book, *Howard and the Sitter Surprise*, and a book on Robert Frost and Andrew Wyeth, *Abandoned New England*. She married into the Midwest and lives with her husband in Northfield, Minnesota. When not writing, she participates in community advocacy and literacy programs, takes photos of birds, and contemplates (fictional) murder.